Acclaim

"Few writers chronicle the Korean-American experience, and even fewer are as talented as Kim . . . A good eye for detail, an excellent prose style, and the ability to create compelling characters . . . luminous . . . hypnotic . . . an intriguing, tortured portrait of a second-generation Korean-American by a promising young writer."
—*Publishers Weekly*

"Kim zeroes in on the debilitating tensions of interpreting between languages, countries, childhood and adulthood, lies and secrets, sex and hurt, anger and love."
—*Daily News* (New York)

"Utterly absorbing . . . stylish and elegant psychological mystery."
—*Toronto Globe and Mail*

"Kim is a precise, patient observer. . . . A sleek, nearly hypnotic glimpse into the world of a Korean family ruptured in translation to America."
—*Kirkus Reviews*

"Riveting . . . No mere whodunit, Kim's debut also examines the myth of the 'model minority' and what it's like to live in cultural limbo."
—*Glamour*

"Kim has come up with one of the most original and disturbing motives for murder that this reader has ever encountered. It brings into play loyalty, cultural differences, and the sometimes lonely existence of our nation's many immigrants."
—*USA Today*

"Outstanding . . . Most admirably, Kim avoids identity politics entirely. She is not interested in ghettoizing her protagonist. Suzy is a character first, a representation of human psychology, one that Kim has studied too carefully to label simply as Korean, or Depressed."

—Max Watman, *The New Criterion*

"*The Interpreter* is a melancholy study of a young Korean-American woman's alienation from both her Asian roots and her American environment. It's also a murder mystery. That Kim makes these two aspects of the novel work together suggests that she's a writer to keep an eye on."

—*San Jose Mercury News*

"Amazing . . . The author's a master tease, surrendering details so slowly that you'll find yourself in such a frenzy to get to the next chapter that you'll skim the one you're on."

—*Jane*

"In Suzy Park, Kim has fashioned a moody, memorable misfit who both captures our heart and twists our guts in one of the new year's more complex and rewarding novels."

—*The News-Press*

"To readers of this compelling, cryptic novel—[Kim's heroine] Suzy is a gorgeous enigma, simultaneously sophisticated and naïve, corrupt and pure."

—*Shout*

"Part murder mystery, part psychological thriller, the novel grippingly explores damaging trade-offs made by people desperate to survive in a strange new place . . . *The Interpreter* opens out into vistas of human complexity that will captivate readers from any culture."

—*The Tennessean*

THE
INTERPRETER

THE
INTERPRETER

SUKI KIM

PICADOR

FARRAR, STRAUS AND GIROUX
NEW YORK

www.picadorusa.com

Picador® is a U.S. registered trademark and is used by Farrar, Straus and Giroux under license from Pan Books Limited.

For information on Picador Reading Group Guides, as well as ordering, please contact the Trade Marketing department at St. Martin's Press.
Phone: 1-800-221-7945 extension 763
Fax: 212-677-7456
E-mail: trademarketing@stmartins.com

Designed by Abby Kagan

Library of Congress Cataloging-in-Publication Data

Kim, Suki, 1970–
     The interpreter / Suki Kim.
          p.   cm.
     ISBN 0-312-42224-5
     1. Korean Americans—Fiction. 2. Women interpreters—Fiction.
3. Parents—Death—Fiction. 4. New York (N.Y.)—Fiction. I. Title.

PS3611.I457 I58 2003
813'.6—dc21

                                                    2002072120

First published in the United States by Farrar, Straus and Giroux

First Picador Edition: January 2004

10   9   8   7   6   5   4   3   2   1

For my parents

THE
INTERPRETER

1.

CIGARETTE AT 9 A.M. is a sure sign of desperation. Doesn't happen to her often, except on mornings like this, November, rain, overcrowded McDonald's in the South Bronx off the 6 train. Like a block party, this place, with those dopey eight-year-olds who should be in school, and their single mothers sick of shouting, and the bored men at each table still not at work. Morning is full here. Everyone's in it together, a communal experience, this day, this life. It is not her life, though. She does not know this. She does not want this. She looks up, instead, at a huge sign for the breakfast special across the window. Not much mystery there, food is plenty. Ninety-nine cents for hash browns, an English muffin with microwaved egg yolks, and a miniature Tropicana. Too good to be true, such abundance for barely a dollar. This is a generous neighborhood.

She is twenty-nine, and it is November. She is overdressed, as usual. The black cashmere coat that costs double her rent, and the pin-striped pants are sleek enough for any Hollywood starlet. Across her shoulder is a navy tote bag that matches the steel shine of her leather boots. Her face bears no trace of makeup. She is morose in black and blue. These are power colors.

November, and she stands facing the entrance of McDonald's on Burnside Avenue. In her left hand is a black vinyl umbrella, and in her right, a half-smoked cigarette she barely sucks on. Five minutes past nine. She is too early. The subway was unexpectedly fast. Only when she is running ahead of schedule should this happen, should the local suddenly reroute to express and drop her off at the Bronx stop within minutes. Fifty-five minutes to hang outside McDonald's in this part of town, a world away from her apartment back in downtown Manhattan. Fifty-four minutes and counting; she is stuck in this wilderness and peeks at her watch again.

But a rescue is handy, a cup of fresh coffee, a slab of butter on a toasted muffin. All she has to do is walk through that door and wave a dollar. A long drag on a cigarette, longer than necessary. She is stalling. She has not yet bought into this place.

Rain keeps on, halfhearted, barely soaking. She is Cinderella-at-midnight, and her chic ensemble a pumpkin dream ready to pop. There is no glass slipper in this part of town, no Prince Charming in search of a princess. The crossover is final. Beyond that door is the wrong track, whose morning begins with a dollar and a jaded appetite.

Looking in is easy, to stand out in rain and take note of what unfurls from a distance.

Instead, she is inside now. There are several lines, which all reach several faces taking orders. The line in which she stands moves fast enough, but she has time, enough time to stand and wait. Oh, but time is plenty here. People sit around in all corners. No one dashes out to a merger meeting at the head office. No one screams double espresso with a touch of skim milk. No one fumbles with a tray balancing a Motorola on their right ear.

None of that happens here. This is a place of leisure. She's in no rush.

What do you want after all, do you want me to tell you? Damian had lunged at her in his final message, as if he were pushing himself into her once more.

"What do you want, miss?"

She did not hear the man the first time. Such mishaps keep happening to her lately. She keeps missing the cue. She sets an alarm for eight and bolts out of bed at seven, or she presses "3" in the elevator and finds herself on the second floor, or she runs to answer the phone only to realize it is not ringing. Here she is dumbstruck before a man in a brown uniform who is shaking his head now, repeating for the third time, "What do you want, miss?"

"Coffee, a medium-sized cup of coffee, please." She thought she had said it. She thought he knew what she wanted. The big-haired teenager behind her is popping her pink gum, visibly annoyed. The man in the brown uniform snatches the dollar from her, shaking his head once more. The coffee costs seventy-nine cents. Twenty more cents, she could have a complete break-fast; what's she thinking? She can sense the man's disapproval. Bitch, he must think. A cup of coffee for seventy-nine cents when a whole tray comes for a dollar, Miss Too-Good-for-a-Discounted-Meal, Miss Stuck-Up-Coat, Miss Can't-Hear-for-Shit!

Bitch it is, this 9 a.m. Marlboro high. She needs to sit down, but the place is jam-packed, and no one is leaving anytime soon. But a miracle, it must be. There is someone waving at her, pointing at the empty seat across from him. Once she plops her-self down and takes a hot sip of coffee, she notices that the man is in fact the only other Asian present.

He is reading the paper. *Hangukilbo*—the *Korea Daily*—she recognizes the bold type. Beneath the thick Walgreens reading lenses, his eyes appear puffy and reddish. Lacking a good night's sleep, she thinks. They all do, these immigrant men. He wiggles his nose, which is too small for his spacious face, before glancing up at her for a second. She smiles, grateful for the seat. He does not return the smile but continues to stare at her awhile before turning back to his paper. He knows, she thinks. They always do. It's one of those things, the unspoken recognition among the same kind. She can tell who's Korean from miles away. Of course, she's been wrong before, though only a handful of times, mistaking a Japanese person for Korean. She is not sure why, perhaps something in the history, a possible side effect of the sick affinity between the colonizer and the colonized—Japan had once ruled Korea for thirty-six years, her father never forgot to remind her. Or it might simply be the way their facial bones are shaped, Koreans and Japanese more oval while Chinese seem flatter. All she knows is that she can always tell, and he can tell, and they both know that they are the same kind, sitting so close amidst a roomful of the rest of the world.

He is not interested in conversation, and she is glad. He does not harangue her with "Were you born in the States?," "What do your parents do?," or "Why is a good Korean girl like you not yet married?"—the prying questions that fellow immigrants often feel entitled to ask. Buried behind his newspaper now, he is no longer visible to her. It's almost noble of him, she thinks, to offer her a seat and leave her alone.

Nothing comes for free, look closer, you always find a tag, Damian had whispered into her ear while pulling at the last button on her dress. Then he took five steps backward and stood gazing at her first nakedness as if he were an artist before a muse. His eyes had appeared awfully blue then, bluer than they justifiably were, almost aqua, the ocean color, so different from her own black eyes that she looked away in a sudden wave of embarrassment, thinking the whole time, "Even this has a price, even his lips on my skin, even his bluest eyes on me."

Rain this morning is an accomplice. Even at the edge of the city through a cloudy window across which hangs a ninety-nine-cent-breakfast banner. The coffee is cooling. The waiting is not so bad after all. This might be her break. No one will find her here. A perfect hideout.

Then the man across from her shuts his newspaper. He picks up his tray without meeting her eyes. She watches him walk away. It is the shrunken walk of one who had once been a young man but is no longer, who has not spoken his language for longer than he can bear, who no longer believes that he will ever see his homeland. She can feel the weight of each step. She wants to look away. Yet she is relieved when he stops outside and lights a cigarette under the orange awning.

He is not gone. He is not yet gone from her. He stands with his back turned to the window, which she is facing now. The back of his hair is thinning. He is older than his actual age, perhaps. She notes the wrinkled seams of his gabardine pants and the shiny leather of his dress shoes, which are long out of style. He is awkward in his clothes, she thinks. Those are not his everyday shoes. When was the last time he put those shoes on, what was he like then, what was the rest of his life? But this is a terrible habit, to wonder upon a past, to dig into a history of anything, anyone, even a passing stranger at a fast-food joint in a neighborhood that is not hers. A lack of reserve, or boundary. Yet she still cannot look away. She knows men like him. She imagines how he might have fumbled through the back of his closet to pull out those black leather shoes, which might have sat in the dirt of his buried past for as long as a decade, or even longer, depending on when he had moved to this country, and how he might have shined them all morning with a bit of paper towel and wax, thinking to himself, "Ah they are fine still, they fit still, I am not such an old man after all, this mute delivery guy from Queens whom no one ever looks at, including my own wife, who hasn't had a day of smiles since she made that bad slip of following me so far, as far as this McDonald's land in the middle of nowhere, to this bad-food, bad-mannered country where I am nothing but a frail old man, smoking the last butt of a Marlboro in the November rain, as if my life depended on it, as if this life were a thing I could have known when I last wore these shoes."

She knows men like him. She knows what his days are like, the home he might return to at night, the daughters to whom he no longer reaches out.

She glances at her watch again. Quarter to ten, time's almost up. Didn't take so long after all. They must all be waiting for her. The case is nothing without her. She looks up and notices that the man outside is gone.

2.

FORTY-FOUR BURNSIDE AVENUE is a three-story concrete building east of McDonald's, the sort of place where an insurance agent or an accountant keeps an office, filled with ancient filing cabinets and dubious clientele. The elevator has not worked in months. The "Broken" sign is ripped halfway across, and a tiny scribble in red ink proclaims not so shyly "Your Ass." The staircase to the basement leads to a chunky wooden door adorned with a musty gold plaque that reads DIAMOND COURT REPORTING.

Inside, a Hispanic receptionist with bright-pink lips is screaming something into the phone. Then she looks up for a second and snaps, "You here for *Kim* versus *Santos*?," pointing her matching pink-manicured index finger toward the room marked "3" without waiting for an answer.

"Your name?"

Name is always the first thing they ask, not out of personal interest, but because everything has to be recorded here, stamped and witnessed. This is a mini-court. A place of honor, justice, and underpaid lawyers who didn't make the grade at hundred-thousand-dollar firms.

"Suzy Park," she answers automatically.

The stenographer scribbles the name in her note and adds, "Love that name Suzy, with 'z-y,' right?" Stenographers are always such chatty characters, mostly women from south-shore Long Island, mid-thirties with blond highlights. This one is no exception, although the blond streaks on her head appear almost natural against her blue-shadowed eyes. "As in Suzy Wong?" one of the lawyers blurts out with a chuckle, quickly realizes that no one is laughing, and tries hard not to blush. He is the young one, freshly out of law school and awkward in his crisp tan suit and the awful green tie with tiny boats on it that must have come from Macy's sale rack. "You mean the Chinese prostitute in that Hollywood classic?" Suzy is tempted to throw back at him, but she ignores him, grabbing the seat next to the one reserved for the defendant, who is still not here.

"Oh, Mr. Kim just went to make a phone call, but he'll be right back. Nice fella. Too bad about the union mess, though." The stenographer nudges, as if any of this is Suzy's business, as if the details of the case matter to anybody in the room at all. "Poor guy, he really doesn't speak a word of English. I don't know how they carry on. Amazing, don't you think?" The stenographer addresses the young lawyer, who is still blushing and is now glad at the chance to redeem himself. "Well, he does know a word or two. A smart man, though. Just because he doesn't speak the language, it doesn't mean he's dumb." With this declaration he is quite proud of himself, and turns to Suzy, grinning.

The other lawyer glances at his wristwatch with the insolence of a student ready for the bell. He is older, perhaps in his late forties. He is not interested in the Ping-Pongy chat across the table. He's heard it all, and he is not having it today. He is worried that he might have parked his car in the wrong spot. What the hell, if he gets a ticket, he'll just bill Santos. But where's Santos anyway? Should be outside waiting for his line of questioning, even if he doesn't want to sit face-to-face with this Kim guy! But he's not sure he turned the headlights off before getting out of his car. Damn rain, shouldn't have brought his brand-new Honda Accord to this pissy neighborhood. Then he remembers what his wife said to him this morning, about the loan on the car and how she's not going to help pay a penny of it if he doesn't pitch in for their Florida vacation this Christmas. And he thinks, Florida. They've gone every winter, dragging the kids, well, not really kids anymore, but brooding trench-coated teenagers who'd much rather stay online in their chat rooms than follow their mom and pop to the package hotel where they lie around the pool arguing over loans that seem to tag along with everything they own, from their Forest Hills house to the kids' prep-school tuition to the brand-new Honda, which is possibly sitting on the wrong street corner with sparkling headlights calling to any thugs who watch from McDonald's across the street, killing time.

With a mumbling moan, he rushes out. The stenographer, raising an eyebrow, is about to say something and then changes her mind. The young lawyer appears nonchalant, as if this sort of thing happens all the time at a deposition. "Oh well," he says, "we're gonna have to start a bit late. Why don't you ladies take a little break?" Then he excuses himself and walks out also. "A cigarette?" the stenographer suggests, grabbing her white leather bag to head outside, and Suzy declines. They smoke like high-school girls, these Long Island women, usually Virginia Slims or Capri, menthol if they are over thirty-five and newly divorced.

So it's Suzy all alone in the windowless room, staring at the stenograph mounted on a tripod, which is the only object other than the oversized conference table. The pay is by the hour, so it hardly matters if the case is delayed. Depositions never start on time anyway. Witnesses are rarely the problem. In fact, they usually show up early, nervous and guilty by association. The confusion begins with the whole arrangement of such interested, or disinterested, parties. Lawyers behave like children at a playground. Some are bullies flying on a verbal roller coaster like kids on speed; and others, bored and sullen, reluctantly finish up homework under supervision. Stenographers are jesters, butting in with needless commentaries and inevitably running out of ink or paper right at the crunch of a testimony. The interpreter, however, is the shadow. The key is to be invisible. She is the only one in the room who hears the truth, a keeper of secrets.

In fact, that is why Suzy has stuck with the job thus far. She has never before held a job for more than six months. She's done what college dropouts do—lie and get on with what she can scrape together. Waitressing required too much smile, although she did give it a shot for a few weeks at a sushi restaurant on Bleecker Street, only to get fired for refusing to pretend to be Japanese. Nightclub hostessing was a disaster, and she hated sleeping through the day and missing the sun. Internet sales made her head spin, as if her life were being gambled on fictitious credits. An artist's model meant being grabbed in the wrong places by the wrong hands. Copyediting ruined her eyesight. Copywriting was a hoax. The latest gig was a factchecking stint at a literary magazine. She lasted barely four months. She only got there through the connections of an old college roommate who was an editor and declared Suzy's career phobia to be "so nineties." "Get over it," Jen told Suzy over the phone. "Damian must've fucked with your brains." It was Jen who begged her to reconsider when Suzy packed her bag in the spring semester of their senior year. "Everyone will forget soon, it'll soon blow over." Jen had always been the sensible one. She never seemed to suffer from hangovers or PMS. Jen was right, of course. Except forgetting came with its price, as Damian had said. Was it a premonition? How did he know?

It wasn't that the fact-checking job was necessarily boring. Suzy didn't mind reading the copy all day. She could pretend that her cubicle was a waiting room at a doctor's office or an airport lounge as she scanned articles about the President's latest run-ins with that big-haired intern, or Philip Roth's ex-wife's tell-all book about Philip Roth, or the usual groundbreaking news, most of which she forgot instantly. Every day she had to call the New York Public Library and ask them to verify the year of publication of *The Bell Jar* or *The Crying of Lot 49* or the exact number of literary texts mentioned in Harold Bloom's monstrous canon book. The line was always busy, and she had to keep redialing. She thought it was kind of a miracle, that someone somewhere across the city was looking up all the gritty facts for her, as if it mattered to anyone, except Mr. Bloom, whether the magazine should print 100 texts or 101. What she did mind, and could not stand, in fact, was the voice of the researcher who came on the phone in the third month. It was a new person; by then, Suzy could recognize all voices on the other end. There was a shy, whispery girl-voice that answered in the morning, which Suzy imagined might actually belong to a tall woman in her fifties with wavy silver hair and a pleated skirt. Another was a husky male who often answered during lunchtime, whose intonation of words like "chiaroscuro" and "serendipitous" made Suzy swallow hard before saying thank you. But the new voice was without much character: monotone, matter-of-fact, flat. Suzy cringed when he answered, and was not sure why. She would forget the question and mumble whatever came into her mind, or, worse, she would hang up instantly. But it bothered her, this ominous voice she had to hear every day, almost every hour on busy days. Finally, in her fourth month, she quit. She did not explain why, and she was never asked. Fact-checkers are a dime a dozen. They come and go. Some get real jobs at the women's magazines around town, and a few actually sell the novel they've been slaving away at for years. But most move back home to Wichita or Baltimore, swearing never to return to New York. Jen laughed when Suzy told her later and said, "Damian, he must've been some fuck." Sure, something about the researcher's dark drone reminded her of Damian, but that was almost an afterthought.

Interpreting, Suzy finds, is somehow simpler, freer to be exact. The agency calls her when there is a job, and she shows up wherever the deposition happens to take place. Most cases are banal: automobile accidents, slip-and-falls, medical malpractice, basically any misfortune that might generate cash. The details are almost always predictable. The plaintiff wasn't really hurt at the time of the accident, but now, six months later, cannot move his head. Or the plaintiff had surgery and is now suffering from complications. Suzy never finds out what happens to these cases, whether they actually end up in trial or settle out of court or lead to another set of depositions. Her job is just to show up and translate into English verbatim what the witness testifies in Korean. She often feels like the buxom communication officer in *Star Trek*, the one who repeats exactly what the computer says. Except Suzy's role is neither so fleshy nor so comical. The contract, which the agency made her sign, included a clause never to engage in small talk with witnesses. The interpreter is always hired by the law firm on the side opposing the witness. It is they who need the testimony translated. The witness, summoned to testify without any knowledge of English, inevitably views the interpreter as his savior. But the interpreter, as much as her heart might commiserate with her fellow native speaker, is always working for the other side. It is this idiosyncrasy Suzy likes. Both sides need her desperately, but she, in fact, belongs to neither. One of the job requirements was no involvement: Shut up and get the work done. That's fine with her.

Except it doesn't go as smoothly as that. Suzy often finds herself cheating. Sometimes the witness falters and reveals devastating, self-incriminating information. The opposing counsel might ask how much he makes a week, and the witness turns to Suzy and asks what he should say. Should he tell him five hundred dollars, although he usually makes more money on the side? Suzy knows that the immigrant life follows different rules—no taxes, no benefits, sometimes not even Social Security or green cards. And she also knows that he should never tell lawyers that. So she might fudge the answer. She might turn to the lawyer innocently and translate, "My income is private information; approximately five hundred dollars, I would say, but I cannot be exact." Or the opposing side might try to make a case out of the fact that the plaintiff, when struck by a car, told the police that he was feeling fine and refused an ambulance. "Surely," the lawyer insists, "the injury must not have been severe if you even refused medical attention!" But Suzy knows that it is a cultural misunderstanding. It is the Korean way always to underplay the situation, to declare one is fine even when suffering from pain or ravenous hunger. This might stem from their Confucian or even Buddhist tradition, but the lawyers don't care about that. "Why did you say you were fine at the time of the accident if you weren't? Were you lying then, or are you lying now?" the lawyer presses once more, and Suzy winces, decides that she hates him. The witness gets all nervous and stammers something about how he's not a liar, and Suzy puts on a steel face to hide her anger and translates, "I was in shock, and the pain was not obvious to me until I got home and collapsed." Then the lawyer looks stumped and moves on to the next question. Suzy knows it is wrong, to embellish truth according to how she sees fit. In fact, she will be fired on the spot if anyone discovers that her translation harbors a bias. But truth, she has learned, comes in different shades, different languages at times, and lawyers with a propensity for Suzy Wong movies may not always see that. The job comes naturally to her. Neither of her parents had spoken much English. Interpreting is almost a habit.

Suddenly a light tap on her right shoulder. Suzy turns around to find a man standing there. It is the Korean man from McDonald's, the one with the freshly polished shoes, with a tired wife and unreachable daughters. "Mr. Kim?" She is delighted at such a coincidence. Breaking into a shy smile, he nods. He looks meek and timid now, no longer the grave man sitting across from her buried in his newspaper. "*An-nyung-ha-sae-yo.*" She makes a slight bow, the way Koreans do when addressing the elderly. Then he stares at Suzy's face intently, as he had done earlier this morning, and says in the unfamiliar midregional Korean accent, "You remind me of someone I used to know, a good woman, too young to be killed like that." Before she can ask what he means, the stenographer and two lawyers charge in as if they have been hanging outside together the whole time. "Shit, a ticket." The older lawyer shakes his head, waving a piece of paper. The younger one frowns, trying to appear sympathetic. The stenographer ignores both and adjusts the paper into her machine with the efficiency of a pro, turning to Suzy.

"Raise your right hand. Do you solemnly swear that you will translate from Korean to English and from English to Korean to the best of your ability, so help you God?"

"I do," Suzy answers, thinking to herself, *Yes, please help me, God.*

On the way home, Suzy calls Jen from Grand Central, which is just a few blocks from Jen's office.

"Do they always let you out this early?" Jen smiles when she greets Suzy at the Starbucks counter in the north wing of the station, sipping a Frappuccino. She is impressed that Suzy has stuck with interpreting for eight months, but she also makes it clear that she is not fooled.

"You're hiding," Jen says after ordering a chocolate-dipped biscotti with her decaf. "This is your little revenge, to make him find you, but you know Damian's far too decadent for that."

Suzy pretends to not hear and blows the foam on top of her Frappuccino into a little bubble, which makes a perfect round circle for a blinking second, then pops.

"The witness today said that I looked like someone he knew," Suzy says almost in passing.

"Another married asshole with a midlife crisis?" Jen rolls her eyes.

"No, he looked sad. He reminded me of Dad."

"Why, was he . . ."

"No, not angry, just sad."

"*Suzy . . .*"

"I've gotta go," Suzy says, sucking on the straw to get the last taste of the sugary bit at the bottom. "Michael's calling me at three."

"Where's he this time?" Jen asks with a smirk, creasing her perfectly powdered face.

"London. He loves calling me from there. He says that his cell connects clearest from Heathrow. I don't know. He might be right. Last week, he called from Lisbon and I could barely make out a word."

"Why doesn't the big guy just call you from a regular phone?"

"Because he thinks anything's traceable, and at least with his cell, he's on top of it."

They both burst out laughing then, like two coy college girls picking on the cutest boy in the room.

3.

THE PHONE CONTINUES for four rings and stops as Suzy reaches the fifth floor and stands at the door looking for the key. It rings again as she inserts the key into the hole, and stops at the fourth ring. Then it begins again. Whoever it is does not want to leave a message. Whoever it is does not know that she never picks up the phone, a habit that started the year she left school and moved in with Damian. He always let the machine take the call. It was from neither arrogance nor aloofness. During the first few months, it was a necessity. There were too many people hot on their trail, acquaintances with too much spare time who would call periodically to alert them to exactly what other people were saying about this "terrible situation," which they would repeat in a conspiring whisper as though it were not they who thought it "terrible" but everyone else. "New Yorkers aren't busy," Damian mused. "They just don't have enough time for themselves." Then there was the family. Damian's one sister lived in Lake Forest, Illinois, and had rarely been in touch over the years; Professor Tamiko would only speak to him through the lawyers. What Suzy feared was hearing her father's silence on the other end of the line. But it soon became clear that her parents would not try to contact her. Grace left a message a few weeks after the eruption of the scandal: "Suzy, you must get out of there. God will only forgive the ones who forgive themselves."

God had become Grace's answer by then, although she had been the bad one all through their growing up. Grace was the one who got grounded for being found naked with that Keller boy in the back of his dad's Toyota when she was fourteen. Grace was the one who hid her marijuana pouch inside her tampon case, which she nicknamed her "best friend, Mariana," and then, to Suzy's surprise, declared so boldly at the dinner table, "May I be excused? I promised my friend Mariana that we'll do our homework together." It had also been Grace who told Suzy that the only reason she applied to Smith College on early decision was that no decent Korean boy would want her now, because everyone knew Smith was for sluts and lesbians. But somehow, during her four years away, God found his way into Grace's untamable spirit, and Suzy could no longer recognize her older sister, who left such an inappropriate message on her machine, as though salvation lay somewhere on the stoop of a Presbyterian church on Sunday mornings. Suzy began to dread the phone. Damian said that if he could help it he would live without the damn thing. He was distrustful of people anyway. The thought of Damian being stuck on the phone with any of her young friends—although, after a few months, Jen was the only one who called with any consistency—was almost painful.

When Suzy enters the apartment, the phone begins ringing again. She waits for the click at the fourth ring, but instead the machine takes it.

"Babe, it's me, pick up!"

The voice is cheery and confident.

"Suzy, I know you're there."

She is not sure why she does not pick up immediately, but there is an unmistakable moment of hesitation. For a second, she is tempted to leave Michael at Heathrow, sliding down the moving sidewalk, shouting into his Motorola. For a second, that seems to be the most obvious thing to do, the only thing to do—to leave him there.

"Hi, I just walked in." The hesitation is over.

"See, I knew." Michael is all happy.

"London?"

"Yeah, it's fab, brilliant. Those Brits just ate it up, man. They fucking love the whole crap. They've got it all mixed up. They think Java's some coffee from the Caribbean, and HTML a code name for the newest hip-hop nation. They're sure I'm their Bill Gates, and I told them, 'Bill and me, we're like brothers.' "

"Good," Suzy agrees, as she always does when Michael's had a shot of whiskey or two.

"I sent Sandy out to Harrods to get you some stuff, some slinky things here and there, for my pretty girl back home, I told her. I'm sure she thinks I'm a pig, so I told her to get some sexy stuff for herself too, although you make sure my girl gets the best of the pile, I said."

Suzy smiles, imagining Michael's curt, crisp, forty-something-and-single secretary lingerie-shopping for her boss's mistress. Sandy often calls for Michael when he is stuck in a meeting or on the plane. Sandy is efficient and excessively private. Although, Michael has said, the minute she finds a man, she will quit in a flash. He is sticking with her, he has claimed, just to see that happen.

"Babe, you listening?"

"Michael, I miss you." Suzy is surprised at this sudden confession and thinks that it must be true.

"Meet me in Frankfurt. Sandy will arrange the ticket."

"I can't. I don't have a passport." In fact, she has never been out of the country, not since she followed her parents to America as a child. At twenty-nine, Suzy has never been abroad. Partly for fear of flying, and partly because she can no longer leave New York.

"Suzy, I'm being serious." Michael does not believe her. Why should he? He knows practically nothing about her.

"I really can't. Family business."

"What family? Babe, you haven't got any . . ." Michael is good at dodging serious conversation. "Except for me," he adds almost peevishly.

You're hiding. That is what Jen said this afternoon.

"When are you boarding?" Suzy asks, trying to shake off Jen's voice.

"Right now. Gotta go, call you tomorrow!"

Michael is gone before she can ask if it was he who kept hanging up at the fourth ring.

Suzy's apartment on St. Marks Place is at the hub of downtown. It was the first place she saw when she moved back to the city five years ago. She had been in such a rush then that she just grabbed the first thing offered, although there had been a few more apartments to check out. Apartment hunters in Manhattan are truly desperate. At 7 p.m. on Tuesdays, they line up outside Astor Place Stationery, where the first batch of *The Village Voice* is delivered upon printing. That is where the apartment war begins, everyone grabbing the first issue and running to the nearest phone booth to call the handful of landlords who fill the ad space with "No broker, low rent!"

For three consecutive Tuesdays, Suzy stood in line with no

luck. Although she had been worried that such a collective panic would make her so nauseous she would run straight back into Damian's arms, she actually found it comforting to see that she was not the only one looking for a new home or new life in the streets of New York. Mostly they were college graduates fresh from Middle America who had watched too much MTV and decided to try their luck the minute they could scrape up some money to get to the city. They often appeared even hipper than the city kids. Clad in vintage velvet and leather, they looked everything they said they were. "We need a loft where me and my girlfriend can both paint; our paintings are huge, bigger than the stuff Pollock used to do," one goateed boy declared, so loudly that everyone in line turned to him, as though he and his girlfriend were the newly crowned postmodern Abstract Expressionist royalty. Then others chimed in competitively: "New York rocks, man. I wrote like two hundred songs about it," or "I'll take anything on Avenue A; how could you be a poet and not follow Ginsberg?," or "This casting agent says that I look just like Monica from *Friends*, and I'm, like, no way would I ever do TV!" Suzy would listen and wonder how many of them, if any, would attain their dreams, and she would realize that she, in fact, envied them all, these buoyant kids for whom life was just offering its first mysterious glimpse, while she, at twenty-five, had already given up. Then, one day, a boy who stood behind her tapped on her shoulder and asked if she needed a roommate. He was the first true redhead she had seen in a long time, and he wore a sky-blue bowling jacket that had "Vince" stitched above its right pocket. He could not afford to live alone, he said, and did not trust strangers to share an apartment, but she looked nice and he'd always wanted to live in Asia, and perhaps she was the closest thing he'd come to the continent. Then he held out his multi-ringed hand and said, "Hi, I am Caleb, I'm twenty-one, a philosopher and a performance artist." She tried not to laugh as she shook his hand with "Suzy, twenty-five and unemployed."

She liked Caleb. He was honest and surprisingly shy. He also brought her luck, because on that very night they found the apartment on St. Marks Place. She was amazed that it had been so easy, considering that she was unemployed, and as far as she could tell, his day job of working at a vegan restaurant on the Lower East Side did not quite fulfill the criterion of a desirable tenant. Then Caleb told her that his doctor parents who lived in Scarsdale co-signed the lease. When she asked if they knew that the beneficiary of their generosity was an unemployed stranger their son had met outside Astor Place Stationery, Caleb winked. "Darling, I told them that I had a mad crush on you. They would've bought the apartment for us if they thought we were actually doing it."

The apartment was a typical East Village walk-up railroad, an elongated stretch of three connecting rooms. Suzy had to pass through Caleb's bedroom to get to the kitchen, which led to the bathroom that was missing a sink. Neither noticed the missing sink until they finally moved in, when Caleb walked out into the kitchen with a seriously distraught look on his face and exclaimed, "There's no place to put a toothbrush!" Suzy thought it could have been worse. Better a sink than a tub. She could not imagine surviving New York winters without the relief of a hot bath.

Caleb often brought home leftover tofu pancakes and non-dairy crème brûlée from the restaurant. The only edible things there, he explained. The rest tasted so depressingly dull that it was simply cruel to put his taste buds through such an uninspiring challenge. A cleverly concocted diet plan, he claimed. Imagine working at a restaurant where the food is actually good! The philosopher-and-performance-artist bit was hard to figure out,

though. Caleb never read books and was certainly too cynical to
perform in front of a crowd. When Suzy finally approached the
subject without wanting to sound either dismissive or disre-
spectful, he burst out laughing. "Oh, it's a private joke with myself. My dad once said that homosexuality is for philosophers or
performance artists. How could you grow up in Westchester and
end up fucking boys? He wept when I came out at my high-
school graduation, really. Imagine this Jewish optometrist in
his fifties with tears streaming down his face. He didn't use the
f-word, of course."

Suzy found it almost comforting to hear about Caleb's unending drama with his parents, who phoned every Sunday and
yet always managed to avoid addressing her directly. Soon they
stopped calling. Caleb's therapist, whom his parents hired and
paid for, thought it was unwise for them to keep up with this
weekly communication, which only encouraged resentment in
both parties. "Once the homosexual issue is 'solved,' Dr. Siegel
told them, then they can call!" Caleb exclaimed with the cheeky
smile of a kid who has just pushed the bully off the merry-go-
round.

"What about your parents? Do they know that you never get
laid?" Caleb asked one night after three months of living together. It must have been Thursday, the crème brûlée night,
which they often celebrated with an Australian Chardonnay
from the "Deal of the Week" shelf at First Avenue Liquor.

"They're both dead. But, no, I guess they never knew, or
never wanted to know at least," Suzy answered in the most
matter-of-fact tone she could muster, which she hoped would
make him feel less sorry about asking.

"Gee, I'm sorry, Suz, I didn't know . . ."

"Don't worry about it. It's been a while. Besides, we never
talked much when they were alive anyway."

With that, Suzy polished off the last scoop. Caleb sat still, waiting for her to say more. But she didn't. It was the first time she had said aloud that they were dead. It came out just like that, almost naturally. She had not talked to anyone she knew since the funeral. She had not seen anyone, except for Jen. She certainly did not plan on finding herself in an East Village walk-through kitchen with a twenty-one-year-old boy whom she'd met three months ago and casually saying, while picking at a bowl of crème brûlée, that her parents were dead.

Suzy never mentioned her parents again, and Caleb never asked. Instead, she asked him about his. She inquired after his progress with Dr. Siegel, and if his father still occasionally cried, if his mother was curious at all about the supposed girlfriend who lived with her son. Suzy asked to see their photograph, which Caleb then stuck on the refrigerator door with a magnet that said "From Here to Eternity." They looked almost exactly as Suzy had imagined, with Caleb's red hair and extra-long eyelashes, posing before their unmistakable Stanford White house and the nougat-colored Mercedes Benz. Caleb would tell her all about his father's glass-walled office in the center of Scarsdale, and his mother's book club, which included other doctors' wives from the better part of Westchester County. "Whatever's on the *Times* best-seller list they'd read, especially the lewd ones, you know, books like *Hollywood Madam*, which I'm sure they took home to pore over only the dirty parts." Caleb would steal a glance at Suzy as if he knew that she kept prodding him with questions so that she would not have to talk.

Then, three months later, Caleb started dating an older man who one day walked into the restaurant and fell in love with him, and three weeks later, he packed his bag and moved into the man's spacious one-bedroom apartment in the West Village. "He has a real sink, with gold faucets and everything. I feel like I'm back in Scarsdale," Caleb said, chuckling into the phone on his first night away.

Suzy did not bother looking for a new roommate. There was still some money left over in the savings account that Damian had set up for her during the later stage of their escapade. It occurred to her that she should send it back to him, but she knew that he also expected her to. It was Damian's way. It was his hook, his excuse to keep her in his tow, and she knew that he waited patiently for a day when she would throw the money back at him with a letter, a memo, a phone call, so Suzy would not do it. She kept it instead, and paid her landlord $966 each month with Damian's money. She thought this ensured her as his kept woman, as everyone had believed, including Professor Tamiko and their mutual colleagues, including her parents and Grace, including Damian himself, although Suzy was the last one to find out.

Suzy spent the first year back in New York doing nothing. She lay around the apartment all day and called no one. Caleb dropped by once in a while, after his day shift at the restaurant. They would walk around the neighborhood on sticky evenings and sit on a bench at Tompkins Square Park munching on crème brûlée wrapped in tinfoil. Caleb would buy her a Starbucks Frappuccino, which he said was her Jappiest habit and that if she ever met a decent boy, she should keep it a secret from him until he was well hooked on her Asian charm, and she would laugh, realizing that her own laughter sounded almost foreign to her. Caleb would tell her all about his new boyfriend and the incredible sex they were having: "Three courses a night, darling. I tell you, you ain't seen nothing yet until you fucked someone your dad's age."

But everything comes with a price, Suzy thought. She was twenty-five then, unemployed, goal-less, an orphan.

At the funeral, Grace avoided Suzy. They sat next to each other and did not exchange a word. No one spoke to Suzy, not her parents' acquaintances, not the man with gold-rimmed glasses who had helped Grace out of a car, not Mr. and Mrs. Lim, whom Suzy grew up next door to when they lived in Flushing years ago. It was as if they considered her also dead, as if respecting the wishes of her parents, who had disowned her the minute she ran off with Damian in her senior year. Quite a crowd had gathered at the Korean church in Fort Lee, New Jersey, where Grace now lived. There were no relatives, because they did not have any except for a few aunts back in Korea whom neither Suzy nor Grace had ever met. Her parents barely had any friends, never liked people much, but their death had been shocking, scandalous, tragic, and people, especially church-going immigrants, loved tragedies. The only thing Grace said when Suzy went up to her to say goodbye was, *Don't bother showing up for the ashes, they are with God now. Do me a favor, Suzy; leave us alone.*

The phone starts ringing again. Whoever it is does not want to leave the evidence. Whoever it is is desperately looking for her. The Caller ID says "private." But she knew that without even looking at it. Suzy finally takes off her coat, throwing it on a silk hanger from the pricey Madison Avenue shop. Took Sandy all afternoon to find it, Michael claimed. Michael wants Suzy in the latest fashion. He wants the latest of anything. Often she stands in front a mirror, clad in what strikes her as carefully sewn and stitched money, lots of it. She hardly recognizes herself. A bona fide mistress, whose clothing shields her from herself. Suzy brushes her fingers across the array of silk shirts and cashmere sweaters. They come in every shade of black. "To match your hair, Suzy," Michael said. She imagines his wife in the most flamboyant pitch of red and green, a blonde surely, once-upon-a-sorority, maybe a book club or two, that would suit him. Michael never discusses his family. It is taboo, and

Suzy prefers it that way. She knows how to be a kept woman. She got her start early. She even sacrificed her own parents to be one, so she had better be damn good at it. The phone starts again, and Suzy stares at it without turning off the ringer. Then she walks to the end of the railroad and turns the hot water on to the fullest.

4.

THE VOICE ON THE OTHER END shouts, "Delivery." Suzy
presses the intercom button, standing at the door in her
bathrobe with her hair wrapped in a towel. The deliveryman
smiles, as if her wetness suggests a private promise. In his arms is
a bouquet of white irises. "Sign the receipt, please," he says, and
she asks, "From whom?" although she already knows the answer.
No sender's name, nothing. No note, no miniature card with a
happy smile, no heart-shaped balloon with a double I-love-
you's. A bunch of white irises, a rarity in November, but only in
November, always in November. Almost exactly four years ago,
a man first appeared at her doorstep with a bunch of white irises
much like these. It occurred to her that they might be from
Damian, but this was not Damian's style, and delicate white
irises definitely not his thing. Then who? Not Michael, because
she did not even know him then, and not a secret admirer,
Caleb said he hoped, because the joke was too old and she was
not so young anymore. They were always delivered right around

the anniversary of her parents' death. She wonders if they were
sent to Grace also. But why irises, why such insistence? Mom
had liked them, Suzy vaguely recalls. Her parents used to sell
them at their store. Mom said that, among all garden flowers,
irises needed the most care, because they withered quickly and
had virtually no smell. Her mother was not one of those softies
whose hearts melt at the sight of long-stemmed roses or tulips,
and neither was Suzy. They were pleasing to look at, she
thought, but why not leave them wherever they came from, either the perennial fields of the Netherlands or the sloping valleys
of northern California, anywhere at all but primped like a poo-
dle and squeezed into a glass vase on a now-satisfied girlfriend's
mantel in order to reassure her that somebody loved her on this
Valentine's Day or birthday or anniversary? A bouquet reminded
Suzy of a Hallmark card from a corner stationery store, whose
price was preprinted and whose purpose was long prescribed.
Only once she thought that flowers served a purpose, and that
was at the funeral. Grace must have arranged it, which surprised
Suzy, but one could never tell how a sibling might react to one's
parents' death, which sort of coffin, open casket or not, a chorus
of hymns even if they had never believed in Christ. There were
white flowers everywhere around both coffins, either lilies or
chrysanthemums, although Suzy cannot recall if she saw irises
among them. Dad would have thrown a fit, she thought then.
"Frivolous!" he would've screamed. "What a waste! In Korea, no
one would dare to throw away so much for nothing!" And that
must be exactly why Grace chose to do it. Everyone thought
that the flowers were appropriate. But Suzy knew that they were
the last things her parents would have wanted at their final moment.

Grabbing the nearly empty Evian bottle from the refrigerator, Suzy cuts open the top part and sticks the flowers in it. She
is not sure where to put it, although she must have found a spot

for it each year. On the dining table, there, she places the bottle on the corner as if putting it away. Irises are sad flowers, she thinks, neither as glamorous as roses nor as graceful as lilies, just a run-of-the-mill sort. Each flower stalk stands perfectly straight, with slivers of drooping falls. White ones are the worst. Such petals, signaling perpetual mourning. Mom was right. It is eerie how they carry no scent, no trace.

Suzy told no one about the flowers. Somehow she thought that she was not supposed to, that it was meant to be a secret between her and whoever sent them, and that if she were to break this code something bad was bound to happen. Caleb was the only one who knew, because the first delivery came while he was over. "An acquaintance of your parents, probably," he said. "Maybe he owed them money, maybe he cheated your parents a little and feels sorry, who knows, but whoever it is sure isn't very original!"

November is a strange month anyway, not quite the winter, not quite the end of a year, and Suzy not quite thirty. She is happy to be almost done with her twenties. The whole youth thing escaped her. While other girls fretted about noncommittal boyfriends, maniacal bosses, or aimless Friday nights, Suzy was always looking to see who might be lashing at her from behind. It is impossible to insist on youth when your own parents call you a whore. But one cannot blame the dead. Whatever meanness is forgotten, washed away, gone with the ashes. It is their privilege. And here's Suzy, five years since the funeral, still looking over her shoulder, or looking at the screeching phone, which will not leave her alone.

Perhaps it is the last echo of Dad's anger, the way he muttered "*yang-gal-bo*" under his breath, or perhaps the faraway look on Mom, who would not meet Suzy's eyes, but Suzy continues to stare at the phone without turning off the ringer. Each ring is a slash, a slap, a shot or two.

Two shots only; the gun had fired exactly twice and pierced their hearts.

Too precise for a random shooting, too perfectly executed, too clean. There wasn't much bleeding, she was told. The bullets stopped their hearts.

A cold murder, a professional's job, miss, your parents died instantly.

Suzy knows nothing further, and Grace will not speak to her. The Bronx Homicide Unit did the usual investigation, but there was no witness, no evidence, no suspect. There had been several similar shootings around the neighborhood, all unsolved. The case was quite typical, Detective Lester told Suzy: a useless killing by useless thugs. The victims were almost always immigrants, but there were no outstanding conflicts between specific immigrant groups, just the usual squabble. "Don't worry," he said. "We'll get them; these thugs end up in jail anyway, if not for this, then something equally horrendous sooner or later." And that was that. Grace took care of the store, the funeral, and their Queens brownstone. She contacted Suzy only once, through the accountant, about a small sum of money Suzy was entitled to from the sale of her parents' possessions, but Suzy quietly declined. What right did she have? When Dad called her a whore, she stood up and said, *I wish I wasn't your daughter!* That was her farewell to him.

Nine years now, almost ten. She had just turned twenty when she ran off with Damian. Four years later, her parents were shot at their store. Five years have passed since their death. Once you start counting years, the numbers drive you crazy. A decade since she's seen her parents alive, which should make her a credible orphan, and yet one never gets used to being alone. A bouquet of flowers arrives, and she cannot imagine who could've sent it, who would know that irises were her mother's favorite flowers, who would mark each November to commemorate her parents' death, who would care whom she loves, who would cry because she will never marry him because he is already married, who would call her a whore, hoping it would stop her from plunging onto the wrong track, who would lose sleep at night because she is all alone in her railroad apartment afraid to answer the phone.

I wish I wasn't your daughter.

She had meant it, and they knew it. There are words one cannot take back, intentions that are permanent.

It is useless going back to bathe now. The moment is gone, the shock of hot water running over her body has had its fill. She stands in her towel and lights a cigarette instead. She barely inhales before putting it out. The ashtray is filled with half-smoked cigarettes. Lately, cigarettes have begun to taste bitter. She has heard that it happens when one stops longing. Each time one of those righteous ladies comes up to her on the street and clicks her tongue with the cigarettes-are-so-bad-for-you speech, she wants to spit back something equally rude, like "So is your corduroy dress for your sex life." But instead, she throws them the coldest stare, which usually wipes the benevolent smile right off their faces. Damian used to tease her for it. He used to say that Philip Morris should give her a medal for being one of the last true militants. He himself never touched them. He said that cigarettes were for the young, and it would be embarrassing for him at forty-nine to be sucking on something so obviously seductive. But he liked watching her smoke. "Take off your bra." He would surprise her with an order so abrupt, and she would hold on to the cigarette between her lips while unhooking the strap with both her hands. "Take off your stockings," he'd say. And before the end of the cigarette, she would be ready, and Damian would finally reach over and take the cigarette from her lips and stub it out.

Still she refuses to quit, although she can no longer smoke a whole cigarette. Still it is the one thing she recognizes in herself. It's like a line from a Leonard Cohen song, a girl who's been left with nothing but a pack of cigarettes. Nothing is familiar any longer, nothing sinks. Since Caleb left, the apartment became bare. Hardly any furniture except for a futon and a mahogany dining table with two chairs. No posters lighten up the walls, no pretty fabrics cover the cracks in the corner. The only obvious electronic items are the Sony boom box and a fourteen-inch television set. The table and the TV belong to Caleb. "Turns out that a married life needs something more than Ikea," he sighed when she asked him if he wanted his stuff back.

During her first year back in New York, Suzy watched TV all day. It was a new thing for her. Her parents never had time to sit around, because they were always working, and when they did watch, for an hour or two on rare weekends, they would put on Channel 47, which was the East Coast's only Korean programming, whose jokes were lost on her. Grace had no tolerance for it either. It bored the hell out of her, she said, turning back to the book in her hands; the only thing she did with any enthusiasm was read. And when Suzy lived with Damian, of course there was no TV. Despicable, he grunted. American culture is the gutter, worse than drugs, definitely worse than cigarettes! Damian would have turned away in disgust if he saw how Suzy started the day now with *Good Morning America* and continued with *Regis and Kathy Lee* until midday, when the wildly convoluted sagas of daytime soaps unfolded. They had fabulous titles like *All My Children* and *Days of Our Lives.* There was one called *The Bold and the Beautiful,* which she thought was a more appropriate name for a body shampoo or a cologne. She welcomed the whole ritual, to lean back in her futon with a bowl of microwaved popcorn and lose herself in the entangled lives of Yasmina or Desiree or Katharina, who all seemed to have popped out of the Ms. Clairol box, and the occasional black or Asian

ones, who looked even more Ms. Clairol–like with their perfectly coifed hair, which, even though they were definitely not
blonde, still carried the just-walked-out-of-a-salon essence as
they bobbed along with the saccharine smile of the golden girl's
best friend. Her favorite was *One Life to Live.* She tried not to
miss it, only because she found out while watching *Regis and
Kathy Lee* one morning that it was the least popular among the
soaps. She thought this was unfair, since they were basically in-
terchangeable. In fact, even the actors seemed to skip around.
She was sure that she had seen one particular actor in the two
o'clock soap as a handsome but evil doctor, and then, a week
later, she would find him at three o'clock on another channel as
a self-made millionaire. Then, of course, she would quickly discover that he had been killed in a plane crash in one soap but
smoothly popped into another with a newer and nicer character.
She envied their resurrecting lives. They never died, not completely. There seemed to be always a way out, a second, even a
third chance. People did not just disappear without proper explanation. Tragedies came with namable causes and retribution.
Their fate was a puzzle but an easy one, and days, months
would fly by as she watched and toyed with the missing bits.

She stopped watching TV when she got her first job. Or
maybe she got the job in order to stop watching it. No matter
how frequently and closely she watched, she was never sure what
really went on, who had supposedly died only to return with
amnesia, who was cheating on whom with whose husbands and
wives, who was kidnapped on the day of the wedding by the
priest who turned out to be a spy. She thought these dramas required specific minds that could keep up with all the details. Yet
what made her finally turn the TV off had nothing to do with
its mind-numbing spell, but the gunshot. At least one or two
characters were killed on TV each day. Almost always in daytime
soaps, the victims came back alive, and the actual shooting scene

was skipped over. But there were the odd ones that would show the entire gruesome sequence in detail—the index finger on the trigger, the horrified victim shuddering, the squinting of the killer's vengeful eyes, the slow falling of the body as the final ray of blood spurts out. The first time she saw a scene like that, Suzy was fixated. She could not stop thinking about it and wanted to record it to watch again and again. But the second time it happened, she felt sick and lay still on the futon and did not move for hours. And the third time, she shut it off and moved the TV set to the farthest corner of the apartment. She never went near it again.

"You're waiting for a whistle to blow; it'd take you less than five minutes to grab your stuff and run," said Jen when she stopped by a few months ago, which she rarely did. "Deadline," she claimed. "Drop by the office, we'll go to the Royalton for lunch on the company's account." But Suzy knew that Jen did not want to meet at home. When lounging at each other's apartments, they naturally fell into the familiar ways of former roommates. One would get up to pour coffee before the other even asked for a refill, or bring the ashtray before the other took out a cigarette. Yet somehow, sitting on the futon with the coffee brewing, they could not help remembering the way Suzy had quit and left an irreparable hole in their college days. Jen was right, though. The apartment resembles a temporary shelter. There is no sweetness here, no flowery sheets, no matching duvet cover, no framed childhood photos. In fact, Suzy cannot say if she is attached to anything anymore. A jade ring that once belonged to her mother? An album filled with her childhood photos? A videotape of her seventh-birthday party? No such memorabilia in her apartment. Sure, Grace might have retrieved a few items from the Queens house where their parents had lived in their final years—their family having moved frequently through their growing up—but how important were such things if she had rarely missed them all these years? In college, Suzy envied Jen, who went home every few months to her parents' Connecticut mansion, where her childhood bedroom was intact with her Barbie and her tattered Cure poster and a bulletin board filled with the snapshots from her high-school excursion to St. Petersburg. The shrine of such a lovely American past, to Suzy, suggested an emblem, a reference to what Jen would become, what Jen could only become—a successful editor, the one-bedroom apartment on Central Park West, a summer share in the Hamptons, a boyfriend of her own age in his final year of residency at Johns Hopkins. They were all the right, correct things in life, which a smart, ambitious young woman such as Jen, upon finishing an Ivy League education, was expected to find in such a scintillatingly possible ground as New York City.

But those *things* were not what differentiated Jen from Suzy. Two girls of the same age, the same education, the same earnest propensity for Brontë's *Villette*, and yet their makeups were different from the start. It was neither because Suzy spent her early years moving constantly from Flushing to the Bronx to the inner parts of Queens, as new immigrants often did, nor because Suzy's inner-city public-school education suffered next to Jen's suburban private-school history, a deficit that Suzy was bright enough to overcome. But there was something else, something markedly different, something more fundamental, ingrained, almost inborn. Jen seemed to float about their mutual college life with the brightest sunlight, whereas Suzy, no matter how she tried to hide it, was stuck somewhere cold and brooding. And Damian was the first one to notice, and was not afraid to tell her about it.

On their first date, sitting on the bench in Riverside Park—although "date" might be a misnomer, since they had just slept together for the first time that day—Damian gazed at her awhile and said, "Stop looking at me for an answer; you're not going to be happier." Suzy knew that he was telling the truth and kept silent, because she still did not know what she wanted, and could still feel the pain between her legs, and felt no regrets. She looked away instead at the afternoon calm of the Hudson River, across which New Jersey loomed with not much promise, and remembered that she had missed language lab that afternoon. Damian was forty-nine then, a married scholar whose picture she had seen framed at Professor Tamiko's office. Suzy had just turned twenty, a comparative-literature major, a virgin, which strangely did not matter at all. Neither discussed it. Suzy's virginity was the last thing on their minds. From the first meeting, there was no doubt that they would make love. What bothered them was the darkness they sensed in each other, which pulled them together, which let them know almost instantly that their union was not a good thing, was doomed, was bound to hurt people and leave scars that might not go away no matter how much time passed, how they reorganized their lives so that one might forget that the other had ever happened at all.

The phone is persistent, and Suzy is not sure what makes her finally answer it. Perhaps she hopes it is Damian after all, perhaps she imagines that he has gotten softer with years and will break down just once. She tightens the towel grip and walks over to the end of the room and picks up the receiver before its fourth ring. She does not say hello. She waits for a voice, a signal. But instead, a pause, a drawn-out silence. She will not speak. She will not give up easily. Then, finally, comes the click—she knew it—a smooth, intentional hang-up. Must've been a wrong number, surely a prank call. And yet, for a quick second, she cannot help looking to make sure that the blinds on both windows are drawn.

5.

NO MATTER WHAT TIME OF DAY, it seems, the north wing of Penn Station is packed. Eight a.m., and a horde of men and women in suits and briefcases pour out of Long Island Rail Road trains and rush into the subway to reach their cubicles on Wall Street or the Avenue of the Americas by nine o'clock sharp. The commute costs them the better part of the day, the better mood of their lives. But a small sacrifice for a two-story house with a basketball hoop in the backyard and a cozy public school whose PTA meets for a monthly picnic in the town park. It's worth one and a half hours each way, three hours combined. Who would want to raise kids in the city, who could afford it? So they recline in their seats with *The Wall Street Journal*, the *Long Island Weekly*, or the *Times*. The clever ones make the best of the lull by balancing their checkbooks, or reading over contracts or invoices, whatever they do all day at work and still take home extra of because there never is enough time, because time is what such commutes are all about. And amidst crowds who reappear from the LIRR each morning like ants out of mounds, Suzy stands waiting for her 8:25 to Montauk, glad to be going in the opposite direction.

Montauk is the final stop. Suzy finds a seat easily enough. The train leaves exactly on time. She will have to make the connection in Jamaica, which is about twenty minutes away. Leaning back, she looks out the window, although the view is nothing, just the outskirts of the city, impossible to place. And yet she keeps on staring, because she is sitting by the window and there is nothing to do except follow this motion and let the barren scenery pass like a dull movie.

Outside is a mess of twisting highways and cement buildings. Some bits seem familiar. The train passed by Long Island City, where they had once lived, many years ago, when her father got a job at a Korean deli for a few months. It was an ugly, depressed part of Queens, and she was glad when he finally quit, or was he fired? Suzy is not sure anymore, but she recalls the fiercely unpleasant drive through the neighborhood and the oversized man with the overlapping front teeth named Mr. Yang who owned the store, who tossed a dollar at eight-year-old Suzy to run along and get him a slice of pizza from across the street, and how Dad had put a hand on the man's right shoulder and said in a quiet but menacing voice, "Don't tell my daughter what to do."

The memory seems slightly skewed. What had she been doing with him at work? Why wasn't she at school on that day? Did he really say those exact words? Perhaps he mumbled with an awkward slouch to his shoulders, "Please don't order my daughter around," or lashed with a stone in his voice, "Who do you think you are, ordering my daughter about?" Or is it possible that he did not say anything at all? It's been so long, over twenty years. Hard to remember now how it had really been between a father and a daughter, how he might have taken her small hand and stormed out of the store with the parting spit at the rotund man, "Don't you *dare* tell *my* daughter what to do!"

Outside, the familiar streets are gone now. The train is moving swiftly, almost gliding. She cannot recall the last time she was inside a moving vehicle in such tranquillity. Perhaps Dad's Oldsmobile had felt this safe, pure. All you had to do was just hop in and let him take you. Mom never drove, although she kept saying that she should learn, since she could not get anywhere on her own. But she never did, because they had only one car anyway and she had gotten used to being driven around. Dad was the best driver, never got a ticket, never got into an accident, never drove in the wrong lane. Later on, Suzy expected the same when she first rode in Damian's Volvo, and was shocked to discover that she had to check her seat belt several times before settling down. Luckily, she rarely found herself riding in cars. New Yorkers don't drive. The city is all about smelly subways and screaming taxis. Subways often get stuck in the middle of dark tunnels, and cabs, of course, are driven by a breed of wild men who zoom through the grids with a certain unexplained rage. The train remains ancient, Suzy thinks, like Dad's Oldsmobile. It sticks to the right course, from here to whatever its destination.

The first time she went to Montauk was for the ashes. She did not know that her parents had ever been there. Like most immigrants, they never took a vacation. Long Island for them ended in Bayshore, a seedy town where a few Koreans owned dry cleaners and fish markets. Dad once mentioned in passing that the business was not bad over there and the schools were better than the ones in Queens. But both Mom and Grace were fiercely against the idea. Mom could not imagine having to take a car to the nearest supermarket, which meant having to learn to drive immediately, and Grace said she would rather die than divulge that she was from Long Island. Suzy did not care one way or the other. They moved so often that it did not seem to matter where they went, for she was sure that they would move again before the year was up. Besides, she did not feel that she came from one particular place. When someone asked where she was from, she would pause and run through her mind the various apartment complexes in Flushing, the Bronx, the inner parts of Queens, even Jersey City, where they had lived for a few years when Mom got a job at a nail salon during their first years in America. None of them fit the bill, she thought. Korea, she would ponder, but that also seemed far away, for they immigrated when she turned five, and Grace six. Suzy could hardly remember the place. They had lived in a tiny apartment complex on the outskirts of Seoul, she was told. Oddly enough, the only detail she remembered about this childhood home was the elevator. Their apartment was on the fifth floor, which was the uppermost floor, according to her parents, because the top-floor units usually cost less; most young families did not trust the elevator and feared that kids might fall from the windows, which had happened in some buildings. What Suzy remembered vividly was the tiny box of the elevator, which was not so tiny in her child's eyes, and the mirror that had hung on its wall. She always wanted to look at the mirror, but it hung so high that she could never reach it. She would ask Mom to hoist her up on her shoulders, but Mom was always carrying bags of groceries and was busily pressing the numbered buttons, because the elevator would never respond to the first try. Sometimes Dad would give her a lift—although this happened rarely, for he came home long after the kids went to sleep—but then she was too high up on his shoulders, and the mirror reflected only her dangling feet. Suzy was not sure why this mirror should stick so distinctly in her mind, but almost always she would look for a mirror upon entering elevators and would immediately feel a lack, or a pang of something distant and impossible to name.

They never did move to Bayshore, and Long Island remained a distant place she never thought much about until shortly before the funeral, when she was told that the ashes would be scattered over the Atlantic from the Montauk Lighthouse. She thought it was a bizarre idea; there had been no will, and she had not realized that her parents had ever been to Montauk. Grace would not explain, and everyone assumed that it was fully discussed and understood between the two daughters. When Suzy pressed the matter, Grace cut her off in mid-sentence and snapped, "That's what they wanted; since when do you care about their wishes?" Suzy took the LIRR to Montauk three days later and watched Grace scatter the ashes. Suzy merely walked alongside Grace and let her conduct everything, as the older child, which was what her parents would have wanted, she thought. There were only a few people who seemed to have known her parents through work, and a reporter from the *Korea Daily* who showed up uninvited. It was exactly five years ago. November, rain, and her entire world had just ended.

Why Montauk? No one told her anything. Maybe Mom had mentioned something about it to Grace, or Dad had left a diary somewhere in the back of filing cabinets, or Grace knew things about their parents that Suzy did not—but it was a mystery, and there was no one Suzy could ask other than Grace, who, even five years later, would not speak to her. The one thing Suzy knew was that Grace disapproved. Grace was a fervent Christian, and burning the body was unacceptable. If Grace had had her way, they would have been buried in a sunny lot somewhere in New Jersey, preferably near her own church, where the funeral was held, as though her parents had ever believed in Christ.

Her parents had been floaters. They went to churches on a whim. Good for business, Suzy thought. They always had a specific reason for each visit. Either a job connection from one of the elders or trade gossip or market information. A church was where most Koreans gathered on Sundays, and it would have been foolish to ignore its usefulness. But they were atheists at heart. More than once, she overheard Dad cursing off Christians. "Bastards," he'd say. "They'd even give up their own mother if they thought it would guarantee a spot in that nonsense called heaven." Sometimes Mom would say a prayer to Buddha when Suzy or Grace got sick, or Dad would say something about the ethics of Confucius at the dinner table, which all seemed confusing somehow, but the message was clear: Jesus was not for Koreans. One night, Suzy walked into the kitchen to find her father in a heated argument with someone on the phone and overheard only the last bit before her mother pointed to her to get back in her room. He was screaming into the phone, "Your ancestors would weep if they knew you were pushing this Christ shit on your countrymen!"

"Ancestors"—that was a familiar word. Suzy heard it again and again while growing up. If she got a B instead of an A on a test, the shame lay on her ancestors, who watched from their graves. If Suzy and Grace fought and did not speak for days, it was again the ancestors, who lamented over these descendants who were not only girls but bad-mannered as well. And of course it was due to the watchful eyes of the ancestors that Suzy and Grace were forbidden to speak English at home. "You must never forget your language; once you do, you no longer have a home," Dad told them. It was not easy to keep on speaking Korean when English came so naturally, and Suzy and Grace often cheated, falling into English when their parents were not around. But in the end, Dad got his way. Ancestors or no ancestors, the girls never forgot Korean. They were even sent to a Korean-language school every Sunday afternoon, though there was almost no need. The girls spoke Korean with near-fluency.

. . .

The train is slowing down again. Everyone is getting up at once. Outside, the sign reads "Jamaica," a stopover station with several platforms. The morning started out overcast, and now the sky is turning black. Each time she comes out here, the rain follows. Or perhaps she has come only when it was raining. With each year, she can bear the rain even less. It makes her terribly aware of being alone. Her father had said that remembering one's own language ensures home, but was that true? She wonders if her parents would approve of her coming out to see them so often. Suzy at twenty-nine, still single, still careerless, still stuck with a married man—would they turn away in shame?

From here on, it is a smooth ride. Two hours and fifty minutes, and the train will arrive in Montauk.

Once she boards the second train, she shuts her eyes and pretends that this ride will continue forever. She is on her way to see Mom and Dad. She imagines their new home, a pastel oceanfront house they have just moved into. Dad's newest whim, the beach, the lighthouse, the moonlight, the edge of New York. "Oh, who would've ever thought," Mom would say, laughing, picking up Suzy at the train station in her brand-new Jeep. Mom behind the wheel in her Christian Dior sunglasses and a sky-blue tank top with tan lines showing through its straps despite the November rain, while Dad is out fishing for fluke, which he would then get the local fishermen to fillet for sushi later. Suzy would present them with a bag of Korean groceries, which her parents would delight in opening; Montauk is not Flushing, definitely not Woodside or Jackson Heights, no Oriental goods within miles. They would gloat over a jar of *kimchi*, dried squid, salted pollack eggs. They would laugh like children, and Suzy would squint from so much sun in their faces. But then, always, Suzy remembers that she is nineteen still, and college is not easy at all, and she's come home to tell them: *Dear Mom and Dad, I don't want to stay in school anymore, I'm afraid of the rules and of breaking them all, I'm afraid of the boys who want me and the men I desire in return, I'm afraid of being stuck out there and not finding my way back unless I hide with you for a while, stay in the bedroom upstairs, and let you take care of me, I will wait for you all day while you fish, while you sunbathe, I will mop the floor and vacuum the living room and even fillet the fish if I can stay just a few nights or weeks or years until I am okay, until I can stand on my own and chase her away who stands in dark with wet hair and a cigarette, afraid of the phone that keeps ringing, until her fingers turn red from the ashes.*

The screeching of the engine signals a stop, and Suzy looks out through the rain-streaked windowpane to find one of the Hampton towns. Even in November, she can spot the white-and-khaki ensemble on the platform. This part of Long Island has nothing to do with Bayshore and its Korean immigrants. This is Ralph Lauren land, the *crème de la crème* of Madison Avenue. "Why call this a country? Disneyland would be more accurate!" Damian ranted as they drove across the entire coastline one summer in search of the antique shop where the missing Edo print was found. It was a research trip for the book he was working on. Suzy thought he was overreacting, but she liked that about Damian, his refusal to forgive the tiniest flaw or weakness. She believed that it was a sign of honesty, his unwillingness to compromise, his search for the ideal. She admired his intrepid pursuit of beauty, which she thought was his faith in love, the very essence of what she lacked.

The first time they made love, Damian began with her hands.

I've always believed that a woman's hands should tell me nothing, to keep me from the rest of her, but you, yours surprise me, a sign of temper, tenacity, such long, angry fingers.

He was running his index finger across her face. He was whispering the whole time. He kept talking, not so much to her as to himself, as though it was he who needed convincing.

I would've recognized you anywhere, your sad eyes, the ones marked for tragedy, your nose is emotional, the angle tells me so, your forehead is high like mine, you're ambitious like me, your lips are too small for your face, so imperfect and afraid, you're a beauty full of holes.

Suzy lay still and watched the peeling of her skin with wonder. She had just turned twenty. It seemed miraculously natural, and Damian the wrong man for the job. Afterward, she shuddered at the possible consequence of this love, if that is what it really was. She was not sure if she was frightened or excited at the prospect. Their lovemaking was an escape. It was passionate certainly, not in the usual lusty way, but with a fierce current of sadness, for they both knew that they would be alone at the end of each other.

People later said that Suzy was the precocious thing who ruined the most celebrated marriage of academia. Damian Brisco, the foremost expert on East Asian art, and his wife, Yuki Tamiko, the renowned translator of the newest edition of *The Tale of Genji*. Some blamed a midlife crisis, how Damian, at forty-nine, seemed to have lost his head over a mere student at the expense of his career, which had been crucial for everyone, including himself and his marriage. The couple had collaborated on many groundbreaking studies. They were the authors of the three volumes of *East Asian Art and Literature*, which was the main text for every university's Asian-civilization course. Most agreed that their marriage catapulted the field of East Asian studies, which up until their prolific partnership had been in a vacuum. Although it was Yuki Tamiko who held the chair position in the East Asian Department at Columbia University while Damian Brisco took an extended leave to work on the fourth and final volume of the text, it was clear that any major decision had to pass through both. Their names were forever linked together, always in the context of "edited, researched, compiled, translated, written by Brisco and Tamiko." Their joint lecture series on "Trekking Buddhist Art Through East Asia" was immensely popular, and their marriage admired by those in the field as the perfect union between East and West.

But Suzy knew otherwise. She had been one of Professor Tamiko's advisees since the beginning of her junior year. Yet it was nearly impossible to get Professor Tamiko in person. Twice a semester, Suzy was supposed to meet with her to discuss her impending thesis, but so far, she had been greeted by a different TA each time, someone who seemed merely a few years older than Suzy herself, and rather flustered at having to advise anyone at all when his own dissertation lay forgotten somewhere between the hands of the university's bureaucratic committees. She saw her in lectures, of course. Postwar Japanese Fiction was one of the few standing-room-only classes on campus, and even though Suzy had actually registered for the class whereas half the attendees seemed to be auditors, she was always stuck at the farthest distance from the podium, on which stood Professor Tamiko, whose profile seemed almost ethereal.

It was true that she was beautiful. Yuki Tamiko was stunning. At forty-nine, she had retained much of the delicate-boned, high-cheeked, ultra-slender, and immensely haughty girl whom Damian Brisco had met at Harvard when they were both freshmen. The coy-girl beauty might have long passed the woman, but there was something regal in its place, something strikingly soft and compassionate and yet impenetrable, edged by the vastness of her knowledge as she stood before the hundreds of eager minds and recited lines from Mishima's *The Sea of Fertility* as though Western scholars had done the most unthinkable injustice by declaring *Ulysses* the ultimate fiction when the real thing lay shrouded in this Japanese tetralogy, which cast its spell over everyone in the auditorium while she, Yuki Tamiko, towered from her highest ground, suddenly demure and fiercely competent. Everyone was at her mercy. The boys looked up at her with awe and admiration—Yuki Tamiko was not the sort of woman one dared to have a crush on—and the girls marked her every word in their spiral notebooks in red ink with double exclamation points, as though everything would be different now that they knew what they had not realized merely fifty minutes ago, when their literary scope lacked the passionate breadth of that remarkable woman up on the podium. Suzy, however, remained untouched. The lecture was perfect, and Professor Tamiko's seductive banter mesmerizing, but Suzy felt somehow left out. There was a twinge of coldness that Suzy sensed in the older woman's face, guarded by the finest words of Japanese literature. Suzy felt claustrophobic and was struck by a distinct desire to get up and walk out. It was during one of these rash walkouts that she saw Damian for the first time.

She had slipped out the door and skipped down the steps facing Dodge Hall when she sensed that she was not alone, that another person had just taken the same steps and was walking behind her. Resisting the temptation to turn around and look, Suzy kept on walking. It must have been April. The first two weeks of April were always deadly. Finals were just on the way, the summer was around the corner, and a strange mix of excitement and panic spread through the campus as students crammed for exams. It had rained for a week straight, and the afternoon looked unnaturally bright. And it was during these nervous hours that Suzy, instead of returning to her dorm room, turned right onto Amsterdam Avenue. Now a few more people were on the street, mostly campus people still, but a bit older, because beyond the actual gates of the campus, yet still within the ten-block radius of 116th Street, most passersby were graduate students or school employees or faculty family. All seemed to be hurrying, although it was Friday afternoon, and the rain had finally ceased. Suzy ambled with not much feeling at all, or with so much feeling that she felt breathless. This extreme ennui came upon her with no warning, a dark hand moving onto her heart. Sometimes she would suddenly get up and leave, even though Professor Tamiko's lecture was faultless and there was no reason for such an impatient exit.

Along Amsterdam Avenue there were two usual stops for wandering, restless undergraduates—St. John the Divine and the Hungarian Pastry Shop. The former was more a construction site than a cathedral, under renovation for as long as anyone could remember. Although it was one of the largest cathedrals in the world, its imperfection, Suzy thought, was really what soothed and attracted visitors. There was something oddly comforting about a cathedral whose façade was forever being repainted or repositioned. She liked sitting on a pew while listening to the usual banging of hammers and drills coming through the stained-glass windows. She hoped that the cathedral would never get done, that it would always remain half finished with steel wires sticking out. God had problems too, Suzy thought, and his cavernous sanctuary was a mess. God belonged more in the café across the street. It was the typical underground hangout often found in college neighborhoods, where goateed boys and hand-knit-sweatered girls sipped their refills of double Hungarian, which was a shot of espresso with a squirt of amaretto, and discussed the usual suspects—Derrida, Kierkegaard, Wittgenstein, even Said—although for a break they might bring up Woody Allen, whose latest film had been shot in this very café only a few weeks ago; they agreed that it sounded rather dull—a middle-aged professor falling for one of his students—so typical, so jaded, so hopelessly redundant that they all got tired of talking about it, and the conversation shifted right back to Derrida.

But Suzy entered neither that day. She was about to, and then something stopped her. She had climbed the steps to St. John the Divine when she became aware of the man next to her. He had been walking behind her; although she could not see his face, she knew he was there all along. And then, suddenly, he was on her right, almost directly parallel, facing the entrance of the cathedral. The entrance was wide enough for two people to pass without having to impose on each other, and she feared it was an aggressive gesture from a stranger who seemed to have followed her all the way from the lecture. She was cornered, and was left with no choice but to turn and face him.

His eyes are unhappy—that was her first thought. Deep, penetrating blue eyes that did not appear exactly hard, but somehow absent, even heartless. The rest of him she noticed much later: that he was considerably older, stood quite a bit taller than her five-foot-five frame, had a faint dimple on his left cheek that seemed out of place, and a face marked by permanent stubble that would graze against her thighs when finally opening her up into complete honesty. But in that initial second when she saw him standing so near that she could almost feel his fine-lined, insistent fingers on her, she thought, *I must seem so terribly young.*

Certainly an odd reaction to a stranger, as he was to her then, an older man, neither particularly handsome nor striking, a passerby possibly her father's age, although her father always seemed older than those around him, whose conviction was the absolute law by which everyone must abide, because he was the sort of man no one in the family disobeyed. But when Suzy saw Damian that first time, she felt hopelessly young, almost silly, naked, as though she knew that he could see through her own flaring vulnerability as she stood there in her brown suede jacket and faded Levi's, looking so lovely and tortured the way nineteen-year-olds can look on wet April days, staring up at this older man who seemed to have appeared from nowhere.

In fact, Suzy had never really known men. The boys around her age never showed much interest in her. It did not help that her father forbade dating. "School dances? Whatever for? Schools are not for dancing around!" In Korea, he said, girls did not frolic like these American ones. In Korea, he said again, girls stayed clean, as girls should. Under Dad's "Korean girl" rules, nothing was allowed: no lipstick, no eye shadow, no hair dye, no perm, no perfume, no miniskirts, no cigarettes, and absolutely no boys, especially American boys. The family's frequent moving seemed to guarantee all that. The girls never stayed in one school long enough to develop a crush. No time to get attached to sinful American habits, Dad used to say. Suzy thought he was justifying all the years of moving his family around. He might have even been trying to blame them. There never was a doubt that, when the time was right, Suzy and Grace would marry decent Korean men. Once, during a drive to a church on Sunday, they nearly hit a puppy, a curious mix of terrier and chow. It looked strange as it whimpered away, a hybrid with pointy ears and a moon face. Dad declared, laughing, "See what happens when you mix blood? Even dogs turn out a mess, stupid and ugly!"

Grace somehow managed to sneak around with boys behind Dad's back. She would make up excuses about the yearbook committee or student-council meetings and tumble in long after the nine o'clock curfew, and Suzy knew where she had been just by looking at her rumpled skirt and tangled hair. Grace had always been the daring one until she found God and moved to New Jersey. Suzy, on the other hand, never even kissed a boy until her freshman year in college, when she moved out of her parents' house into the dorm. His name was Brad. Suzy never even knew his last name. He was her first roommate Liz's boyfriend and stayed over every weekend; each time Suzy turned to the wall to sleep, she would hear moans and giggles from the other bed. Then, one day, Suzy came back from class and found him waiting for Liz. It was awkward to be puttering about with him sitting on Liz's bed. The silence hung heavy as Suzy sat facing the desk, still feeling his eyes on her. It was when she decided that she'd had enough and began gathering her books that she felt his hands on her shoulders. He said nothing at all, and Suzy just froze. He slowly turned her around and kissed her without hesitation, not the sweet and soft kind, but the forceful probing of a tongue that was confident and mechanical. Then he walked away from her and lit a cigarette and asked when Liz was coming back. "Any minute now," Suzy answered without looking at him, and threw the books in her bag and walked out. He never kissed her again, and Liz never knew.

Later, Suzy would recall that first kiss as if it were an omen. *What was it about her that marked her as the other woman? What did he see?*

What Suzy never forgot was the smell. It was a sick smell, like something dying almost, like instant powdered milk, non-dairy creamer, the milky-baby smell but fake. It leaped into her throat and would not wash away, no matter how fiercely she rinsed her mouth afterward. Each time she kissed boys after that, she looked for the smell. She pretended to kiss them and looked for the smell. Sometimes she would sniff the awful smell and would push the boy away violently and never speak to him afterward. But when the smell wasn't there, she would be curiously disappointed. It was as if nothing quite erased the initial shock of being kissed by someone who was not hers, a kiss that was stolen, claimed from her flippantly, a kiss so abrasively illicit that she seemed to deserve it, as though she was not worth much to begin with. It stuck with her, the shame, the smell, and came back at odd moments, such as when she stood on the steps of St. John the Divine and saw in the older man's eyes a clear reflection of herself, terribly young and terribly dissatisfied.

Damian would later confess that he had indeed followed her from the lecture hall. What made him do it? He would never say. He might have been bored, or simply tempted by a young woman who seemed as unmoved as he was by his wife's lecture, or, more likely, he really had nowhere he wanted to be on that afternoon. Perhaps he wanted Yuki Tamiko to notice him following the girl; that Suzy reminded him of Yuki at nineteen was a minor detail he would have preferred not to see. But he did follow her, which was embarrassingly impulsive for someone so much older and supposedly more sensible. He followed her all the way down the College Walk and along Amsterdam Avenue, to stand before her finally with an awkward smile, which only accentuated his lone dimple, and seemed to her somehow heartbreakingly sad. His stare did not waver, and she stared back, because she thought it might make her appear less young. Finally, one of them burst out laughing—Suzy is not sure which—and soon both were laughing like kids who had cut class and gotten away with it.

Ten years since, and it seems impossible now that she should be alone, no parents, no Damian. She thought that the choice was one or the other, and it was up to her to decide. It never occurred to her then that she would lose both, that she would not be able to keep the one even after sacrificing the other, and that the choice was never really there from the beginning.

All around her, people are gathering their things. 11:37 a.m., Montauk. Outside is the November beach town, empty and forlorn. Between the rain streaks on the windowpane are her parents buried at sea, half rising to meet their daughter here at last.

6.

NOTHING IS AS DESOLATE as a late-autumn beach. The motels with "Vacancy" signs wear the dejected face of the abandoned. The fish-and-chips stands have pulled down their shutters, closed for the winter. Fickle and selfish, the rest of the world has skipped out. Gone are the flirtatious smiles, the bronzed bodies, the neon beach balls flopping down on the bluest water. Girls with names like Tracy and Cindy and Judy no longer hang out at McSwiggin's, which is the only bar near the train station still open for business.

Even at this early hour, a few men are stooping at the bar, nursing pints. They glance at Suzy but soon look away with the stolid faces of small-town men. Most fishermen hang out at the dock, on the other side of the town, where many bars remain open, lobster and swordfish being their prime catch this season. But the nonfishing locals, mostly Irish descendants, prefer the bars in town, where the grime and sweat of the fishing crowd remain far away, where they might hang on to their Montauk as a sort of Hawaii for Long Island's working class.

It is lunchtime when Suzy enters. "Catch of the Day = $4.99" seems underpriced, and Suzy points to it immediately upon settling on a stool. The bartender is a grinning man in his mid-forties. She has seen him before, the same time last year, when she peeked in for a cup of coffee. Suzy remembers thinking how perfect that he should be called Bob, such a compact guy with a barrel chest and permanently tanned forearms.

"You want that poached, right?" he asks with a good-natured hearty smile.

"Pardon?"

"Lady, I told you we don't poach our fish, just fried, plain and good!" He is still smiling, so he is not annoyed, perhaps teasing a bit.

"Fried, yes, that's fine."

He must be confusing her with someone else. He thinks she's been here before, which she has, but a year ago, just for coffee, could he remember that?

"And coffee, right?" He is already pouring a cup. He then brings her packets of cream and sugar and says, "Oh, I forgot, you want Sweet'n Low, sorry, we're out."

Suzy stares at him awhile before reaching for the mug. She takes a sip and winces at its burnt aftertaste. The coffee's been brewed for much too long. Black, which is the only way she takes her coffee.

"No seltzer with a straw today?" Bob taunts with a wink.

Grace it must be. Grace must have been here recently. Grace, who never touches fried food and never takes sugar, who never drinks anything without a straw—he must be confusing her with Grace. When was she here? Does she come here often?

The sisters look fairly alike. When they were young, they often passed for twins. "Stupid fucks," Grace fumed, "they think all Asian girls look alike!" But Suzy was secretly happy, for she knew her sister was a beauty. They had similar features, but Grace had longer eyelashes, a finer complexion, sleeker cheekbones, poutier lips, and blacker, straighter hair. At first sight, there was no doubt that they were sisters, perhaps even twins to those who did not have an eye for beauty. But upon a closer inspection, it was clear that Grace had far superior features, the sort of face a man might die for, as Suzy thought and often witnessed through high school, when the boys would steal glances at her older sister, who remained aloof and haughty, as though her beauty were reserved for far better things than a mere boy with his dad's Toyota. The odd thing was that Grace had a reputation for being easy, but only with the older boys, the sort of boys who had cut out of school long ago, who hung in front of the local pool hall on their motorbikes, which probably did not even belong to them to begin with, who waited for Grace outside the school gate with helmets on, not for the sake of safety but to remain faceless, Suzy thought. Grace managed to hide it all from their parents. This must have been because the family moved so often. Before Grace could settle in with any of her troubled boys, they moved again, and Grace would find yet another pool hall, to which she would disappear on evenings when her parents worked overtime. Even more impressive was that Grace kept up her grades. Grace would sit by herself in the corner of the cafeteria and study furiously, while Suzy was cozily tucked in with her set of meek friends. Grace would never sit with Suzy. She said that it was embarrassing. She said that Suzy with her geeky friends embarrassed her. Everyone called Grace a stuck-up bitch, especially the girls who could not stand how their boyfriends kept looking at the new girl in the corner. All Suzy felt was distance. They must have been close once, but that seemed impossibly far away.

"So how about it, one order of fried cod!" Bob is all smiley, as though he is proud of having initiated this young woman into the art of fried cuisine. Suzy peers at the oversized piece of fish drenched in grease. She takes a bite while eager Bob dotes on her for approval. She gives him the sort of satisfied smile that makes him happy, then takes a long look around the bar. It is a typical beach-town dive, with a jukebox and a pool table. Against the wall is a laminated poster of a buxom blonde holding up a can of Budweiser. A few stools away from her are a couple of older men whose eyes are fixed on the sports updates on the TV screen suspended from the ceiling.

"So did you find what you were looking for?" Bob pretends to be nonchalant, but Suzy can tell that he is curious. She is not sure what to say. Is it really Grace he is taking her to be? What had Grace been looking for? She is tempted to tell him that he's got the wrong girl, but it seems too late now, and Bob looks too earnest. So, instead, Suzy drops her gaze at the plate of fish before her.

"Thought you went back to the city. Twice in one week in this lousy weather—whatever it is, lady, you've gotta find it fast, so you don't get that pretty head of yours wet again." He pours more coffee into her mug, although she does not want a refill. Suzy runs her fingers through her wet hair, realizing only now that she left her umbrella on the train. Perhaps it is not Grace he takes her to be, but another Asian girl who had wandered in one rainy afternoon. Perhaps Grace was right after all, white men can't tell one Asian girl from another. The fish is good. They all taste the same once fried like this. She did not realize she was hungry. She left the apartment in a hurry this morning, barely time for coffee, definitely no breakfast. The alarm did not go off again, and she woke up panicking, certain that she had missed her 8:25 train. It wasn't until she wiped the sweat off her face and took a sip of cold water and glanced at the clock again that she

realized she had more than an hour to kill. So she lay there recalling the strange phone rings and the bouquet of irises that
had come accompanied by a drill or a hissing noise, which she
failed to identify, which grew louder and louder until she could
not stand it anymore and finally bolted out of bed, only to realize that the deadly shrill had, in fact, been the alarm chiming
seven.

"See, nothing like a good piece of fish on a day like this!"

Bob is dying for her to say something, anything, so that he
can say to his regulars, "That girl over there, she's from the city,
after something, she won't say what," or "See that Asian girl? She
wanted cod poached until I told her, no, miss, we won't have
that here, not in Montauk, not at Bob McSwiggin's place!" But
all Suzy is capable of is another vague smile, a nice-girl smile so
that he knows there is nothing personal as to why she won't let
him in on what she's looking for. It would not take much to give
him the one-line answer, a simple acknowledgment: "Yes, the
fish's good; yes, I'm glad you talked me into it; yes, nothing like
a plate of fried fish on such a dreary afternoon." But even that
she cannot manage, for she is suddenly dying to get out of here.
It is as if her parents know that she has arrived, that she is here
to see them, and that not a day goes by when she does not wonder who shot them, who wanted them dead, who knew exactly
how to pierce their hearts.

The numbers on the TV screen flip with a dizzying speed:
Knicks 88 Bulls 70 Lakers 102 Spurs 99 Giants 21 Saints 10. The
coffee is tepid now and tastes somewhat less burnt.

"Did I leave an umbrella here last time?" Suzy ventures cautiously, hoping the question might bring light to when Grace, if
it was indeed Grace, was here. Something inside Suzy cannot re-
sist. Become Grace for a moment. Embrace Grace's trace, which
might lead to Grace.

"Beats me. I keep whatever people forget in that bin." Bob

points to the plastic crate by the entrance. "You were here when, on Friday? Should still be there, but if you don't see it, just take any umbrella you find."

Suzy walks over and makes a pretense of looking through the crate before picking out the only umbrella among the torn jackets, chipped pocket knives, soiled bandannas, and baseball caps, the sort of leftovers no one wants. Friday, just three days ago. Did Grace come to see Mom and Dad early so that she wouldn't run into Suzy? Does she still hate her so? *Leave us alone,* Grace told her at the funeral, without once meeting her eyes. Hasn't Suzy done exactly that, hasn't she stayed away all these years as though she had no family left in the world?

The umbrella is a weapon. She can leave now, out into the torrential sea where her parents wait. Bob looks happy with his five-dollar tip, almost as much as the whole bill. But today is not a day for calculating the 20 percent, and Suzy is holding on to the nameless umbrella left by a drunkard on a rainy night.

"Oh, I knew I forgot something," Bob hollers after Suzy. "Kelly's back, tell him Bob sent you and he'll give you a deal. Make sure you tell him you can't even swim."

Crazy to hit the beach in this rain. The lighthouse is on Montauk Point, the easternmost tip of New York. From here, Suzy can either follow the shore for about six miles or just hop in a taxi. An impossibly long pilgrimage, but Suzy cannot bring herself to call a cab, not now, not on her way to see her parents. One of the wires of the umbrella hangs loose, through which the precarious sky threatens to break. It seems almost perfect, that the rain should follow each step and erase the trace of this mourning.

So it had been Grace after all. On Friday, while Suzy was interpreting in the Bronx, Grace had shown up at McSwiggin's looking for something. Neither Grace nor Suzy can swim. Their bodies simply will not float. Suzy tried to learn a few times, but her body would tense immediately upon hitting the water. Grace is terrified of the water—as far as Suzy knows, possibly the only thing she is afraid of. So it had to be Grace: poached cod, Sweet'n Low, seltzer with a straw, can't swim . . . Then who's Kelly? Three days ago, Grace may have stood on this very path. She may have continued up the shore holding the umbrella with a broken frame. She may have cried a little, praying for a miracle.

Suzy has a hard time picturing her. She has not set her eyes on her sister for five years. In fact, she has barely seen her since they both left for college at seventeen. Grace came home only twice during the four years. Suzy saw her just once, during the Christmas break one year. Suzy was struck by how thin her sister looked. Even Dad commented on it, telling Mom to give her an extra scoop of rice at dinner. Grace mostly kept to herself during the four days she stayed. A few phone calls came for her from the same husky-voiced guy, who would only identify himself as a "friend," to whom Suzy had to lie each time and say that Grace was not home. Grace seemed somehow subdued, a bit nicer. The only time Suzy glimpsed the familiar cynicism was when she expressed her surprise at Grace's choice of major, which was religion. Grace smiled faintly, as though it were a private joke that Suzy did not understand, and muttered, "What does it matter?" Although the visit went smoothly, without much commotion, Suzy was relieved when Grace took the bus back to Northampton.

Grace is thirty now. She will turn thirty-one at the end of this month, only two days after Suzy's birthday. Suzy the 24th, and Grace the 26th. Grace always resented their birthdays' falling so close together. She said it took all the steam out of her day. To appease both, Mom used to make them *miyukguk*, the traditional birthday seaweed soup, on the 25th. Kill two birds with one stone, Grace would grunt as she slurped her soup with a vengeance. What Grace really could not stand, Suzy suspected, was that they were the same age for those two days. They were equals suddenly, neither younger nor older. Grace no longer had the upper hand. Last year, for Grace's thirtieth birthday, Suzy bought a card for the first time in years. She stood for a while before the Hallmark section of the stationery store and looked through the ones with the gold-engraved "To Dear Sister." She chose instead a plain white one, but she never sent it.

The walk is not easy, increasingly rocky. On Suzy's left is the dramatic formation of eroded cliffs, the land broken by years of water. To her right is the ocean. No one is around. One o'clock on a rainy November afternoon, who in their right mind would be out here?

Except someone is. Far in the distance, Suzy can see a figure walking ahead. Either a man or a woman under the umbrella, but a tinge of familiarity in the shape, in the way each step is dragged. Where did the person come from? Had he or she been walking ahead the whole time?

For a second, Suzy imagines that it might be Grace, and that she will run and catch up until finally the two will be joined, holding hands, together to see their parents, a family as they had never been, as they should have been—Mom and Dad, Grace and Suzy. *Since when do you care about their wishes?* Grace will never let her forget. It was Suzy who had cut out first, the first escape, the first hole in the foursome. It was Suzy who had ruined it all, Suzy who ran off with her professor's husband and left everyone back home in shame, Suzy who disappeared for four years, until the day the police tracked her down at Damian's Berkshire house with the news that her parents were dead. Grace never forgave Suzy for ditching Mom and Dad in their final years. Jen found Grace's resentment toward Suzy unfair. "I thought your sister never came home either when she was at Smith. Why is she suddenly the good daughter?"

But of course it cannot be Grace walking ahead. Grace must be tucked safely back in her Godly New Jersey home. What happened at Smith? What happens at her church, where Grace must spend all her time now? In the spring of 1991, over nine years ago, when Suzy chose Damian over everything, Grace had just moved back home from Northampton, where she had tried a few jobs with not much luck. Suzy was surprised when she learned that Grace was home. Suzy thought that Grace, more than anyone she knew, would have some grand plan waiting for her upon finishing college. Moving back to her parents' house seemed like a desperate decision. Grace was living in New Jersey when her parents were shot in their Bronx store in November 1995. She taught ESL at Fort Lee High School. Most of her students were Korean kids who had recently landed in America, whose parents were often gone, working overtime. The same kids also attended Fort Lee New Joy Fellowship Church, where Grace was in charge of the Bible study Wednesday nights and Sunday afternoons. Grace was a good teacher supposedly, exceptionally competent and quick with her lessons. That was her style, never sentimental, never messy. Suzy overheard all this on the bus after the funeral. The older women who sat opposite Suzy must have been the parents of Grace's students. "So what about the other daughter?" one of them asked. "Shhhh." The second woman made a hush motion with her finger on her lips, glancing at Suzy.

Definitely not Grace up ahead. Someone entirely different, a stranger with his back toward Suzy. Quite a distance separates the two, and with the rain and all, Suzy can barely make out the shape of the other. The rocks are getting sharper, and from here on, there is no choice but to follow the steps to the road, which continues for a few more miles parallel to the shore. The path is uphill, slippery. Whoever's ahead must be heading in the same direction. Whoever's ahead keeps an even distance without once turning around, or perhaps it is Suzy making sure that she keeps up. Perhaps there are other ashes scattered from the lighthouse; perhaps it is the locals' favorite burial spot. Why scatter the ashes from the lighthouse? Whose romantic notion was that? Suzy, of course, had been left out of the decision. It seemed like a good idea, a comforting idea, but definitely not her parents'. But, then again, what did Suzy know about her parents?

Barely two in the afternoon; the darkness is menacing. When she first came here five years ago, she saw nothing. All she could focus on was the urn Grace was carrying, in which her parents' ashes were mixed together. Dome-shaped, wrapped in stiff white linen, the way the dead were kept in Korea. Suzy could not stand looking at the thing that held her parents, and was relieved when Grace assumed all responsibilities for handling it. Neither cried. Suzy was still in shock, and Grace, being in charge, seemed unable to cry. Suzy had no doubt that once they found themselves finally alone in their respective apartments each would burst into tears. Afterward, Grace must have gone straight to church; Suzy packed her bag and left Damian's house immediately. He was not around when she left. During their final six months, she had stayed at his Berkshire house while he spent much of his time abroad. She left without a note, and he did not try to find her. She went straight to Jen's apartment and slept for several weeks. When she was finally able to get up and walk outside, she wandered into the East Village and found the apartment on St. Marks Place. And still Suzy had not cried.

The path cuts into the main road, where the sign reads "Montauk Highway." Definitely not the smartest thing to walk along the highway, not in this rain, not alone, not dreaming of tears. But Suzy is determined; so is the person ahead. Hardly any cars pass. The road may continue this way, and Suzy will have circled the edge of New York, down to its rocky bottom.

Then, suddenly, without warning, emerges the lighthouse, up there in the distance, beaming into the brooding sky. The white tower is forlorn and majestic, fenced in from all sides. Its silence seems so repressive that for a second Suzy is afraid for her parents, who lie beneath the cliff. Even in this rain, the flag hangs from the pole on its left. The gray colonial house has been turned into a museum with a gold plaque at its entrance which reads "Montauk Historical Society." She soon finds the spot where Grace stood five years ago, holding on to the urn before finally opening its lid. Nothing there now except a lone bench behind a rusty viewfinder.

Tell me what happened, Mom, Dad, what really happened to you?

One thing Suzy has learned in the last five years is that nothing follows death, no revelation comes into play. Death is silent, heartless, heart-wrenchingly unfair. Each time Suzy comes here, sometimes twice, three times a year, she realizes how stock-still everything is, how immutable the lighthouse, how infinite the Montauk sky, how constant the rain, how absolutely unforgiving the water appears from where she stands. Each time Suzy stands here, she cringes at the way the watchtower looms over everything, as if it suggested man's ultimate power over nature, and the star-spangled banner at the edge of the eastern coast, as if this very cliff were the helm of the American dream. And each time, she becomes certain that time has played tricks on her, and those five years—during which Suzy floated from job to job, from one married man to another—happened only so that she might stand and wait for someone, anyone, to step in and say, Look what you've done, look what you've been left with, look what you are, is this what you wanted?

What do you want after all, do you want me to tell you?
Damian had pleaded in his final message.

But she is not alone. Someone else is here, over in the distance by the drenched flag, now facing her direction. It is hard to see the face buried beneath the hooded raincoat under the black umbrella, and so much rain between them. It is a man, she can tell that much. She takes a step toward him. An Asian man. Something about him strikes her as being familiar, the way he stands with his head tilted slightly to his right. She takes another hesitant step. She wants to shout something, say hello, excuse me, anything, but she seems to be choking and no words will come out. He stands there watching her, or perhaps watching beyond, toward the ocean. She follows his gaze and finds the angry sea gaping at her and wonders if it is a signal from her parents, a sign, a code she cannot understand. The sky is burning gray, almost red at its edges. Suddenly frightfully cold, Suzy tightens the opening of her coat. This overly chic trench coat— Michael had brought it from his last trip to London. Michael, whom she never thinks about when he is not around, which he never is. Odd that she should recall him now, so inappropriate, almost irreverent to her parents, who would weep for their daughter, who, after all these years, is hiding with another man who will never be hers. *My dear Suzy, my girl, my poor daughter, where have we gone wrong, where did we go wrong with you?* Mom might plead, which cannot be true, since she would never say anything so self-deprecating, would play dumb instead, avoid Suzy's eyes, turn to Dad, who would take one final look at Suzy with a disgust, an anger that should never be directed by a father toward his daughter, words that should be swallowed instead, erased, so Suzy will not stand here five years later, five long, grueling years that brand her with the echo—*Whore, you whore to a white man, a white married man, don't ever come back.*

But death is silent. Suzy shuts her eyes to the lashing waves.

She still cannot cry, nothing will make her cry. Then, turning back, she notices that the man in the distance is no longer there.

The train back to Penn Station departs at 5 p.m. No time for a drink at McSwiggin's. Twice in one day, Bob might become too familiar with her face, Grace's face, whichever he takes her to be. The taxi pulls up exactly at four-thirty. The driver, with a bright-yellow T-shirt that says "Montauk Taxi," looks no more than sixteen, and she wonders if the kid even has the proper license to be driving a commercial vehicle. He speeds on Montauk Highway along Napeague Bay, passing the dock with its fishing boats and a few bars with rooms upstairs where the fishermen blow the last of their sea-winded dollars. It takes less than ten minutes to get to the train station, and Suzy hands the driver the fourteen dollars before turning around and trying, for the hell of it, "Hey, happen to know who Kelly is?" The kid gingerly counts the dollar bills before replying in the thickest Irish lilt, "Sure, everyone knows Kelly, he rents boats out over at the dock, tiny sloops, two-person max. Why, you need a boat?"

7.

THIRST IS WHAT GETS HER. The clock points to 4 a.m., which is inevitably the hour when she is awoken, breathless. She lingers in bed for a while before dragging herself to the refrigerator. The water is cool, a clean break from sleep. She fell asleep with the light on again. It is hard to believe that she slept at all under such brightness. There was no dream. The night was a black, soundless tunnel. Nothing interrupted her, no crying girl by the shore, no unknown hand shaking her home.

It is a terrible habit, to wake up in the middle of the night and reach for a cigarette. But the world is claustrophobic at 4 a.m., nothing comes to the rescue. The irises on the table still look serenely white, even if there's a hint of wither, the writhing of petals. Averting her eyes, she notices the blinking red light on the answering machine. Several messages. Must be Michael. Suzy wonders why he calls her constantly, if he calls his wife also. The conversation is most often one-sided. He runs through everything he has accomplished that day, most of which Suzy does not really understand. He needs to report to someone, to anyone, to any ear that will listen. He talks about the conference calls with Germany, the merger meeting that busted, the additional clauses in the newest contract. Each feverish rant ends with the inevitable chuckle, "All it means, babe, is that they're suckers and I've got you for love." She wonders if he is lonely, if he ever thinks about being lonely.

The first time she slept with Michael, he got up at five in the morning to catch his train home. His wife and their five-month-old son lived in Westport, Connecticut. He had not seen them in two weeks, and Suzy could tell that he missed them. When he turned on the light to dress, Suzy pretended to be asleep. It was easier that way, and she preferred waking alone in the hotel room. She enjoyed lounging in the strange surroundings, which would become no longer strange, since Michael had a habit of always returning to the same room, 755 at the Waldorf-Astoria. The checkout was at twelve, and Suzy would take a long bath in the marble tub, whose enormous size seemed right out of a fairy tale. Afterward, she would wrap her body in the luscious terry-cloth robe and wait for the room service that Michael had ordered for her before leaving—the poached eggs with hollandaise sauce, a basket of freshly baked scones and croissants, and a tall glass of fresh carrot juice. The ritual seemed to be a good one; it had nothing to do with what she knew.

Except Michael was married, which seemed crucial. Jen, when Suzy told her about the affair, looked at her aghast. "Why?" asked Jen. "You know your parents are no longer watching, there's no audience anymore." Jen said nothing further and stopped introducing Suzy to those hopelessly Ivy League, defensively arrogant, devoutly bookish young men who passed through the magazine where she worked. None of them took to Suzy anyway. They would come along for a drink with Jen, which Suzy knew was all for her benefit, and ramble on about another young author on the verge of fame. Their tales of the author's propensity for run-on sentences and waify poet girls bored her. Most of all, she could not stand the tinge of jealousy in the bookish man's voice as he repeated, with a vengeance, the exact numbers of the six figures that the author's first book had garnered. Suzy remained silent, trying her best to suppress a yawn, and Jen would play the moderator by cracking jokes, which was not her style. Suzy was relieved when Jen stopped her matchmaking gestures.

"Getting older, Suzy, means just getting more selfish all the time. Does my heart break anymore because you're fucking another Damian? What if you're hiding with another asshole? What can I do really, how does that change my life?" Jen cried one night when they had emptied half a bottle of Jack Daniel's that had been sitting on Suzy's kitchen shelf for several months. *But nothing changes my life either, nothing touches me.* Suzy may have mumbled in a drunken stupor. The night was vague and easily forgotten.

No Jack Daniel's tonight, nothing at all but this empty kitchen and the Evian bottle of wilting irises. Why did Grace want a boat? Did she sail out into the shallow sea to mourn their parents? Has Grace become lonely over the years? For a second, Suzy is tempted to reach for the phone and dial Grace's New Jersey number. Over the years, Suzy tried calling Grace a few times during afternoons when she was sure Grace wouldn't be home. Each time, she secretly hoped that Grace might have stayed home from school by some sisterly telepathy and would pick up the phone. Instead, the machine clicked on with no outgoing message whatsoever, just a plain, long beep, and Suzy would hang up immediately. Perhaps Grace never answers her phone either; perhaps the sisters have that in common.

Sleep is impossible. Not quite the night, and interminably far from the morning. But Suzy is used to this sort of wait, a

meander, a break with no end in sight. The ring of smoke casts
a mournful veil around the flowers. A perfect white on white,
but death over life really, as if the smoke is seeping through each
pore of the iris.

The sisters wore white *hanbok* on that day in Montauk. They
gathered their hair back with white cloth pins, following the Korean tradition for immediate mourners. *White is the color of sadness, the color of remembering, of home,* Mom had told Suzy when
she asked why she wore a white cloth pin in her hair on each anniversary of her own parents' death. The delicate silk of their
dresses appeared almost transparent against the lighthouse towering above. They must have looked hopelessly small on that
day, two newly orphaned girls in white carrying the urn, their
blackest hair rippling in the wind, suddenly alone amidst a vast
country. Watching Grace scattering the ashes, Suzy thought that
her sister seemed more Asian than she had ever remembered.
Had it rained that day also? Did her parents disappear into the
Atlantic, which kept calling her through that day and each day
after?

To an insomniac, night crawls in secret. Suzy can hear each
second tick so loudly that the anticipation of the next second
makes her heart beat even louder. Sleep eludes her. It comes either all at once or not at all. During her first year in this apartment, Suzy slept all the time. She would watch TV and sleep.
She had no trouble at all. She would close her eyes, and then,
upon waking, she would realize that it was the next day. And
then she would turn on the TV again, the continuation of pro-
grams from the previous day, and then, so naturally, a soft,
smooth sleep would engulf her. Day by day, month by month,
in fact, that whole year went by with a blink, as if she were not
there at all, as if it were not she who slept and ate and watched
TV with such mechanical efficiency. And then, at some point,
almost overnight, she found that nothing would happen when

she shut her eyes. Just as she could not bear to watch TV one day, sleep also failed her. No matter how hard she tried, as now she had to make a conscious effort to will herself to sleep, nothing came. And soon sleep missed her at all hours. It would come suddenly and grip her. She would collapse onto bed, often fully dressed, as though she were under a spell, a forgetting spell that would wipe her out. Such flickering, intensely invasive sleep never lasted long, never sank into her, and here she sits at 4 a.m. wide awake at a kitchen table, making herself smoke a cigarette because there is nothing else to do.

Michael helps. Sex helps. Suzy wonders if that is why she so willingly accepted his suggestion of a date when she first met him. Even he seemed taken aback when she said yes without a glimpse of hesitation. Suzy served as the interpreter at one of his joint-venture meetings with the executives from a giant Korean corporation. The Korean side brought their own translator, but Michael's firm had hired Suzy as a backup. It was one of Suzy's first interpreting jobs, and she masked her nervousness with cool detachment. During the lunch break, Michael turned to her and asked, "Ms. Park, are you not allowed to smile on duty?" Suzy looked at him for the first time then and noticed that he was attractive, the way men are when they are successful, late-thirties, and obviously married. His angular, almost square face was deeply tanned, as though he had just returned from a weeklong vacation somewhere tropical, and his sandy-blond hair set off his mischievous green eyes, which made him seem younger than he actually was. He was much shorter than he had appeared sitting down, about five feet nine perhaps, which might make him feel self-conscious, because he had a very tall air about him, which Suzy could not help but find endearing as she stared back at him without an answer, still with no smile. At the end of the meeting, Michael tossed his card at Suzy with, "Call me if you wanna show me your other face," which was not exactly romantically inspired, as he admitted later, but more like a dare, a brutish proposition, to see if this rigid, aloof girl would break rules for him, on whose fourth finger a wedding ring shone like a big fat warning sign. Instead, Suzy shot back at him with, "Forget the call, how about tonight?" She might have been waiting for someone like him, so bold, so crudely unseductive, so unlike Damian, that love never came into the question.

Michael found Suzy's acquiescence intriguing. He took her to the "21" Club that night, not the sort of place a married man should take a girl whom he had just picked up on a job. He gazed at her over the preposterously priced salmon zapped with mint-flavored sauce and said, "You've got issues, but I don't wanna know about them, not because I'm an asshole, but because you think I am." Suzy reached over and kissed him then, a light, fleeting kiss, and remembered that it had been years since she had kissed a man. He broke into laughter as if to cover his embarrassment. "You're a funny girl, Suzy Park; that clears it, we're not gonna fuck tonight." Michael was a romantic in his own way, Suzy thought. She went along with whatever he wanted, and it bothered him, she could tell. It took a few more dinners before they finally slept together. He wanted a bit of resistance, something befitting a mistress, some temper, some tears, but Suzy gave none, and he turned to her afterward and said, "That was like fucking a ghost, a very sexy one, but a ghost nonetheless." He kept coming back, though. He liked her. He admired her, even. He was a generous lover, and Suzy slept well afterward.

Yet here she sits still, listening to the radiator tap again, as it always does at this hour, an ambulance siren, a train engine, an evenly paced knock that will not stop, which she has gotten used to through the years, which comforts her on winter nights, as though its hissing noise were the only sign familiar to her, the closest thing to a home. The heat comes on slowly, and she is no longer sure if it is Michael she craves or the kind of warmth only another body can offer, the embrace afterward as his hands curl into her arms, as his breath caresses her neck, as his thighs are wrapped into her own. It is sleep she wants, perhaps, the sleep of a spent body, sleep buried in the body of another who's been so close, who's entered so far, who's moved back and forth with such insistence, emptying her of anything she might still remember.

Of course, Michael never holds her like that. He always rushes off afterward, to a meeting, to an airport, to his family. On the rare occasions when he dozes next to her, he will kiss her once with a note of finality, then turn to the wall and be fast asleep. Theirs is not that kind of intimacy. She knows that it would be false for them to cling to each other afterward. She knows that she would leave him if he ever reached out that way. She knows this because she lies next to him recalling another's hands, which had held her afterward, which had stroked her face so precisely, as though making sure that her eyes were closed now, that her lips were smiling with the sated ripple of what had just occurred, and her fingers still following his as if reluctant to let him go, as if her body had finally found the right angle, the right corner where it might rest until she would awake again and again find him whose hands had held her no matter how often she tried to leave, how far she ran, as far as this 4 a.m. apartment where she sits alone with a dying cigarette, wanting Michael instead, wanting Michael again and again, as though dispelling the dream of another's hands.

Four a.m. is a haunted hour. *Suzy, come back to bed,* Damian would plead upon finding her on the porch. She often did that then too. She would awake at this exact hour and retreat so easily into where Damian could not enter. He hated it. He hated seeing Suzy lost in what he dismissed as a "purgatorial suspension of guilt," for neither he nor she should suffer for what they had to do. *Suzy, I need you back in my bed.* He claimed her, the way she sought him above anything else in the world, above her parents, her college, her youth, and it was this desperate claim that made her feel uneasy, almost doomed. *Suzy, enough.* He was never afraid to say what he wanted. He was fearless. Most of all, he was fearless with her, which she thought could only be love.

The same unending night, the same uncertain hour in which Suzy sat in the wicker chair on Damian's porch many years ago, afraid of the ghosts who were living then, who had such short lives left before them, who have now returned as though they've been waiting inside her all day, watching her along the Montauk shore, riding beside her on the Long Island Rail Road, fighting through the evening crowd of Penn Station, hailing a cab to downtown, following her up the steps back to her apartment, and finally settling into this repose where nothing seems familiar except their darling daughter and a bouquet of white irises.

Suzy climbs between cold sheets, back in her futon, which floats like a tiny boat burying her inside the room. Is this what Grace sought? Out there in the sea? A burial for her who cannot swim?

Two shots only; the gun had fired exactly twice and pierced their hearts.

What happens when a bullet pierces a heart? What happens in that eternal second? What happens to a body falling so instantly, as a perfect answer to a perfect finger that pulled the trigger as if counting one, two, first the man, then the wife, or the woman, then the husband, whichever order, for it is all the same who goes first, they will fall together, the bullet never misses, a clean shot, two clean shots, no messy stuff, no pool of blood, no heart-wrenching cries, no crying daughter whose body lies five years later still hoping for the third bullet, which was surely fired, which will reach her heart with dead certainty, as it did once, twice, so easily, so conclusively, two shots only, exactly twice, and how Detective Lester turned to Suzy afterward with a sorry face and informed her, "Miss, your parents died instantly," as if to say, *Miss, your bullet is on the way; miss, be patient, your time will come; miss, we're sure of it, whoever never misses, whoever is a professional, the shot is a sure thing.*

The silence is deceiving. The hissing of the radiator has stopped. The night is a perfect calm. Soon the dawn will break. Already there is a faint light smudging the black sky. Already the next day is a possibility. She thinks she hears the shrill of the phone, the rings, the four desperate rings, though she cannot be sure, though she must be dreaming, this must be the hour when no one calls, no one listens, except for her who follows the sea in piercing rain, who craves a warm body despite love, who lies in the dark pretending to live.

8.

"THIS IS THE INTERPRETER HOTLINE SERVICES for the Korean interpreter Suzy Park. Client, Bronx DA's Office at the Criminal Court on 215 East 161st Street. Time, twelve-thirty p.m. tomorrow. Take Number 4 to 161st Street. Call back in one hour if there's a scheduling conflict."

The message on the machine sounds as if it belongs to one of those computerized answering services. The details vary, but the voice is always the same. Suzy has never met the one giving orders. She was hired over the phone after a forty-minute mock trial in Korean. She sent them the signed freelancer's contract and began working immediately. The procedure is always the same. They tell her where to go, and she shows up at the designated location. After each job, she faxes them the details of the case, including the file number and the contact information of the attorneys and witnesses present at the deposition, and they send her a check every two weeks. Unlike a fact-checking job, which can last through nights, depositions are over in just a few hours—longer if the case involves a serious medical-malpractice suit, for which both the doctor and the hospital dispatch their individual lawyers, whose redundant questionings can make the whole thing tedious. Then there are the occasional cases where an interpreter is hired as part of a legal strategy even though the witness speaks English. When such a witness is caught lying, he can always point a finger at the interpreter and claim that it is she who translated incorrectly. Or the witness might double-talk and confuse the interpreter, thus making the testimony impossible to translate. These types of depositions can drag on for days, at which point it is no longer the truth the interpreter delivers but a game of greed, in which she has become a pawn. Luckily, such cases are rare, and almost always she walks out of a job within an hour or two.

At first, the agency recommended that Suzy get a beeper or a cellular phone, but she told them that it would be unnecessary. She was always home, she admitted to a mere voice, a stranger with a tab on her life. The message was left yesterday. While Suzy walked along the shore in Montauk, the subpoena was drawn, the witness summoned, the investigation scheduled. A little after midday, an odd time to start a job.

The machine is still blinking. The second message is from Michael. He groans about his dump of a hotel in Frankfurt, the food is glorified grub, and there're too many Germans everywhere. It is Michael's way of filling up the silence. When he cannot think of anything else to say, he complains. It is easy to find a man endearing when one's heart is not at stake. "I'll call you tomorrow, around four p.m. your time, after my meeting. Be home." Michael always volunteers his exact whereabouts to Suzy, as though he is afraid of disappearing between the airport runways somewhere in the world. He might do that with his wife also, and she might never suspect him. Suzy has no idea what he tells his wife on those nights he stays at the Waldorf.

Suzy never asks. It is an unspoken rule. She imagines Michael to
be a good husband and father. He probably arrives at the front
door of his Westport home with an armful of presents each
time. On his wife's dressing table is surely an array of duty-free
perfume bottles in every color and shape. She probably laughs
and tells him to stop, a cute joke between the two, she refusing
to wear the airline-sponsored scent and he promising never to
buy another, and then, upon reaching home after a whirlwind of
flights, with a cheeky smile, he takes out another crystal bottle
from his coat pocket. The baby, now almost a year old, is on the
lap of their nanny while the handsome couple in their late thirties kiss.

But his white-picket-fenced Westport house, his blonde wife
in her primary-color outfits, and his baby boy who so resembles
Michael have nothing to do with Suzy. Connecticut is a long
train ride away, and her cell-phoning lover remains her secret
through the cool winds of November. Oddly, no guilt, no sleep
lost over his family, who really have nothing to worry about.
Suzy is only happy to send Michael home. She has no intention
of keeping him, as she had with Damian.

They didn't see each other until seven months after meeting
on the steps of St. John the Divine. It happened in the third
week of November of that same year. There were only a few
weeks left in the first semester, and Suzy was anxious, still un-
sure about her senior thesis, which focused, of all things, on
Shakespeare. The comparative aspect had to do with the Eastern
treatment of *King Lear*, as adapted by Akira Kurosawa in his
minimalist film *Ran*. Suzy had been intrigued by the fundamen-
tally opposite viewpoints expressed in the two interpretations of
the same plot, which supported her central argument of the impossibility of harmony between the East and the West. It seemed
a militant way of analyzing the problematic relationship, and
Suzy was not sure how much of it was really her idea, or if it had

been Professor Tamiko who encouraged such a position. Suzy had met her only once privately, for half an hour. The scheduled twice-a-semester meetings never worked out. Back in September, soon after the senior year began, Suzy sat before Professor Tamiko, feeling awkward, if not slightly terrified. It was the first time she saw her up close. Of course Professor Tamiko showed up late and offered no apology.

"So you believe that Shakespeare was exhibiting a secret Zen desire through Cordelia's insistence on 'nothing,' or by declaring so boldly, which is really to negate the premise of 'nothing,' he was illustrating the very Western ideal of negative space?"

No warm-up chitchat, no polite hellos; Professor Tamiko liked to get straight to the point. Suzy was not sure if she expected her to say anything in reply. Besides, she really did not know what she thought about the whole thing, if she had any concrete position. Certainly, it was her thesis. She was still brewing with thoughts, some interesting, some absurdly minor, and yet, sitting before this woman who was now spewing infinite possibilities, Suzy felt dumb, as if she became Cordelia herself, who could declare nothing over and over as if it were the only conceivable cry against all that had brought her there, to this ground-floor office whose window revealed the sunny autumn outside, which seemed suddenly impossible to believe. Professor Tamiko was now saying something about Kurosawa's use of the scene depicting a tree as the Eastern answer to Cordelia's verbal filial piety. The tree, yes, Suzy liked that scene in the movie, how the younger son stands holding up the bony branch that casts a soft shadow over the old king's sleeping face. It was a heartbreaking scene, the son's last gesture of love for his aging father, the old immutable tyrant on whose face death has begun its menacing grip.

It felt unbearably hot suddenly, and Suzy took out a tissue from her bag to wipe the sweat off her face.

"Yours is quite an interesting thesis, but anything can be interesting if you just put your mind to it, even Shakespeare. Let's take it one step further . . . How effective is Cordelia's 'nothing'? How pure is Shakespeare's intent? Or perhaps have we all been fooled by Shakespeare, could he be the biggest con man of the world's literature? Why is it always the white man?"

The sudden tightness in Professor Tamiko's tone surprised her. No one uttered the words "white man" with such contempt, except perhaps her father. Suzy thought she had seen the fleeting anger across the older woman's pale face, whose violet lipstick shone so brightly against the cream silk blouse and the matching cardigan, and the afternoon sun almost too faint against her piercing black eyes.

"Don't look so timid, now; it won't get you very far, not with me, and definitely not with them."

Suzy realized that she was being dismissed. What did she mean by "them"? Her father often said things like that. He would say "us" and "them" as though there were always a line between the family and the rest of the world. The implication was clear. The guilt lay with "white men," as he never forgot to tell her: "Don't ever trust them, don't you ever let them touch you."

Suzy got up to leave. The meeting seemed to have nothing to do with her thesis. Shakespeare and Kurosawa seemed to have so little bearing on what had just been confessed in the office; she would be glad never to return. And it was then that Suzy saw the black-and-white photo of Damian on the corner of the bookshelf. He appeared very young, his chestnut hair down to his shoulders, the flared collar of his flannel shirt so unmistakably seventies. Next to him was Professor Tamiko, girlish with clean bangs and no lipstick. She looked happy, her head leaning against his shoulder, shockingly youthful, and clearly in love.

"It's from a long time ago. I should've put it away."

Professor Tamiko muttered as though she were excusing herself, as though she thought Suzy had already left the room.

The next meeting was not scheduled until November, which was when Suzy saw him. She had been waiting in front of Professor Tamiko's office. The thesis was going nowhere, and she was seriously considering dropping the whole topic. Their meeting was supposed to be at two o'clock, but upon arriving she found the door locked. Suzy crouched on the floor with her bag at her feet, hoping that someone would show up eventually, perhaps one of the TAs who usually answered the door during her office hours. But half an hour passed, and no one came, and Suzy began to feel hungry and sleepy. She had not slept for days, sitting up all night before the blank computer screen, glancing at the familiar tree scene from *Ran*, which was now on her VCR permanently with its sound muted. She was beginning to get sick of it. Filial piety or not, what did it matter to her, who really cared if Shakespeare was a con man or not, why lose sleep over something so abstract and ancient? Suzy was never a rebel, never imagined herself as one, and now was certainly not the time for her to behave as such, when her college degree was down to just one more semester.

Suzy must have dozed off, for she suddenly opened her eyes to furious knockings nearby. He did not seem to notice her crouching on the floor against the right wall. He was banging on the door repeatedly, stamping his feet, muttering something under his breath resembling a curse, though Suzy could barely make it out. A few minutes went by before he stopped.

"She's not there," Suzy volunteered hesitantly. He looked down at her as if he could not understand where she might have come from. His face lacked any discernible expression. But there again—she could not help noticing it—the hollowness in his eyes, the sort of loneliness collected for years, why should it seem so familiar to her? Even back in April, when she first saw him on the steps of St. John the Divine, even as they both burst out laughing, she found, in his shockingly blue eyes, the mark of something absent, akin to resignation, irrevocably past innocence. And now, sitting here, gazing up at him with her arms hugging her bent knees, she wanted to get up and take his hand and lead him away from this dark hallway, this locked office to which she had hoped she would never return. So, instead, Suzy fired a shot, with a boldness that surprised her: "I hope you didn't follow me again."

He stared at her intently, as though he had not recognized her until then. Of course, it had only been a chance encounter. He had once followed her out of his wife's lecture on a whim, on a silly, crazy, shiny April whim. Call it spring fever, call it the aging scholar's midlife confusion. The girl had caught him then, red-handed and guilty, and the two had laughed with an understanding that neither could really explain, and continued on their separate ways, innocent and strangely rejuvenated. And here was the girl again, sitting in front of his wife's office, watching him lose his temper with such sweet tenderness on a face frighteningly young. He was embarrassed, but not terribly.

Suzy watched his face soften, and took a chance: "I'm starving."

When they sat across from each other at Tom's Diner at 112th Street and Broadway, they were both silent. Gone were her smooth Lolita talk and his seething discomfort. There was nothing more to say. Whatever should be was happening. Damian sat before his tea, watching Suzy biting into a cheeseburger with the sated face of a child.

"I'll be twenty in one week," she told him when she cleaned off the plate, now toying with the last fry that remained free of the pool of ketchup surrounding it.

Will you make love to me then, I have never done it before.

Surely she could not have said it. She had never been so reck-

less. She did not even want him in that way. He did not fill her
with lust, as she later learned to feel after learning his body as if
it were her own. But that afternoon, leaning on the orange
Formica table at Tom's Diner, she invited him to imagine her. It
seemed necessary, almost understood between the two, that it
should take place, that a part of him should pour inside her, a
significant part of him, not that fresh-faced, long-haired guy he
might have once been to Professor Tamiko, but instead this
much older, visibly distraught man nearing fifty, bad-mannered
enough to kick his wife's door open, who now sat opposite, un-
dressing her silently, wishing he were not doing so.

Certainly she seduced him, but he encouraged her with silence. He gazed at her, not laughing, not making light of her
suggestion, not saying anything to distract her maneuver. He
simply watched her eat and waited patiently until she stumbled
on her words. Once the waiter took the empty plate away, Suzy
felt a slight panic, not knowing what to do with her hands or
where to rest her eyes. She thought of taking out a cigarette
from her pocket, but she could not decide if that would make
her seem even younger. She was afraid that he might get up and
leave, although she knew, on some basic level, that he wouldn't.

"What is your name?" he asked, matter-of-factly, as though
he was finally beginning to see whatever lay between them,
which had been quite unspoken, quite imagined, which was yet
to be convinced or confessed, and the only thing left to do was
to say her name, the first uttering of her name, which might be
the first decision on his part.

She hesitated. She did not want him to say her name yet. She
was afraid of its permanence. She dropped her gaze as if to hide
her blushing face from him.

"I'm terrified."

Later that night, when she lay back in her dormitory bed
counting the creeping clock, she wondered what had pushed her

so far. Later, much later, when he did say her name once, twice, and again, she shut her eyes and thought that everything was different now, everything had changed permanently: the hollowness she had seen in his eyes at their first meeting, the passing of innocence she had so aptly sensed might have been the premonition of the escape.

What do you want after all, do you want me to tell you?

He might have said before touching her face, before gathering her in his arms. But that happened a week later, on November 24th, her twentieth birthday, when she stood before him like a small, trembling bride and let the white cotton slip off her body.

This body, as he had known so completely, remains now with no vestige of such nights, such hands, coyly innocent in her white terry-cloth robe, which Suzy pulls over any exposed skin as though she cannot bear such a glimpse.

She plays the final message as she steps into the kitchen and scoops coffee into the filter.

"Ms. Suzy Park, is this Ms. Park's residence? Detective Lester here, from the Forty-first Precinct. How're you? Listen, could you come on up to the station later this week? Nothing urgent, just a few questions. I'm out on a case but will be back by Thursday. Extension III if you wanna call before coming in."

It has been years since she last heard from Detective Lester, not since the case was filed away unsolved, which he never admitted. He kept assuring her that these "thugs" would sooner or later be caught. But she has not kept in touch with him either. There was no point. If any new development occurred, she was sure he would find her. Why such faith? She stares at the brewing steam of the gurgling Mr. Coffee machine. Why does he want to see her suddenly? Has he also contacted Grace?

Mr. Coffee lets out a big sigh. The pot is ready. Suzy leans over the boom box and presses the knob marked AM. "1010-

WINS!" the announcer is shouting at the morning audience. "The most listened to station in the nation!" It must be true. Every time Suzy hops in a taxi, she is sure that she hears the same greeting on the radio. "The time at the tone will be ten-thirty." The announcer is a pickup artist. "You give us twenty-two minutes, we'll give you the *world*!"

She had lain awake well into the morning. It must have been around seven o'clock when she drifted off to a second round of sleep, which always leaves her feeling groggy and oddly anxious. Suzy pours herself a cup of coffee. The morning is familiar: black coffee, the 1010-WINS cheers, the traffic watch every ten minutes.

Except for Detective Lester. What could he possibly tell her?

Criminal courts are not fun. Just getting past the security is a big hassle. They might as well strip-search you. It's even worse than downtown clubs on Friday nights, the way those biceps-heavy security guards block the door and make everyone wait in line. Pockets are emptied. Bags are scrutinized. Bodies are felt up and down. It is useless explaining that she is hired by the court, or that the assistant DA is waiting for her inside. It is useless fighting through the crowd. She is easily the only Asian person here. Everyone around her seems to be black, including the security guards, the guys in handcuffs being led by officers, and the rest in line, whose purpose for being here God only knows. Attorneys, though, often are not black. Judges, almost never. None of them are here. They must use a separate entrance, hidden in the back. The power structure is pretty clear. Between those who get locked up and those who do the locking is a colored matter. There are no two ways about it.

She has been to the Bronx Criminal Court once during the last eight months of interpreting. This past summer, she was hired for the investigation of a Korean deli in Hunts Point that burned down overnight. For some reason, there had been no insurance, and the poor guy who owned it was out on the street. He'd lodged a complaint against the Albanian landlord, who, now that the neighborhood had picked up and could fetch a higher rent, had been trying to force him out for years. The case had all the makings of a racial conflict. The store owner claimed that the landlord had brought in the neighborhood's Albanian gangs to threaten him physically and set fire to his store. Suzy never found out what eventually happened to the case, but it appeared serious, one of those racially charged incidents that, with a bit of brutality from the NYPD, could end up on the cover of the *New York Post*. For a few weeks afterward, she glanced at the *Post* whenever she passed newsstands, but she found nothing.

Once past security, Suzy is told to wait in the windowless reception area on the third floor. People pace about. Something urgent is in the air. She sits in the corner until finally a small, slouching man with a drooping mustache peeks out from the door behind the reception desk and waves her in.

"Hi, I'm Marcos," he says. "Interpreter? So young. We never get young ones like you for Korean." Given the way no one pays attention to him, he is clearly not the assistant DA. "Follow me; we're running a little late." Marcos points to the long hallway beyond the door. On both sides are rows of identical doors marked only by double-digit numbers. Inside, there must be different investigations under way. Burglary, murder, kidnapping, random shooting, all collected behind each door. It would be impossible to find her way back, she thinks, suddenly glad that Marcos is leading her through the labyrinth. After taking a few turns, he stops before a door that is missing its number. "Wait inside; the ADA's on his way with the witness." A quick pat on her shoulder. Marcos scurries into the abyss.

The austerity of the room suggests a typical municipal agency. The lack of windows is intentional. This must be what a prison feels like, she thinks. The walls are sealed in off-white paint. The table and chairs are so generic that they appear to have been hauled right out of a Kmart window. Curiously, it reminds her of her own apartment, the bareness, the chilling stillness, the unspecified waiting. It could be 4 a.m. still, and Suzy, alone, wishing for sleep.

"Ms. Suzy Park? James Richards, Assistant DA." He is tall, somber, in a dark suit that matches the furniture. He hands her his card and points to the man standing next to him. "You'll be interpreting for Mr. Lee here."

Against the ADA, whose six-foot-four frame seems unsettling under the low ceiling, Mr. Lee looks timid, although he is not small for a Korean man. In a stiff black suit and a starched white shirt, he could almost pass for a lawyer, or an undertaker. Koreans tend to overdress at depositions. Lawyers and judges, in fact, anyone to do with the law, are taken ultra-seriously, and witnesses put on their cleanest, smartest outfits, as though these meetings were Sunday mass. It is their way of showing courtesy before the law, although such effort might mislead the opposing council to assume that the witness's claim of economic hardship must be a fabrication. But a deposition is an event for these immigrant workers. A brush with the American law does not happen every day, never mind the summons from the Office of the Attorney General. For those who labor seven days a week at groceries, nail salons, dry cleaners, when, if not now, would they ever get a chance to don their fake Gucci, Armani, Rolex?

His face looks too tanned for a dry cleaner. Deli or grocery, maybe. But his hands have seen too much dirt and sun, which could only mean fruits and vegetables. The mystery does not last long, for the ADA sets down the folder he's been carrying: "Case 404: Office of the Attorney General Labor Bureau in the

Matter of the Investigation of Lee Market, Inc. of Grand Concourse, New York."

Mr. Lee nods slightly, the way Koreans greet each other in formal settings. Suzy nods back, a bit more deeply, since he is obviously older and requires more respect.

"Ms. Park, this is just a preliminary questioning, so no stenographer will be present. Will you ask him if he understands that he has the right to be represented by a lawyer under the law?"

James Richards has a kind voice, and Suzy is glad for Mr. Lee, who looks nervous, almost rigid, the way he knits his eyebrows as if trying to understand the flow of language that escapes him.

It's okay, she tells him. *Don't worry too much,* she says before translating what has been uttered by the ADA.

He answers, "Yes, I understand, I cannot afford a lawyer, I have no time to find a lawyer, I work twelve hours a day, I work seven days a week, I barely have time to sleep, I've done nothing wrong."

Suzy translates his answer, and the ADA nods eagerly, as if to acknowledge the man's concern.

"Mr. Lee, no one's accusing you of wrongdoing. You've been summoned here for a few questions in response to the complaints we've received, the source of which I cannot reveal to you due to the laws of confidentiality. The investigation has only just begun. This might lead to depositions and hearings, but for now all we are here to do is to ask you some questions, and to have you tell the truth."

Suzy scribbles a few key words into her notepad while the ADA speaks. No matter how long a sentence, she must not leave out a single word in her translation. An interpreter is like a mathematician. She approaches language as if it were an equation. Each word is instantly matched with its equivalent. To ar-

rive at a correct answer, she must be exact. Suzy, unbeknownst
to herself, has always been skilled at this. It cannot be due to her
bilingual upbringing, since not all immigrant kids make excellent
interpreters. What she possesses is an ability to be at two
places at once. She can hear a word and separate its literal meaning
from its connotation. This is necessary, since the verbatim
translation often leads to confusion. Languages are not logical.
Thus an interpreter must translate word for word and yet somehow
manipulate the breadth of language to bridge the gap.
While one part of her brain does automatic conversion, the
other part examines the linguistic void that results from such
transference. It is an art that requires a precise and yet creative
mind. Only the true solver knows that two plus two can suggest
a lot of things before ending up at four.

But she is being more flexible than usual when she turns to
the witness and repeats the ADA's words, adding at the end, *You
should really bring a lawyer next time; in fact, if you want, you can
stop this right now and request one.*

Mr. Lee meets her eyes and says, "No, I will be fine, I will tell
it as it is, tell this guy here I don't lie."

From the way the ADA twirls the pen between his thumb
and his index finger, Suzy can tell that the real questioning is
about to begin.

"What is your full name?"

"Lee Sung Shik."

Koreans put their last names first. It is the last name that
matters. The last name determines the status, the family history,
the origin. Older people often refer to each other by last names
only. All last names come from different roots. There might be
twenty separate sects of Lee, or fifty divisions among Kim. Lee
of the Junju sect bears no relation to Lee of the Junuh sect. Each
sect carries its own registry of thousands of years, which documents
the class status. Americans love to say that all Koreans are

named Kim, but Koreans do not look at it that way. To them, all Kims are not the same. In fact, there is often a world of class difference between two sects of Kim. For example, Kim of the Kyungju line descends from noble blood, whereas another sect of Kim might trace its ancestry among the commoners. It is all in the last name. So it is not unusual for Koreans to skip first names altogether. Many deposition transcripts get mixed up because of this switch of the name order. Lawyers who often handle Korean cases immediately ask Suzy at the beginning of a deposition please to put last names last in her translation. Do it in the American way, they say.

"Mr. Lee, what, if any, is your involvement with the store located at 458 Grand Concourse?"

"I am the owner," Mr. Lee answers.

"How long have you been the owner of the store located at 458 Grand Concourse?"

"Four years."

"Before that, where did you work?"

"I was unemployed."

"For how long?"

"For approximately a year."

"Before that, did you work at all?"

"I was employed at a fruit-and-vegetable store."

"By whom?"

"They are dead now."

"What were their names?"

This is where Suzy falters. This is where Suzy is afraid she will know the answer.

What were their names?

It takes her a second longer to translate the question, so easy, although the answer is even easier. She really should not be here.

"Mr. Park and his wife, over in the South Bronx; I never knew their first names."

So he had known her parents. He'd worked for them five years ago, which must have been right around the time of their death. This man here, with stubby fingers and swarthy face, had seen Mom and Dad every day. It should not surprise her. The Korean community is not big, after all. Many workers passed through the store in the South Bronx during the eight years in which her parents owned it. Turnovers seemed unusually frequent. When Suzy asked Dad why, she was told to stay out of their business. They had bought the store the year Grace went away to college. Before that, they kept changing jobs almost every year. Neither of her parents stuck to one job for long. One of them always got fired for one reason or another. With each new job came a move. Sometimes the relocation made the commute easier for her parents. But more often, they moved for no reason whatsoever. The family never stayed in one address for longer than a year. It was as if they were on the run. From what, Suzy had no clue. Once they bought the store, things calmed down a bit. They moved less often, although by then both girls had moved into dorms at Smith and Columbia. Suzy was surprised that her parents had saved enough money to buy a store finally, and was even more shocked when Mom told her about the brownstone in Woodside, Queens. They closed on the house soon after she ran off with Damian. Suzy never got to see it.

Now the questions have moved on to the store Mr. Lee currently owns. Suzy translates with mechanical efficiency, as though each question simply filters through her, each word automatically switching from English to Korean.

"How many employees are there in your store total, including both day and night shift?"

The ADA is looking through his notes. Suzy wonders why he asks such questions, when the answer must be right at his fingertips.

"Seven, including myself."

Mr. Lee is no longer thinking about Suzy's parents. He's back in his own fruit-and-vegetable store on Grand Concourse, where the underpaid illegal immigrant workers must be slaving away twelve hours a day, seven days a week, much the way he has been doing since he arrived in this country.

"Can you name the workers and their responsibilities, along with their salaries, weekly or bimonthly, however they are paid?"

So the issue at hand must be the violation of the minimum-wage law, for which countless Korean store-owners have come under scrutiny lately. Some have been forced to shut down, some so bombarded with back payments that they deteriorate into bankruptcy. Suzy has served in several depositions brought on by the union. She once overheard the lawyers gossiping about how the Labor Department has been tightening its watch, something about the elections coming up and the mayor needing a new shakedown. "Get them behind bars or back in their own country," one lawyer chortled, imitating the mayor, known for his tough-man act.

Mr. Lee is rounding up the names now. Jorge, Luis, Roberto, inevitably Hispanic names. The hierarchy becomes even more marked. The white prosecutors, the Korean store-owners, the Hispanic workers, and Suzy stuck in between with language as her only shield. He is now producing the record of all payments, scrawled in ink, for workers are always paid in cash. Of course they are. How many of them actually have working papers or even bank accounts? How many are legal in this country anyway?

Suzy is desperately hoping that the questions will go back to five years ago, back to when this man had worked for her parents, while they were still alive, while they were still swearing to disown her. But the ADA is zeroing in now. This is the moment the investigation has been leading up to.

"No benefits, no sufficient evidence of pay, no adequate va-

cation or sick days. Have you, Mr. Lee, been exploiting these illegal immigrant workers?"

The questions become more accusatory as they drag on, well
into the late afternoon. When the assignment lasts this long,
which must mean something serious, it is the interpreter who
tires the most. The ADA only asks, and the witness answers accordingly, but the interpreter must do both, must keep her ears
open at all times. Mr. Lee says nothing in return, and James
Richards lets out a deep sigh, twirling the pen faster. Each question takes her a bit longer to translate. She is beginning to slow
her words. They have been doing this for over three hours.

"Can you describe to me again the ways in which you hire
and fire your workers?"

He has asked that before. The answer could only be just as
tedious. Through word of mouth, Mr. Lee will say, through acquaintances I find them, and I let the worker go when he's not
good. How predictable, such a question, such an answer. So, instead, Suzy makes up her own question, surprised even as the
words escape her lips.

*Five years ago, you said, you worked for people who are now
dead. Can you describe to me what happened to them?*

Mr. Lee casts a quick glance at the ADA's face, as if slightly
confounded by such a turn of questioning. But he appears un-
suspecting and gazes at the wall as if reaching back to five years
ago, which is exactly what Suzy wants to see.

"They were killed. I had stopped working for them by then,
been fired, actually. I only heard about it later. It was all over the
Korean news."

Turning to the ADA, Suzy repeats the same response Mr. Lee
had given previously. Her heart is pounding. She cannot stop
herself. She is being guided by an impulse that is beyond her.
James Richards nods, as though he's been expecting such an
answer. Undeterred, he continues. "Mr. Lee, when a new em-

ployee is hired, do you offer him a set amount of time for training?"

Training, what a useless question. These jobs don't require sophisticated skills. Just strong muscles and a willingness to sweat for a bit of cash.

Instead, Suzy asks, *What was the nature of the murder?*

Mr. Lee answers grumpily, "They said that it was some sort of a random shooting. But I wouldn't be surprised if it wasn't. I shouldn't talk this way about the dead. But that Park guy, he had it coming to him."

Mr. Lee does not notice Suzy's face turning pale at his last words. She needs to register this information quickly, discreetly. She faces the other and gives him what's been answered before. Yes, she tells him. Yes, for about a week, all the new worker does is watch how the work gets done and do whatever the others tell him to do.

James Richards sees nothing. He is setting up the next question. He seems to be moving toward his mission: get them behind bars or back in their own country. The evidence is all right here in this terrible man who cheats on those illegals who should be sent back to their country immediately. What's the INS doing?

"Mr. Lee, can you describe the manner in which a worker is fired at your store? Do you offer him unemployment benefits?"

What does he think a fruit-and-vegetable market is? A Wall Street office? A nine-to-five, suit-and-tie job? Does he actually assume that working twelve hours a day, seven days a week, comes with that kind of privilege? Does he believe that the same rules apply to those who don't have the right papers, don't speak a word of English? Does he believe that the American dream is that easy? Unemployment and health benefits? They were never designed with these immigrant workers in mind. No one, not even the owners, have those!

So, instead, Suzy asks, *What do you mean? What makes you believe that the shooting was not random?*

Mr. Lee spits out the answer, as though the whole business is distasteful to him: "He had friends in all sorts of places. He and his wife, they were up to something."

It is clear that the man is not enjoying these questions. What had her parents done to evoke such strong feelings?

James Richards is patient. He keeps on. He wants evidence. Not those scribbled notes the man has brought with him, but a record, a receipt, an invoice, none of which seem to exist.

"Mr. Lee, how would you notify your worker when he is being fired?"

But Suzy barely hears his question as she asks instead, *Why did they fire you?*

Mr. Lee's face reddens a little, as if he cannot control the sudden rage as he recalls, "That Park guy had it all planned. He owed me two months' pay, so he decided to throw me out instead. He looked as though he could kill, the way he screamed what a lazy lout I was, so I walked out. I took off my apron, which they made me wear for the work around the salad bar, and just walked out. Of course he never paid me, and I didn't pursue it. I knew I didn't want to mess with him. I'd seen what happens to guys who stand up to him, like this delivery guy out in Queens, Kim Yong Su I think his name was. Man, was he really screwed by that Park guy! Let me tell you, half the Korean community didn't exactly shed tears when they heard about his death!"

It is hard to keep her composure, but Suzy must try, improvising an answer as long as the heated monologue. She repeats what Mr. Lee had said earlier, about firing a worker when he's not good. She repeats it a few times to make up for the length. It actually works, this repetition, and discourages the ADA from poking into what is quite simple and obvious.

"I understand," the ADA is pleading now. "I can see how you fire your workers, but tell me again about the hiring process; is there any contract which you or your employee enter into, a written contract, I mean?"

A written contract? Has he forgotten that no one, neither the one who does the hiring nor the one who is hired, speaks, never mind reads, a word of English?

Suzy turns to Mr. Lee without meeting him in the eyes. She is afraid that he will see the resemblance, find her father's face in her lowering gaze. She is afraid to ask further.

Tell me, who do you think was responsible for their death?

Mr. Lee snickers as he barks, "The brave one. Someone so righteous that eliminating them would've been a necessity. Even the police wouldn't touch the case. Random shooting, my ass; what idiot would believe that?"

Suzy believed, and Grace. Or maybe they wanted to believe.

Turning to the ADA, she tells him no, no written contract, no such thing. It is shocking how she manages to maintain her calm through all this. It is shocking how easily she lies.

James Richards appears exasperated at last. The questioning is going nowhere, or going so smoothly that his answers will haunt the trial as falsifying evidence.

"I am asking you one final time, Mr. Lee, are you claiming that you have always paid your workers the minimum wage?"

Suzy translates the last question quickly, wanting to be done with this.

"Yes," Mr. Lee shouts back with a vengeance. "You can see from all the record."

He's lying. He has clearly broken the minimum-wage law. It's her instinct. An interpreter knows almost instantly when a witness is lying. She is the most astute listener in the world. She listens between the lines, between the words. Nothing goes unnoticed. The first time Suzy interpreted for a lying witness, she was surprised how much it hurt. It happened at a trial, before a judge and a jury. Suzy stumbled, causing the entire room to stare at her. An interpreter must be neutral, and anonymous. It is not up to her to make judgment. Except the bitterness was on her tongue, and Suzy was not sure if she would be spared with her heart intact. Afterward, she could not help noticing that it was the lying party that won.

But now Suzy wonders how much of her averse reaction might be due to his confession about her parents. She repeats his answer, which fools no one.

Shaking his head, James Richards declares that the questioning is over. Closing his file, he tells her what a great job she did. Knowing two languages so well, that cannot be easy, he says. You need to interpret not only the words, but every nuance, don't you? Yes, every nuance, Suzy replies. *Every goddamn nuance, so I might know much more than I was meant to.*

It is Marcos who leads them out at last. The corridor is a maze. Suzy wants to lose Mr. Lee in its tangles. He'd hated her parents, although, according to him, there are more, many more people out there, who hated her parents even more passionately than he did, who hated them enough to risk everything in their bravery, their righteousness, whatever he declared was the motive for wanting them dead. She is dying to get out of here. When Mr. Lee calls after her "Thank you," she runs past the door without looking back.

Kim Yong Su, the guy from Queens. Where has she heard that name before? Where has she met him?

9.

"SUZY, MY DARLING, you're looking way too ravishing for an old maid!"

Caleb is grinning when she opens the door. She has not seen him in a few months, not since he started his first nine-to-five job at a gallery in Chelsea. "A bitch shopping mall," he whispered on the phone after the first week of working there. Caleb at twenty-six, much changed from the shy art-school graduate Suzy met outside Astor Place Stationery. He's let his hair grow out, gentle ginger waves down to his shoulders. "It's the Botticelli look," he tells her with a wink. "The curator adores it, and those Eurotrash buyers keep saying 'divine' in their phony accents." She pours him a glass of red wine while he looks around the apartment as if expecting to find an improvement since the last time he was here. "Suzy, my God, we need to get you a subscription to Martha Stewart, fast!" Suzy laughs and gives him the warning look, which he once said reminded him of his great-aunt, if he had one. When he finally sits down before her,

Suzy remembers how nice it is to have someone here. Another person sitting with her, listening to her voice, to her breath, to her silent walks around the kitchen. It's been so long since anyone's stepped into her apartment. She has almost gotten used to being alone.

"So the admirer strikes again!" Caleb points to the irises in the Evian bottle.

"It's that time of the year, remember?" Glancing at the drooping petals, Suzy realizes that she should throw them out.

"No, I didn't remember, but obviously *somebody* has." He takes a sip of wine from the glass, still looking at the irises. "So any idea who's the anniversary freak? I mean, it's grossly old-fashioned, and getting a bit creepy too."

"Maybe I'll never know, maybe I'm not meant to."

Suzy opens the plastic bag he handed her upon entering. Inside are small yellow balls with glimmering surfaces. The bag is filled with all kinds of cheese wrapped in cellophane. Blue cheese, goat cheese, Brie, Gouda, Swiss, Stilton, even fresh mozzarella. "What's all this?" Suzy turns to him, her black eyes wide.

"Call me the cheese fairy; oh no, that sounds *so fag*." Caleb chuckles, happy to see Suzy's face brighten. "I would've gotten you crème brûlée, but gallery openings don't do desserts, since you know the art groupies don't eat, and there's nothing close to a pastry shop on Tenth Avenue."

Leaning over, she kisses him on the cheek and then begins unwrapping the cheeses onto a plate, one by one. "Blue cheese is good," she says without looking up. "It's sad somehow, almost melancholy. I can never eat it, really."

"Darling, I don't think you're getting laid enough. When a piece of cheese in Saran Wrap makes you cry, you know it's time."

"Michael's coming back soon."

"When?"

"I don't know. I never know until the day before. He doesn't know himself usually."

"Oh, *please*, let him feed that one to his wife."

It is true. Michael never knows his schedule. Suzy has no doubt about it. But she does not protest when Caleb rolls his eyes. It is more fun that way, to pretend that the man who is cheating on his wife is also cheating on his mistress. Michael left three messages today. He sounded irritated, impatient, the way he gets when she is not where she is supposed to be.

Hey, pick up the phone, I know you're there.

Then, *Suzy, pick up the fucking phone, where the fuck are you?*

Finally, *Suzy, babe.*

She'd left the court by four, but did not arrive home until half past six. She had not planned it. It was an impulse. She was on the Number 4 train, a downtown express from the Bronx, forty minutes maximum. The familiar drone announced Grand Central. Change here for the 5, 6, 7, and the shuttle to Times Square. Watch out for the closing door! It was the Number 7 that stuck out at her. Flushing-bound, passing through inner Queens, which she used to take to visit home from college. She got out almost automatically. Grand Central. A little past five in the afternoon. Its crowd heading to Metro North instead of the Long Island Rail Road, to upstate New York, the mountains and rivers instead of the ocean. Grand Central was more civilized, its corporate-sponsored orchestra playing Bach, Beethoven, Mozart. The fresco of constellations on its vaulted ceiling shone in lime green with freckles all over, as though these comings and goings made sense, a divine sense. It must make the commuters feel better, to rush along with the universe hovering above. That's why Suzy preferred the drab Penn Station, where a commute remained a commute, a train a train, nothing more, nothing even remotely artistic or celestial.

Soon she was back on the platform, the Number 7 train

platform this time. She could get out at different stops on the Number 7, which would lead to the various neighborhoods where she grew up. Queensboro Plaza, 46th Street, Jackson Heights, Junction Boulevard, and Woodside, although she had never seen the house there. The Number 7 line is for immigrants, the newly arrived immigrants, the ones they call FOB, fresh-off-the-boat, the ones who have to seek out their own kind for a job, a house, everything foreign in this new land. Hardly any whites on the Number 7 except for their seasonal outings to Shea Stadium, and blacks favor the 2, 3, 4, 5, the lines bound for the Bronx and Brooklyn. The Asians rule on the Number 7, mostly Chinese, many Koreans, some Indians, few Hispanics. Even the subway regulations on the steel door are written in Chinese.

When Suzy hopped into the last carriage, there weren't many people at all, despite rush hour. Immigrants keep different hours. Nine-to-five is a luxury. Rush hour is only relevant to the commuters with desk jobs. Suzy slouched in the empty seat in the middle, not knowing where she planned to go, why she got on to begin with. There was a couple sitting opposite her. A pair of high-school sweethearts, a willowy Chinese girl with shiny braces and bell-bottom jeans leaning in the arms of a Hispanic boy with a pimply face and a diamond stud in his left ear. Times were different now. You rarely saw couples like that when Suzy was growing up. Hispanic boys never looked at her. They might have checked out Grace, but they still wouldn't ask Grace out— not because they thought she was a bitch, which they might have, but because they just didn't do that. Different racial groups didn't mix. In fact, a war was often declared between rival groups. One school would be dominated by the Chinese kids. In another, Puerto Ricans were the bad and popular ones. The mood was multicultural, certainly, but all it meant was that there were fewer white kids, and the rest just stuck to their own.

Suzy and Grace moved schools too frequently to really grasp any of it; Grace often broke the taboo, although, for the sort of boys she hung out with, nothing was much of a taboo.

Once the train glided out of Manhattan, it emerged into the open, no more tunnels, no more underground darkness. The sudden sunlight was ruthless. The sallow faces of the passengers became too visible, and the faded graffiti on the walls appeared sad and past its glory. Outside revealed the uneven surface of Jackson Avenue, the first stop in Queens. The gray buildings crammed against the pale-blue sky, and the interweaving highways jutted forth in confused directions. The first stop she recognized as one of her past neighborhoods was Queensboro Plaza, but it was merely a stop, a place where they had lived for less than a year, like all the others. She barely remembered it. Soon the train passed another. But there was no reason to get out, no real recognition that sank into her heart. Woodside was next, where her parents spent their last days. But this was no homecoming. Homecoming didn't happen on the Number 7 train. When it pulled into its final stop in Flushing and all passengers scattered out, she noticed a man still sitting opposite her. His hand was pointing at his open fly. She quickly averted her eyes while he got up and walked sluggishly to the next car. Suzy sat motionless in her seat, dreading the long return trip back to the city.

"He's only thirty, a baby really."

Caleb is now telling her about his new boyfriend, whom he met two months ago. He left the man from the West Village last year. "It just fizzled out. We were like roommates after the first year. He spent all his time trading stocks on the Internet, and I got sick of crying for his dick, which wasn't much to begin with, really." Suzy admires Caleb's way of downplaying everything. She knows that he suffered after the breakup. She knows it was his first love.

"I'm thinking of bringing Rick home for Thanksgiving. I mentioned it to Mom the last time I called her. You know what she said? The phone goes dead for like five minutes, and then she comes back in this super-snotty tone, 'Must you do that?' Can you believe it? *Must you do that!* Sounds almost British, doesn't it? My mom, the queen of the Japs! She suddenly turns British 'cause she might have to meet her son's gay lover!"

Suzy stares at Caleb as he chatters away. His parents have finally come around, not fully still, but trying. It's taken years, but he is talking with them—not every Sunday, not as his therapist had once suggested, but talking. She enjoys Caleb's stories about his parents. She pretends that it is she who is fighting with her parents, who insists on bringing Damian home for Thanksgiving, who sits here telling whoever how ridiculous, how silly her parents are.

She sips the wine. It's tart. It tastes of half-ripe raspberries.

"So have you found out if your sister gets a bouquet also?"

Caleb changes the topic, as if sensing Suzy's mood. He pours more into his glass and also into hers, although she has barely taken a sip.

"No."

"Does she not talk to you still?"

Suzy shakes her head. Grace, she meant to call Grace today. She wanted to check if Grace had also heard from Detective Lester, if she was also summoned. But Suzy has changed her mind. She has decided to wait until tomorrow morning, when Grace will be gone to school, when she can safely leave a message without having to confront her on the phone. Suzy is afraid of the chilly silence. She is afraid that Grace may just hang up on her. Right after the funeral, right after Suzy moved out of Damian's house, she had tried calling Grace a few times. She wanted to explain, although there was really nothing to explain. She wanted to talk about their parents, anything that might have happened during the past four years of her absence. Anything at all. But Grace hung up each time. Soon Grace stopped picking up the phone altogether. The message was clear: Grace did not want to speak to Suzy. With each year, it became clearer that Grace intended *never* to speak to Suzy.

"She's family. This will pass. It can only pass."

Suzy is comforted by Caleb's optimism, although she does not believe it. The thing about newer friends is that they have so little reference. You might give them the synopsis of the life you've led up until the point when they met you. But it doesn't quite sink in, not really. How could it? Your past is only a story for them.

"I don't think she's ever liked me."

She did not mean to say it. Why say it? The truth might even stick and become truer.

"Why do you think that?"

"I just do," Suzy whispers, sharpening the end of the cigarette against the edge of the ashtray. The ashes fall, and the flame comes alive. Suddenly the orange-red tip of the cigarette looks almost transparent.

With Mom and Dad gone most of the day—sometimes through the night, depending on their job of the moment—the only one Suzy had was Grace. Yet they were never close, never comrades. It is impossible to tell why. It wasn't even jealousy. Sure, Grace was better in many ways, prettier, smarter, and often wiser. But jealousy would only happen if the sisters were willing to engage with each other. No, their distance has had nothing to do with jealousy. There has never been any room for warmth between the two. They had different friends. Grace knew boys; Suzy didn't. Grace's favorite book was *Moby-Dick*, which Suzy gave up after trying the first few pages, bored and confused. Grace had a life outside school. Suzy could not even fathom where she would go. They shared bunk beds always. Grace on top, because she said that she didn't want anyone seeing her when she was asleep. When she was not whispering into the phone with one of her many secret boyfriends, she would disappear up there and read. Grace was always reading. Even when Dad got drunk one night and ripped down her posters of Adam Ant and Siouxie and the Banshees, Grace did not flinch but climbed up to her bed with a book. When she was grounded for being found naked with a boy in the back of a car, she repeated, "Sorry, I'll never do it again," with not a hint of regret on her face, and read for a month straight. She read just about anything. Novels, newspapers, sometimes even the Sears catalog or a copy of the neighbor's *TV Guide.* She would flip through them for hours, which seemed unfathomable. Suzy once made the mistake of buying her a book and spent most of her allowance of twenty dollars for a new edition of *Anna Karenina.* Suzy could not decide what to pick at first, but she thought that the cover looked mature and that Grace might like the fact that it had originally been banned in Russia. It also looked promising that the volume was impossibly thick, like *Moby-Dick.* Grace, though, was hardly grateful. She handed it back to Suzy without a word. When Suzy began protesting, Grace said quietly, "I don't want you choosing my books." They were only about fourteen or fifteen then. That was the first time Suzy suspected that it wasn't about books after all. Grace's obsessive reading might not have had anything to do with books. It didn't matter what she read, as long as she was left alone. Reading was a refuge, a shield, an excuse to avoid facing the family, and Grace would not let Suzy be an accomplice.

The only regular interaction between the sisters concerned chores, as though they were two strangers with one thing in common—the house rules. Grace, being older, was in charge of most housework, while Suzy helped with whatever was left unfinished: vacuuming, dusting, taking out trash, preparing rice.

Grace was quick with everything. The house was spotlessly clean by the time she stood at the door in a skirt too short for a fifteen-year-old, telling Suzy, "The rice is rinsed. Stick it in the cooker in ten minutes. The rooms are vacuumed; make sure you put away the vacuum cleaner in the broom closet. Tell them that I've gone to the AP-English study group." That was the extent of their conversation. Sometimes, in the morning, Suzy would ask her where she had gone on the previous evening. "The study group," Grace would snap before walking out the door.

Then there was the interpreting. Neither of her parents had spoken much English, which meant that they relied on the girls to break the language barrier. But almost always the job fell on Grace, because she was the older one, and smarter. Grace, since she was little, had to pore over a letter from the bank trying to make sense of words like "APR" or "Balance Transfers," or call Con Edison's 800 number for a payment extension. Suzy would sit by her side, scared and anxious. There was something daunting about undertaking what should have been delegated to an adult. Not only was it nearly impossible to understand the customer-service representatives, but often they would not release information unless it was the account holder calling. Grace would plead, to no avail, that her parents were at work and that they did not speak the language. Sometimes Mom and Dad would sit by the phone, dictating exactly what Grace should say. But often such demands did not work, because their request was so anachronistic that it defied translation. After all, their understanding of such transactions was steeped in Korean ways. Finally, Dad would scream at Grace, "Tell them no late fee, they'll get their money by next week!" Then Grace would look helpless as she repeated, "But he said that the balance was due last week, so next week will be considered late!" At those times, Dad never seemed grateful for Grace's instant interpreting service. He seemed frustrated, even suspicious. He was certain that if he could speak the language he would resolve all matters with a quick phone call. He seemed to resent Grace for relating to him what he did not want to hear, that the debts must be paid instantly, because that's what most of those calls were about—money owed in one form or another. But most of all, he seemed angry at his own powerlessness. The ordeal of having to rely on his young daughter for such basic functions humiliated him. He never seemed to forget that humiliation.

Their parents' lack of English and the family's constant relocation only made things worse. There were always red-stamped notices in their mailbox. Once or twice a month, Grace skipped school to accompany Mom and Dad to the Department of Motor Vehicles or an insurance company or some other bureaucratic nightmare. They were often gone all day. Afterward, their parents went back to work while Grace returned home alone. Suzy would often notice the red in Grace's eyes, as though she'd cried all the way. Almost always, upon arriving home, Grace would confine herself to the upper bunk without speaking to Suzy. Or she would stay out and come home much later. Curiously, on those nights, Dad never said anything. He pretended not to notice that Grace was missing at the dinner table. Suzy never asked Grace about the exact nature of those interpreting tasks—because they seemed so scary to little Suzy, and because Suzy felt guilty for letting Grace do all the work.

"You know, I sometimes wonder . . ." Caleb's voice turns suddenly low, almost flat, the way it gets when he is serious.

Suzy keeps her eyes on the cigarette burning in the ashtray. The red wine, the plate of cheese, the smoke slowly rising.

"I wonder . . . why you never talk about your parents." Caleb is cautious, uncertain if he should bring it up at all.

She had told him about her parents once, briefly. But that was it. Nothing more. No heartfelt anecdotes, no tearful monologues. Suzy avoided the topic, and he had never asked. Instead,

Caleb would chatter on about his parents, his lovers, his uncertain careers, and Suzy would laugh. They have grown comfortable with that.

"*My parents*—I never think about them."

Suzy holds the cigarette between her index and middle fingers without actually bringing it to her mouth. She is hesitant. She is not sure what else to say, although Caleb is quiet, listening.

She recalls how she had abandoned them in their final years. She recalls the last time she saw them and how Dad had called her a whore, just once, but it was enough to slash her. She makes up little stories in her head about how happy the family would have been had she not run off with Damian, had her parents not been at the store on that final morning, had her sister forgiven her. Yet she cannot remember the sound of Dad's laugh. She never longs for Mom's Nina Ricci perfume. She never craves the empty late afternoons when Grace had gone out and her parents were still not home from work. She can barely picture her parents' faces in daylight; she rarely saw them before dark.

"Strange, isn't it?" Suzy lets out a small sigh, so thin that it sounds like a gasp. "I can't stand myself for letting them go that way. I blame Damian. I blame myself for choosing Damian. But at the end of it all, they're not here. I can't stop thinking about it. That they're gone, that they disappeared while I wasn't even looking, while I hadn't yet had a chance to solve anything, solve me, solve Damian, solve why I had to run away all those years. I thought I was the one leaving them, but parents, they always have the last word, don't they? Still, I never think about them. Not really. What I'm not sure of is if I miss them. I'm not sure if I can honestly say that. I'm not sure if guilt has much to do with love." Suzy is glad that there is a cigarette. She is glad that she is not here alone. "I'm a horrible person, aren't I?"

Caleb does not respond. He is playing with the plate of

cheese, separating the mozzarella into little braids, making the holes in the Swiss bigger. Finally, he piles the bits of blue cheese into a little heart shape before pushing the plate toward Suzy.

"Sagittarius? In two weeks, the 24th?" Caleb's eyes are on her now. Soft eyes. He wants to say something clever, something that will ease the moment. "The stars are in your favor, darling, you can't be horrible. Nope, they won't let you."

The night is deeper. The wine bottle is nearly empty. The heart-shaped blue cheese looks ruffled and strange, like the map of the universe on the Grand Central ceiling. It feels good to be with Caleb.

"So you think Michael's lying to me?"

"Absolutely."

"What a scum."

"What a two-timing bastard!"

They both start laughing when the phone starts ringing. Four times. Exactly. Then the click. Suzy is almost relieved. Whoever has been waiting. Whoever is still watching. Whoever is not letting go.

10.

MICHAEL, IT CAN ONLY BE MICHAEL at this time of the morning. The phone is an alarm. Seven a.m. Probably lunchtime
wherever he is. A miracle that he's even waited until now.
He probably thought to let her sleep a little. He is being consid-
erate.

"So where were you yesterday?"

He is not happy, Suzy can tell. His voice is tight. Something's
up. He never gets so tense unless it has to do with his work, the
nature of which Suzy barely understands.

"The case took longer than usual. I was stuck at the DA's office." Balancing the receiver between her right ear and her shoulder, Suzy opens the refrigerator and takes out the Brita pitcher
to fill a glass. Her head sways with pins and needles. The wine
last night took its toll. They had opened another bottle after the
first one. She vaguely recalls Caleb urging, *Why not, drink it up
before thirty!* He kept pouring more, and Suzy kept giggling,
emptying each glass much more quickly than she should have.

"I called the whole fucking day!" He is fuming now.

"*Michael*, it's early." Her head is caving in. She is not up for this battle.

"I'm tempted to just get on the next fucking flight to see you."

He can be such a child, so wildly different from Damian. Is this what Jen meant by "hiding"?

"So why don't you?"

Suzy is good at handling his moods. That must be why he calls three times in a row. He knows she will never humor him. He knows she will never let him in.

"Four-point-three million, Suzy. Four-point-three fucking million on the line. Germans are fucking snakes. Everything's all ready to go, and, boom, they need another fucking meeting, another fucking review, another big fucking waste of my time. And I'm fucking stuck here rather than fucking you, tell me the logic."

Michael hates Germany. He hates almost everything, but he hates Germany more than most things. He thinks all Germans are Nazis and penny-pinchers. Suzy has no idea where his resentment stems from; she's never quite bothered to ask. He is stuck in Frankfurt and can't bear it. Thus his petulant mood. Suzy could see Michael lounging at a hotel lobby, a cell phone in one hand, with the other stirring two sugar cubes into his espresso. The top button of his shirt would be undone. No tie, since he would have taken it off immediately upon storming out of the meeting earlier. His feet up on the table. His eyes glancing at the *Herald Tribune* as he rants into the phone. Suzy suddenly misses him.

"I've got my period. We can't do it anyway."

That gets the abrupt silence, and then a chuckle. He's already better, she can tell.

"*Christ*, Suzy, is that all you can say?"

"No, there's more. I also have a pounding headache." She pops two tablets of Advil into her mouth.

"A hangover?" He sounds doubtful. A bit suspicious, a bit jealous. But all an act, Suzy knows. Jealousy is not a part of their arrangement.

"Umm. I celebrated my twenties, the passing of it, I mean, or that's what Caleb said at least." Suzy is grinning. She might still be a little drunk.

"But your birthday is not for another two weeks?"

Of course he would remember. He would probably send her a dozen long-stemmed roses, boxed. He would make a reservation at the Rainbow Room. He would slide across the table a blue Tiffany case in which there would be a set of sparkling diamond earrings. He would do everything so that she would feel the weight of a mistress.

"I began celebrating early. I wanted to be happy yesterday."

Maybe that's what Suzy wanted. Maybe that's why she circled on the Number 7 train for two hours. Maybe she was doing everything she could to stop the gushing sadness. *Half the Korean community didn't exactly shed tears when they heard about his death!* Mr. Lee did not spare his words. So many people had hated her parents. One of them might have hated them enough to want them dead.

"Babe, you listening to me?" Michael is shouting. He's forgotten about her headache.

"Sorry, what did you say?"

"I said, save your celebration for me. I said, wait."

It is a game for Michael, to pretend to claim her. Suzy goes along with it because she knows what happens when it isn't a game, when the claim is for real, when the claim takes over and plays out. Damian would never have asked her to wait. He would have taken it for granted. He would have expected nothing less. And she would have, almost indefinitely, if he had asked.

"I'll wait, I promise."

"*Christ*, I'm really fucking dying to see you."

When Suzy puts the phone down, it is still early, too early for anything. But Grace would be up. She would be getting ready for school. A little after seven. Suzy cannot remember anymore when high school starts, probably eight, or maybe eight-thirty. Teachers always come in before students, or at least they should, although, as Suzy recalls from the schools she attended in Queens and the Bronx, kids were often made to wait for teachers who sometimes didn't show up at all. Grace wouldn't be like that. Grace would show up on time. Her lessons would be well prepared, all set to go. Her hair would be neatly trimmed and coifed, and her dark-navy two-piece suit freshly pressed and buttoned. Or at least that's how Suzy pictures her.

Grown-up Grace, born-again Grace, thirty, the ESL teacher at Fort Lee High School—her only family.

It must be an impulse. Or last night's alcohol still in her blood. There is no other explanation for such courage, such longing to hear her voice. Suzy begins dialing the number. 7:15 a.m., what is she thinking? There's the ringing, once, twice. Something lurches inside her. Her heart seems to be made up of tiny wings which all begin to flap at once. The sudden ocean inside. The waves breaking. She can feel the tightening in her throat. They have not spoken in years, not since the funeral, not since she was twenty-four and Grace twenty-five. Suzy keeps counting age, as though each year pushes her farther away from her parents.

The voice that comes on is unexpected.

The computerized operator.

"The number you have dialed is no longer in service. Please check the number and dial again."

So Grace has moved once more. Like their parents, she never stays at one address long. Each time Suzy has tried calling her, the operator would come on instead with the new number, which Suzy imagines is a sign, a message from Grace telling her that she has not completely given up on Suzy. Although Suzy also knows that Grace, as a teacher at a public school and a church, needs to have her number listed. But this time, Grace didn't. Nothing, no further information available. Suzy dials the operator. Grace Park, she insists. I need a number for Grace Park. Yes, the area code 201, Fort Lee, her last name is Park, my sister. The operator tells her, no, nothing; there's Grace Park in Edgewater, Grace Park in North Bergen, but not in Fort Lee, no one under such a name. Maybe Grace has moved to a town nearby. Maybe she has found a deal in one of those riverfront rentals along the Hudson. 7:30 a.m., not a good time for a wrong number, not surprising that they would hang up: Grace Park? I am Grace Park. I don't have a sister; you've got the wrong person; do you know what time it is? The school, then, she must try the school. Fort Lee High School. Surely the school must be listed. Surely there would be a secretary who would take the call and deliver the message. It is then that the thought flashes across her mind—*why not go?* Why not just go there, why not tell Grace in person that there might be more to their parents' death, that it might not have been random after all, that a guy named Lee had known their parents, that another guy named Kim out in Queens might know even more, and that Detective Lester, he called for the first time in five years, he might know something, he might even have found a clue?

But then Suzy is not so sure. Grace would surely just walk away. She would pretend not to have seen Suzy and hop into a

car with one of her colleagues. Who's she? the colleague would
ask. No one I know, Grace would answer without once glancing
in Suzy's direction. Worse yet, she might get mad, furious. She
might drive off after telling Suzy never to come near her. *Do me
a favor, Suzy; leave us alone.* Those were Grace's parting words at
the funeral.

Suzy throws her coat on anyway. It has not occurred to her
that Grace would move without leaving a number, or that Grace
might one day become unreachable. It is as if the phone number, or just having the phone number, or the possibility of the
phone number, affirms Grace's presence in Suzy's life.

The headache seems to be getting worse. A bit of fresh air
might not be such a bad idea. Fresh air, who's she kidding? Fort
Lee, a half-hour bus ride from the Port Authority, not the freshest outing. Before she loses courage, she is out on First Avenue,
waving down a cab to Port Authority, where the Number 156 departs every twenty minutes.

It takes all her concentration not to get sick on the bus. The
constant lurchings, the reek of gasoline, the jammed traffic in
the Lincoln Tunnel—none of it helps. It does not seem to
matter that the bus is moving in the opposite direction from
the Manhattan-bound traffic. The tunnel keeps spinning. Suzy
holds her breath, thinking that it might keep her stomach from
rising up again. Two bottles of wine, not so smart to get on an
interstate bus the first thing in the morning. A man on the other
side of the aisle keeps fumbling with the paper bag in his lap. He
takes something out and begins nibbling it, exuding a distinctly
crunchy noise. Hash browns, wrapped in the McDonald's cover.
Soon he takes another out. Suzy wonders how many are in
there. How many hash browns can a person eat at once? The
sudden pungent smell of its microwaved, fried grease rushes up

her nose, and Suzy swallows hard, pressing her forehead on the cold windowpane to push the nausea away.

The hard surface against her skin seems to help a little, but then a gigantic billboard emerges on which lies a striking blonde in a neon-green bikini that looks electric against her implausibly copper tan. WELCOME TO NEW JERSEY, it says across the top of the blonde. It is impossible to tell what the advertisement is for exactly, but the bus swerves past before Suzy can study more closely. Suddenly it is not clear if the chill in the air signals the winter's coming or leaving. Could the summer be just around the corner?

She hasn't had enough water. She wonders if Hash Brown Man has some spare water in his paper bag. She wonders if he will share it, although she can't decide if she wants water that has been stuck in there with all of his other fried snacks. She is thirsty, shivering. The summer is definitely nowhere near, she thinks, huddled in her coat with her face pressed back against the window.

It is impossible for her to raise her head. When the driver tells her that this is Fort Lee High School, this is where she should get off, Suzy inhales once before running out, holding her face in her hands. Then she is not exactly clear how she pushes through the main entrance, bypasses the security, makes it up the stairs, finds her way down the corridor, and finally, bending over a toilet bowl in the first-floor ladies' room, heaves up the contents of her stomach, her hair stuck on her wet face.

Her mouth tastes sour—that is the first thing she remembers thinking. After flushing the toilet, she staggers out of the stall, turns on the tap, and dunks her face in the cold water. Something gives inside her, a horrible knot, a twisted froth. She swallows the water, and it is surprisingly refreshing, this tap water in the ladies' room at Fort Lee High School. Then Suzy lifts her face with water dripping from her wet hair, only to see that she is surrounded by a roomful of young faces peering at her.

"You okay?" One of the girls steps forward, offering her a piece of brown paper towel from the dispenser.

"Yes, fine now, I'm fine. Thank you." Suzy wipes her face, and feels suddenly wide awake. The first period must not have begun yet. Around her are a group of girls, now scattering back to their corners to wait in line for a stall, to stand before mirrors holding aluminum cans of spray to their highlighted hair or applying another layer of lipstick, mascara, eyeliner on such youthful faces. A commotion. Teenage girls all getting ready at once. Suzy had been like that, long ago, so impossibly long ago. And Grace. Of course Grace. What would Grace say if she knew, if she saw her right now? The thought alarms Suzy, and she quickly rinses her mouth again and smooths her hair. It is better now. The sick feeling has passed. And most of all, she is finally here, at the Fort Lee High School, where her sister must be standing before a class, before a roomful of boys and girls who are now rushing out at the loud thud of a bell.

"Wait, please!" Suzy calls after the one who offered her the towel. The girl turns around, the glitter on her eyelids twinkling under the fluorescent gleam. "Do you know where I can find Miss Grace Park? She teaches ESL."

The girl turns to the group around her as if to say, Do you know? No one seems to know; their faces are blank. Of course, ESL, only for the kids whose English is not fluent. Then a tiny voice pops out of nowhere and volunteers in Korean, "I do."

Suzy turns around to find a small, round girl to her right, who seems to have been standing there all along. She is curiously short, barely over four feet tall. She is alone, unlike the other girls, who all seem to be traveling in groups.

"Are you one of her students?" Suzy stoops a little to face her.

"No, not anymore," the girl answers, lowering her gaze as though she is not used to making eye contact with an adult. Her jeans are belted too high, definitely no hip-huggers. No piercing in her ears. No makeup whatsoever. A true FOB. There were girls like this even back in Suzy's school days. They spoke very little English and only hung out with each other. They carried Hello Kitty bags and kept photos of Korean pop stars in their wallets. They looked frightened when white boys spoke to them and avoided girls like Suzy and Grace, whom they secretly called Twinkie.

"But you know where she might be?"

The girl nods, still without looking up. She seems suspicious of Suzy. Why wouldn't she be? Here's an adult who spent the better part of the morning throwing up in the school toilet. In the world of teenagers, just being an adult is reason enough for suspicion. To appease her, Suzy asks softly, "So is Miss Park a good teacher? Do students like her?" She is not sure why she wants to know, but she does. Grace's life. This bashful teenager in front of her. This first-floor ladies' room. This concrete building filled with ebullient sixteen-year-olds. This suburban town half an hour away from Port Authority.

"Yes," the girl answers with surprising eagerness. Then, as if suddenly aware of her own voice, she drops her gaze and mumbles, "They said I'm ready to quit ESL, but Ms. Park lets me sit in her class sometimes. She says it'll get rid of my headache."

"A headache?"

"Ms. Park says that so much English all day is what's giving me a headache."

A strange thing for an ESL teacher to say. Suzy has never quite thought of it that way—the English language being a headache-inducer. She wonders if such a reaction might also happen at depositions. She wonders if her translation sometimes sends the witness home with a migraine. Then she realizes that her own headache has faded. She probably threw up all the alcohol. Her stomach must be spotlessly clean, emptied.

"Can you show me to her class?"

The girl nods again, leading the way. The classroom is on the third floor. The stairs are steep and wide, the way they often are in old buildings. The students obviously get enough exercise, walking up and down between classes. The second bell must not have rung yet. Kids are rushing from lockers to classes, some grumpy and morose, some clapping high fives with dramatic facial expressions. Those are the popular kids, Suzy can tell. The ones who are not afraid to be seen, the ones used to being seen.

Neither Suzy nor Grace had known such teenage years. Theirs was the darkness surrounding home, the brooding silence before a storm. Suzy is not sure if her parents had always been so uninterested in each other, or if they just ran out of things to say over the years. It did not help that they were always tired. By the time they came home, around nine or ten, they had been working for over twelve hours. By rule, Suzy and Grace would have to sit at the table while they ate, although almost always both girls had already eaten. Often Dad burst into a rage, the violent, vicious thrashing of words. He would lash out at whoever happened to be near. Sometimes he would grumble about the *kimchi* being too sour, the rice not cooked enough, the anchovies too salty. He would take a bite and make a face, and then storm out of the kitchen, slamming the door behind him. Sometimes he would scream at both Suzy and Grace for sitting there like idiots while he slaved all day to put food on the table. Mom would never say anything back. She would sit there and finish her rice to the bottom of the bowl, and then get up to clear the dishes. She would never ask Suzy or Grace for help. She would never apologize for Dad's moods. She would pretend that nothing had happened. Then, finally, she would turn to both and say, "Go finish your homework and get to bed, it's a school night." Suzy can still hear Mom. *It's a school night.* She would say it sometimes even on weekends. Both her parents often worked seven days a week. They rarely had weekends.

With each job, with each endless hour they labored at dry cleaners, liquor stores, fruit-and-vegetable markets, nail salons, delis, truck-delivery service, car service, they seemed to have lost something of themselves, a sort of language with which they had communicated with each other and their daughters. Sure, it could have been the claustrophobia of immigrant life, being stuck in Korean enclaves that remained ignorant of English-speaking America. But there was something deeper. Something terrible that seemed to have haunted both. Something resembling fear that stirred Dad's rage and Mom's pointed absence, and always the two girls were made to sit and watch. Everything always came to the same end. The reason was Korea. The final answer was Korea. All of their discontent, their misery, their endless wanderings through the slums of outer New York happened only because they had left their country. The girls were bad girls because they spoke English, rather than their native Korean. The houses they kept moving through were temporary shelters with torn mattresses on the floor, because America could never be home. But of course her parents had no intention of returning to Korea. It was an excuse, Suzy thought. Korea was a crutch. It was what they used to keep the girls on their own terms.

Yet the one thing both Suzy and Grace so desperately wanted was to be American girls, full-fledged American darlings, more golden than the girl next door, even cheerier than the prom queen, definitely sweeter than all-American sweethearts. Far, far away from their parents' Korea, which stuck to them like an ugly tattoo.

How misguided such a dream: neither even made it to the prom. Dad would never have allowed it, but it did not matter really, for the girls were always new in their high school and had hardly any friends. No boy would have asked Suzy, and the ones Grace knew would have laughed at the idea. Besides, a prom was a luxury at the sort of schools to which they transferred. Most kids came from immigrant homes. No boy could dish out a hundred bucks for a night. No girl looked good in ruffled dresses. Pink satin was for white girls. A limousine? Why hire one when your father's the cabbie? A prom belonged in those Molly Ringwald movies, in which the prettiest girl, pretending to be a geek, ends up winning the rich, handsome, sensitive football captain for the last dance. High schools, as Suzy knew, had nothing to do with sweet sixteen. You were lucky if you didn't get mugged on the way to the locker. You were lucky if you didn't get frisked by the policeman at the gate ready to crack down on drug gangs. The golden girl, the girl next door, the all-American sweetheart didn't get made in the gutters of Queens.

"Here we are." The girl turns around, stopping abruptly in the middle of the hallway.

"The prom . . . when's your prom?" Suzy blurts out, then quickly regrets it, realizing that this might be too far-fetched for the girl.

"Prom?" asks the girl, her eyes widening.

"No, never mind," mutters Suzy, finding herself before Grace's classroom.

It is hard to believe that Grace must be inside. It suddenly occurs to Suzy that she might be too early. 8:50 a.m., not the best time for a surprise visit. But, then, it might even work to her advantage. Grace would have to greet her politely, first thing in the morning, showing up before her entire class. But it would not be fair to walk in on her like that, nor would it be wise. In-stead, Suzy suggests, "Could you ask Miss Park to come out-side? Tell her someone's here to see her." The girl is still vexed by Suzy's question about the prom but seems relieved that the subject is being dropped. Before disappearing inside, she turns around once, as if making sure Suzy is still there.

A few minutes later, the door opens to reveal the girl, followed by an older woman. Short-waisted and blotchy-skinned, she reminds Suzy of Michael's secretary, Sandy. Although Suzy has never seen Sandy in person, she imagines Sandy to have a similar look, the nervous look of a woman who's been on her own too long.

"May I help you? I'm Ms. Goldman," she says, peering at Suzy as if searching for a clue.

"I'm here to see . . . Grace Park. Is she not available?" Suzy stammers, barely hiding her disappointment, and a tinge of relief.

"Miss Park, well, she's not here today." Ms. Goldman glares at the little girl, as if shooing her away. The girl turns bright red, embarrassed for overstaying her welcome. Then she makes a slight bow in Suzy's direction and slouches down the hall, glancing back a few times.

"I'm a family member. Is she ill?" Strange that she should say "family member" instead of "sister." But Suzy cannot bring up the word "sister" with this woman who seems irrelevant, too irrelevant to be standing in Grace's place.

"Family? I didn't realize Miss Park had any family." Ms. Goldman raises an eyebrow, sizing up Suzy. "She's not ill. She's gone on vacation." Obviously Ms. Goldman does not notice the resemblance, unlike Bob out in Montauk. Perhaps Grace was right. Perhaps it is only white men who can't tell one Asian girl from another. But Suzy is used to this look, this subtle look of disappointment. Often it came from other Korean women. *Sisters?* They would repeat, scanning Suzy once more, as if they felt sorry for the sibling who fared so poorly, by comparison, in looks.

"A vacation? Did she say for how long?" It is as if Grace knew Suzy was coming, and had slipped away just in time.

"Two weeks, although . . . well . . ." Ms. Goldman is about to say something but quickly changes her mind.

"I've sort of fallen out of touch with her because . . . I've been away. Do you know where I can find her?" Suzy puts on an apologetic smile. People are suckers for family values. They don't like to hear about a sibling falling-out. They want reconciliation, and if it takes a slight breach of promise, oh well, it's all for the good of getting a family back together.

But Ms. Goldman is not so easy. She is not moved by Suzy's smile, and instead dismisses her with a firm note: "No, I have no idea. I must go back inside now. I'm sorry, I can't help you."

And just like that, Suzy is left standing alone in the hallway. Teachers, that's what she remembers about them. Never answer questions that matter; never give anything away unless they have to. Perhaps Grace had warned her. Perhaps the whole school is hiding Grace from Suzy.

With students gone, the hallway is endless. Eerily quiet, except for the occasional murmur and laughter from classrooms. She would now have to try the administrative office, which is located at the east end of the first floor. Its formidable door opens to a reception area, and another door farther back which leads to the principal's office. The haphazard state of the desk indicates that someone has only just stepped out. The carpeted sofa feels more plushy than it looks. Suzy is tempted to stretch out, eyeing the stack of newspapers and magazines on the table. *The Jersey Journal, Education Today, Child Psychology*, some of them dating back to the previous summer. There couldn't be a duller selection. Resting her head on the cushion, she is about to recline when she notices an odd one sticking out. It is barely a newspaper. A slim volume entitled *1.5 Generation*, which is just a bunch of legal-sized sheets stapled together. The first page reveals "A letter from the editor" that ends with an exaggerated signature. Across the top runs, "A Quarterly of News, Arts, Ideas and Colleges: published by the Asian American Student Union." It is an amateurish rendition of an alternative weekly. Its format is familiar, down to the last page filled with ads from local Korean restaurants and tuxedo rentals—not surprising, considering more than 30 percent of the student body is Korean. The 1.5 generation—the immigrants caught between the first and the second generations. They used to call Suzy that too. But it never sounded right. "1.5" still meant real Koreans, she thought. Ones who were born and raised in Korea long enough; ones whose fluent English will never forget its Korean accent; ones who, without a second thought, would root for the Korean team if the two countries were to ever meet for the World Cup. It's these kids who proudly call themselves 1.5 and brandish the word "multicultural" with the surest sense of allegiance. Definitely not Suzy, who has never even made the proper minority.

It is then that her eyes stop at the photo under a column called "Locker Talk," whose caption reads, "Check it out, BMW M5! Is this dude rich enough for Miss Park?" A gossip page in which recognizable names are highlighted with photos to match. The photo reveals a car parked in a lot; if there's a man inside, it is impossible to tell. Suzy quickly scans the article, searching for the corresponding paragraph, but the rest is the student stuff: who's going out with whom, who was at whose slumber party, who's likely to end up at Harvard on early decision. No more mention of Grace. No explanation of the car or the man.

"May I help you?"

Behind the reception desk sits a thirty-something redhead in a pink sweater set, holding a cup of coffee. Odd that Suzy did not even hear her come in. Which door did she appear from?

"Hi, I'm here to inquire about Miss Park," says Suzy, rising from the sofa while discreetly shoving the quarterly in her bag.

"Yes?" Her lips curl up in a simper. She is a natural. The sort of face any school would be glad to have.

"Miss Grace Park, she teaches ESL."

"Yes?" The parrot smile. The woman is custom-made.

"Do you have a number where she can be reached?"

"Have you tried her class?"

"Excuse me?"

"All teachers are in their classes now."

"But she isn't. I just checked."

"That's strange, I swore no teacher's absent today." The redhead punches a few keys on her computer and says, "Oops, sorry, our systems are down. Let me see, Ms. Gibney told me there's a list somewhere on this desk . . . Oh, here it is. Park, you said her last name was . . . Oh, here it is, try Room 302!"

"I've tried and was told she's not in."

"I'm sure there's been some mistake. You must've gone to the wrong room. Try Room 302." Then, with a toss of her fiery locks, she chirps, "Sorry, I have to take this call," picking up the receiver with "Fort Lee High School, may I help you?"

Useless; the redhead knows nothing. Suzy is not even convinced that she punched in the right keys before. Obviously a temp filling in for the real secretary. Room 302, exactly where Suzy just came from. What does it mean that no teacher's absent? What is Ms. Goldman not telling her? What about the car in the photo?

Reluctantly, Suzy climbs back to the third floor. Being sent around in circles—that's what she remembers about high schools. She was always the new girl, and the first day of a school happened too often. Soon she would be transferred to another school much like the one before. And through each step, each loop, each journey, Grace was her witness. And now this third-floor hallway of Grace's school seems no longer unfamiliar. That's what happens to people who keep moving homes. Everything becomes familiar; yet nothing is. It is possible that Suzy might also have attended this school at some point, somewhere between Jersey City, Jackson Heights, Jamaica, Junction Boulevard, and how many others were there? It is also possible that Grace might have chosen a school, any school, so that she could finally put a name, a face to their childhood, which seems to have gone missing in the vertigo of repetitions. Is it, then, fair to say that all of this, all that lies before Suzy—the hallway, the ESL class, the screaming sixteen-year-olds inside each classroom—might signal Grace's mourning?

Suddenly a bell. Doors crack open and happy faces begin pouring out. They are elated. The end of a class is always cause for celebration. The end of the first period. Three more to go until lunchtime. The last one to emerge is Ms. Goldman, whose face stiffens at seeing Suzy.

"Miss, I told you I have no idea where she is, and if you'll excuse me, I must get ready for my next class." Ms. Goldman walks briskly, heading for the elevator marked "Staff Only."

"Why isn't the school notified? How come you're teaching her class and the office knows nothing?" Suzy follows in quick steps, afraid that Ms. Goldman will disappear into the elevator without her.

Pressing the "Down" button, Ms. Goldman heaves a sigh and says impatiently, "Ms. Gibney, the school secretary, is out on maternity leave, so it's all chaos there. But that's not my problem."

"Why does the secretary downstairs seem to think Grace is in today?"

"Well, I don't know anything about that."

"Does any of this have to do with the guy she's seeing?" Suzy is tempted to pull out the quarterly and show it to the woman, but she decides it's better to let the question hang.

Ms. Goldman skips a minute or two, then says wearily, "May I ask how you are related to Miss Park?"

"She's my sister."

Just then the elevator arrives. Ms. Goldman motions Suzy to get in and snaps, "Fifteen minutes, but that's it, I have papers to grade."

The door opens to a cafeteria. Empty except for the kitchen staff and a few students at the far end, either waiting for a class or just killing time. Ms. Goldman returns to the table carrying two mugs on a tray. When Suzy declines the packets of cream and sugar, she dumps all into hers and stirs quickly. She knows Suzy's eyes are on her. She lets the coffee sit without taking a sip. Finally, she looks up and says, "It was Miss Park who asked me to keep quiet. Without Ms. Gibney keeping track, no one has to know she's gone as long as her class is covered. She didn't want the absence on record, 'cause, you see, she's used up all her vacation and sick days. She was afraid she might lose the job. Don't get me wrong. Miss Park is very conscientious. I don't know if I should even be telling you this, since you say you haven't seen her in a while, but she hasn't been herself lately, not since that guy started coming around, I guess for about a month. She's been missing classes. Then, a few days ago, this past Sunday night, she called me out of the blue.

"She was quite upset. She sounded frantic. She said that she couldn't come in for a while, and could I cover for her? You see, with ESL, the school doesn't provide substitutes. It's just not in our budget. So, when she's sick or something, we're all supposed to cover for her, the English teachers, depending on whose schedule works best with her class. So it was not a problem, except that she said 'for a while.' You see, I have my own class to teach, and it wouldn't be fair for me to teach someone else's class 'for a while.' So I asked her, for how long? She said two weeks. She'll be back by Thanksgiving. I told her flat out that it was impossible, it just wouldn't work. I told her to try Mr. Myers from English III, or Mr. Peters, who teaches remedial English. She's got her ways with men; I don't mean that in a strange way, I just mean that she has her ways."

Ms. Goldman talks fast, in nervous bursts, as though she is glad finally to be getting it all out.

"That's when she started crying, which surprised me. You know what she's like, she's always polite and proper, but I've always found her to be, well, a bit cold. But here she was, crying into my phone on a Sunday night. I'm a woman, I can hear it when there's trouble. She said that she didn't want to ask the other teachers 'cause she didn't want them to talk, and that she was calling me 'cause she respected me more than others. Well, I never knew she'd felt that way about me, although I guess I've always treated her with respect, much more respect than either Mr. Myers or Mr. Peters, who both look at her in ways not exactly decent, if you know what I mean. Besides, at large schools like this, students gossip, and especially with Miss Park—you know how she is—she's rather, well, much talked about, let's say." Ms. Goldman will not say it. She will not say that Grace is popular because she is beautiful. She is a woman, after all. She will not let herself go there.

"Then she told me she was getting married. She said that it was a secret from everyone, more like eloping, because they wanted to do it quietly, especially with her parents gone. Of course, everyone remembers about her parents. I asked her then whom she was marrying, although I've heard about the guy picking her up in a fancy car lately, which I have to say I found inappropriate, these young people showing off money, especially on public-school grounds. She told me not to worry, 'cause he was like a new family for her. I asked her if he had a proper job, which concerned me, you know, since he'd been coming around in the middle of afternoons. She said that he was in the music business, which I found odd. I can't remember why I found it odd, but I did. She then said that she was planning to announce it when she came back, but until then I was the only one she was telling. Poor girl, she was still crying. My heart just went out to her, a single girl getting married finally, without a family to help her, it must be overwhelming." Ms. Goldman's eyes flicker at Suzy, as if she blames her for Grace's tears, as if asking, *Where the hell were you when she needed you?* Then she quickly adds, "So I felt sorry for her and told her that I'd take over her class, just for two weeks, though, not any longer!"

Grace.

Married.

It never occurred to Suzy.

Surely one of them would marry first, someday with someone. Yet Suzy never thought of it. Suzy never imagined that Grace would one day start a new family. But why go away to do it? Why in secret? Why would Grace suddenly confide in this woman?

"Did she leave any contact address or number? His phone number, or his name, anything about him?" Suzy can just about muster the question. There's the sudden loosening, the hollowness inside.

"No, I thought of getting an emergency number, but then I thought it would be better to leave the girl alone through this. Let her have this moment, I said to myself." Ms. Goldman lifts her chest a little, as though she is touched by her own magnanimity, and then she whispers, as if she just remembered, "I know nothing about him, although, when I asked her if his family minded the wedding being so sudden, she told me that he was alone too. What a lonely wedding, I thought, and asked her how come he was so alone, and she said that he was an orphan, just like her."

Ms. Goldman is now studying Suzy a bit closer, contemplat-

ing her hair, all stringy from the sink water, and her overcoat
still wrinkled from the bus. *Too bad*, her eyes seem to be saying.
A sister? You don't quite measure up to Grace Park, do you?

Before Suzy thanks the woman, she writes down her own
phone number and hands it to her. "Just in case Grace gets in
touch," she tells her. "She's all I've got."

Although she is the one who insisted on sparing no more
than fifteen minutes, Ms. Goldman appears to be in no hurry to
end their conversation. It's probably been the biggest drama in
this whole week of her otherwise single, paper-grading teacher's
life. As though still jittery from all the excitement, Ms. Goldman knocks over the mug while getting up from her seat.
Instantly there's brown liquid everywhere, spilling over Ms. Goldman's tan PBS tote bag and the piles of papers. Suzy immediately reaches over and pushes the papers off the table.

"Oh my God, I'm so sorry, did it get to your coat? Let me
go find some tissues." Ms. Goldman scowls, running to the
kitchen.

Too bad the mug was full. Ms. Goldman never even touched
it.

Squatting on the ground, Suzy begins picking up the papers.
Essays for the ESL class. Each cover sheet bears the student's
name followed by "Miss Grace Park," underlined. Strange to see
Grace's name typed so neatly. Then *"Assignment #3"* in italics,
many with a single "s," which seems to be the common spelling
error. It is then that Suzy notices their titles. "MY PERFECT
HOUSE," says one. "MY SWEET FAMILY," says another. Slowly,
Suzy surveys the papers strewn around her. They are all about
one thing. The glorifying, larger-than-life capital letters celebrating home. "MY AMAZING FATHER." "MY BEAUTIFUL
MOTHER." Then, finally, "MY GOOD SISTER."

11.

THE WATER looks burnt again. The color of weak coffee, twice run through a filter. It's not good for a bath. She should not be lying in it.

On some days, the water turns strange. Something about the rusted pipes and the clogged drain. When it first happened, Suzy called the super in panic. Wait a few hours, he told her, groggy from a nap. The clear water did come back, about seven hours later. Suzy waited, eyeing the pile of dishes in the sink and the empty pitcher of Brita on the table. It kept happening, though, every few months, only just as she's stepping into the shower or about to rinse the toothpaste out of her mouth. She has never gotten used to the burnt water, which has become a source of mystery. Why should it happen? What's going on inside the pipes? She asked Michael about it once. He had no idea. He'd never lived in an old tenement. Pipes? he asked. What do you mean by "burnt"? Suzy changed the subject. She didn't want to get into it. She would have to invite him over if she wanted to explain better. But that seemed wrong, Michael in her apartment. He would look awkward. He wouldn't fit.

She sinks lower. The tub is so small that she has to bend her knees to get her shoulders wet. Her body looks almost tanned under this water, like the bikini-clad blonde from this morning's billboard. From the minute she got out of the bus at Port Authority and into the taxi downtown, she was desperate to reach her apartment. She ran up the stairs. She was trembling when she stepped inside. But the water that trickled out of the tap was hazy brown. She jumped into it anyway. She lay in it. It seemed necessary.

Already, Fort Lee feels distant. Not even noon yet. The whole day before her.

Grace.

Detective Lester.

Mr. Lee.

Kim Yong Su, the guy out in Queens, as if half the Koreans do not live in Queens. Where has she heard that name before?

The water is cushiony, almost velvet. She must be imagining it. Her headache is lurking. She recalls the girl who thought that English was a headache-inducer. Why would Grace tell her that? Where did Grace go? Did she stop in Montauk to see her parents one final time before the wedding? Did she sail out into the sea for their permission? Would Grace fill her wedding with white flowers, as she had the funeral? Would she stand tall and make a vow, not once breaking into tears?

Suzy has never imagined herself married. By the time Damian's divorce was finalized, it was too late. They never brought up marriage. For Damian, it reminded him of Yuki Tamiko and the life he'd left. Suzy felt it was wrong. She kept hearing her father's last words. Whore, hers was the life of a whore. Marriage was never an option, which might have been why she chose Damian.

Suzy saw Professor Tamiko just once more, at the Greenwich Village apartment that belonged to Damian's friend who was out of town on sabbatical. It was Suzy's first day there. She had not quite intended to move in, although she arrived with a suitcase. Now it occurs to her that he might have set it up. She had thought then that it must be chance. An awful, unfortunate chance. Yuki Tamiko had known, though. She had seen it coming. She might have wanted to warn Suzy, but she also knew that the younger woman would never listen. It was the end of January. It had all happened too fast.

They had slept together once. Back in November. Then, right afterward, he was gone. A research trip to Asia. She only found out from reading the *Spectator*, which ran a small article on the upcoming expansion of the East Asian Wing at the Metropolitan Museum, for which a few experts had been selected to form a research committee. That is where she saw his name. Damian Brisco—Former Chairman of the East Asian Department at Columbia University, Professor of East Asian Art, on leave for the past three years. He was gone, somewhere, some city in China, Japan, even Korea. She could not stand it. He had told her nothing. He had held her afterward. She had lain in his arms, thinking about the blood, thinking it might have stained Professor Tamiko's sheets. Dusk was setting when they walked to Riverside Park. They didn't speak much. She was no longer a virgin.

She had no idea when he would be back. No postcard, no phone call. Somehow she knew that he would not get in touch, but she still waited. With each day, she was becoming less certain whether he had indeed made love to her, whether any of it had actually happened. But then she would recall how he had kissed her, in such quiet steps, until he was sure she was ready. It was embarrassing, how clearly the picture came back to her. She could recall his every breath. Her body held him intact. It was all in her body. She threw herself into her thesis instead. She would stare at the computer screen without seeing a word. She would replay *Ran* without remembering a scene. "First-class asshole," Jen said, wincing, when she finally told her. "But, Suzy, you're not any better."

Two months later, in January, Suzy ran into him on Broadway. She was on her way to buy books for the new semester. It was the first time she had left her dormitory room in days. She was wearing a sweatshirt and jeans. An oversized blue hooded sweatshirt with "Columbia Crew" on its front. It had belonged to Jen. Suzy had thrown it on because it was the first thing she saw hanging across the chair. She was turning the corner at 114th Street. He was leaning over a stall of books outside the shop. It was him. She knew even before she saw his face. She felt something slip inside her. Her breath caught in her throat. She thought of her silly sweatshirt.

"Hi," she said first. His eyes looked pained, she thought, neither surprised nor overjoyed by this chance. "Looking for books?" She tried to smile, although her face felt stuck, every muscle suddenly locked. She was afraid that she looked obvious.

He continued to gaze at her. His eyes still cold. She wished she had worn something else. "You look thinner," he said finally, his right hand moving up slightly, as though it was about to reach her face.

"The thesis . . ." she stammered, unable to think of anything else to say. There were silver sparkles in his dark-brown hair which she had not noticed before. Neither spoke, although neither looked away. She wanted him to say something. She wanted him to explain why he had gone away so abruptly, why he had not been in touch. But she also knew that he had promised her nothing. He owed her no explanation.

"Come," he said then. He took out a piece of paper and

wrote something on it and handed it to her. His hand barely touched hers. It was an address. A downtown address. He was already hailing a cab. "Come stay with me for a while," she thought she heard him say, but the cab was already speeding away. He did not turn around once.

Three days later, when Suzy rang the buzzer of the three-story brownstone on Hudson Street, it was Professor Tamiko who answered. Neither had expected the other. It was Yuki Tamiko who broke the awkward silence. "May I help you?"

Suzy just stood there, not knowing how to respond. She wanted to turn back. She felt caught, guilty, humiliated, all at once. She had never expected this.

"Here to see Damian?" Professor Tamiko asked, with an edged smile, as if she finally understood. This girl. This young girl in front of her.

Suzy nodded, feeling stupid more than anything.

"Come in; he won't be back for a while." Professor Tamiko moved away from the door, her eyes quickly taking in the suit-case in Suzy's right hand.

"I am . . . I didn't . . . I can come back another time." Suzy had never expected to see her. She simply never thought about her. Here she stood with a suitcase that contained her life, and yet she never considered Professor Tamiko in relation to Damian. She had made the first move. It was she who had asked him to make love to her. She had even lost her virginity on this woman's bed.

"Don't look so frightened. You're obviously not a child if you've come this far." Professor Tamiko sat on the sofa, crossing her legs, her long slim legs, shimmering in off-black silk tights. Suzy stood still. She felt confused. She was not sure what she should do, or say.

"Come in, for God's sake." Professor Tamiko shot a quick glance at Suzy at the door. "I'll be leaving soon anyway."

Suzy put her suitcase down at the door and walked in. She did not know where to sit, although she did not want to keep on standing either. Her legs felt as if they would collapse any minute, as did the rest of her. She finally slouched in the love seat, which was farthest from where Professor Tamiko was sitting.

"A drink?" Professor Tamiko got up and walked toward the kitchen. She seemed to be familiar with the place. She seemed to be wanting to move away from the younger woman.

"No, thank you," Suzy answered in a near whisper.

Professor Tamiko poured herself a glass of water. For a second, Suzy was afraid that the older woman would offer her something heavy. Whiskey would make sense.

"How's your Cordelia?"

The question caught her by surprise. Suzy had hoped that she wouldn't remember—Professor Tamiko had over a hundred students. But women like Yuki Tamiko remembered everything. Suzy remained silent. She had made virtually no progress on her thesis.

"I guess you've been busy." Professor Tamiko took a quick sip, as though she regretted the remark, which came off sounding almost bitter. Then she asked, facing Suzy from across the room, "Tell me one thing, why do you think he asked you here?"

Suzy avoided her eyes, uncertain what she was driving at. He had asked her to come. He had not told her when. He had not even given her the phone number. She had assumed that the downtown address was his own, a sort of place apart from his wife, where Suzy could drop in without calling ahead or making a special arrangement. Such an illicit suggestion, strangely, did not scare her. She had been dying to see him. She could not think of anything other than wanting to see him. She had waited so long. *Come stay with me for a while.* It was an open invitation.

"Or did he make you think that it was you who chose him?" A smile formed around her dark-rouged lips, a sardonic smile.

Certainly she made the first move. She came here of her own will. Was that not her own decision? Did he somehow will her here? Was Professor Tamiko hinting at some kind of manipulation that had escaped Suzy?

"Don't think so hard. You're not breaking up a marriage. This has nothing to do with you." Yuki Tamiko took her gaze away, as though she had finally lost interest. Then she finished the glass of water and grabbed the cream leather handbag that had been sitting on the counter. She stopped at the door. She seemed to hesitate. When she turned around, her eyes were no longer cold. Almost apologetic, Suzy thought.

"Damian's not capable. He cannot love an Asian woman."

The water is getting cold now. She climbs out of the bath and wraps herself in a towel. The mirror is her own face staring out at her, oddly unfamiliar. The lines have crept under her eyes, tiny threads of years which have not been there until recently. Her chin appears sharper, almost angular, no longer innocent. Her breasts are looser, facing downward slightly, a note of gravity. She's become a woman suddenly. She will turn thirty in less than two weeks. Her mother had never warned her. "Asian girls don't age, do they?" a painter for whom she had posed once told her, moving into her face a bit too closely. He was wrong. He implied that being Asian was a different destiny. He thought that it bought her time.

Suzy stares at her own reflection. Ms. Goldman seemed to think that she looked nothing like Grace. Bob had mistaken her for Grace. How could two people think so differently? Then it comes back to her.

You remind me of someone I used to know, a good woman, too young to be killed like that.

The witness from the other day.

The deposition in the Bronx.

Diamond Court Reporting.

Forty-four Burnside Avenue.

The man who had saved a seat for her at McDonald's, whose gabardine pants and shiny shoes had reminded her of Dad, whose name, if she is remembering correctly, was . . .

Suzy runs to the kitchen table, where she had dropped her bag upon entering. She unzips the side pocket and pulls out the yellow legal notepad. She flips through the pages. November 10th. Last Friday, November 10th. Five days ago.

Case name.

File number.

Witness information.

Kim Yong Su. Born: 6/10/36. Address: 98-44 Woodhaven Boulevard, Apt. 8F, Queens, NY 00707

12.

THE BUILDING NUMBERED 98-44 is a red brick co-op. Built in the 1950s, probably. Solid and grim, although here, among the residential complexes called Lefrak City, it is just one of many identical blocks. Two o'clock in the afternoon. Kids running here and there who should really be watched by parents. Old women's faces at windows who spend their days looking out. Distant howls of stray cats, although in this chill they've all gone hiding. From across the street, Suzy counts up to sixteen, roughly. A sixteen-story building. His is situated right in the middle, on the eighth floor. Better there, she thinks. Not too close to the ground floor, where bored hands loiter with not enough cash. But not too high up, for one can never trust the elevator.

She is used to buildings like this. Two-room holes for the entire family. Her parents in the bedroom, and the bunk bed in the living room for Suzy and Grace. Who needs a living room? her parents claimed. They might have had a point. How much living could one do when working seven days a week? Suzy had just started sixth grade when they moved to a real two-bedroom for the first time. From then on, their two-room days were over. Her parents must have been doing better.

It was also around then that Grace began to change. Grace had always been quiet. She had been one of those shy kids, at her happiest when left alone in a corner with a book. But it was in that year, when Suzy and Grace finally got a real bedroom, that Grace began to show signs of withdrawal. The change did not occur overnight, but she became increasingly dark and sullen. Suzy did not understand why, nor did she question. She just got used to her sister's prickly moods. Later, Suzy thought that it must have been teenage angst, the heightened adolescent sensitivity, which must have hit upon Grace much more severely than it had Suzy.

Once, Suzy tried to draw her out. It was when Grace was getting ready to choose a college. Smith was an odd choice for Grace, who could have gotten into any college she wanted. Although they had moved through countless schools, both girls had always maintained top grades. In fact, it did not take much effort to be the best in class when most students either spoke no English or lacked proper teachers. Smith was certainly good enough, but why not look into other schools before making the early decision? Grace was not interested. She said that she'd had enough of men, which might have been true. But she also mentioned that Smith offered her a full private scholarship. Grace would not accept any other aid. No federal grant. No financial aid. No support from parents. Suzy failed to understand the reason. They were more than eligible for financial aid. Who really cared whether the scholarship came from a government agency or a private donor? What difference did it make, Suzy thought, as she herself went off to Columbia a year later with a good enough aid package to cover her entire tuition and dorm fee.

But Grace was adamant. When Suzy tried to point out the absurdity of her insistence, Grace lashed out, "You're so fucking stupid, Suzy, you wouldn't care what kind of money it is as long as it puts food before you, would you!"

During her first year away, Grace phoned only once, to say that she wouldn't be coming home during the breaks. Oddly, her parents did not seem too upset. If they were worried about her, they did not show it. In fact, they avoided mentioning her name altogether. Once, Suzy remarked casually at dinner, "I wonder how Grace is settling in." They just ignored the comment. They seemed almost relieved that she was gone. For the final few months, Grace had barely spoken to the rest of the family. She seemed ready to leave home forever. Suzy did not think that her sister would ever come back, certainly not move back home, the way she did a few years later.

Without Grace, the house became unbearable. Although Grace had never been a source of warmth for Suzy, her absence made Suzy feel strangely alone. Her parents had just bought the shop on Tremont Avenue. Both had been working at different fruit-and-vegetable stores for a few years, Mom as a cashier and Dad doing delivery. None of the other jobs had panned out. Dry cleaning didn't bring in enough cash; fish markets smelled nasty; clothing repair was taxing to the eye; nail salons were toxic; liquor stores got robbed too often; car services were too prone to accidents. Miraculously, they seemed to have saved enough to buy a store, which also meant that they came home even later.

Running their own business made them perpetually anxious. There were nights when they did not come home at all, because the store was open twenty-four hours. Suzy never got to see it. The less she knew, the better, Dad said. A fruit-and-vegetable market, nothing to see, nothing to learn. When Mom mentioned how other kids helped out, Dad balked: "I'm not slaving

away in this goddamn country to have my kids cut up melons!"
And that put an end to that. Suzy was secretly relieved. She'd
seen Korean markets. They were familiar sights around the city.
While the rest of the country had 7-Elevens and Pathmarks,
New York City had Korean markets, where one could find almost anything at any hour, fresh and cheap. They all had the basic setup of fruits and vegetables, bunches of flowers in buckets,
stacks of groceries on shelves, and salad bars and fruit cups. But
the key was that almost all the food items were fresh; nothing
was ready-made. They even sold freshly squeezed carrot juice.

The thought of seeing her parents at work made her uneasy. The twenty-four-hour market. The sleep-deprived wife behind the cash register. The bossy husband in a baseball cap hauling boxes in the back. The confused customers gesturing to
workers, none of whom speak English. Such an absolute immigrant portrait terrified her. And she knew that the only one who
would understand such fear was Grace. Grace had been her
American ally. Grace had always been there as a shield. Without
Grace, her home became a refuge for two overworked immigrants and Suzy, the interpreter of their forsaken lives.

And then there were those bills to sort out. Grace had always
taken care of them. Suzy was suddenly lost without her. She had
never had to calculate deductibles from the balance due or fill
out loan applications. Luckily, by then her parents had learned
to operate within the Korean community. There were people
whom they could consult in Korean, an accountant or an insurance agent. When they absolutely needed to communicate in
English, they got by in their broken English. Her parents never
relied on Suzy the way they had with Grace. Because Grace was
older, Suzy assumed. Grace knew how to get things done. But
sometimes it almost felt as if it was Grace who wouldn't let her.
All those times when Grace was stuck having to translate for
Mom and Dad, she never once asked Suzy for help. When Mom

suggested Suzy take a turn, Grace snapped, "Leave her alone," and then said loudly, so Suzy could hear, "She's too slow, she'll never figure it out." That did it. Suzy never offered to help. Let *her* deal with the mess, she thought sulkingly. But now that Grace was gone, Suzy thought perhaps Grace had been right after all. On the rare occasions when Suzy had to read over a confounding notice from creditors, she wondered how Grace had managed, gone all day as Mom and Dad's personal interpreter.

The elevator reeks of urine and sweat. The floor appears not to have been swept in years. The loud bass line from a boom box vibrates through each floor, accompanied by the occasional shrill of a woman, either joyous or dying. Suzy pauses before the door marked 8F.

Kim Yong Su is a truck deliveryman, which means that he should be home now. A deliveryman's day begins around 10 p.m., when he drives his truck to the wholesalers in the Bronx Terminal Market or the Hunts Point Market and purchases the goods that have been ordered by his client stores. He then loads the boxes of fruits and vegetables onto a truck and starts making deliveries through the early-morning hours. On average, one driver has five or six stores on his roster. A regular truck won't hold more than six stores' worth of goods. He is the middleman. All deliveries must be made by at least 9 or 10 a.m., when the stores finish stocking inventories. By noon, he must rush home, eat quickly, and go straight to bed, so that he can rise again at sunset.

Suzy rings the bell once. Nothing happens. No sound comes from the inside. Maybe he is not home yet. Maybe he is already asleep. She rings again. Somewhere from the end of the corridor comes a hissing noise. A kid up to mischief. A curious neighbor looking on. Finally, a shuffling sound against the door and an eye through the peephole. "Who is it?" the voice asks in Korean. "Suzy Park." She brings her face close to the door. "I met you the other day at the deposition, I was your interpreter." Then a clatter of bolts, and a face emerges, the same face that beckoned her at McDonald's only five days ago.

He looks surprised, if not wary. He does not invite her in. Not yet anyway. His face seems to be asking, What are you doing here? Do interpreters make house calls now? Did my lawyer send you? Did the court? Am I in trouble for something I am unaware of? Whose side are you on?

"I would've called, but I had no phone number for you," she says finally. It is hard to know where to begin. She hopes that she is not imposing too much on his sleep time.

He appears even more puzzled. He is not sure if he should let her in. Why is she here?

"I think you knew my parents," she comes straight out. "They had a store on Tremont Avenue in the Bronx. They were killed five years ago."

A flicker of something in his eyes. A flash of recognition. He looks her over once, lingering on her face, and says, "I've got nothing to say." He is about to shut the door when Suzy blurts out, "Mr. Lee from Grand Concourse sent me. He told me that you know things, that you were wronged by my parents." It is not true, of course. No one sent her here, only her own suspicion, and poor Mr. Lee, he will never know what exactly ensued from his testimony. The man behind the door pauses mid-step, his eyes boring into her once more. Then he moves aside, reluctantly.

Inside is a small studio with a bed against one wall, along with a table and a tattered brown sofa. On the other wall is a kitchenette barely wide enough for one person. It is a shabby place, but not without a semblance of order. Obviously he lives alone. But of course that must have been in his testimony; she never recalls details afterward, one witness's life often blurring with another.

He motions for her to sit on the sofa before bringing a chair from the foot of the bed. He then sits opposite her with a table between them.

"I would offer you something, but all I've got is water."

"I'm fine," she tells him. "I'm not thirsty."

From the lack of expression on his face, it is impossible to tell what he is thinking. If he is still wary of her, he no longer lets it show.

"I didn't know when I met you at the deposition. I didn't know that you'd known them. I guess I don't know many people who knew my parents," she says, choosing her words carefully.

He takes out a pack of Marlboros from his shirt pocket and grabs the blue plastic lighter from the table. When he inhales, there is a hint of a gurgling sound from his throat. He has a weak heart, Suzy thinks. Weak lungs. This man should not be smoking.

"The police claim it was a random shooting. But the murder was professional. It was precisely executed. It was obvious. It made no sense that no one was getting to the bottom of it." Suzy raises her eyes, fixing him with a clear, steady gaze. "I'm not sure what I'm asking you to tell me. But I know you might've had reasons to hate my parents."

He is looking down at the black plastic ashtray on the table, the kind that belongs in a bar, not in the solitary home of a man well past sixty. When he exhales, the smoke casts a fog between them.

"So you think I had something to do with your parents' murder?"

The question comes so abruptly that Suzy does not know how to respond, except to continue staring at him. He does not return her gaze. He looks tired. Of course, he must have just come home from work. A man of his age should not be hauling boxes all night.

"Your father . . ." He pauses, as if just a mention, the uttering of the name, brings up memories he'd rather do without. "He'd worked with me many years ago. About eight years before he was killed, so I guess thirteen years now. A fruit-and-vegetable store, the only kind of work I know how to do."

He takes a deep breath, as though it is not easy for him to talk at length. Suzy wishes now she had asked him for that water. Her throat feels dry suddenly. She swallows hard, looking across at the red glow of his cigarette.

"Whatever you've heard is your business. It's been thirteen years, a long time. Nothing left now, nothing left to say." When he says "nothing" in Korean, the word leaves an echo, the peal of hollowness. Looking around, Suzy is again struck by the austerity she observed upon entering. It is obvious that he is not attached to his living quarters. Nothing gives a clue, nothing personal here. Except for a photograph framed by his bedside. A snapshot of a middle-aged woman with a short permed hair and pursed lips. Koreans rarely smile before a camera. It makes them uneasy, such a mechanical documentation of history.

"Is that your wife?" she asks, hoping to engage him, who seems determined to end this talk.

"*Was* . . . She's been dead for thirteen years," he mutters. Suzy cannot tell if he is annoyed by her interest.

"I'm sorry," says Suzy, vaguely recalling something about it from his testimony. A suicide, it was. The plaintiff's lawyer, the older one with a brand-new Honda Accord, brought it up a few times, only to back away when pummeled by objections from Mr. Kim's attorney. Nasty ones do that. Any tragedy in your past can be used to bring down your case. The more tragic, the easier it is to paint a bad character. A man who cannot be trusted, a man who's driven his wife to death.

"Thirteen years . . . seems like yesterday," he adds, contradicting what he said earlier. Suzy cannot help noting the coincidence. Thirteen years ago, he'd known her parents. Thirteen years ago, his wife committed suicide. Suzy was sixteen then. A junior in high school. They were living in either Jackson Heights or Astoria.

"I understand," she says softly, surprised at her own confession. Sometimes tragedy throws people together, even when they must stand on opposing sides and guard their ground.

He glances at her for a while and then lowers his eyes again. He taps the cigarette against the edge of the ashtray. Not because he really needs to, but because it gives him something to do, a slight motion of fingers, a scatter of ashes.

Suzy takes note of his every move. It is a habit. An interpreter must listen always, even when no words are being spoken. Language comes in all forms. A witness's sighs and hesitations might determine the tone in which she interprets his claim.

"A brave woman, but not brave enough maybe," he says as if to himself. It is obvious that just the mention of his wife brings him home, if only for a moment. Suzy says nothing. She knows that this is his moment, that his mind has drifted far from here.

"Some guy once told me that the airport is where the American dream begins. It's all up to whoever picks you up there. If it's your cousin who owns a dry cleaner, you go there and learn that business. If it's your brother who fillets fish for a living, you follow him and do that too. With me, it was my wife who'd come before me and found a cashier job at a fruit-and-vegetable store. Women are harder than men. The only thing I thought she knew how to do was be a housewife. She was eighteen when we got married right after I was released from the army. I never doubted that we'd grow old together. People who marry that early, they often do."

In his mind, he is a young soldier stationed at a remote

country near the 38th Parallel. Every night, before falling asleep
in his barracks, he takes out his wallet to steal a glimpse at a
photograph. Even in the wrinkled black-and-white photo, he
can tell that her lips are the shade of a cherry blossom, the rib-
bon in her hair is a matching pink. A bashful girl smile. Antici-
pating her lover's gaze, she forgets the usual reserve before a
camera.

"It was always the two of us, from the beginning, all the way
until . . ." His voice is a bit shaky now, as though he is over-
whelmed by the rushing memory. "We'd never had any children.
She couldn't conceive. Neither of us knew when we got married,
and later, when we found out, my wife was more terrified than
me. She thought it was a sin. She even said that I should divorce
her. In Korea then, and maybe even now, those things mattered
a lot, having kids, carrying on a family name. Sure, I was upset.
I never thought that I'd be without a son, or even a daughter.
That was what one did, get married, have children. But then,
once I accepted the fact, I wasn't so bothered. I even told my
wife that it worked out better, imagine dragging children
through the pain of it all, of leaving Korea and getting here. My
wife, I don't think she ever got over it. She felt forever like a sin-
ner. She thought she'd wronged me by not producing a son.
Sometimes I think that might've been why we left Korea. Leaving a homeland, it cuts into you like nothing else. It's like an
illness, haunting generations. But I wonder if we hadn't also
hoped that America might make us forget, that in this new
country a tradition wouldn't shun you because you're a middle-
aged couple with no children.

"I'd been a manager at a small trucking company in Korea.
I was forty-one when they went bankrupt overnight and left
me with nothing, no severance pay, no workers' compensation.
Jobs were scarce then. It was the late seventies. They say that
it was our economy-building era, but I tell you, the only econ-

omy that was building was for the rich, Samsung, Hyundai, Daewoo, the megacorporations, *chebul,* you know. It was the rest of us, the working people, who paid for it. No small company survived. Bank loans, mortgage rates, trade regulations— everything worked against you. It was the time. There wasn't much any of us could do, except wait for a better time, or get out, which is what I did.

"I'd heard of a guy who'd moved to a place called Brooklyn in America and made a good life. Korea is a small country; once you lose your chance, there's nowhere you can run to and start over. So we looked for ways of getting to America. Not legally, of course, because obtaining the American visa was even harder than finding a job. We found a broker who hooked my wife up with this church group whose yearly choir tour to New York was due in just a few months. I followed, about a year later. The same broker got me in through the Canadian border. Fake papers, fake names, it's a miracle what those immigration brokers can fix. I landed at JFK in the fall of 1980. My wife wept at the airport. I couldn't believe how much older she looked in just one year. Those first years were hard, the things I saw and did when I first got here, this country called America, this number-one country in the world, it had nothing to do with home.

"I started out as a setup guy at the Bronx store where my wife was working. The owner was a good man, hiring me when he could've gotten anyone much younger. It was a favor to my wife. She was an honest worker, and he knew that. In a few years, I was basically managing the store. A tiny store, just my wife and I, and a few Mexican kids. The work was hard, but we were happy. We were building something together, finally a new life in a new land. I wonder sometimes if that wasn't the happiest time of my life. She and I, starting a life together for the second time, like newlyweds almost . . ." He pauses suddenly, as if struck by the image of the two together. An early morning, and the sun gloriously shining upon the stalls of fruit. The ripe yellow of plantains, the green hills of Hass avocados, the firm blush of McIntosh apples. Fruits were a sign of home then. A different kind of home from what he had known before, from what he knows now, not this studio apartment he crawls into for sleep.

All Suzy can do is listen. She is afraid of breaking his spell, although she cannot quite make sense of his story. Was that why his wife committed suicide? Because she could not conceive? But why thirteen years ago? The woman must have been in her late forties by then. What does this have to do with her parents?

"Sometimes I think maybe she was right. If we'd been able to have children, she might not have been so rash, or so heartless," he mutters as if to himself, as if he's reached the limit of his memory. He never talks this much. He never gets visitors. He is sucking on his Marlboro as though it is the only life left in him. He then says without looking up, "But that didn't help your parents, did it, to have you and your sister."

Suzy is startled by this sudden turn. She stares at him, although she cannot see his eyes. Finally, she asks, "What makes you say that?"

"Because you wouldn't be here otherwise. You wouldn't be so sure they'd wronged me."

It only occurs to her now how odd it is for her to be here, to show up at the house of someone who might have had reasons to hurt her parents. Why did she come to him instead of notifying the police? Why was she so quick to believe Mr. Lee's claim? Why didn't she give her parents the benefit of the doubt? By showing up here, by asking this strange man for an explanation, she seems to have already made up her mind. Behind the murder, the guilt lay with her parents.

Whose side is she on?

The air feels stuck. Its lumpy clouds surround her, and she can barely breathe. She walks over to the sink. She takes two glasses from the shelf and fills them with water. She puts one glass in front of him before sitting down.

"Thank you," he says, reaching for the glass. He looks exhausted. Aged, she thinks. It is clear that he is done talking. Almost three o'clock, long past his bedtime. Although, today, it does not seem likely that he would be able to fall asleep. The cigarette has burned itself out, the ashes drooping limp and long, still hanging on to the filter. The room has gotten much darker, as though the sun outside has given up. And the two mourners in their devastated corners.

Neither will speak. He won't speak anymore. He is waiting for her to leave.

Why is she here?

She suddenly becomes aware of her parents gazing at her from all corners. She can almost hear them, feel their eyes on her. She rises abruptly, as if fleeing. With her right hand, she brushes back a strand of her hair falling in her face.

"I should've recognized you right away," he says, walking her to the door. "You take after your mother, more than your sister does."

Suzy pauses, turning to face him.

"Has Grace been here too?"

"Yes, several years ago, a few months before your parents' deaths maybe. She wasn't like you, though."

"What do you mean?"

"She had only one question." He smiles faintly, his hand around the doorknob. "She asked where my wife was buried. Montauk, I told her."

13.

IT IS AFTER FOUR O'CLOCK when Suzy finds herself sitting on a bench at Bryant Park, on 42nd Street. The wind is cold against her skin, crisp, refreshing. Darkness sneaks in with a tinge of green, the way it does when autumn turns to winter overnight. The trees are drained of color. Suzy prefers the parks in winter. Their bareness comforts her.

It's been a long day, from the morning bus ride to New Jersey to the trip to Queens. She would have been happy to go straight home. But while waiting for the R train at Rego Park Station, she noticed Mr. Lim on the opposite platform, their next-door neighbor when they lived in Flushing many years ago. He and his wife had shown up at her parents' funeral, which surprised Suzy because she vaguely recalled a sort of falling-out between him and Dad. He did not exactly acknowledge her then. He seemed aware of the circumstances in which she had shamed her parents. Korean elders never look kindly at daughters whose filial piety is in question. His wife tried to meet her eyes a few times, but Suzy pretended not to notice, not feeling up to polite greetings.

Mr. Lim had also been a truck deliveryman. During his early years of delivery work, Dad used to call him for tips. The selection of fruits and vegetables depends on the neighborhood. Harlem stores needed more bananas than others. The ones in the Hispanic neighborhoods couldn't do without yucca roots and plantains. And the Manhattan stores, the Upper East Side especially, carried the most expensive fruits, like mangoes and raspberries and papayas. The trick is to figure out which wholesalers carry the best grapes, and which ones to avoid for melons. It was Mr. Lim who showed Dad where to go for half-priced bananas on Friday mornings, and whom to enlist for extra help during Thanksgiving seasons. But then, at some point, Mr. Lim bought a store on Lexington Avenue. Manhattan, Dad exclaimed, where rents are steep and employees cost a fortune! After visiting his store, Dad couldn't stop talking about his impeccable salad bar. From grape leaves to California rolls to vegetable tempura to *kimchi*, imagine charging as much as $4.99 per pound! Whoever knew Americans would develop such continental taste buds? You'd think they had never lived without salmon maki or chicken tandoori! Koreans are responsible for that, you know, the craze over world cuisine at your fingertips, it all started with our salad bars! But then, soon afterward, Dad stopped calling Mr. Lim. In fact, the mere mention of his name made Dad twitch in anger. Something to do with money. Dad needed a loan, and Mr. Lim seemed to have refused.

Suzy was about to wave at him across the track when she noticed something strange. A group of boys and girls were straggling around him, as though a nearby school had just let out for the day. Amidst the giddy teenagers in oversized parkas and baggy jeans, he cut a lonely figure, huddled in a dark overcoat, facing the black tunnel from which a train might come hurtling any minute. He hadn't seen her yet, or if he had, he was pretending not to have. She had been only nine or ten when she last saw him in Flushing, and at the funeral she barely paid him any attention. But now, in the dimness of the underground, she noticed something oddly familiar about the way he stood with his head cocked to one side, about thirty degrees to his right. What was he doing here anyway, on a subway platform in the middle of the day? Why wasn't he at work? Has he moved to this part of Queens now? At that very moment, the R train flew down the track with a roar, landing at her feet. She jumped in automatically, quickly turning to the window to find him still on the other platform. She thought she saw him turn to stare directly at her as the train gained speed. And it was not until a few stops later—between Elmhurst and Jackson Heights, where the train got stuck for fifteen minutes—that it dawned on her that Mr. Lim's peculiar posture had reminded her of the man who'd stood by the Montauk lighthouse in the rain.

Montauk, I told her.

Kim Yong Su's last words, circling in her head. What could it mean? A few months before their death . . . did her parents send Grace there?

Montauk.

Where her parents' ashes are scattered.

Where Kim Yong Su's wife is buried.

Where Suzy two days ago walked to its lighthouse, where a strange man had stood watching, a man resembling Mr. Lim, the next-door neighbor from her childhood.

Where Grace had shown up last Friday to rent a boat. Kelly's boat, over at the dock. A tiny sloop. Two-person, max. And Grace can't even swim. And the secret wedding. Somehow Suzy is not convinced. Just a gut feeling. No evidence to the contrary, no reason to disbelieve . . .

"Sorry, have you been waiting long? What a dreary day!"

Jen stands before Suzy, carrying a brown paper bag in her arms. She's gotten older, Suzy notices for the first time, but in just the right way. Her blond hair is pulled back in a simple ponytail; the light-mauve lipstick complements her creamy glow. Looking at Jen bundled in a knee-length camel coat, Suzy can see a woman reaching her prime in her thirties. Jen has never looked more radiant, Suzy thinks. So confident, so knowing, so perfectly compassionate. The same does not apply to Suzy herself, of course. Linear age eludes her. With her parents' sudden death, Suzy skipped her youth entirely.

"Thank God, I was worried you might've gotten us coffee too." Jen slides by Suzy's side and takes out two large cups from the bag. "Decaf. I didn't think you'd want the caffeine kick so late in the day."

Suzy recalls how they had both been such fervent coffee-drinkers in college. They spent most of their junior year huddled in the dark corner of the Hungarian Pastry Shop, sipping double espresso while writing their Eighteenth-Century Novel papers. They were both literature majors. Back then, they would have sniffed at the mention of decaf, as though caffeine were the sign of a true soul. And now nothing is that absolute, nothing evokes such a conviction. Must be the years. Comforting to know that they are gaining in years together.

"Soooo nice to be outside!" Jen takes a deep breath, handing Suzy one of the paper cups. "I didn't know that I'd end up wasting all of my twenties in a cubicle."

Earlier, when Suzy called from the subway station, Jen sounded flustered, even slightly panicked. Meet you at the park in twenty minutes; any excuse to leave the office for a bit, Jen groaned. The writer for the cover story was a total control freak, which explained the painful late hours this week. But that could not be the reason for her panic, Suzy thought, detecting a slight tremor in Jen's voice, which suggested trouble.

"You love it. You'll say the same thing when you turn forty," predicts Suzy, taking the hot cup with both hands. The heat is nice. Half the fun of hot coffee is holding the mug.

"Maybe not . . ." Jen looks away at the pair of musty pigeons tottering along the green patch nearby. "So how was your day?"

Suzy can tell that something is wrong. Jen always defers the subject to another when something is bothering her.

"I went to see Grace today." Suzy does not elaborate. It is obvious that Jen has a load on her mind.

"And did you see her?" Jen looks surprised, and intrigued. She has never met Grace, but she has never approved of Grace's hostility toward Suzy.

"She wasn't there. She's gone off to get married, supposedly."

"And you don't believe that anyone would want to marry her?" Jen is being cynical. It is a sign that something is definitely wrong.

"I don't know what I believe. I haven't seen her in five years. More like ten, if you count those years she was at Smith and I . . . took off. Ten years, then—I guess people must change a lot, no?" Opening the lid, Suzy blows on the coffee once before taking a sip. The hot liquid trickles down her throat, warming the inside. The park is a good place at this time of the day. The late-autumn sun is setting.

"Have we changed in ten years? Am I different now than I was in college?" Jen asks without taking her eyes off the pigeons.

"No, I guess not, because you still can't hide anything. What's the matter?"

"Is it that obvious?" Jen gives up pretending. "Nothing too serious. Just a job thing." Jen smiles, trying to appear nonchalant. Suzy remains quiet. This job means a lot to Jen. Suzy knows from having worked there herself, although for just a few months.

"There have been reports about me. The insider report, because only the insider could know the stuff, even though they're a bunch of silly lies really. How I purposefully leaked the Baryshinikov feature to the Sunday *Times*. How I've been assigning articles to one particular writer since his wild book party last April. How I've been ripping off the story ideas from freelancers. They all sound just absurd enough to get me weird looks. I don't know who's making these up, but I don't like it. It makes me feel . . . trapped." Jen pauses, taking a sip of her coffee. "I mean, the magazine world isn't innocent. Editors fuck writers, and writers fuck their subjects. That's the way mass journalism works. But these rumors about me, I'm not sure. Actual e-mails were sent to the editor-in-chief's private address, although no one knows from whom. At least that's what I was told by my assistant, who's up on office gossip. Who knows, maybe everyone knows who it is and is not telling me. Maybe no one's telling me the truth. Sure, someone could be jealous, someone could want me out." Jen turns to Suzy with a tight smile. "But I'm no longer sure who's on my side."

Whose side is she on?

When Mr. Lee testified that her parents' death was not random, that someone must have had a reason to plan and execute the killing, she did not doubt him. When he claimed that half the Korean community didn't mourn their deaths, it did not surprise her. When he swore that her father had had it coming to him, she did not defend her father. Instead, she sought out Kim Yong Su, as if to confirm her suspicion.

"Funny how life turned out much simpler than it promised to be in college," says Jen, smoothing the wrinkled end of the white silk scarf which wraps around her neck a few times to drape down to her lap. It is a dramatic sort of look, not quite Jen's style. Suzy wonders if that is why she suddenly noticed Jen's beauty, not because of the scarf itself, but because of such a subtle change, which seems no longer so subtle. "It was never about

Faulkner or Joyce or even Derrida or whatever they jammed into our brains for four years. What a superb con job, feeding us a fantasy for our hundred thousand dollars' tuition! Literature and semantics don't make us cry. It all comes down to such basic fights, like holding on to a job despite an infantile enemy, sucking up to the editor-in-chief for a higher profile. The survival has nothing to do with your brain. It's about who has the thicker skin. It's about shedding all the ethics and righteousness that we learned in college. It's about the resilience of your needs and fulfilling them even if it costs all your moral conviction.

"You might've been smarter after all, Suzy. To cut out when you did, when you followed your asshole Damian to the ends of the earth. At least you stuck to your heart. You did what you wanted to do, no matter how you reproached yourself afterward. Who's to say what's right and wrong? Who's to say the right path is so right after all?"

Suzy stops biting the rim of the paper cup and stares at Jen. It is unlike Jen to be so filled with doubt. Jen has always been confident, and right. She has always been the image of what Suzy was not, what Suzy could never be—the ultimate emblem of the American dream. It was Jen who begged her to stay when Suzy packed her bag in her senior year. "This isn't love," Jen repeated with unflinching certainty. "You don't love him; love shouldn't make you run." Four years later, when the escapade with Damian was over, it was also Jen who took her in without asking any question. She cleared her study so that Suzy could sleep through those unfathomable weeks following her parents' murder. Jen always knew exactly what to do. It is not fair, Suzy thinks, for Jen to retreat like this suddenly. It is not fair for Jen to break down before her.

What do you want after all, do you want me to tell you?

Damian had struck the right chord. The impossibility of desire might have been at the core of their union. The escape with

Damian, why did it happen? Did he manipulate her into their reckless affair, as Professor Tamiko had once suggested? Did he claim nineteen-year-old Suzy in order to punish his wife, whom he failed to love? Would he have wanted her still had she not been Asian, so much younger than Yuki Tamiko, and definitely less fierce? What Suzy had wanted in return is still not clear. Neither an act of courage nor mindless passion. In fact, it was very mindful, each step measured. It had to be Damian. It could only have been Damian. No one would have claimed her with such absolute disregard.

"But I had no choice." Suzy is not sure how to continue this, how to explain the inevitability of the past. "The difference between you and me is that you've always been on the right side. You say that you're not sure anymore. But you are. Because you're outraged still. Because you're sad, not for fear of losing your job but for its injustice. You search for explanation. You won't give up until you find the way. You have the eye to discern what is good and what isn't. You can point a finger and tell me where and when and why. You're confident in that knowledge. You're secure. No one can take that away from you." Suzy draws a quick breath and glances at Jen, who is quietly listening. Jen has one thing Suzy could never have: a sense of entitlement, the certainty of belonging. It was not a quality Suzy could learn to adopt, or even pretend to assume. Jen belonged, Suzy didn't. It was as simple as that. If Suzy had resented Jen for it, she would have hated herself, because it was easier to blame the one who lacked. And such resentment would have been so lonely that Suzy could not have borne it. Jen, Suzy knows, would understand this.

"Me, I'm not sure if I ever had it in me. For a long time, for as far back as I can remember, something was amiss, something fundamental. It's as if I've never had a home, as if I've never known what it is to have faith, as if I was never taught what's right from wrong, or if I was, then somehow the difference didn't matter. Why is it that I never felt guilty toward Professor Tamiko? Or Michael's wife? Why did I choose Michael? Why did I run with Damian? Why did I run from my parents?"

She did not mean to bring up her parents. Kim Yong Su. His dead wife out in Montauk. Her poor, sad parents. Missing Grace.

Jen stares at Suzy, meeting her eyes for the first time. She is about to say something, but she looks away instead at the empty green patch of grass where pigeons had flocked only minutes ago. The late-autumn breeze is sharper now. The bare branches have formed hard shadows. The lamps along the fenced path appear bright, giving off a warm glow when everything else is shutting down. Finally, without turning her face, Jen asks, "Do you still hate your parents, Suzy?"

It is useless to pretend with an old friend. Yet there are things one should never say aloud, never admit. So, instead, Suzy says with forced clarity, "But they're both dead; it's been five years."

"Five years, but you're still hiding," Jen mutters slowly.

"Not any more than what you're doing here with me," says Suzy, changing the subject.

Jen is smiling now. The first real smile since she got here. "Decaf sucks, doesn't it?"

"It was your idea." Suzy puts down the cup, which has gotten tepid too quickly. "So you still have to go back to the office?"

"Yeah. The issue ships tomorrow, and Harrison still hasn't faxed in his corrections."

"The control-freak writer?"

"More like the pain-in-the-ass writer. If he didn't have such a stunning mind, we would've severed our ties with his last piece, which came in three months late."

"What's this one about?"

"Nabokov. The pre-*Lolita* years, when he was teaching at Cornell. Harrison was one of his students then and makes a case about how Nabokov had hated America, and, even worse, how he despised writing in English. Harrison claims that Lolita was really a metaphor for how Nabokov felt toward the English language. The strange mix of desire, subjugation, remorse. It's an interesting theory, although I'm not sure how much of it I really buy. Nabokov wrote in English almost exclusively, you know. Once he moved here in the forties, he dropped his native Russian, which was a peculiar decision. But he'd been raised trilingual—English, French, and of course Russian. As far as I can tell, he was at ease with all three languages. The man ended up retiring to Switzerland, of all places, talk about neutral ground! They only okayed this article because it's controversial, and of course because it's Harrison. He even claims that Nabokov's decision to adopt American citizenship was little more than a pretext, that it gave him cover for his anti-Americanism. It happened in 1945, not exactly an innocent year. It offers a totally new reading of *Lolita*. I'm not convinced, though." Jen turns to her, knitting her eyebrows. "Does it mean all that much? What does it mean to adopt a new citizenship?"

American citizenship. Of course, Suzy, having come to America at five, had to have become a naturalized citizen at some point. The question rarely came up. She has never even applied for a passport. The idea of flying seized her with vertigo, but in reality, the opportunity never arose. Damian talked about their taking a trip together, since his research often took him to Asia. But it soon became obvious that he did not want her along on his trips. Without a passport, nothing proves her citizenship. She has always checked off the "citizen" box on financial-aid forms, because she once asked Mom and was told that she was a citizen. Since she herself was a citizen, wouldn't her parents and Grace be as well? When did they all become citizens? How did it happen? She was told that they had left Korea in 1975. They had followed a family member who had been living in the United States, a cousin on Mom's side, who must have applied for their visa. When Suzy asked the whereabouts of this cousin, Mom said that she died soon after their arrival. Suzy remembers feeling bad about it. Since they had no relatives in America and had not kept in touch with anyone from Korea, an aunt nearby would've been nice. But as it turned out, the family had no one. When other kids boasted about visiting a grandmother or a cousin or an aunt, Suzy just shrugged. She had never had any, so she felt no terrible loss.

Contrary to their insistence on everything Korean, her parents rarely discussed their life back home. Dad had been an orphan. A war orphan, a leftover from the 38th Parallel, he used to say. He'd been all alone from birth, and yet he'd managed to get himself to the richest country in the world, so how about that!—Dad would grunt at little Suzy and Grace on nights when he downed a whole bottle of *soju*. On those nights, Dad seemed to forget that they were there at all. The rage they often witnessed was gone too. He seemed to be fighting the urge to remember and yet could not stop recalling the demons from his Korean past, which had nothing to do with his daughters or his wife or this faraway land, as far as the ocean, as far as the length of a decade or two decades or however long it took to call it a home, a place called Queens, a place called the Bronx, a place called America, none of which assuaged whatever stuck in his heart unturned. What Suzy saw was a kind of sorrow, so raw that it felt contagious. Had his recollections at such times signaled the seed of all his angers, she could not have known, because he would not have told, because he was a type of man who should never have had a family.

Mom, though, had not been so alone. She still had family left in Korea. Two sisters. A couple of nieces and nephews.

Everyone comes from somewhere. But it seemed that something bad had happened, and she stopped talking to them years ago. When Suzy asked Mom why, she was told to stay out of the adults' affairs. Family feud, Suzy later assumed. Probably about money—what else? Couldn't be much money, though. Mom did not come from wealth. Suzy gathered that much.

The subculture of immigrants had nothing much to do with the rest of America. When the girls took sick, Mom would get a concoction from a local Korean pharmacy where they never asked for a prescription. When Dad lost his appetite, he would visit an herbalist in Astoria for a dose of bear's galls. When her parents had some money they could put away, which was hardly ever, they would turn not to a bank but to a *gae*, which was a Korean communal-savings pool where a monthly lottery was drawn to grant the winner a lump sum. It was beyond Suzy's understanding why her parents, like most Korean elders, preferred Maxwell House instant coffee to fresh coffee, or why they wouldn't touch grapefruits or mangoes, though they kept boxes of dried persimmons at home. Had she stayed in just one neighborhood long enough, had she been allowed to build intimacy with one friend, one neighbor, one relative, then perhaps this perpetual Korea, which hovered somewhere in the Far East, might have seemed more relevant. She kept up with the language. She followed the custom. But knowing about a culture was different from feeling it. She would bow to the elders without the traditional respect such bows required. She would bite into the pungent spice of *kimchi* without tasting its sad, sour history. She would bob her head to the drumbeats of the Korean folk songs without commiserating with their melancholy. But how could she? She recalled nothing of the country.

Yet American culture, as Suzy was shocked to discover upon leaving home, was also foreign to her. Thanksgiving dinners. Eggnogs. The *Mary Tyler Moore Show.* Monopoly. Dr. Seuss.

JFK. Such loaded American symbols meant nothing to her. They brought back no dear memory, no pull of nostalgia. Damian hailed her as the ultimate virgin. He laughed when, at one Thanksgiving dinner, he saw Suzy's face brighten as she tried turkey covered in cranberry sauce for the first time. A blessing, he said, to be raised in such a cultural vacuum. But the blessing came with its price. Being bilingual, being multicultural should have brought two worlds into one heart, and yet for Suzy, it meant a persistent hollowness. It seems that she needed to love one culture to be able to love the other. Piling up cultural references led to no further identification. What Damian had called a "blessing" pushed her out of context, always. She was stuck in a vacuum where neither culture moved nor owned her. Deep inside, she felt no connection, which Damian seemed to have understood.

"Nabokov . . . If he hated America so much, does that mean that he loved Russia?" Suzy is fingering the pack of cigarettes in her coat pocket, but this is not a cigarette moment. That would be too close to home. A late-afternoon park in November. A cup of coffee. Jen sitting by her side.

"I don't believe he did. I don't believe he was capable of that kind of love or hate for a country. He was too selfish. You can see that in his writing. He picked each word as though his entire life was at stake. He was notorious for jotting down every thought on three-by-five index cards. His life was a string of exile, from England to Germany to France to America to Switzerland. It was right after renouncing Russian that he threw this verbal masturbation of a novel called *Lolita* at the American public. Here's this Russian guy who's only been living in the U.S. for a decade or so, tripping on English prose like Faulkner on acid! What's worse, just as the American readers can't get enough of him, he skips out to Switzerland. The reason? His obsession with butterflies. Of course he was strange, no doubt about it. But I think Harrison is wrong. Russia versus America would've been too simple for Nabokov. If he'd been tortured, which I believe he was, then it was about something less obvious. The Cold War might have contributed, but his oddness, that something which doesn't quite add up about him, goes way deeper. No, I'm not talking about the sexual perversity of his book, which is hardly relevant, but something else, the neatness, the systematic design of his life, like those index cards. Did you know that he lived exactly twenty years on each continent? Twenty years in Russia, twenty in Western Europe, twenty in America, before his final attempt in the neutral Switzerland, where he ended up dying in his seventeenth year? If he had lived, would he have moved again once he filled his twenty-year quota? Where would he have gone?"

Suzy is hardly listening anymore. *Too selfish for exile.* Was there a bigger reason behind her parents' constant moving? Or had they always been fleeing from one situation to another? Were they skipping out on unpaid rent? Why did they leave Korea?

Once, when Suzy was either seven or eight, she was awoken in the middle of the night. "Get dressed," Mom whispered, shoving the clothes and books into big black garbage bags. Both Suzy and Grace stumbled out of bed and threw on whatever they found, grabbing their favorite dolls before following Mom out. Dad was waiting outside in his dove-gray Oldsmobile. When they stole into the night, both Suzy and Grace fell asleep, only to wake up a few hours later at a roadside motel along Route 4, off the New Jersey Turnpike. The family stayed in a tiny linoleum-floored room for about a week before moving into the studio apartment in Jersey City. Her parents never talked about it afterward, but the silence of the night road stuck with Suzy. The hurried steps of Mom gathering things in their old apartment; the clammed-up face of Dad behind the wheel.

Before Suzy fell asleep in the back seat, she remembers, Mom turned around a few times to look through the rear window. Suzy wanted to look as well, but she felt too sleepy and afraid.

Strangely enough, the weeklong stay at the motel was not so bad. Neither Suzy nor Grace minded much. It didn't happen every day that they could skip school with their parents' permission. It was almost fun to be stranded in a strange room with all their belongings stuffed in bundles. It felt like playing house, to search through the bags for toothbrushes and a matching sock. They amused themselves with whatever they found curious in that motel room. There was an airbrushed painting of Jesus Christ hanging above one of the beds, which Suzy and Grace tried to copy onto a piece of paper. Neither could draw, and their finished sketch revealed a scary-looking, bearded old man. Suzy remembers the drawing vividly, because it belonged to one of the rare moments when Grace laughed with her, when they had no school, no house chores, no Korean-language lesson. Both Mom and Dad would set off each morning, presumably to look for housing and work, leaving them with a bag of food, mostly from the fast-food counters along the highway, a couple of burgers, a bag of potato chips, and a family-sized Coke. It was a treat. McDonald's every day, like eating out for each meal. Grace still ate things like that then. Only later, when she started high school, did she become obsessed with dieting.

Fat was not what concerned Grace, not the way it did other girls. She simply cut out things that she considered extra. No chili-pepper paste, because it contained sugar, which ruled out practically all Korean food except white rice and a few odd dishes. No oil of any kind, which Mom used generously in cooking. No soy sauce, because its black color looked artificial. It did not matter whether the dish contained meat or fish or vegetables as long as it was steamed, poached, or broiled, seasoned only with salt. Grace would blame it on an allergic reaction as she sat picking at a bowl of white rice and not much else. Dad called Grace crazy. Did she realize what he had to do to get that food on the table? Once, he tried to force-feed her a plate of fried dumplings. He sat before her and ordered her to eat. When Grace would not budge, he forced her mouth open and stuffed the dumplings in one by one. Mom sat at the end of the table and did not say a word; Suzy began to cry. Neither intervened, partly because they were afraid to disobey him, and partly because they were both secretly relieved. Grace's food problem had become increasingly noticeable. It seemed to harbor a certain brooding anger, which then manifested into an overwhelming tension around the dinner table. Her silent rebellion broke the code of whatever had held the family together. By rejecting the food they all shared, Grace was declaring herself separate, apart. It was impossible to ignore the weight, the terrible mood of discord that would be cast over the family each time Grace pushed the food away with her chopsticks. As they watched, Grace vomited every mushy bit of meat and dough onto the floor. Finally, Dad slapped her once and stormed out. After that, he never commented on Grace's eating habit. They all learned just to ignore it. That might have been the beginning of their silent dinners.

With each year, Grace became more and more withdrawn from the rest of the family. There was a certain anger Suzy sensed, but nothing palpable enough to put a finger on. The only thing she knew was that if Grace had had a choice she would not have wanted to be her sister, or, more clearly, her parents' daughter, and it was this realization that always came between the sisters. The coldness, or the unassailable distance between them, was in fact a clear desire for separation.

But why, even now, even years later, Suzy cannot say.

"Sorry, I got carried away. Maybe you're right. I could turn forty and still be obsessing over dead writers." Jen is getting up.

It is now past five o'clock. The fax from Harrison might be waiting for her. The day is far from over.

"Thanksgiving. I guess it's Thanksgiving soon." Suzy suddenly recalls the holiday with Damian. He did not believe in it,
she knew. He hated holidays. But he seemed to derive a certain
oblique pleasure from celebrating this particular American tradition with her, as though he were maneuvering a young woman
onto a sordid path. He claimed it an *éducation sentimentale* in
the American way. He would fuss over each stage of prepara-
tion. The ten-pound turkey that was too big for the two of
them, the bread stuffing baked with yellow raisins and mac-
adamia nuts, the cranberry sauce simmered for exactly half an
hour, the pumpkin pie he had preordered from Balducci's because he did not bake. He loved watching her eat. He himself
hardly touched the food. "Dreadful memories," he said. "You
cannot imagine the atrocity of the Midwestern Thanksgiving.
Everyone gorges on the feast, because there's nothing else to do.
No one has anything to say, because overeating does that to a
mind. Remember, it's the core of the American culture, the
barest of food, the big slab of what barely qualifies as a bird." No
one was more cynical about America than Damian, which must
have been why he became fascinated with Asian art. But did it
mean that he loved Asia? *He cannot love an Asian woman,* Professor Tamiko had warned her. Yet it took the death of her parents for Suzy to leave him.

"But you don't celebrate Thanksgiving . . ."

Jen is careful. In college, Suzy used to stay behind while
everyone went home for Thanksgiving. Jen would come back after a week, grumbling about having gained five pounds. But
things are different now. It is no longer a choice. There is no celebration, no family. Holidays always make people feel sorry for
Suzy. Even Jen, who should know better.

"No, of course not. I just remembered, that's all."

"Come to Connecticut. I'm going to Colorado first with Stephen, which makes Mom and Dad furious. But with his insane schedule at the hospital, this is probably the only time I'll get to meet all his family. So I promised Mom that I'll fly back early and spend at least three days at home. So come. We can lie around the house and eat leftovers and play Monopoly. They always ask about you."

Colorado with a boyfriend. Connecticut to see Mom and Dad. Suzy cannot help feeling a little envy. She has never had that. Not even when she had parents. Damian was not exactly a boyfriend, the same way Michael isn't. Damian would never have brought her to his childhood home. Suzy was what he chose in order to run from all that, as she did him. The two of them together could never have built a family. How could they, when neither believed in it? But why? Where did her parents go wrong?

"Thank you. I'll think about it."

They both know that Suzy won't come. But it is nice to dream about it anyway. Sitting around the parents' house eating leftovers. Doing nothing for three days except playing Monopoly with Mom and Dad. But in such a dream, the house is in Montauk, and everything appears the same—the pastel house, Mom's brand-new Jeep, Dad's fishing rods, the bag of Korean goodies Suzy has brought from the city—except for someone else, someone standing in the rain against the lighthouse, in so much November rain that for a second it looks as though the person is quietly weeping.

14.

THE 41ST PRECINCT is located on the better part of Gun Hill
Road. The sidewalk is freshly swept. No one honks as though
his mother's honor depends on it. No one fires a shot just for
the hell of it. Even the boom-box blasters stay clear. Any half-
brained crook knows better than to defile its sanctimonious
ground. This is where the mayor's fury takes out its revenge.
This is where his soldiers plot out their games. This is where the
NYPD rules.

Two officers are leaning against the patrol car smoking cigarettes when Suzy approaches the two-story concrete building. Across the trunk of the white car are the big blue letters of
allegiance: *Courtesy. Professionalism. Respect.* One of the officers
skims her over with a whistle, nudging the other with his elbow.
They both appear to be about Suzy's age, maybe even younger,
the local boys who grew up watching way too many episodes of
S.W.A.T., whose sweethearts must be waiting at home with a
couple of toddlers.

"May we help you?" asks Whistle Boy. He is the joker, the one who is not ashamed to ogle any passerby in a skirt.

"Not really." She is not up to this hide-and-seek right now. She is about to enter the station. Hardly any help necessary.

"C'mon. We can't let a lady walk in by herself!" Whistle Boy won't let go. He must be bored. This must be his off-time from ticketing double-parkers. Beneath the uniform and the badge, he is still a mere boy. The sweet dimples. The awkward crew cut. Suzy can't help smiling a little.

"See, I made you laugh. You must let us escort you inside. Let me tell you, it's a jungle in there! Ain't I right, Bill?" He turns to his partner, who laughs along. Bill is the shy one, even handsome. A black man with a clean-shaven head. A set of twinkling brown eyes.

"Sorry. No escorting for me. But maybe you can tell me where I might find Detective Lester in the Homicide Unit."

Then another set of whistles.

"Oh well, she's here to see the boss!" shouts Whistle Boy, turning to Bill, who finally straightens up from the car and says, "Please excuse him; not all of us are like this jerk over here. Follow me inside. I'll take you to Lester."

Suzy is glad that it is the quiet one who is leading her inside. Before following Bill through the door, she turns around once as Whistle Boy hollers after her: "See, I knew it. The bastard always gets the girls!"

Once inside, she is led upstairs, away from the commotion of the general area. Detective Lester is being held up with a real head-case, Bill tells her, motioning her to wait in one of the wooden chairs in front of the door marked "Private."

"A thirteen-year-old, just brought in for blowing some grandpa in the back of his Nissan for twenty bucks," he says, shaking his head. "It's the fifth time we've taken her off the street in the last six months. A kid hooker with her pimp daddy on crack. The city's filled with them, and the juvenile agencies are way too swamped and fucked up, and the kid ends up back out on street in a matter of days. Except this time somebody's popped her daddy." He brings her a can of Coke from the vending machine. Too cold, it is the last thing she wants, but she takes it anyway.

The corridor is curiously designed so that the end appears interminably long, although the distance couldn't be more than thirty yards. There are three rooms on each side of the corridor. Each room is marked "Private," which must mean that inside is where serious questionings take place. She can hear nothing. No noise escapes. It is eerily silent, as if the entire building were soundproof, and bulletproof.

Two bullets total. Not one wasted. Not one straying off its course. Not one missing its target.

"So you here for a case?" Bill is making small talk. He seems reluctant to leave her, or perhaps he is not allowed to leave anyone unattended. After all, this is the inner world of the police station. It is probably not safe for her to be here alone. Who knows, one of those being questioned inside could set himself free and burst out the door. Imagine, to be held as a hostage while waiting for the Bronx detective who's done nothing at all for the past five years.

"Yes, a case," answers Suzy, taking a fuzzy sip from the can.

"Which one? Maybe I know something about it." He is trying to be helpful. He is not being cocky, like most policemen she's met before. But she knows that he could not possibly know anything. Five years ago, he must have only just finished the Police Academy.

"I doubt it. It's an old case." Suzy smiles, not wanting to sound dismissive.

"Unsolved, then. Parents?" he asks placidly. It is the first time, she thinks, someone has mentioned her parents' death without the inevitable gulp of hesitation and stammer.

"Yes, both of them. How did you know?" She is surprised at the casualness with which she answers him.

"We get a hunch in our field. A smart-looking young woman like you showing up here in the middle of the day looking for Lester, it's gotta be serious. Besides, you being Asian helps. Model citizens, hard workers, all that stuff is pretty much true, except for some of those punks out in Queens. You've got no business coming in here unless it's family trouble. Parents most likely, since you don't look married to me."

His voice is soothing, she thinks. A young man of her age. No wedding ring. Polite, straightforward. She never talks to men like him. They remain out of her range, always. Something about them belongs in another world. Something about them suggests a home, a different kind of home from what she knows.

"I'm not trying to impress you, although maybe just a little. But the real clue is your face. I hope you don't mind me saying this . . ." Bill takes a gulp from his can of Coke and says, "You've got the face of a mourner."

Even that does not deter the sudden calm of the moment. Face of a mourner. He is probably right. The years must wear on her face, the five-plus immense years.

"Why, you feel sorry for me?" she asks with a tight smile. Desperation. This must be what desperation is, to beg a stranger for his heart.

"No, I don't. But it's okay to let people feel sorry for you." Then he adds quickly, "But don't get me wrong, I'm not pulling my friend Don Juan out there."

"I know." Suzy nods, to reassure him. She wants him to know that she understands.

"Listen, if you have any questions, or just wanna talk or

something, feel free to call me at the station. Ask for Officer Edwards. Bill Edwards. I'm usually here, unless out there hauling kid hookers off the street."

He grins bashfully. A nice guy. The sort of guy who probably won't make a good policeman. Too soft. Too sincere. She will never call him. It would not be fair to him.

"Hey, sorry to keep you waiting."

Detective Lester emerges from the room, wiping the sweat off his face. He motions Bill to go inside; Bill waves at Suzy with a big warm smile before following the order. And just like that, the momentary calm breaks. She is back here now, back in the Bronx police station where the record of her dead parents has been gathering dust among the forgotten files.

"C'mon. We should go into my office for a talk. You look good. Five years, hah! Long time. I swear, the only thing that flies is time. How're you doing, married yet? Any kids?"

He is one of those jovial older men who ask several questions at once, none of which is meant to be a real inquiry. He is stocky, not quite big, but solid. His balding head is supported by a remarkably rotund neck. His dark-brown bomber jacket squeaks each time he moves.

"Good to see you. What you been up to? Are you never home? We tried you several times last week." He removes a dusty leather armchair from the corner, filled with stacks of paper and a few gold medals and piles of photographs. Suzy just smiles in return. She knows that he is not expecting a response.

"I gather you don't know why you're here?" He finally sits down, facing her across the desk. He looks suddenly more alert. No more of the avuncular chatter. He means business now. That's the tricky thing with these guys who work for Uncle Sam.

You never know what they are thinking. You can never be sure which side they are on.

"I know coming here like this isn't exactly a ball game for you. Believe me, I haven't forgotten your parents' case. I know you haven't either." His voice is almost deadpan, as though the speech is already rehearsed, as though he has run these lines before with another sad girl, another heartbroken family member.

"But something funny turned up. Or not funny at all, in fact. About two weeks ago, I got a call from the AOCTF in Queens, that's Asian Organized Crime Task Force, the special unit of the FBI. Supposedly they got a tip about some sort of trafficking and raided a pool hall in Flushing. During the search, they found, hidden underneath a pool table, a bag filled with ice. Twenty kilos, probably the biggest stash of ice they've seen in Queens in years. You know what ice is?"

She shakes her head. A sort of drug, obviously. Cocaine. Heroin. Suzy's never been into that culture. She tried pot once in college and threw up violently. It didn't suit her system. A lucky break, which confirmed nicotine as her only vice.

"Crystal methamphetamine. You might be familiar with its other names. Rock candy. Shabu Shabu. Tina. Krissy. Same thing. Speed, the nineties version. Lethal. Harder than cocaine. Ice has always been the West Coast thing, definitely not the drug of choice around here, which means that those boys in the pool hall were up to something bigger than what we've seen recently, a much higher game than the usual gambling and racketeering. So, right away, the Narcotics Squad goes ape-shit. They round up the suckers and narrow down on three connected to Triad, the international Chinese gang. Except these are Korean. Three former members of Korean Killers, which disbanded in the early nineties. You following all this? You wondering why I'm telling you all this?"

He talks fast, too fast for her. Ice. Triad. None of it rings a bell, except for Korean Killers. They were notorious around Queens high schools, although nobody Suzy knew had ever met one.

"During one of the all-nighters, your father's name popped up." He stares straight into her face. "Got any idea why?"

She stares back, not clear whether he expects an answer. He does not budge. Nothing on his face. No help there. Finally, she breaks: "No."

"Neither do we." He rises suddenly from the chair, as if needing fresh air. "Mind if I smoke?" he says, lighting one of his Lucky Strikes. "What's funny, or I shouldn't say funny, okay, what's peculiar is that one of those KK boys brought up your parents' killing from five years ago. The one called Maddog, the ringleader. Maddog kept saying that they didn't do it. He swore that they had nothing to do with it. He claimed that when they arrived at the store your parents were already dead. He even went on to say that it was a setup, a conspiracy. Then he just clammed up. He realized that he'd slipped up. The squad had no idea about any of this, of course. They knew nothing about your parents' case. Their sole interest was the source of that bucket of ice they found. But now they've got possible murder suspects on their hands for an unsolved five-year-old crime. So I'm the man they turn to, and I go over there and sit up with those assholes for three straight nights, and nothing, none of them will say a goddamn thing, especially Maddog. These are hard boys. Triad. Korean Killers. Any idea what they do to the one who squeals? These boys have been trained to shut their mouths. They'd rather die than betray their honor. Honor, my ass, their monthly paycheck revolves around trafficking either drugs or counterfeits or women. Still, these Asian gangs mean business. They've done their homework. They're even more tightly organized than the Italian mobs. Nothing in the world can get a word out of them at this point, which is why I called you a few days ago." He sucks hard on his Lucky before stubbing it out, as though the monologue has brought him beyond a point of frustration.

"Because?" Suzy is at a loss. Asian gangs. Her parents shot at the store. Anything is possible.

"Because you might know something. Because you might remember if your father had owed the KK a few thousand dollars, or if he'd used their service for one thing or another, or if he had some secret drug habit, or if he'd gotten himself on their bad side for whatever . . ."

"Excuse me, Detective, but I know nothing like that."

Five years of silence, and now a gang connection. Except her father might not have been so innocent.

"Think, though. Was there any point at which you might've seen something or heard something? Did you ever see any strange set of people coming in and out of your house? Did your parents ever talk about a private loan from somewhere?" He is groping for a clue. No more Mr. Deadpan. Each question is a bit more heated. Each question resembles a threat.

"Nothing at all." She can barely contain the anger rising within her.

"Work with me, Suzy. We might've found the answer. These boys vehemently deny any involvement, which can only mean one thing, that they were involved somehow. It's got KK fingerprints all over it. The way they do away with their enemies. The exactness of the shooting. Did they do it? I don't know yet. But I sure am gonna find out. So you've gotta cooperate. Try to remember something, anything." He is turning into the nice uncle again. He is pleading with Suzy. He wants desperately to pin the murder on these boys. Why not? It's the only lead he's got.

"No, I can't help you. I remember nothing." Suzy is tempted just to get up and walk out, but she continues, "What I'm curious about is why you didn't see any of this five years ago. If the shooting method seems so familiar, why didn't you suspect them then? Why did you call it a random shooting and ignore it for five years?"

Turning his back on her, Detective Lester faces the window, a tiny slit between the metal filing shelves which Suzy has not even noticed until now. He stays silent for a while with his arms folded across his chest, and then, without turning around, he says, "I'm not surprised that you're upset. But we're not God here in the Police Department. We're not Sherlock Holmes. We might not always get to do the right thing. Several hundred murders in the borough every year, it's hard to go after each one."

The last bit gets to her. *Hard to go after each one.* So they haven't even tried. It's taken five years to look for a motive. This incompetent detective. This idiot of a man who called the execution random. And the murderer still somewhere loose, still so far from their grip. But nothing is fair. Nothing has been fair for so long. Five years. Why?

"I just don't understand why you're suddenly so interested in finding my parents' murderer. The Asian Organized Crime Task Force. The Narcotics Squad. All of that means nothing to me. Are the stakes bigger now? Now that gangs and drugs spice up what happened five years ago; now that all the higher branches of your police force are having a field day with whoever might've murdered my parents; now that my parents might be more than just a middle-aged Asian couple shot dead in their store? Tell me, Detective, do you get a medal if you score this one? A promotion?"

He must be used to such outbursts. He may even expect them. When he finally turns around and faces her, the furrows between his eyebrows look deeper. He does not like doing this either, she can tell. It is a hard job, to pick up after the most hideous of all crimes. "We didn't ditch them cold, Suzy."

A sudden fatigue washes over her. Nothing more will come out of her. Everything seems to be crashing down at once. Damian, she misses him infinitely. Damian, what happened to Damian? Wasn't he supposed to take her away from all of this? Wasn't that why she lay in his matrimonial bed at twenty, letting the blood trickle down her legs? Wasn't that why she went with him despite everything, despite her youth, despite her then-living parents, despite her Ivy League college, despite all good common sense that had told her to stay still, stay where she was, stay in her rightful spot as the good Korean daughter? Wasn't that what she had wanted after all? To run away from all of this?

"Listen, Suzy, we've gotta work together on this one. Your father, whether you wanna face it or not, must've had some gang connection. It might not even have been a bad one. Many immigrant store-owners pay dues, for protection or whatever. Your father might've just been one of many victims. He might've owed them some money. Maybe business was slow, and he took a loan and couldn't pay. Something as little as that. But we need evidence. We need some concrete motive. You've gotta think, and think hard. You've gotta try to remember everyone your parents knew or had dealings with. Someone somewhere must know something. I've already sent some men over to the Hunts Point Market and the Korean Grocers Association. Something's gotta give. It'll just be faster if you can recall some names, so we can finally resolve your parents' deaths."

He is making sense, of course. He is even convincing. But Suzy is not sure. She still cannot buy into such sudden enthusiasm. Five years is a long time to do nothing. Any evidence must have long been erased.

"I thought you said that Korean Killers disbanded in the early nineties. My parents were shot in 1995. What dues would they have owed? To Triad? I thought they were Chinese. Do they collect dues from Korean stores too?"

He is glad that Suzy seems to be coming around. The shadow of guilt that had clouded his face is gone. He looks almost grateful when he tells her, "No. New York Triad mostly operates within Chinatown. But these ex-KK guys seem to have been sort of working under them for years, at the bottom of the rung since the breakup of their own group. Who knows, there might've been old debts, old scores to settle."

"What about their claim that it was a setup? Isn't it odd that they would bring it up only to deny it? I mean, if they're guilty, why mention it at all, when they weren't even being accused?"

"That's why it was a slip. One of them thought that we'd already linked them to the murder, when in fact we had not a clue. He thought that was why he was taken in for questioning."

"So you're convinced that it was them?"

"I didn't say that. But I'll tell you this, I certainly wouldn't give much weight to their denial."

"And you've known nothing at all about these three guys until now, until they got raided in the pool hall with enough drugs to spread alarm through the entire New York Narcotics Squad?"

"It's like this." He begins pacing around the desk, as if shuffling the bits of information in his head. "KK disbanded nearly a decade ago. We know much more about the other groups, like Korean Power and Green Dragons, who're both still active in the Flushing area. Korean gangs operate differently from either Chinese or Japanese gangs. They tend to keep a lower profile. They often have links to the bigger international groups, like Triad or Yakuza. They might occasionally do some dirty work for the big guys, but mostly they keep to their own. They raid their own Korean communities, who are infamous for never using banks, just hoarding cash in their homes. Easier for them, since Koreans rarely report gang crimes. The AOCTF calls it a 'collective shame.' A sort of responsibility, immigrant guilt for not having properly reared their second generation. You might understand that one better than I can. So, according to the AOCTF, it's always harder to keep track of the Korean gang movements. They don't know much about these ex-KK ones except that all three have done time for fraud, extortion, money laundering, the usual stuff. No murder, though; they've never been charged with murder. One interesting thing is that they used to call themselves the Fearsome Four. They obviously fancied themselves as a bit of legend in their own little-league way. They once each cut off their little fingers to honor their brotherhood, copying that crazy Yakuza ritual. But it seems that's as far as their legend ever got. Other than doing a little time here and there, we've heard nothing about them until two weeks ago."

"What happened to the fourth one?"

"Which fourth?"

"The Fearsome Four. If only three have been arrested, what happened to the fourth one?"

"Oh, he faded out of the picture long ago."

"How?"

"Deported. Gone without a trace. He seemed to have split from his brothers soon after the KK breakup; anyway, it's all hazy, who knows, maybe it was Maddog or one of his many 'brothers' who dropped a dime on him. But somebody reported him, and the INS tracked him down at a motel on Junction Boulevard and packed him home. Turns out the guy never even had a green card. One of those orphans who'd been shipped into the country, probably through the KK's adoption fraud of the early seventies."

"Which was?"

"The typical trick. They'd charge between ten and twenty grand for each Korean orphan adopted by an American couple, and then, once the deal goes through, pocket the money and sneak the kid away."

"Why the kid too?"

"Human resource. Child labor. They usually traded boys over the age of four. I guess the younger ones proved useless. You can't really stick two-year-olds into sweatshops, can you?"

"But why would the orphans be left without a green card? What about the visa that had been issued to them to begin with?"

"*Please*—there never was an orphan, don't you see? The orphans weren't real. Those were just some random kids kidnapped off the streets of Seoul or wherever they were taken from. Whatever papers they had with them were all fake anyway. The visa was only useful to smuggle the kids into America. After that, these kids filtered through the system as nonentities. They truly became the orphans of the world, no name, no nothing, which was exactly what the gang wanted. To pin these kids with nowhere to go. These were the very ones recruited as the next generation of KK. The true brothers. The little boys with no ties in the world except for their gang brothers. Desperation. That's what pulled them together, which is why it's so hard to get any of them to speak."

"When did you say that he was deported?"

"November '95. Roughly five years ago. He was in his twenties. I guess he should be about your age now. Why? You think you've heard of him or something?"

"No, all of this is news to me. What was his name anyway?"

"They all called him DJ. No last name. None of them ever have real names."

An orphan kid smuggled into the country.

No one except for his gang brothers.

She must be getting tired. The day may have dragged on too long.

"Two possibilities, assuming we've got the right boys." Detective Lester suddenly stops pacing. "Either the gang acted on

their own, or they were hired by someone. But gangs don't kill
for debts. They might threaten or hurt the victims, but they
wouldn't just get rid of them. What would be the point? Where
would they get the money? So let's assume that they were following someone's order. Then we've gotta start looking around
at the people your parents knew. Employees. Other store owners. People with enough reason to want them dead. Can you
think of anyone with a grudge against your parents? My men
doing rounds among the Korean markets might find something.
But Koreans don't tend to trust policemen. They don't wanna
tell us anything, which unfortunately doesn't help your parents'
case."

Kim Yong Su. And the other witness at the deposition, Mr.
Lee. Even Mr. Lim, who'd had a falling-out with her father, who
resembles the strange man in Montauk. In fact, the entire Korean community might be filled with people who had hated her
parents. Yet no one will talk. No one will cooperate with the investigation. No one wants the murderer to get caught.

"No, I don't know anyone with a reason to kill my parents."
She may be like the rest of them. She won't confide in police.
She may even be shielding the killer.

"Well, if you remember anything, call me." Detective Lester
extends his hand with a smile. If he suspects her of withholding
anything, he does not show it. Instead, he asks, "So where's your
sister?"

"She's . . . away."

"Vacation?"

"Something like that."

"Funny, she didn't mention it on the phone."

"You spoke to her?"

"Just last week. I told her it was perfect timing."

"*She* called you?"

"Sure, she was just checking in, she's done that before," he muses, as if to say, What about you? "She wasn't much help either. I was hoping to see both of you here today."

So Grace knew about it already. Grace was told.

"When did she call last week?"

"Gee, I don't know. Friday maybe?"

Grace showed up in Montauk the same day. Bob the bartender seemed to think that she then returned to the city. On Sunday, she called Ms. Goldman to say that she was not coming in.

"Well, tell her to stop by when she gets back. She's older, right? Maybe she'll remember more." He shows her to the door. It is not much of a door. A narrow crack, just like the window. The whole building is tightly woven. No sound, no bullet, no room for escape. Before shutting the door, he says, almost in passing, "You look different from how I remembered. I don't know what it is. I can't quite put my finger on it." Then, gazing at her once more, he adds, "Don't worry. It'll come to me."

15.

"INS, MAY I HELP YOU?"

The 800 number was the only viable option. Since eight o'clock this morning, Suzy has kept dialing the local branch, whose computerized operator put her on hold for what seemed like the entire morning only to route the call to the toll-free number. New York City must be one of its busiest chapters. They probably have their hands full, having to answer all the immigrants, whose panicked questions in broken English must get tiresome pretty quickly.

"I'm trying to find out about my status, and that of my parents, who are . . . both deceased."

"Are you a U.S. citizen?"

"I think so."

"Were you born in this country?"

"No, but I'm sure I am a citizen."

"What's your file number?"

"I don't know. But my name is Suzy Park, and my Social Security number is . . ."

"Miss, I didn't ask for your Social Security number. Do you have a filing receipt or a certification paper?"

"No."

"Did you file for citizenship yourself?"

"No, I believe my parents did."

"Were they citizens?"

"I think so."

"Miss, I can only help you if you are certain of the situation."

"I'm almost sure that we are all citizens, I mean, that they were also, until they passed away."

"Miss, I can only help you if you are certain of the situation."

What did she expect? It is the INS, after all. The iron gate of America, and the gatekeeper is on the other end, not sure if he wants to let her in.

"Look, if I were certain, I wouldn't be calling you in the first place. My parents are both dead. They can't tell me a thing. They never showed me any certification papers. I just want to know when they might have filed for citizenship and under which circumstances. You tell me, am I a U.S. citizen or not?"

Then the silence at the other end. For a second, Suzy is afraid that he may have hung up. She is half expecting the usual "Let me call the supervisor" move. Instead, the man comes right back on. Obviously, in his line of work, her level of outrage must be almost expected.

"Miss, there's nothing I can do for you. It sounds to me like you need to apply for G639 papers. Freedom of Information Act. Please hold, while I transfer you."

With that, she is put on hold again. Several minutes later, when she is put through, it is to a machine telling her to leave an address to which the G639 application can be sent out. The application will take two to three weeks in the mail.

The INS, not the most open organization, not exactly known for efficiency. It was naïve to think that she could just call and find out anything. Not surprising that no one is jumping to her aid. Looking up a citizenship-status file cannot be as urgent as deporting an illegal immigrant. A few weeks to get her hands on a bunch of papers called G639, a few weeks for them to process, and then who knows when they would get back to her with a response? Freedom of Information Act. Freedom, sure, in the most roundabout way. There must be an easier way.

Her first instinct is to call Detective Lester. He should be able to pull up the record in a second. Aren't they all in league with one another? Would the INS refuse him speedy access when the information might be pertinent to a criminal investigation? *If you remember anything, call me.* He sounded almost chirpy. The police. It is impossible to guess what they know or how much they pretend. Where has he been for the last five years? Why did he declare her parents' deaths random? Why has he ignored the case all this time, until now? Korean Killers. Fearsome Four. On second thought, maybe she shouldn't ask him for help. Why bring him into something that might only be personal?

Grace. Only Grace would know. Grace, the sole evidence of her family.

Without Grace, there remains no trace of her parents. The Woodside brownstone. What did Grace do with all their parents' things? Whenever Suzy pictures Grace sorting through them, she imagines her amidst a pile of blankets in rainbow colors. They each owned thick winter blankets, which Mom called "mink blankets." Fake silky furs with complicated flower designs in pink and orange. They were very warm, but Suzy found them too heavy and flashy. Both Suzy and Grace left the blankets behind when they went off to college. That was one thing Mom objected to. Although nothing aroused her reaction much, she seemed hurt when her daughters would not take what she considered to be the family heirlooms. Suzy felt bad when Grace cut her short with, "Please, Mom, it's not mink and it's not an heirloom."

A few months after the funeral, Grace contacted Suzy once through the accountant. It should have been handled by a lawyer, but Korean accountants often extended themselves over all matters, from inheritance rights to tax returns. There was money, he told Suzy over the phone one morning. Not a whole lot, but a good enough sum to see her through for a few years. Suzy refused her share. They had disowned her up until their death. It seemed unthinkable to take their money. "Sleep on it for a while," the accountant dismissed her refusal. "Heirs often react this way. Inheritance evokes guilt. You think you're compromising your parents' death. Especially when their death isn't natural. But believe me, you'll change your mind in a few months." The accountant was adamant. When Suzy said no for the third time, he barked, "That won't bring them back, you know."

What is his name? She had not thought to write it down. During those few months after the funeral, nothing quite stuck with her. It is still a wonder how she managed from day to day. Getting up each morning. Finding a place to live. Finding something to do. Finding ground to stand on. You'll regret it, the accountant warned. But he was wrong. She could not have taken her parents' money. It did not belong to her, although it might not have belonged to them either.

You're so fucking stupid, Suzy, you wouldn't care what kind of money it is as long as it puts food before you.

It wouldn't be a bad idea to look up the accountant. The guy might know something. He had done paperwork for her parents for a few years. Not for long, he insisted. He made a point of emphasizing "few years," which, for an accountant-client relationship, was not a long period. Later, it occurred to her that he might not have wanted to be associated with her parents' death. At their only meeting, she found him abrasive. But no one seemed to be on her side then. Everyone appeared unsympathetic, unfeeling, including Suzy herself, who remained living while her parents were shot down in a remote corner of the Bronx.

Suzy is about to grab the Yellow Pages when it dawns on her that most Korean accountants would not be advertised in it. What would be the point? No American clients come to them anyway. She would do better with the Korean Business Directory or Korean newspapers, neither of which she has in her apartment. His office had been located in Koreatown, above a restaurant that specialized in bone-marrow soup, 32nd Street in midtown Manhattan. A part of the city she rarely visits. The pervading smell of *kimchi* along the street. The posters on windows displaying jubilant Korean movie stars. Bright neon signs in Korean letters. Too close to home, although her home had never been that festive. Suzy had been to his office once to sign papers. It was a simple procedure. It took five minutes, and all her claims to her parents were over. Afterward, she sat before a bowl of oxtail soup and wept.

She is zipping up her knee-high boots when the phone rings. Ten-thirty on Friday morning. Who else but Michael? His daily phone call. His daily declaration of love, or need. It is good to have a routine. The only problem is that, by the time you get used to it, something inevitably happens to break it. She picks up the phone on its third ring. He should be impressed. He knows she is bending rules for him.

"Michael, I'm on my way out, can you call me later?"

No response. His phone must be acting up again. He must

be out of Germany now. The connection is never a problem from there.

"Michael? Your cell's not connecting. I can't hear you."

He must be calling from Southern Europe. Portugal, maybe Spain, if he is lucky. Michael chuckled when Microsoft announced the downsizing of their Madrid office. "Those hot-blooded Spanish will rock you with their fiestas and siestas. But are they Web-ready? Do they care? They'll be the last civilization to hook up. Why should they, when they actually prefer their world to the virtual one?"

"Michael, it's useless. I'm hanging up."

Then she hears it. The perfect silence. No static. No distance on the connection. This call could be coming from down the block. It is not Michael. It is not Michael on the other end.

"Who is this?" Dropping her bag, she throws a quick glance at the dead irises dried up in the Evian bottle.

"Damian?" Part of her is hoping. Of course it cannot be Damian. He would not be calling her. Not like this anyway.

"I'm going to hang up if you don't speak."

She is about to take the receiver off her ear when the voice stops her. A male voice. Shaky and unnaturally low, with a distinct Korean accent.

"Don't." It is not clear if he just has a feeble voice or is talking in a whisper.

"Who is this? Who are you?" She speaks slowly, strangely calm, as though she has been expecting him.

"I call to tell you . . . No more. Stop. No more talk with people. No police." His English is just barely comprehensible. But he won't speak in Korean. Maybe he is afraid that she will recognize his voice if he speaks with fluency. Maybe he is calling from somewhere not private. She tries anyway and asks in Korean, "Stop what? What're you talking about?"

"Your parents dead. No more. Stop now." He insists on his

broken English. Barely a whisper. She won't recognize his voice even if she hears it again.

"What do you mean? Who are you?"

"No. Nothing. They do not kill your parents. So stop."

He is about to hang up. She can sense it. She cannot let him get away. He is the only clue she's got.

"Wait! Who's they? What did they have to do with my parents' death?"

"Your parents dead. Nothing change. They watch you."

He is gone. She can tell even before she hears the click.

Stop poking around, unless she wants to get hurt.

Is it a warning, or a threat?

Who is watching her?

Who are *they*?

Who is he?

She is slumped on the kitchen floor staring at the phone when it rings again. She snatches the receiver almost instantly. Has he changed his mind? Is there something he forgot to say?

"Wow, what's with you?"

It is Michael. The real Michael this time.

"Babe, what's going on? You been waiting for my call or something? Suzy, are you there? *Suzy, hello?*"

Her heart is beating too fast. She shuts her eyes and counts to three.

"Suzy, what's the matter? You sick or something?" He is not used to a sick mistress. He sounds uncertain suddenly.

"Hi, I . . . I'm just a bit out of sorts."

"Shit, I thought I'd have to jet over, scoop you in my arms, and lick your wounds!"

"Michael, I'm a bit scared." She cannot help it. Sometimes the truth is easier with someone for whom it won't matter much.

"*Christ*, Suzy, what's going on with you?" He sounds more

alert now. He is not used to vulnerable Suzy. He is not sure how to respond.

"Nothing at all. I think it's my period." She quickly changes her mind. It is not fair to dump it on Michael. It is too late for them to be anything but what they are. It is really not his fault.

"*Christ*, sometimes you fucking surprise me." He breaks into nervous laughter. He is relieved.

"I think I better go lie down."

"You do that. But I'm gonna call and check up on you."

"Don't. I'm gonna sleep for a while." She does not want any more calls this morning.

"You need anything? Should I get Sandy to send you a doctor or something?"

Suzy laughs at his suggestion. How absurd, a doctor making a house call to her East Village flat? Michael. He will try anything. He will make anything happen. *Anything*. Of course, why hasn't she thought of it before?

"There is something, actually."

"Just name it." Michael is trying to hide his surprise. Suzy has never asked for anything. She has never had a request for him.

"I need to find out about my citizenship status. And that of my parents. I need to know on what grounds those citizenships were issued, if they were issued. I need them fairly soon."

"Done. Sandy will call you in five minutes and take down the info. I'll tell her to send you a doctor also. What else?" He is a good businessman. Gets the job done. No questions asked.

"Nothing else."

"Sure?"

Suzy is suddenly so grateful that she wants to cry. She must have been alone for too long. She is not used to getting help.

"Michael?"

"What?"

"Thank you."

"Shut up and go get some sleep. And for God's sake, don't act so fucking polite."

From her seat at the window, she can see the bustle on 32nd Street. The same bone-marrow-soup restaurant, just downstairs from the accountant's office. Several tables are occupied already although it is barely noon, not quite lunchtime. Whereas Americans crave eggs and bacon on bleary mornings, Koreans go straight for a steaming bowl of bone soup topped with freshly chopped scallions. They swear that it magically heals the unsettled stomach, the best cure in the world for hangovers. Koreans are known as the Italians of the East. They drink hard and eat to their heart's content. Indeed, the faces bending over the clay bowls appear quite pale, as though they have not yet recovered from the night's triple rounds of *soju* and karaoke. Some of them sneak glances at Suzy sitting alone, hiding behind the *Korea Daily*, which she bought from the dispenser upon entering the restaurant. The sudden flash of Korean letters confuses her for a second. She glares at the print without making sense of it. She stares instead at the row of restaurants across the street. The second-floor windows are plastered with neon signs for hair salons, acupuncturists, even a twenty-four-hour steam bath. The third and fourth floors continue up the same way, cluttered with shops that only Koreans frequent. It is a way of cramming the immigrant life into one tiny block. One could stroll back and forth along this quarter-mile stretch and find anything, from bridal gowns to Xerox toners. Nothing is missing. No craving is hard to fill. It's all here, right on 32nd Street.

The accountant was useless. Mr. Bae was his name. A smallish man with a shocking amount of grease in his neatly parted hair. He barely looked up when Suzy entered. Although she introduced herself three times, he continued to ignore her. Even his assistant seemed embarrassed by such an outrageously rude reception. When Suzy started to ask him about her parents' file, he cut her off in the middle, "First, your sister specifically asked me not to engage in any talks with you. Second, your sister has terminated her business with me as of last week, so I'm no longer working on her case, which naturally includes your parents' file. Third, I told you once that you'll regret giving up your inheritance rights, but, just like your sister, you thought my advice wasn't worth a dime. Fourth, as you can see, I'm a busy man, with more than enough work to do for my clients, so I'd appreciate it if you'd stop wasting my time." Then he turned back to the stack of files on his desk, leaving Suzy standing there tongue-tied. His hostility seemed unreasonable and clearly immutable. So Suzy walked out, feeling wounded, as though she had just been scolded by someone dear, and it wasn't until she reached downstairs that she remembered bone-marrow soup and felt suddenly hopeful.

Once she sat down, the smell of brewing bones from the kitchen tugged at her. A taste from her childhood, although her mother rarely made such a variety: *sulongtang, komtang, kori-komtang, doganitang.* From tail bones to knee bones and cartilage to tripe, the choice depends on taste. A true connoisseur would swear by the subtlety of each, but for Suzy they all taste somewhat similar. Just a tinge of Korean flavors inevitably brings her back to Memory Lane. A pinch of garlic, scallion, ginger would sure enough do the trick, although her house had never been filled with such culinary extravaganza. The family usually made do with white rice and a couple of side dishes, maybe a stew or two, either of tofu or miso. Always *kimchi* on one side of the table, and on the other, fried anchovies and salted pollack eggs. They were almost always store-bought.

Mom barely had time for sleep, never mind brewing oxtail bones or marinating *kimchi.*

After Suzy moved out of her parents' house, she often stopped by this neighborhood, whenever she craved Korean food. She would sit alone with a book or a newspaper and order a bowl of *sulongtang.* People would stare at her, because Korean girls rarely ate alone. Back then, there was no way one could get ahold of *kimchi* on 116th Street. Sure, Columbia was filled with students from around the world. Along Broadway, there were a number of Chinese takeouts, as well as a few sushi bars. And if you really wanted to splurge, it wasn't hard to find all kinds of exotic food, from the candlelit Tibetan parlor on Riverside to the hole-in-the-wall Ethiopian takeout near the Law School building. Yet for Korean food you still had to travel down to 32nd Street. It was still the end of the eighties. The *kimchi* trend had not yet begun among students. It soon stopped mattering, though, because things changed almost overnight. First, when Damian happened in her life, she stopped craving anything except him. She would go wherever he suggested. She would skip food all day if that was what he wanted. Besides, they would not have dared entering 32nd Street together, for fear of bumping into anyone they knew. Then, later, with her parents' death, everything lost its color. On certain rainy days, she would wander into this corner of the city, wanting so much, wanting anything on the menu. She would experience such an immense hunger that she wouldn't know which dish to choose. It was as if she was looking to fill a certain longing, a certain desperation. Yet, by the time the food arrived, she no longer had any appetite. In fact, she could not bear the sudden rush of Korean flavors. It was impossible. It hit too close to home. It fell upon her like a sad awakening. Soon she just stopped coming.

But the soup tastes so good today, tangy, with lots of juice. It is a perfect soup for the cool weather, milky white and hot. The lumpy bits must be cartilage, rolling so smoothly on her tongue. She may still be the same girl after all, the one who would skip classes and hop on a subway all the way from 116th Street just for a bowl of soup and a plate of *kimchi*. She is so comforted by this thought that she almost forgets about the mean accountant, and the hushed tone of the caller who seemed afraid for her life. She is about to ask for another plate of *kimchi* when she notices the ad at the bottom of the *Korea Daily*'s front page. "The New Joy Fellowship Church," it reads. "Join us for the Thanksgiving Sermon at our God's House, the largest Korean church in New Jersey! Parking spaces available. Live Broadcasting on www.newjoyfellowship.org."

All Korean churches advertise. The competition is fierce. Sometimes a newspaper is sponsored by a specific church, like an allegiance to a political party. The prime missionary spots are restaurants and airports. At entrances to Korean restaurants, there are often boxes of sermon tapes provided by different churches. At the JFK's KAL lounge, it is not unusual to find Korean missionaries approaching those freshly arriving, like the zealous hostel-owners at tourist islands when the ship comes in. So the ad is nothing new, except that Suzy knows the church. Grace's church, where her parents' funeral was held. Suzy does not remember its being the largest Korean church in New Jersey. Surely it has grown in the last five years. Grace must have worked hard. All those Bible studies. All that hard-earned cash. A safety-deposit for heaven. Maybe someone there will know of Grace's whereabouts. Maybe Grace will even show up, if she has not gone too far away.

It is then that Suzy becomes aware of the face at the window, a young woman peering in as if trying to get a better look at her. She is more like a girl, in fact, twenty at most. A down coat with fur trim and a matching scarf. It is odd that so many Korean girls seem to dress the same. A crushed-velvet ponytail holder, the sure sign of an office girl. Finally, she breaks into an awkward smile and mumbles something. Then she seems to realize the absurdity of speaking through the window and moves toward the entrance.

"Hey, sorry about that," the young woman says, pointing upstairs with her eyes. "He's been like that for days."

Quickly swallowing her mouthful, Suzy stares back, realizing that the girl is Mr. Bae's assistant. Suzy feels compelled to say something, but she is embarrassed at how long it took for her to recognize the young woman.

"Good choice. *Sulongtang*. No other restaurant on this block throws in as much cartilage, and they even marinate their *kimchi* with fresh oysters. For *doganitang*, though, try the place across the street. Ask for ginseng between the knee bones. Costs more, but you won't get cold all winter."

The Asian youth these days are so confident, so full of life. She must be only about ten years younger than Suzy, yet there seems to be a gulf of generations separating the two. Suzy wonders if this girl considers herself 1.5 as well. Suzy has noticed fresh radiance among the NYU kids around her block. The Asian-American hip-hop kids. The petite girls in platform sneakers parading their dreadlocked boyfriends. The goateed boys in bandannas scooting around Tompkins Square Park. Being Asian is no longer embarrassing. Being Asian no longer suggests a high-school chess team. Being Asian might even be hip, trendy, cool.

"What if your boss sees you talking to me?" asks Suzy, cautiously.

"He's in a client meeting. Fuck him. He can't fire me anyway." The young woman plops down opposite her. She then waves at the waitress, raising her index finger to gesture one order of *sulongtang* for herself.

Something about her insolence reminds Suzy of Grace. Young Grace. Suzy feels a sudden rush of affection for the girl.

"Besides, I sort of followed you . . ." Then she blurts out, "By the way, what's up with those glasses?"

Earlier, leaving the apartment in a hurry after the strange phone call, Suzy threw on a pair of black sunglasses and some dark-red lipstick. A clumsy attempt to hide her face. She rarely wears lipstick, especially red. It came out of the last package Michael had sent her. Every possible Chanel beauty product wrapped in the newest Prada. Sandy's choice obviously, although for a second Suzy wondered if the gift might not have been intended for his wife instead. There was a matching nail polish, which she gave away to one of the stenographers on a job. It was silly to think that she would feel less conspicuous behind the shield of glasses and lipstick, but she did feel better as she tumbled onto the N train with the acute sense of someone following her. Apparently, she's kept the glasses on the whole time. No wonder people seemed to be staring at her. A woman alone sitting by the window, slurping soup while wearing dark glasses indoors.

"A hangover?"

Suzy nods, uncertain what to say.

"I can run to the pharmacy next door and get you a bottle of Bacchus. Or maybe they can fix up something even stronger. One shot of it, you'll feel as good as new," says the younger woman, who is now staring at Suzy with concerned eyes despite her tough-girl talk.

Suzy declines, finally taking the glasses off. Bacchus. It's been years since she's heard that name. A sort of miracle cure, like those tiger balms in Chinatown. Except Bacchus is a tiny-bottled drink, used mostly for hangovers or indigestion or anything to do with stomach troubles. Mom used to send Suzy to pick up a box of a dozen on mornings when Dad lay sick from *soju* the night before. Strange, the way Korean pharmacies just give out whatever they consider a cure. Prescriptions are never really an issue there. If you get sick, you just describe your symptoms to the pharmacist, who fixes up a concoction with whatever he has available behind the counter. It is a leftover habit from a Third World country, where prescription drugs were not carefully monitored. Although Korea has long since risen above its Third World status, the people never seem to have gotten over their easy access to antibiotics such as mycin, which, as Suzy recalls, Mom used for everything, from a common cold to a sore. The whole thing sounds dubious, even terrifying, but for Suzy it brings back yet another bit of her childhood. Illogical, yet sadly familiar.

"Hey, now that the glasses are gone, you look less like your sister." Leaning close, the young woman squints her eyes theatrically. "That's funny; if you really look, you don't look like her at all."

The spell of the good soup is over. Suzy asks instead, "So why did you follow me?"

"He was so nasty to you. I felt bad."

"To tell me that?"

"Also, I thought maybe you'd want to know that your sister's in some sort of trouble."

Suzy puts down her spoon.

"She called last week to liquidate her assets. Stocks, real estate, everything. Bae's furious, 'cause he's been playing the market and she pulled out all of a sudden. I don't understand why it's such a letdown, after she did away with all that cash just a month ago. I saw it coming. Between you and me, I smell drugs." The young woman lowers her voice, as if suddenly aware of the people at other tables.

Stocks. Real estate. Was there more money than Suzy knew about? Whose money is this? Her parents'? Has Grace been in-

vesting her inheritance? Suzy is not sure what to say, but the
young woman makes it easy by talking constantly. She may be
one of those people who talk in order to fill the silence.

"She was supposed to come by Monday to sign the papers,
but she totally flaked out. Then I find out her phone's been dis-
connected," she says, shaking her head. "I don't think liquida-
tion's a good idea right now."

Is Grace in some kind of debt? Is that why she has vanished?
Selling off everything for cash is what people do when they are
planning a drastic move—not a wedding. Last Friday, Grace
called Detective Lester out of the blue. Later the same day,
Grace showed up in Montauk looking for a boat. Then, on Sunday night, she called Ms. Goldman to say that she was getting
married. On Monday, she failed to turn up at the accountant's.
If Grace had planned to take the money and run off somewhere
with her new husband, why did she not follow it through with
the accountant? Was the wedding a sudden decision? What is it
that Ms. Goldman said? *A secret from everyone, more like eloping,
because they wanted to do it quietly, especially with her parents
gone.*

"How much?" Suzy asks, reaching for the glass of water on
the table.

"How much what?"

"How much a month ago?"

"A hundred grand. In one shot."

Something must have happened to Grace a month ago.
Something changed. The guy. But he didn't sound as if he were
in need of money.

"She won't sell the house, though. That, she won't touch."

"Which house?"

"Your parents' house, of course."

"Grace never sold it?"

"She won't even charge rent. Maria Sutpen lucked out. I need a friend like your sister!"

Maria Sutpen. Suzy has never heard of that name before, but, then again, she knows virtually nothing about Grace's life.

"Maria's totally useless for an emergency contact. I called like a hundred times this week, but she's never in. I got so frustrated that I almost went there myself. After all, the house is not too far from mine."

"You live in Woodside too?"

"No, in Jackson Heights. But it's just a couple of stops on the Number 7."

Jackson Heights. Woodside. The Queens neighborhoods where the Korean population makes up nearly 50 percent, where a woman named Maria Sutpen has taken over her parents' house.

"How long have you lived in Jackson Heights?"

"Since I was seven; why?" the young woman asks, glancing at the waitress who is heading over with a tray.

"No, nothing, it's just I've lived there too . . ." Suzy mumbles, studying the lipstick smudge on the rim of her glass. She lets a few minutes pass before asking, "So why are you telling me all this?"

" 'Cause I'm an only child, I guess." The young woman shrugs. "I don't get it when sisters don't talk to each other. I think that's like way twisted."

"So you thought to run down here and warn me about Grace's financial problems? So that I might track her down and convince her to keep Mr. Bae managing her money?" Suzy says quietly, meeting the other's eyes.

"No!" the young woman exclaims, her face turning bright pink.

"It's okay, nothing wrong with trying to help your father, or uncle, or whoever he might be for you. He seemed like he could use it," Suzy says with a smile. "Honestly, though, I have no idea where she is. And you're right, it's really twisted that she won't talk to me."

The younger woman looks sullen, pretending to be having difficulty splitting apart her wooden chopsticks.

"Listen, if you don't hear from her by Thanksgiving, call me," says Suzy, writing down her phone number on the girl's napkin.

Give it a few days, she thinks. If Grace turns up to sign the papers, then all must be fine. If she doesn't, Suzy will be notified. That is, unless Suzy finds Grace first. Then, rising from her seat, Suzy asks, "And one more thing, what's the name of that famous pool hall in Jackson Heights? Used to be a big deal in the eighties. Is it still around?"

The young woman looks up, befuddled. "You mean East Billiards on Roosevelt Avenue? Sure, they reopened a couple of years ago. Why? You play pool?"

16.

THERE IS NOTHING REMARKABLE about the brownstone at number 9. A two-story family home. The hexagonal living room protrudes with a fake-Victorian charm. Bright-pink lace hangs across each bay window. The only notable feature is the stoop. Seven steps in total, with newly painted railings. Shiny black layered with white stripes, like a zebra or a snake. It's not a house but a zoo. A miniature animal-farm, right here in the heart of Queens.

It's been half an hour. Late Friday afternoon. No one's home. The adults are at work; the children have gone out to play. This must be the high time for robbery. Where are those Asian gangs? They raid their own people, Detective Lester said. But no gang in sight, hardly anyone on the block. It is not such a terrible neighborhood. Not a bad corner on which to spend your final night.

The sky is turning charcoal gray now. The threat of an imminent shower. She has no umbrella, and it is really not appropriate to get soaked on a stranger's stoop. Her wait is numbered. It is good to have a limit. Otherwise, she might never walk away.

Across the street is a row of identical brownstones. She wonders if her parents knew any of the people there. Neighbors who saw them, who sat across the street while they ate, slept, worked. She wonders if any of them exchanged words on their final morning. Maybe someone's car was parked in their driveway as her father was pulling out. Maybe a jogger waved at her mother walking out the front door. Maybe a newspaper delivery boy on a bicycle saw the light on in her parents' bedroom and wondered who was getting up as early as he.

But no such evidence; it's been five years. When they finally closed on the house, Suzy was long gone. Their first house in America. Their first home. The only evidence of home, although she's never even seen it until now. From the outside, it appears no different from the countless apartments and brownstones in her childhood. A bit nicer, perhaps. A slightly better neighborhood. Woodside, not as bad as Jersey City or Jamaica. Never as bleak as the South Bronx, where her parents worked every day. Except the curtains are wrong. Mom would never have put up such pink frills across the window. Too happy. Too American. Maria Sutpen must be an all-American girl, one of the only whites on the block. A strange neighborhood for such a girl. A strange thing, to choose to be a minority. But, then again, a rent-free house does not come by every day. What does it mean that Grace just let her live here? What was their arrangement exactly? Has Grace always been so generous?

Grace never even let Suzy borrow her clothes when they were growing up. After all, they were only one year apart; it should have been natural for the sisters to share clothes. But Grace would not have it. She said that it creeped her out to see the same jacket, the same skirt on Suzy. Mom did not make it easier.

She would often buy the same clothes for both girls. The same
V-neck sweater in different colors, the same Jordache jeans in
different sizes. Everything seemed to have been found on a two-
for-one sale rack. It never occurred to Suzy to make a fuss. In
fact, she could not understand why Grace was so bothered. Sure,
they resembled each other, in that general way siblings do, but
Grace was the one everyone remembered. On Grace, even the
drabbest Woolworth's finds turned into one-of-a-kind. It was
like watching Cinderella at a touch of the wand, and Suzy
would not have dared to try on her glass slippers. Yet it was
Grace who marked her territory with vicious insistence. It was
Grace who could not seem to bear the thought of being Suzy's
other half. It was always Grace who pushed her away first. So
Suzy was completely taken aback when Grace left her most of
her wardrobe upon leaving for Smith. When Suzy asked why,
she shrugged and said, "Doesn't matter anymore." Not an act of
generosity, Suzy thought. The exact opposite. A silent declaration of the end of sisterhood. What Grace wanted was to leave
everything behind, including her own clothes, including Suzy in
those same clothes. Suzy is still not sure what made her retort so
sharply, " 'Cause you're never coming back." Grace was in the
middle of packing, the suitcase wide open on the floor. She
stopped trying to fit the huge volume of the *American Heritage
Dictionary* in between the set of writing pads and looked across
at her with what Suzy thought was almost concern. The coldness was gone too. Finally, she said, as if in apology, "Not if I
can help it."

Grace had not spoken to the family for a few months by
then. Not since the incident. No, not that Keller boy with
whom she had once been found naked in the back of his father's
car. No, that had happened much earlier and was quickly forgotten once they moved away, soon after. Grace had come up

with some story about having been forced by the boy, which Suzy suspected was a lie. The possibility that Grace might have been violated drew the matter to a taboo. It might even have secured Dad's trust, for he no longer seemed to suspect Grace. No, the real thing happened when they were living in Jackson Heights. Suzy never learned what actually triggered such an outburst of violence, but one night, Dad dragged Grace in through the front door, gripping her by the hair. Grace's hair reached down to her waist then; she often wore it in two long braids, like a mean version of Pocahontas, as some girls at school said. But that day, she must have worn it loose, because Suzy can still remember the black silk fluttering through the air as Dad took out the scissors and slashed through it. It had all happened so quickly that neither Suzy nor Mom could stop him. They simply backed against the wall and watched in horror. Grace did not even flinch. When she finally spoke, her voice carried such rage that Suzy felt suddenly afraid. Dad had begun shouting how she was ruining her life, to which Grace shot back, "But you've already made sure of that." Strangely enough, Dad said nothing in return; Mom looked away. Grace turned to leave when she caught her own reflection in the mirror. Her face was all red from Dad's burning hands. Her hair was cropped so close to her head, like a boy's. For a second, Suzy thought she glimpsed a glint of smile on her sister's face. It was a fleeting gesture. A flash of something akin to resignation. But a smile nonetheless.

It had to have been only one thing. Boys. Dad must have found Grace with one of her leather-clad boys. He must finally have stumbled upon the truth. He must have dragged her out of wherever with the fury of a father betrayed. On the surface, Grace had the markings of the perfect daughter. She had just been named the valedictorian. She was off to college on full scholarship. Even Dad was left with not many grounds on which to vent his anger. So he did one thing that defied all words. He took away her hair. Her iridescently black, luscious, seventeen-year-old hair.

Grace never sneaked out afterward. A point had been made, it seemed. What that point was, Suzy never knew. Suzy never asked what really happened that night. It is hard to fathom now why she didn't. Ironically, Grace looked even more radiant with her newly cropped hair. A girl monk. An odd transformation. She would sometimes brush her fingers across her bare neck while reading. She seemed freer somehow. She seemed ready now to go out into the world. Dad had done her a favor. For whatever it was worth, she managed to fool him until the end.

Later, when Suzy heard about Grace taking on the job as an ESL teacher, she recalled the rage in Grace's voice on that night many years ago. English as a second language. Fort Lee High School, whose student body was over 30 percent Korean. Exactly what Dad would have despised. The pursuit of English. The job of rescuing kids whose Korean language got them nowhere. The mission of spreading English into all those newly arrived Korean minds. Grace was still trekking their parents' wishes, but in the opposite way, in the only way that would hurt them. Only Suzy knew this, of course. Only Suzy could tell that Grace was not okay. Only Suzy suspected that whatever Grace sought in Jesus had nothing to do with God.

No one would have guessed that Grace would go off to a New England college only to get hooked on the Bible. The whole thing seemed strange, almost spiteful. Yet church was what Grace chose, with shockingly fervent enthusiasm. Jesus Christ—the impostor whom Dad had always rejected as the antithesis of everything Korean, the source of what threatened to destroy Korea's five-thousand-year-old history, the Western conspiracy to colonize Asia and its Buddha and Confucius. Grace picked Jesus, while Suzy threw herself at Damian, the white man, the older married man, the one she was not supposed to love. But Suzy had assumed that Grace would be smarter. She had always believed that Grace would be freer of their parents.

During one Christmas break, Grace came home and read the Bible for four straight days. It was the first time Suzy had seen her since they both went off to college. Suzy assumed that Grace's Bible-reading was for a paper she had to write. After all, Grace's major was religion. The only time Grace left the house was to attend Christmas Eve services. Dad didn't mind, surprisingly. He even suggested that Suzy go as well. He said that, now that they were both of age, college girls, a church was as good a place as any for finding decent Korean boys. He believed that most Koreans, like him, attended church for convenience, for getting work tips or finding someone to marry. He told Mom to iron the finest silk dresses for both girls, which were not only too fancy but also inappropriate for December. But Grace obliged without as much as a grumble. When they arrived at the Union Pacific Church on Queens Boulevard, Grace reached over and held Suzy's hand, which surprised Suzy. Through the entire service, Grace sat staring elsewhere. She did not seem to be listening to the sermon or the chorus of hymns. Suzy noticed that at one point, while the pastor was speaking, Grace ripped a page from the Bible and folded it over the gum she was chewing. It seemed almost purposeful, as if she wanted Suzy to witness her, as if she wanted to tell Suzy something. Suzy could not take her eyes off the Bible with the missing page, which Grace put back neatly on the shelf as the service came to an end.

On the way home, Grace remained quiet. She looked sad, Suzy thought. And thin. She had never looked thinner. Her eating habit must have gotten worse at Smith. With her bob that came down half an inch below her ear, which accentuated her sharp cheekbones, and her pale face even paler against her dark-red lips, she looked intensely angular, and yet somehow hauntingly elegant. Then, as they were nearing the house, Grace turned to Suzy and said in a clear, bright voice, "One day, if you find yourself alone, will you remember that I am too? Because you and I, we're like twins."

That was it. Grace never opened up to her again. But for the first time in years, they had held hands like sisters. Grace seemed almost concerned for Suzy, almost afraid. What did she mean? Why twins? Could that be why she hadn't been able to stand Suzy all along? Because Suzy was the most exact reminder of home? The next time she saw Grace was at the funeral, and it was clear that nothing would ever bring them together again. Or at least that was what Grace indicated.

Strange that all of this should come rushing right now, here on the stoop of Maria Sutpen's house, the last place her parents had called home. Still no Grace, no parents. So many afternoons, she had sat like this alone waiting for them. She would be done with homework by then. She knew no one in the neighborhood, always the new girl on the block. Sometimes she wished that she were an avid reader like her sister. She wished her parents would buy a new TV to replace the one with the constant buzzing noise. Even the chores would be done in no time. She was a master at rinsing rice. She'd learned how to vacuum the entire floor in less than ten minutes. Still no one came home. It would be hours before anyone came home. She was good at waiting. She was the obedient one. She stood and watched as Grace's hair fell to the ground. She played mute while Grace became the designated interpreter. She hid in a corner while Grace got thinner and thinner. She never even wandered off until later, much later, when she could no longer stay.

Looking around, she finds it odd that the block should be so empty, even for a Friday afternoon. The whole world seems to have disappeared to give her this time, to leave her just once more with her parents.

Five years, it has taken her five years to bring herself here. After the funeral, after their ashes were scattered across the Atlantic, Suzy kept imagining her parents' last home. But she could never picture them in such a cookie-cutter brownstone in Woodside. No Flushing, no Jersey City, never the Bronx. In her dream, she wanted to get them out of those immigrant neighborhoods. In her dream, she wanted to rewind their immigrant trekking. So she made up their pastel Montauk house. A shiny Jeep rather than the used Oldsmobile. Sunbathing and fishing instead of peeling-cutting-stocking fruit. TV before bed, like all other aging couples. *Nightline*, *Late Night*, the *Tonight Show*. Thanksgiving dinners. A game of Monopoly. For years, she has stayed away from this house. She has been afraid of shattering their last chance for life.

But a dream remains a dream always. Nothing alters the fact that she never got to see them again. She never held Mom's hands and asked why irises brought a smile to her face. She never let Dad explain what made him leave Korea, why he was so tortured by his old country. She never begged them for time, just a little more time to understand. She never told them that she had to run because she could not see ahead as long as they were there. She could not embrace this place called America while they never forgot to remind her what was not Korea. She could not make sense of her American college, American friends, American lovers, while her parents toiled away twelve hours a day, seven days a week at their Bronx store. She could not become American as long as she remained their daughter. *She betrayed them, so she might live.*

Rain on the brink.

Sky churning.

Empty, gray asphalt in its last light.

There is no such thing as a warning. No gentle first drop. When the rain comes, she crouches on the stoop, her arms hugging her bent knees, her hair now hanging below her waist.

17.

"BABE, PICK UP."

Almost noon. She had lain awake most of the night. The rain must have gotten to her. She sure asked for it. Over an hour on that stoop, much of it under the threat of the storm. Maria Sutpen never even showed up. The girl at the accountant's office was right. For an emergency contact, Maria Sutpen was useless. Friday afternoon, silly to think that she would miraculously turn up just to greet Suzy.

"Suzy, pick up already, will you?"

"Hi, I was still in bed."

"You sound like hell. Apparently, you told Sandy to forget about the doctor."

Sandy called right after his phone call yesterday. She took down all the information and promised to get back to Suzy as soon as she finds out anything.

"Michael, I'm fine."

"*Christ*, Suzy, you never listen, do you."

She can hear the tone of disapproval. He does not like things to be out of control. He does not want Suzy sick in bed.

"I'm listening right now, aren't I?"

That puts a little spunk in his voice. "Then where the fuck were you yesterday? Sandy called you all afternoon and you never even picked up!"

"I was asleep. I was out cold." She does not want to get into it. She does not want to rehash the whole business of the anonymous phone call and the accountant on 32nd Street. The house in Woodside. None of it would mean a thing to Michael.

"*Hey*, I was worried sick yesterday."

These are the terms of their relationship. Contrived intimacy. Lots of it. The sort of things a man never says to his wife. The sort of things he can freely admit without sticking to the consequences.

"Well, don't you have other things to worry about over there? Where are you anyway? Frankfurt still?"

"Fucking Germans. Everything's such a goddamn secret. No one tells me a goddamn thing. They think all Americans are out to fleece them, which I might just do so fucking gladly."

Suzy smiles, comforted by Michael's familiar grunt. Suddenly everything seems a bit simpler, easier.

"I swear, babe, the minute they come begging, I'm outta here. The bag's all packed. The chauffeur's getting antsy."

"Then where to?"

"Why, you miss me?"

Typical. He ducks the question again. He never shares his itinerary beforehand. He lets her know where he is each time, but never before getting there.

"Does it matter?" She does miss him, but she won't say.

"Babe, you have no idea."

She is beginning to miss him more. It is all in her body. She must still be dreamy. "So what did Sandy have to say?" She changes the subject.

"Not good, I'm afraid." He is hesitant.

"She didn't find out?" A pang of disappointment. But it is hardly surprising. The INS, not the easiest place to crack.

"Believe me, she tried. Actually, it was some INS stringer who did. But the damnedest thing. It's all blank. Nothing comes up." Michael sounds unconvinced. "Yeah, you're a citizen all right. So were your parents, and your sister. But that's all there is. No past record of green cards or even visas. The guy said that it could be a case of special pardon or amnesty, or even NIW, which means National Interest Waiver, but that's usually for only serious professionals like scientists or academics—you know, the sort of gigs considered to be of 'national interest,' which I assume wasn't your parents' case. But that still doesn't explain why the file draws a blank. Whatever it is, it's all classified. Suzy, take my word, leave it alone."

That Park guy, he had it coming to him . . . He had friends in all sorts of places . . . I knew I didn't want to mess with him. I'd seen what happens to guys who stand up to him.

"Babe, you okay?"

No one is as sharp as Michael. He can estimate any situation to its *n*th degree and react accordingly. A born businessman. A gift. So entirely different from Damian.

"Hey, forget it. It's all in the past, useless."

But the past is all she has.

"Thanks anyway. I appreciate this."

"*Christ*, you sound like you don't even fucking know me."

When she puts the phone down, her first instinct is to grab her notepad to look up Kim Yong Su's phone number. But then she remembers that he did not have a phone number, only a pager, which never picked up. Besides, he is probably not at home right now. There was something in his testimony about working part-time on weekends. Moonlighting as a watchman at a fruit-and-vegetable store. The Hunts Point Market closes on weekends, and he needs the extra cash. She can feel the sudden aches coursing through her body. She puts her coat on, although she cannot remember where Kim claimed that he works on weekends. The Bronx, she vaguely recalls, near Yankee Stadium. That doesn't tell her much. There could be at least twenty Korean markets around there. Korean store-owners generally tend to know each other, especially if they compete in the same neighborhood. Maybe one of them would direct her to him. It would be crazy to roam the streets of the Bronx in this rain, in her state, when she is shivering even here in the warmth of her apartment.

Once outside, she immediately realizes that she has the wrong shoes on. The rain is mixed with something resembling hail. Pelting ice drops. The pavement is a mess, wet and slippery. Hardly anyone on the street, a rare thing on St. Marks Place. Gone are the usual brunch crowds who flock to the East Village on weekends. Some have skipped town altogether for an early Thanksgiving break. Some are holed up in their railroad flats with movies and takeout. Just two more blocks to the Astor Place subway stop. It is then that she remembers she meant to get a bottle of cold medicine. Benadryl, Sudafed, even echinacea, any of them will do.

So, instead of walking straight, she turns north on Second Avenue. There is a Korean market on the east side of the avenue. They sell fruits mostly, but, like all other Korean stores, they also carry almost everything, from candies to cashew nuts to condoms. The prematurely balding man behind the cash register always tries to speak Korean to her, but she never engages. She is not good at small talk, especially not with a stranger from whom she buys fruit almost daily. The storefront reveals a colorful display of clementines, cantaloupes, plums, strawberries, even cherries. New York is the Garden of Eden. Even in such November rain, most tropical fruits are all here, right on Second Avenue. She shuts her umbrella and picks up a few clementines before going inside, where the cashier stands grinning at her. He must have seen her entering in the surveillance mirror on the ceiling.

"*An-nyung-ha-sae-yo*," he greets, as if daring her to answer in Korean.

"Cold medicine, please, anything you think good is fine," Suzy says in English, hoping to discourage him.

"Anything?" he responds in Korean. He is extra-friendly today. Or he is bored, not many customers this afternoon.

"Anything," she repeats in English. Now that she is inside, she can feel cold sweat running down her back. The sure sign of a fever.

"This good?" He grins, handing her a bottle of echinacea. Of course, the East Village's first choice. No one believes in synthetic drugs anymore. She is about to take out her wallet when she notices that the man is still grinning.

"Boyfriend?" As he leans forward, the bald spot on his head catches the ray of the lightbulb.

"Excuse me?" The man's a real pain, she thinks.

"That guy out there, he your boyfriend?" He points his index finger toward the door. Suzy turns, catching a glimpse of someone dashing off.

The clementines tumble to the floor as Suzy runs outside. She looks frantically in both directions, and spots the man under a black umbrella, walking briskly. From the back, he appears to be dragging his right foot slightly, or maybe the ground is so slippery that he is having difficulty running. Even as he crosses First Avenue to head toward Avenue A, he never looks back.

Suzy keeps up at a ten-pace distance, knowing that he will have to stop soon. Ninth Street comes to a dead end at Avenue A, where Tompkins Square Park takes up three blocks in both directions. When he reaches the park, he halts for a few seconds, as if he cannot decide which way to continue. He can either make a ninety-degree turn onto Avenue A or go straight into the park, which is empty except for a few homeless men who've made puddly shelters on benches barely shielded under tentlike coverings.

He quickly enters the tiny fenced-in area between a dog run and a basketball court. He may have decided to give up the charade. He may be planning his next move. From behind, the man is nothing but a collage of a black umbrella and a black raincoat. For a second, she wonders if she is following the right man after all. Maybe the real guy disappeared in a different direction. Maybe he ducked into a cab that had been waiting. Maybe he dodged into the diner next door and watched her follow another man. Anything is possible, as she circles the park for the fourth time, waiting for the guy to make his move.

Suzy is now wondering if she should catch up to him after all. It does not look like he will do anything other than amble through the park. She must be trailing the wrong man. Maybe he's just one of those aimless people who like to meander in parks on rainy Saturdays. As she is contemplating what to do next, he suddenly takes the St. Marks Place exit back at Avenue A. He's decided to leave, obviously, for reasons she cannot tell. He trots along, back toward Second Avenue. The rain is fiercer. She is getting drenched. The umbrella is definitely not strong enough; its spokes keep flipping in whichever direction the wind blows. Already a few of the spines have broken loose, one of them dangling before her eyes at a precarious angle. She might just as well throw it out and take the rain as it comes. Now, suddenly, there are more people on the street. A crowd sweeps past her, which must've poured out of the monstrous Sony Cineplex nearby, or the New Village Theater, where a certain British troupe has been recycling the same sellout number for the past five years. But do shows run this early? Is this the matinee crowd? Then she realizes that it is suddenly impossible to tell which black umbrella belongs to the man. In a mere second, he seems to have gone missing amidst the dancing umbrellas before her eyes. All the strength in her body gives at once, and she is not sure where to turn, what comes next. She knows only how bitterly cold she is suddenly, how wet her clothes are. She is no longer holding the umbrella. What did she do with it? Did it fly off with the wind? She has begun looking around frantically, when something bright and yellow flashes right under her eyes.

It is a flyer, on yellow paper. A club invite. Around here, on weekends, it is not unusual to find kids on street corners passing out flyers. But not now, not in such rain, not when she has just lost someone who's been following her for days. She is about to crinkle it up when a phrase catches her eyes. "HOTTEST PARTY OF THE MILLENIUM"—and underneath it, "COME THIS SAT-URDAY NOVEMBER 18, D WAVE D RAVE DJ SPOOKY & HIS FRIENDS!!!!!"

It is "DJ" that stops her heart.

DJ. The fourth member of the Fearsome Four. The missing KK. The orphan. The name has stuck with her from the first time she heard it. For no reason, really. It is not even his real name.

Instead of trudging through the rain, she runs for the under-ground hole less than a block away. She knows exactly where to go. She is almost elated at this sudden direction. And the man she just lost in the rain? Let him catch up with her if he wants to play real hide-and-seek.

18.

BOLTED ACROSS THE TOP WINDOWS of the three-story building is the dilapidated electric sign for EAST BILLIARDS, trimmed
with blinking red lights. A couple of bulbs are broken; the line is
not as smooth as it should be. The floor below is dark, blinds
drawn, no sign of life. On the ground floor, three stores are
jammed together. A Korean market. A nail salon. Santos Pizza,
the third one is called, and Suzy wonders if Santos is as common
a name as Kim.

The rain has not eased. Her clothes are soaked through. The
forty-minute ride here has only made it worse. She can feel the
chill in the core of every bone. She should have grabbed that
bottle of echinacea. She ran out so fast that the bottle just fell
from her hands, along with the clementines. And the gaping
face of the man behind the cash register—probably the last time
he would smile at her.

Climbing the stairs, she is surprised at how quiet it is. Not a
peek coming from the pool hall above. But, then, she has never

been to a pool hall before. Too decadent, where bad kids congregate and dropouts make trouble. What would Dad have said if he saw her here? And Damian? At least they had that in common, she thinks, quickly averting her eyes from the genitalia-shaped graffiti on the cement wall. When she reaches the third floor and opens the door, she finds a spacious room filled with pool tables. Some with solids and stripes dotting their green tops, and others sitting wide and empty. It is dark inside, the only light belonging to the foggy windows, through which the sky is barely visible.

"Hello?" Her voice rings loud, making an echo. Nothing. No one around. "Hello? Anybody here?" she calls out again. Strange, Saturday should be their busiest day. Maybe it is too early. Maybe they don't open until late afternoon, like some restaurants. But, then, why isn't the door locked? "Hello?" Suzy tries once more. No one still. Not much to see. A rickety soda machine by the entrance. A jukebox to its right that's seen better days. A couple of Budweiser cans on the floor, which no one seems to have bothered to pick up. Farther in the distance is a partition; must be an office of sorts.

She is not sure what she expected. What is it that keeps tugging at her? When Detective Lester mentioned the Flushing pool hall where the drugs were found, Suzy remembered another pool hall, in Jackson Heights, which had been a notorious hangout in the mid-eighties. There were always rumors surrounding it, with gory details of gang rapes and drug deals gone sour. Everyone in her high school had heard of it. The kids whispered its name with awe and fear. The KK had still been active then, along with several other minor gangs whose names Suzy cannot remember now. Back then, it was just a rumor. It belonged to the underground world of the underground kids whose lives would never touch hers. That is, until now.

She is turning to leave when she is stopped by a sound behind the partition. "Hello?" she tries again, to no avail. Yet those rustling steps, an unmistakable murmur. Maybe there is more than one person there. Maybe they are in the middle of an important conversation and do not want to be interrupted. Suzy is tempted to turn around and walk out, but then she remembers the rain outside and hesitates. Besides, she is curious. Why wouldn't the person answer her four hellos? What's he doing there behind the wall? From the doorway to the cubicle is about fifty steps. Five rows of pool tables, two in each row, ten total. It is not such a great distance.

When she finally makes her way across the room and stands before the partition, she can hear a sort of humming from the other side. A staccato rumble, oddly youthful and cheery. She knocks before peering in, although the attempt is superfluous. Rocking in the armchair is a young man, with his feet up on the desk. His eyes are shut, his head bobbing to the Discman whose volume is high enough so that she can even make out the lyric. Some kind of rap. Hip-hop, he would insist. Obviously, calling out to him is useless, but she is uneasy about tapping him on the arm. She is standing there mulling over what to do next when, as if in a miracle, he opens his eyes and jumps out of his seat.

"Holy shit! You scared the shit out of me!" the young man screams, peeling the headset off his ears.

"I'm so sorry. I called you a couple of times, but you didn't hear me." Suzy panics as he flinches from her. "I really didn't mean to scare you."

"Fucking hell you didn't; what the hell were you doing creeping up on me like that!"

"I was just . . . I didn't know how to get your attention."

"Yo, let's forget it." His face is turning red, as though he is embarrassed at getting so easily frightened. Then he reaches for the can of Coke on the desk and gulps it down, struck by sudden thirst. "Don't tell my old man. He'll whack me if he finds out I wasn't minding the door."

"It's a deal, my lips are sealed," she says in a conspiring whisper. His father must be the owner. Family business, not unusual.

"So what do you want? A table?" he says, looking her over once, not without a hint of amusement. He is barely twenty. Boys of his age, they have just one thing on their minds. Even when the woman is old enough to be their aunt.

"Are you open? Looks pretty dead to me," she says, surveying the empty room.

"Sure, we're open. I just haven't bothered turning on all the lights yet. Too early, and no one's here these days anyway. Why waste electricity?" He shrugs, strutting over to the wall to flick the switch. In an instant, the room turns fluorescent.

"Why no one these days?" Suzy asks, squinting her eyes as the white balls beam under sudden artificial bliss.

"Some trouble out in Flushing; the guys're laying low," he says, clicking the "Stop" button on his Discman.

"Can't be good for business?"

"We're used to it. It happens once in a while. Everyone crawls back sooner or later. This time, the deal's bigger, so it's taking longer," he says with a purposeful toss of his hair, which is moussed into a ball of stiff spikes.

"How long has your father owned the place?" she asks cautiously.

"What's up with twenty questions? What're you, a cop or something?" he fires back, then stares hard at her for a minute or two before shaking his head. "Nope, you're not a cop."

"How can you tell?" She asks, half amused.

"Too fine to be one," he says with a wink. "Lady cops are butt-ugly. No Charlie's Angels around here. So you're not one, not a chance. So why twenty questions?" The boy is sharp, doesn't miss a thing. He knows how to use a compliment to get what he wants.

"I used to live around here, long time ago. Went to Astoria High for a while, and then Lincoln High, over on Queens Boulevard." She wants him to know he can trust her. No funny business.

"Fucking hell, Lincoln High? I went there too! Well, didn't quite graduate, but still . . . when did you go there?" the boy asks with a wide grin, as though he now considers her okay.

"You were just a kid."

"No way, you don't look much older than me." He smiles slyly.

"I'm ancient; I was around when the KK was around." She takes the risk.

"That's *old*," he exclaims, teasingly.

"Told you!" Glancing at the room, she says, "Those guys, do they come around still?"

"Who? The KK?"

"Yeah. I know it's been too long, but I was in the neighborhood and thought it'd be nice to see an old face or two," she says, running her index finger along the edge of the table. It is easy to believe this. The familiar place of her youth. The friends long gone. Nostalgia is a powerful thing, even when made up.

"Not really, especially not since Flushing. The trail's still hot. No one wants to get mixed up with a drug mess, you know. The cops are jumping on any Korean kids with a record, which is just about everyone who hangs out here." He chuckles. "Even the room salon downstairs is slow these days. Mina's bumming, she only took over the place not so long ago. Fucking hell, all those booties pining away."

"Room salon?" A call-girl joint. The sort of establishment where hostesses sit around with clients and pour drinks. But "hostess" is really a code word for a prostitute. Implicit in the exorbitant entrance fee are girls as part of the deal.

" 'Seven Stars,' right downstairs, didn't you see it coming up? I guess it's kinda easy to miss, they try to keep a low profile."

"Seven Stars?"

"Don't you remember?" the boy asks incredulously. "Used to be a major KK hangout, long before my old man's time here."

Seven Stars. Why does that sound familiar?

"So you here for old times' sake? Why, the rain get to you?" he asks, as if noticing her wet clothes for the first time.

"The rain, yeah . . ." And the yellow flyer, she remembers, yes, the flyer. "Have you heard of a guy named DJ?" A long shot; the boy's too young.

"DJ? What does he look like?"

Of course she has no idea. An orphan. The last one of the Fearsome Four. The one deported to Korea five years ago, the same month as her parents' murder.

"Doesn't matter, I guess. He got deported."

"Deported? That's fucked up. Fuck those INS assholes!" he says, shaking his head.

Whatever happened, happened too long ago. Whatever evidence has long been erased.

"So where's your father?" Suzy asks, walking to the door.

"A dumb fight, a couple of weeks ago. He should've known better than trying to break up those punks," he answers with feigned indifference. "He got shot."

Suzy pauses, turning around.

"Yo, it's no big deal. He's not dead or anything, besides, he's got me." The boy puts on a tough voice, suddenly looking even younger than his baby face.

It is not until she is halfway down the stairs that she notices the silver dots engraved on the metal door on the second floor. Seven tiny stars in the shape of a loop. A logo. No letters next to it. No explanation. Just a plain circular arrangement of seven stars. She tries the intercom, a neon-green button to the right of the door frame. No answer. Not surprising. If it's too early for a pool hall, definitely sleeptime for a bar. The door will not budge. The video camera glares down like a hawk, patrolling from a corner of the ceiling. The security system is no joke. With the sort of guys who frequent here, everything would have to be bulletproof.

A loop of seven stars. Common enough, not particularly memorable. Yet Suzy is sure she has seen it before. *But where?*

She lingers for a while. The staircase is mute, fully cemented, and dim. Not much use standing here. She makes her way down the steps slowly, hoping that someone will emerge. She keeps looking back at the door, but no one is there. Then she is outside again. Out in the torrential rain.

No umbrella. She is about to run into the Korean market to get one when she notices the warm glow from Santos Pizza. It is inviting, this pizzeria in deepest Queens, right below the pool hall. Like a candlelit cottage in a fairy tale, made of cakes. She could be one of the lost siblings, Hansel or Gretel, following the bread crumbs through the haunted forest.

Inside are a couple of empty booths, and a sleepy man in red and white stripes, kneading the dough. He hardly reacts when he sees her. Maybe he can tell that she does not really want pizza. Maybe he is afraid of the abyss of wanting in her eyes. Maybe she is not the first of the lost children to end up here.

"Coffee, please."

"That's it?" he asks grumpily, as if saying, "Hey lady, this ain't a café, you order pizza at a pizzeria."

"And a slice," she adds, to appease him.

He makes no response, cutting a slab from the congealed pie on the table and flinging it into the oven with hardly a glance.

When the slice finally comes back out, nothing about it signals magic. Drippy yellow on an extra-thick crust. The cottage in the forest was a phantom. No wicked witch. Not a single crumb.

The mushy cheese tastes like fat, a lukewarm chunk, moist and chewy. It instantly turns her stomach, and she washes it down with a sip of coffee, which is so hot that it burns her tongue. She puts down the cup and glances out the window instead. The rain does not seem too bad now, at least more promising than the rancid-fat smell. As she is about to get up, she notices a car pulling up outside. A BMW, too fancy for this neighborhood. From the door on the driver's side, a woman pops out and runs in with her hand on her forehead, covering her face from the rain.

A whiff of candy-sick perfume. The flaring red raincoat gleams too shiny against her yellowed skin. Her copper curls look burnt, in need of a fresh dye job or a perm. With her chapped lips and blotted mascara, she seems to have just rolled out of bed. Someone else's bed, most likely.

The sleepy man, though, perks up. "*Ciao, bellissima*," he greets her with a wide grin.

The woman blows him a kiss, brushing her coat noisily, shaking the water out. "Hey handsome, did you miss me?" she says with a wink.

All gooey now, he asks, "What you doing here so early, Mina?"

"Johnny hasn't come by, has he?" she asks.

The man doesn't look happy when he answers, "Still no news?"

The woman shrugs, glancing at Suzy, as if suddenly aware of her gaze. Suzy quickly looks away.

Mina, the new owner of Seven Stars.

Perched on a stool by the counter, chatting with the no-longer-sleepy man, the woman tackles her pizza and Coke with much gusto. Suzy remains in her booth, trying to listen to their

conversation, which is oddly muffled now. Suzy cannot make
out anything except the occasional giggle and something about
the lack of customers. Then, suddenly, the woman rises, blowing another kiss at her fan behind the counter. Suzy also rises,
quickly trashing her pizza. Rather than hopping back in the car,
the woman dashes next door. Suzy follows, only to be ambushed
by her waiting inside.

"What's the idea?" Mina hollers huskily, squinting as though
she forgot to put her contact lenses on this morning.

Suzy is not sure what to say. She has no business following
this woman. She can play innocent and keep on walking, or she
can make up something, anything that may open doors. Doors
to what, though? What is she looking for, why is she here?

Say something about the KK—a voice in her head. *Be an insider.*

"Those guys . . . Have you heard anything new?"

Glaring at Suzy, Mina asks sharply, "Who are you?" Then
she adds, almost as an afterthought, "I don't know what you're
talking about."

"I've been told to come here for the scoop." Suzy comes up
with the first thing that sounds plausible.

"Who told you that?" Mina asks suspiciously.

Recalling one of the names Detective Lester mentioned,
Suzy takes a chance. "My man's in trouble . . . Maddog."

"You're Maddog's girl?" Mina then steps back a little, contemplating Suzy in her plain dark coat, black scarf, and matching hat. Her eyes pore over Suzy's face, free of makeup except a
touch of rosy lip gloss, most of which has faded by now. It is obvious that Suzy does not belong here. Women like Suzy do not
belong to a gangster named Maddog. Finally, Mina snaps, "I've
never seen you before."

"I've never seen *you* either," Suzy retorts with purposeful
terseness. It works. Mina looks stumped and says uncertainly,

"What's come over Maddog? He likes his girls with a bit more meat on their bones."

"He likes me fine," Suzy says with what she hopes is the right tone of arrogance.

"I don't know who told you to come here," says Mina, shaking her head. "Johnny's got nothing to do with it. Tell Maddog it's not Johnny."

So there must have been some sort of infighting. According to Detective Lester, the AOCTF busted the gang on an anonymous tip. It seems that Maddog believes a guy named Johnny was involved.

"Girl, it's none of my business." She clicks her tongue with a pitying look at Suzy. "But if I were you, I'd wash my hands now. Maddog's a goner." She begins climbing up the steps, then halts suddenly and turns around, leaning closer. Suzy moves away instinctively. Something about the woman's sallow skin makes her cringe, as though its secret is contagious. Scrunching up her face, Mina says slowly, "Wait a minute. I'll be damned."

Suzy stands still, her heart thumping.

A long, cool gaze. Mina cocks her head, muttering to herself, "No . . . she wouldn't dare." Scanning Suzy's face once more, she whispers, "It's not Mariana who sent you, is it?"

"Hey, I told you I'm here for my man . . ." Suzy is about to protest when she remembers.

Mariana.

Grace's code name for marijuana.

May I be excused? I promised my friend Mariana that we'll do our homework together.

"Who's this Mariana?" Suzy stammers. "Maybe . . . I know her."

Mina purses her lips, as if in distaste, and spits out, "Boykiller, we all called her. She used to hang out here back in the old days."

Suzy tries to keep her composure, to stop herself from lunging at this woman with questions. This aging call girl in blinding red. Suzy swallows hard before asking, "And this Mariana—how old was she?" A faint voice, feeble almost.

"Not the legal age, if that's what you're asking," Mina says derisively. "A schoolgirl gone wild. She thought she was something special 'cause she only screwed big shots. That was her thing, she chose her own guys, no money was ever good enough. Johnny should've ditched her when her father took her away."

"Her father?" Suzy repeats, feeling the height of the stairs suddenly.

"I'm sure she put on the whole show just to get caught." Mina rolls her eyes.

"Her father . . . came here?"

"You sure you're Maddog's girl?" Mina says, studying Suzy with a puzzled smile. "Listen, I don't care who you are, but if you see Mariana, tell her to leave Johnny alone." Then, fixing Suzy with a nearly pleading look, she adds, "He's no KK's bellboy. Those days are over."

"Johnny, was he her lover?"

"Lover?" she retorts with a sneering laugh. "More like a chauffeur, the way she always made him drive her home so early. She never gave him the time of the day."

"Because?"

"Because she was a bitch," Mina blurts out bitterly. "If it hadn't been for her, he would've never crossed Maddog all those years ago and . . ." She pauses, as if trying to shake off her anger. "Doesn't matter, 'cause he's come back to be with me now. He won't crawl back to her," she mumbles unconvincingly. "Definitely a changed man."

May I be excused? I promised my friend Mariana that we'll do our homework together.

The girl who used to hang out at the KK's bar.

The troubled one who couldn't wait to get caught by her father.

The boykiller face who slept with the gang for money, and yet picked her own guys.

"Look, I don't want you coming around here again." Mina suddenly lowers her voice, her eyes darting nervously, as though she is afraid that Johnny may show up any minute. She seems to ponder something for a few seconds, then says, "If you run into her, tell her to deal with me instead," quickly scribbling a pager number on a piece of paper and handing it to Suzy. She adds in a softer tone, "Girl, about your Maddog, forget it. Do yourself a favor, get yourself a new man."

The cold sweat running down her back is an icy shock. Suzy becomes aware that her body is trembling. Leaning her right arm against the wall, she tilts her face a little, as though burrowing under a shadow. "And this Mariana—she looked like me?"

A wry smile crinkling the corner of her mouth, Mina repeats, "Weird, the more I look at you, the more you remind me of her." Then she adds, as if in vengeance, "Really, you could be the same girl."

19.

THE HAND ON HER RIGHT SHOULDER is a gentle one. Must be Mom, or Dad finally home. She must have fallen asleep at the doorstep. She must have forgotten her key, and school must have let out early, and Grace must have sneaked out again. So she must have sat here and waited with her homework spread out, and still, when the homework was done, still no one came home, and she must have lain down for a while thinking she was hungry and it was getting darker and the draft from the hallway window sharper, and she was afraid that no one would remember, that no one would find her here, and then sleep must have overtaken her, taken her breath away to an even darker place, where she saw the seven stars in a circle like the misshapen Big Dipper that came loose to join hands to finally surround her, who lay weeping because she remembered where she had seen them before.

But neither Mom nor Dad. Can't be, they've been shot. They

will never come home again. When Suzy opens her eyes, her face still wet with tears, it is Mr. Kim stooping over her.

"I tried to wake you, but you were crying in your sleep," he says.

"Oh," she mutters, blinking slowly.

"How long have you been waiting?" he asks, turning the key in the door lock.

"I don't know, what time is it?" she says, making a feeble attempt to get up; the ground beneath feels strangely muddy.

"Six-thirty," he says, glancing at his watch. "You're lucky I'm home early today."

Following him inside, she recognizes the bareness. The white walls. The single sofa. The single bed. The familiar absence.

"I've got nothing here. I can heat up some water, or maybe *boricha*?" he says, putting a kettle on the stove.

Her body feels numb from the cold concrete corridor. The sleep was a blackout, leaving her spent, hollow, confused. "*Boricha*," she answers. My favorite, she is about to add, and then realizes that it's been years since she had it last. Mom used to keep it refrigerated and serve it instead of water. But it had never tasted like water. It was light brown. It smelled of corn, like an autumn harvest. She seems to have forgotten about it one day. Odd how that happens. You swear by certain things— that particular sundress he first saw you in, or that rose lipstick you wore every day, or that barley tea you once declared you couldn't live without. But then, one day, someone, perhaps a stranger, in a bare, bleak apartment far from home, asks, without a hint of history, "Water or *boricha*?," and you suddenly remember that it's been years since you've even thought of it. But how is that possible? How is it that you could go on fine without what had once been so essential, that you haven't even been aware of its absence? How is it then you could declare, without hesitation, that it is your favorite? Shouldn't love require more? Isn't love a responsibility?

"It'll warm you up," he says, taking a mug from the shelf. Suzy realizes how fatigued she feels, and how cold. For hours, she wandered through the streets of Queens. For hours, she could not get rid of the one thought circling in her head—her parents. What did they do to bring on such hatred? And then there was a girl named Mariana.

"Someone's been following me," she says, surprised that she is telling him.

"Have you told the police?" His eyes are on the kettle, which is taking a long time to boil.

"No," she says, leaning on the cushion, glancing at the ashtray on the table. It is filled to the brim. The butts are smoked to their last skin. The sofa faces the opposite direction from the kitchenette. She cannot see him when she says, "I don't think many people are too upset that my parents are dead, including the police."

Finally, a hissing noise.

"I'm not interested in your parents' death," he says.

Now a shrill from the kettle, but he won't turn it off, as though he is grateful for its shield.

She waits. The final pitch of the boiling water, but she is patient. It's been a long day. It's been a long, long five years.

When he stands before her with a cup of *boricha*, which he promptly puts on the table, he says nothing. He merely sits opposite her, waiting for her to finish. After tea, you may go. He does not have to say it. She knows she is not welcome. He is doing her a favor. A sobbing girl, frozen out of her mind, who can turn her out?

"Someone's been sending me a bouquet of irises, someone's been hanging up on the phone, someone's even called with a threat," she says, holding the mug between her cold palms. "What do you think it all means?"

He lights a cigarette. His hands are restless. A chain-smoker.

"The murderer wants to be found," she says, taking a sip. The tea is instantly familiar, clean and hot as it rolls down her throat. "Not by Detective Lester, but by me."

He won't meet her eyes. He does not want any part of this conversation. The furrows between his eyebrows grow deeper as he inhales harder.

"You told me last time that having children didn't really save my parents. You're right, it didn't." Suzy takes a deep breath before continuing. "I need to know why they couldn't be saved, what it is that they did to you. I guess I'm asking you to tell me before you tell the police, because the police will come sooner or later."

He takes a long drag, longer than necessary. "Is that a threat?"

"No, a plea . . . because I think you understand what it means to try living while circling death again and again," she says quietly, glancing at the photo of his wife, the dead woman guarding his bedside.

The frigid stillness, except for the clock ticking nearby. Her hands around the mug tighten, as though their hold steadies her. When he finally meets her eyes, she lets out a sigh, realizing that she has been holding her breath.

"Your father had enemies. Many, in fact. 'Enemies' might not be the right word. People who held deep grudges against him, let's say. I was one of them. So I can't blame you if you were to discredit everything I say. The ones who know the truth are both dead. So who's to argue over what really happened? . . ." He pauses, his eyes wavering between her face and the rest of the room. He seems to be trying to find the right words, the right place to begin. His face clouds with something indefinite, something akin to resignation.

"When we met your father, we were working at a store on Tremont Avenue. My wife was at the cash register. I was doing the setup work around the store. We were both too old for the job, but we tried to make up for it by working hard, getting the freshest produce, opening the store before anyone else. One day the owner called me in. He was moving back to Korea. He offered me the store at a bargain. I'd saved some money by then, not a whole lot, but enough for a down payment. There was just one problem. We were both still illegal, my wife and I. We had no green cards, and definitely no right to own anything. That's where your father came in."

She recognizes the accent in his Korean from his deposition. Each syllable drags into the next without any inflection. It is kind to the ears. From central Korea, where people speak slowly in a quiet murmur. She was told that its land borders no water, anomalous on a peninsula. The only province kept hidden in the hills. The people there must be full of longing, searching the sky for a glimpse of blue. Their gentleness might belie what is unrequited, and perhaps broken.

"He'd done deliveries for us in the past. My wife remembered how he'd wanted to buy a store but didn't have enough cash. He had once offered to invest some money for renovation in exchange for a part ownership. So we sought out your father, made a partner deal, put his name on the lease."

Who would do that? Why would they trust a stranger? How would they know that he wouldn't put the store under his name and run away with it? But Suzy also knows that the world of immigrants has its own rules. Every man is guide to every other man. They don't speak English, or read English. They don't know the American laws. They might even break them without

knowing. They are forever guilty before the customers, the policemen, the inspectors, the district attorneys, the IRS agents,
the INS agents. Sure, America is the land of opportunity, and
yet they wouldn't recognize an opportunity even if it is waved in
front of them. Only another immigrant can show them, in their
language, in ways they can understand. A fellow countryman
who might understand America better, who might be less afraid,
who might be legal.

"Soon his wife joined us. Your mother. She wasn't much of
a talker. I hold no grudge against your mother. I only say that
because I do believe that, deep inside, she was good. I saw her
smile once, a real full smile. She was looking at a truck passing
by. When I asked her what she was smiling at, she blushed and
said there was a load of irises in the back of the truck, and the
irises brought back some old memories. I never saw that smile
again. Maybe it was too late by then. She seemed tired of life.
Numb. 'Dead inside,' is what my wife said. She always did what
was required of her. She wouldn't work too hard or too little.
She just did her duty with a minimum of fuss. She never talked
back to your father. He'd sometimes call her names, bad insulting names in front of me and my wife. They were both well into
their forties. It really wasn't right to do that."

What Suzy experiences is dread. The absolute dread of what
is to come. It will only get worse, she thinks. *This is not a good
story. This is what I have come for.*

"The business began to pick up after the renovation, although your father put down only a fraction of the money he'd
promised. He also stopped doing the delivery work and hired
someone instead. He was now practically running the whole
store. Both our wives were behind the cash registers, since your
father installed a second one for the night shift. I told him it was
a bad idea. It'd only exhaust everyone. Seven days a week is one
thing, but twenty-four hours? A couple of nights later, he called

to say that our partnership wasn't working, exactly what I'd been thinking, and that it'd be better if my wife and I were to stop showing up. I was flabbergasted. I thought he must've gone insane. It was my store, I mean our store, although he hadn't fulfilled his end of the deal. What did he mean, stop showing up at my own store! That's when he laid it on me—'I could get you deported within twenty-four hours.' "

Sometimes the answer is there even before you are told. You may have suspected it all along. It has only been a matter of time.

"My wife overheard. She snatched the phone and started yelling. She told him he was a traitor, the lowest of the low. I'd never seen her lose control like that. All that work, those sleepless hours behind the register hadn't been kind to her. She was tired, the way your mother had been tired. My wife still had some fire left in her. She wanted to fight out the battle. She didn't want to give up. Your father threatened to report us if we showed up at the store just once more, but we ran there anyway. It's so long ago now, but still so vivid. The ugliest, the saddest day of my life." He takes another cigarette out of the pack. His fingers on the lighter are unsteady. It takes him a couple of tries to get a flame. He can only keep his eyes on the cigarette. Anywhere else will be her face, the girl's face, which is too reminiscent.

"Your father called the INS right in front of us. He reported us while we stood there in our own house. It was like he'd done it before. He knew the number right off the top of his head. He didn't even raise his voice. He looked calm through the whole thing. I saw your mother weeping in the corner. She was silent, even in crying. She didn't want him to hear her cry."

The informers.

No record of green cards or visa.

How many people did her parents sacrifice to obtain their citizenship? How many did they turn in for rewards?

Suzy never questioned why they moved each year. She did not think it odd when they could suddenly afford two bedrooms. She never thought twice when her parents bought a store, a house. She believed that it was the result of their hard work. But hard work, did it really pay off for all immigrants? Reporting an illegal immigrant is a vicious act, an immoral act. No immigrant can do it to another, knowing the fear, the absolutely mind-numbing fright, that a mere mention of the INS brings to those whose underground existence in the forgotten patches of Lefrak City is a source of a collective paranoia. Could her parents have been capable of such a betrayal? Was it out of greed? Could greed be enough motivation for turning on their own people? Why is Suzy not surprised?

"We ran. We shoved our bags into a car and drove to the first place we could think of that was far away. We ended up hiding out at a church member's house on Long Island. That's where my wife fell ill. All that fire inside of her suddenly went out. She kept blaming herself for what happened, for trusting your father. She kept saying that she was useless, that she was a burden to me, and that she was too old to start over. A few weeks later, while I was out looking for work, she took a whole bottle of sleeping pills. She was dead before we even reached the hospital. I buried her out there, in a town we'd never been to before. She was only forty-eight." His voice is small and strained. He is relieved that his story is almost over. "She left me a note, begging me to go back to Korea. But I'm still here, and the only thing I have to show for the past thirteen years is this wretched age, and burying my wife, who wasn't old enough to die. But how could I go back to Korea? Who would look after her? Who would lie beside her out on Long Island?"

From the minute Suzy set foot in this dark, desiccated corner, she might have known that it was her parents who drove him here, who called her here, who wanted her to hear everything, who are now asking her to make judgment on their lives, which, she is finally convinced, could not have been saved.

The tea is tepid. The barley flakes have sunken to the bottom. *Boricha.* It may be years before she tastes it again. Will she like it still? Will she then recall this room, where a dejected man has finally revealed to her what might have been at the root of her parents' murder?

"But I had nothing to do with your parents' death," he says quietly. "That wouldn't have brought my wife back."

What about others? He mentioned that there were many with grudges against her parents. None of them could have gone to the police. How could they? Illegal immigrants, the cheapest target before the law. If her parents had stolen this man's store right under his eyes and driven his wife to suicide, what else had they been capable of? Could her parents have confided to the police as well? Could they have traded information for some sort of protection?

Even Suzy knew that many Korean fruit-and-vegetable stores crumbled in the early nineties. Especially after the Los Angeles riots of '92, relations between Koreans and blacks were at their worst. Over eight hundred Korean stores were destroyed in South Central. Many were torched in Flatbush and Bedford-Stuyvesant. Back then, it was not unusual to find a circle of picketers outside a Korean market, which inevitably drove a store out of business. It was also around then that the Labor Department began cracking down on Korean markets for breaking minimum-wage laws or hiring illegal immigrants, which Suzy learned later through her interpreting. As one wisecracking lawyer put it, "Everyone feeds off the illegals until they get an urge to scratch." Yet, from what she recalls, her parents had never suffered from the upheaval. They thrived, in fact, even bought a house during that time. How did they manage when so many others collapsed? The INS alone would not have guar-

anteed their lucky fortune. It is possible that the police might
have had something to do with it. They could have left her parents alone, in exchange for the names of store owners guilty
of breaking labor laws. It would not have taken much. A few
names. A few handshakes. And how would the police have re-
acted when two of their snitches were found dead one morning
in their South Bronx store? Would they have rushed to track
down the murderer? Or would they have feared the exposure of
their involvement? Why had the police been so quick to dismiss
her parents' murder as random? *We didn't ditch them cold*, Detective Lester told her. Then why so eager now to pin the murder on those ex–KK members? The gang denied the killing.
They insisted that her parents were already dead when they got
to the store. Who had sent them there? Whose order were they
following on that morning of November 1995?

"What about Mr. Lee of Grand Concourse? And Mr. Lim? I
saw him after the last time I came here. He might've been following me. He certainly hated my father. What do you know
about them? What did they have to do with any of this?" Suzy is
surprised at her relentlessness. Leave the man alone, she thinks.
Hasn't he been through enough?

"I don't know," he says curtly. "I'm not like your parents. I
don't squeal on my fellow men."

Of course not. Not many would side with the INS against
their own people. Suzy lowers her eyes, suddenly stumped. It is
then that she notices the full ashtray again. A black plastic ashtray, the kind that belongs in a bar rather than a home. She carefully picks it up and empties it in the garbage can underneath
the table. Immediately she is struck by the haze of stale ashes,
and a pang of disappointment. Nothing, the ashtray reveals
nothing. Just a common circular shape. What did she expect?

"Have you heard of a bar called Seven Stars?" The question

comes out abruptly. Useless—the man will tell her nothing
more.

"Never heard of it."

"And the Korean Killers? The gang that broke up almost ten
years ago?"

"Like I said, I'm not like your parents," he mumbles, avoiding her gaze. Yet, from the way his face tenses for a second, it is
obvious that he is holding back something.

"No, of course not, you weren't shot in cold blood." She cannot help saying it, although she quickly regrets it, remembering
his wife buried in Montauk.

"You think it was me who sent the KK to kill your parents?"
he retorts sharply. "I don't have that kind of money, and even if
I had, I'm too old to get involved with a gang."

So he is aware of the KK's arrest. Who would have told him?
Mr. Lee? Mr. Lim? Someone else? What was it that the mysterious caller had said?

They do not kill your parents . . . They watch you.

Was there more than one person behind it all? Was there a
group of them who had hired the gang? Who are *they*?

"Is that what you told them? When they came to you?" She
is jumping the gun. But there is no other way. Nothing to lose.

"I told them it was a foolish idea," he says wearily. "I told
them they shouldn't get the gang involved."

So it is true. There was more than one. Many who'd been
wronged by her parents, who might have plotted the murder
together.

"Your parents had both the INS and the police behind them.
They were basically invincible. Each time someone got deported, someone's store got shut down, someone's life savings
got stolen, all anyone could do was just look on and hope that it
wouldn't happen to him next. Your parents left them no choice,"

he says, staring vacantly at nowhere particular, as though he has reached the end of his defense. "Except the gang wasn't supposed to kill . . ."

Maybe they didn't. Maybe her parents were already dead by the time the KK arrived at the scene, just as the gang claimed.

"That's as much as I know," he says, stubbing out the cigarette. "I can't give you their names. I won't do that. Besides, I don't know exactly who was involved. All I know is that some of them got together to come up with ways to stop your parents. The KK must've been their only option. You can get the police to question me if you want, but my answer won't change. The police, the INS—they got all they could out of your parents anyway. They went after so many Korean stores for whatever violation they managed to squeeze from your parents. It's all politics, white politics. The police will only be glad to wrap up the case now. How perfect that it should be the pack of Korean grocers getting rid of their snitch, who'd gotten past their usefulness! Koreans killing each other, it only proves their theory that immigrants are parasites." Then he fixes her a long gaze and adds, "Whoever killed your parents were victims. They were desperate, even more desperate than me."

So the end of the story.

So that's how her parents came to their end, she tells herself. A bunch of Korean grocers who'd hired the three ex–KK members to threaten her parents, except their plan didn't go as intended: the shots were fired inadvertently, such shots, such final shots. Except she is feeling no relief.

Nothing remains except for the smoke, thicker than the night. The air is hot, moist, stale. The rain outside, she can hear its knocking. Its relentless knocking. She wants to say something, anything that will ease the pain, for him, for herself. But there are no words. Instead, she glances at the photo once more. The unchanging face of the middle-aged woman who never had a child, who breathed her last breath somewhere in Montauk, whose cry still fills this room after thirteen years.

Suzy finally rises. She is afraid, suddenly terribly afraid of stepping outside.

"Take this," he says, holding out an umbrella.

His loneliness is permanent, she realizes. That must be why she noticed him over a week ago at McDonald's. Recognition among the same kind.

Avoiding his gaze, she says hesitantly, "When my sister came to you . . . how much did she know about our parents?"

He contemplates her for a while before saying, "Your sister— I'd never seen a young woman so haunted by grief." Then he asks quietly, "Who do you think interpreted for your parents all those times with the INS?"

20.

FIRST IS THE HEAT. The unshakable heat inside her bones. The darkness is there as well. Then the wetness. The soaked sheets. The body curling into itself. The eyes are shut. The mouth is so stiff that she must be dying of thirst. Where's the water? Is anyone there? Will anyone find her? Will anyone know if she disappears? The last thought frightens her. It is not death that makes her squirm, but a death with no witness, a death with no explanation.

Before her are the rolling hills. Each one appears so smooth that she wants to reach out and brush her fingers across its surface. She imagines plunging her body between the folds. She thinks if only she could get there she wouldn't come back. She keeps wiggling her arms and feet. But the hills are far away, and she cannot reach them. Her body seems to be stuck to a gigantic futon, mixed in sticky breath. She tries to open her eyes, but the weight is impossible, as though a giant thumb is pressing on her eyelids. It is unclear how long she's been lying here. Hours, even days.

Between the hills emerges a face. An exquisite face behind a chunk of hair. The eyes seem familiar, such sad eyes, they bring tears to her own. The lips are painted in red, so opulent that it hurts to look at them. The fingers between the strands are painfully delicate; she wants to gather them in her palms and kiss each fingertip. Such a luminous face that there must be night surrounding it.

What remains is the heat that will not let go. What remains is the girl who will not lie still. The girl who remembers nothing.

Four rings.

The phone's been ringing all night.

On the wooden floor, next to the futon, are several banana peels and an empty bottle of water. Someone must have carried her up the stairs. Someone must have found the key in her coat pocket. Someone must have laid her feverish body on the futon. Someone must have put the hot towel on her forehead and watched her fall asleep before slipping out the door. Bananas and water. Enough to keep her afloat for days. Bananas; she has no recollection of chewing through their yellow meat.

Who was it?

Damian?

Grace?

It's been days, she is sure of it. A flood of sunlight poured in through the cracks between the blinds, only to slide away several hours later. A clock radio clanged with the familiar 1010-WINS chime. Doors have slammed at consistent intervals, as though the neighbors leave for work at the same time only to return exactly eight hours later. Cats meowed just around midnight, serenading the moon. Even in her deepest exhaustion, she was surprised that such things signaled the passing of time with an astounding accuracy.

But the heat is insufferable.

Now comes another face. The same black hair. The same heartbreaking eyes. The same pursed lips, across which a finger makes a cross to say hush. Now two where there was one. Two identical faces floating parallel. It is not clear which one was first. Upon a closer look, they no longer seem identical. A slight incongruence, although it is impossible to pinpoint what. She thinks she recognizes the one on the left. She is almost certain that one of them is her own, but which? She keeps turning from one to the other. What could be more terrifying than failing to identify one's own face?

White is the color of sadness.

A premonition.

A creepy joke.

Each dried-up bulb is her mother watching.

Dead inside.

Like fucking a ghost, Michael grunted after their first night.

The phone startles her again. The exactly four rings, beckoning her from the world outside. Michael is there. So is Damian. Detective Lester. Kim Yong Su. All those Korean immigrants whom her parents had betrayed, who gathered together one morning to plot their murder. The only way they can get to her now is by dialing the seven-digit number. Instead of whispering her name, instead of kissing her face so gently, they must dial the number first. They must keep on dialing to catch her. She is no longer nineteen. She's learned a trick or two. She's buried herself between the hills from which the faces look on a girl drowning. No one will find her here. A perfect hideout.

But wait, there's someone else. Who's over there by the lighthouse, reading a book? What's she reading? The one book in the world to ward off the dead? Suzy runs up to her to break the news. Look, she's about to say. Look what I've found out, look what I know now. Look who killed Mom and Dad!

When Suzy opens her eyes, her breath catches at the stillness of the room. The radiator has been banging through the night, steaming in excess. Outside is the creeping blue, the first shade of dawn. She can feel her stomach pulling at her with shocking emptiness, the sort of hunger so raw that it has nothing to do with food. She does not bother switching the light on when she stands before the kitchen sink. Turning the faucet, she puts her hands under the running water. She stands still for a minute or two as her fingers get cold. She lowers her face to drink from the tap before reaching for the glass on the shelf. Just then, as she is turning, the glass slips from her grip. Shards bounce off in all directions, over her bare legs. It is then that she becomes aware of the wrenching noise coming from her throat. All air has been choked out of her. Neither the heat nor the hunger, but an uncontrollable sob from the inside. She crumbles onto the floor, burying her face in her hands, lowering her forehead onto her drawn-up knees. It's been years since she cried last. It's been so long that she cannot seem to stop at all.

21.

SUNDAY MORNING IN NOVEMBER. The third Sunday of the month. The Sunday before Thanksgiving. FORT LEE NEW JOY FELLOWSHIP CHURCH. The sign outside looks almost garish, the sweeping gold strokes befitting its status as the largest Korean denomination in New Jersey. Unlike others, who rent their service time from American churches, they actually own their three-story building. It's been five years since she was here last, or in any church, for that matter. Not since her parents' funeral. Not since they took away the coffins to the crematorium. Suzy would have preferred open caskets. The decision had already been made when she arrived at the church. Gunshot wounds. Must not have been easy to clean up. Yet she would have liked to see her parents one last time. She would have wanted nothing more, even though the thought scared her. How could she have faced them? What would she have said to them? Grace might have been wise to block the last viewing.

The church appears different somehow. The altar behind

which the two coffins had been placed five years ago is now empty, with only the towering candelabra flanking the pillars. The vaulted ceiling scoops high in an uneven angle, as though displaying the relic of an ancient cathedral. The stained-glass windows do not reflect sufficient light; their reds and blues seem to have faded in time. The mahogany pews on either side are filled with faces, mostly young, about Suzy's age or younger.

The service is in full swing when she finds an empty seat in the back. Three young women are standing on the pulpit singing a hymn. An easy-to-follow tune that seems to repeat the magic words: worship, praise, seek, follow. People all around begin singing along, some clapping, some muttering "amen" over and over. Suzy cannot bring herself to join them, although the words are right there on the hanging screen behind the singing trio. Glancing around the room, she wonders why everyone seems so young. It must be the youth hour. Grace is supposed to be in charge of the Youth Bible Study. Although the oldest members appear to be no more than in their late twenties, many are couples with toddlers. Koreans marry early. A woman is expected to choose her match right out of college. By the time she hits twenty-five, the "old maid" label sticks fast. Over thirty, the best she can hope for is a much older man on the lookout for a second wife.

Now the song seems to be reaching its climax, or just the high-pitched refrain: "Lord, you're my all, Lord, you're my joy, Lord, you're my righteousness." Suzy cannot recall when she ever believed in anything with such conviction. Damian, she once followed him blindly. But it was love, or at least she thought it was. This church, the Bible—*this is all Grace had.*

As the choir takes a bow, a short, chubby guy in his early twenties strides up to the pulpit. He introduces himself as Presider Kang. "In charge of this segment of service," he shouts into the microphone as though he were Phil Donahue following cues from the audience. He reminds her of the Korean boys at Columbia who roamed the engineering building at all hours, carrying bulging bags on their back and dragging their feet as if sleepwalking. They always wore a set of black plastic eyeglass frames and a pair of white Adidas sneakers. As a literature major, Suzy was never brought anywhere near their circle. Yet, each time she saw one of them, she felt such a desperate need to run, as though their heavily accented English, their awkward disposition, their palpable loneliness threatened her own faltering position on that American campus. Their unmistakable Koreanness seemed to spin her right back home.

Presider Kang commands a prayer for everyone, three full minutes during which he hails the blessing of Jesus. "Without you, Lord, we're nothing," he recites into the microphone with his eyes shut, inspired by the singing trio's lyric. "Without you, Lord, we have no home. Without you, Lord, we have no father. Without you, Lord, we are orphans."

Your sister—I'd never seen a young woman so haunted by grief.

"Now please walk around and introduce yourself to at least five new brothers and sisters. Give them a hug and a warm handshake. We are all family, under the name of our Lord." Presider Kang struts down the nave and puts his arms around each one; their faces light up as though Jesus himself has just descended. Suzy has no choice but to rise and attempt a half-hearted gesture of looking around. She is farthest back, away from the majority, huddled in the middle rows. But churchgoers are not shy. A few are already making their way toward Suzy with beaming faces, as though they have just found their long-lost sister.

"Hi, I am Kyung Hee, welcome!"

"Hi, I'm Maria, what's your name?"

"Hi, I am Paul, so happy to meet you!"

Suzy would never recognize any of them if she were to run into one on the street. No glimpse of family bonding. Family, from what she knows, has nothing to do with handshakes and hugs.

Finally, there's the pastor, who is by far the oldest man in the room. With the sleekness of a pro, he quickly embarks on a heartfelt tale about how scarce the food had been when he was a kid in Korea, and how a mere apple would fill him with tears, as it struck him what wonder God had given us. He is recalling the spirit of Thanksgiving, although most Koreans do not celebrate the American tradition. She has heard it all before, the stories that begin and end with Korea, although here Jesus seems to be the preferred antidote. She rises quietly as the pastor starts reading scripture from the Bible: "The light shines in the darkness, but the darkness has not understood it."

Outside, in the oversized vestibule, Suzy finds a couple of tall wooden chairs lined up against the wall under a large portrait of Jesus on a crucifix. In one of them is a little girl of about four or five sitting with her feet dangling in the air. Like an angel, Suzy thinks, the way the whispery curls frame her face. Odd that a mother would give a perm to hair so young and naturally straight.

"Hi," says Suzy, sitting by her side.

"Is the service over?" The girl turns with a sullen face.

"No, not yet," answers Suzy, leaning back against the green velvet cushion.

"When will it be over?" The girl keeps crossing and uncrossing her legs, in the manner of a lady in distress.

"Why? You waiting for someone?" asks Suzy, amused by the little girl's precociousness.

The girl rolls her eyes, as if she finds adults dull. "It's so boring here. I should've brought my little Suzie with me."

"Who's Suzie?" asks Suzy, surprised at such a coincidence.

"My daughter. I'm a terrible mom, leaving her home alone to hang out in this dump!"

"So where's the father, may I ask?" Suzy puts on a concerned face, pretending to commiserate with the girl's maternal worries for her doll.

"There's no father, of course!" The girl looks appalled by Suzy's cluelessness.

"Oh?" Suzy plays along.

"Okay, promise not to tell anyone," whispers the girl, looking around once to make sure no one is listening. "I'm not Suzie's real mom. The real mom's dead. Poor Suzie's an orphan."

Suzy studies the little girl a bit more closely before asking, "How do you know that?"

"I just know, 'cause she's mine now."

Then, suddenly, the girl's face breaks into a bright smile. From the door emerges a petite woman in a yellow turtleneck and a calf-length navy skirt. The most distinct feature about her strikingly pale face is the freckles that sprout so mercilessly over her tiny button nose. Her dark-brown chin-length bob drapes her face in such stiff angles that it resembles a wig. Something about her seems unmistakably foreign, as though she could be of another origin, half Korean even. Suzy recognizes her as one of those who shook her hand inside.

"Grace, honey, have you been bothering the lady?" The woman bends down to kiss the girl several times before turning to Suzy. "The sermon's not over yet, but I had to check on her."

A daughter named Grace with a doll named Suzie. Too bizarre for chance, too clever for a plan. Then it occurs to Suzy that during the handshake the woman had introduced herself as Maria. *Could it be?* Suzy asks hesitantly, "What's your name again?"

"Maria. Maria Sutpen. And you are . . . Suzy, right?" the woman answers with sisterly familiarity, just as Presider Kang had prescribed.

"Suzy Park," she mutters; the girl does not miss a beat and exclaims, "Like my poor Suzie!"

"Sweetheart, why don't you go downstairs and play with the other children? They have cookies and hot chocolate down there. Mommy will come right down after the sermon." Maria points to the stairs that lead to the Bible-study room, which also serves as a recreation corner for kids.

"I *hate* hot chocolate!" The girl is pouting now, realizing that she will not be going home anytime soon.

"Don't be a baby, now; you love hot chocolate, and if you don't get down there fast, I bet the other kids will drink it all!" It is obvious that she is a good mother. Firm but with enough sense of fun. Loving in the way that she cannot seem to stop gazing at her daughter. Something about her adoring eyes spells a single mother. It has never occurred to Suzy that Maria Sutpen might be half Korean. With a name like that, who would expect an Asian face?

"All right, I'm going, and I'm not a baby!" The girl nods proudly in Suzy's direction, acknowledging her once before taking her leave.

"Both Mommy and Miss Suzy know you're not a baby!" With a wink in Suzy's direction, Maria kisses her daughter once more before letting her go. The girl runs down the stairs, out of their sight. Turning to Suzy, Maria shakes her head. "For a four-year-old, she's a handful."

"Quite a kid," Suzy agrees, still looking in the direction in which Grace disappeared. "Her name, is that . . . after my sister? Grace Park?"

"A sister?" Maria exclaims, staring at Suzy. "Grace's sister?"

"A younger sister," Suzy asserts.

"I didn't know Grace had a sister," Maria repeats incredulously.

"We haven't been too close," Suzy mumbles. "But I was hoping to find her here today."

Maria's face tenses. "I'm looking for her too. I drove here all the way from Queens."

Suzy is relieved that there is finally someone concerned about Grace's whereabouts. Nothing is scarier than an absence that is never noticed.

"I tried her at home, but she's moved." Maria sighs. "She never misses the sermon. I've asked around, but no one's seen her, and Grace is here almost every day."

"Has something happened?" Suzy asks uncertainly.

"Something odd came in my mail," Maria answers nervously. "A letter from her, which at first didn't alarm me, because it was more like a greeting card, except that it contained another letter inside."

"A second letter?"

"She wrote that I should only open it if I don't hear from her by her birthday. The whole thing sounded so strange, although with Grace I never try to second-guess."

Back in two weeks—Grace had asked Ms. Goldman to cover for her. That phone call happened last Sunday, a week ago. Now there's one week left until her birthday.

"Can I see the letter? When did you receive it?"

"It must've been sitting in my mailbox for a while. I was out of town until yesterday." Then Maria adds with an awkward face, "But I don't have it with me . . . Besides, Grace didn't want it opened."

No wonder the girl from the accountant's office could not find Maria. No one had been home when Suzy sat on her stoop in the rain.

Why is this woman living at her parents' house?

The first friend to appear from Grace's life. Perhaps the only friend. "How do you know my sister?" asks Suzy, contemplating the woman.

"From Smith, a swimming class in freshman year. One of those silly phys-ed requirements," Maria says with a smile in her eyes, as though she suddenly recalls the indoor pool where the class used to be held. "On the first day, the instructor, this rather large white woman, turned to both of us and said how some bodies just won't float. She was talking about body fat, of course, how thin girls don't float as well as bigger girls. But what she was really pointing at was the fact that we were the only two Asian girls in the class, that we were different. Strange, I'm not even completely Korean, as you can see, but in white people's eyes, I'm as Asian as they come."

Suzy tries to distinguish the Asian features in Maria's face, although, the more she searches, the whiter Maria looks.

"I bet I don't look so Korean to you either," Maria muses, reading Suzy's thoughts. "Don't worry, I'm used to it. Even Charlie, my daughter's father, left me because I wasn't Korean enough for him; he told me after seven years together . . . Anyway, thank God no one can tell my white blood in my little Grace, although her hair isn't as straight as other Korean girls'. Genes are weird, don't you think? They pop up in the oddest places." Maria sighs, tucking a piece of hair behind her ear. Suzy wonders why she did not notice before that her hair's been heavily blow-dried to appear straight.

"What a useless class; more than ten years later, I still can't swim!" she says laughingly. "It wasn't until after graduation that I started hearing from Grace regularly. She'd send me a letter every six months or so, always with nice little gifts. The odd thing was we weren't even that close. I guess I still can't say I really know her. I didn't even know she had a sister." Maria seems flustered by the discovery.

"What kind of gifts?"

"Oh, random stuff, like an antique jade ring or a pair of fancy sunglasses. Really nice, except they were all hers, clearly things she'd owned for a while. The letters weren't much, though. Just brief updates of her life. I thought maybe she was lonely."

A jade ring? Mom used to wear one on her middle finger. For good luck, she would say, twirling it seven times before whispering a prayer. Did Mom give it to Grace at some point? Why would Grace pass it on to a friend?

"Then, when I was down and out, right after Charlie left me, I was four months pregnant with no job, it was Grace who saved me. She took me in, and later even set me up in a house that used to belong to her parents." Maria pauses, realizing that they were also Suzy's parents. "I owe so much to Grace. I think she felt sorry for me, because . . . maybe she thought I was a bit like her, a misfit, a Korean girl with a name like Sutpen."

"A misfit?"

"She could never stick to a job, temped for years, strange for a girl who graduated Phi Beta Kappa. It's like she was allergic to a permanent situation—until the teaching job, that is."

Like me, Suzy thinks. A waste of college education.

Who do you think interpreted for your parents all those times with the INS?

Grace had never let Suzy know. Grace never let Suzy in. If Grace did not speak to Suzy, then Suzy could remain innocent. But is Suzy innocent?

Even at Smith, Grace was completely alone. Even at Fort Lee High School. No one seems to have gotten through, not even Maria Sutpen, with whom her friendship still feels guarded. Perhaps Grace was freer with the man who she claimed was alone, orphaned, just like her.

"What about her boyfriend?"

"What boyfriend?"

"It seems that she went off somewhere to get married, although—"

"Married? That's ridiculous," Maria cuts her short, looking dismayed. "Grace is appalled by anything remotely domestic. It's a stretch for her to even be my baby's godmother. I pretty much had to force it on her. She certainly wouldn't be getting married overnight!"

How peculiar that the whole school seems to be aware of his existence when her only friend has no clue.

"She's never mentioned a guy she was seeing?"

"Back in college, boys from U. Mass. and Amherst were always after her. She never went out with anyone, though. Boys used to say that she was a lesbian. But she had someone from home, some guy who used to come and see her every few weeks."

"A guy from home?"

"I never met him, but I've heard people say he was bad news."

"Why?"

"He picked fights with strangers because he thought they were checking her out. Right on King Street. I remember hearing about it, because in downtown Northampton pretty much everyone belongs to one of the Five Colleges." Maria pauses. "Why, you think she's still with him?"

"I don't know."

"That's over."

"How do you know?"

"She told me," answers Maria, squinting her eyes as if reaching back to a remote past. "She mentioned something about him finally giving up on her. She said that he was better off without her, because he knew too much about her. She looked so lonely when she said it, though. That's when it occurred to me that she might've had some feelings for him after all. I thought he was just some freak stalking her, but maybe they had a real thing. She hasn't been with anyone since. Especially after what happened to her . . . your parents."

"Why do you think she couldn't?" Suzy mutters, as though posing the question to herself.

"Something in her died with them. She seemed permanently lost without them. Years ago, when she moved back home after college, she used to write to me about how great her parents were, how much she loved them. I remember being envious. My mother died when I was five, and I never even met my father. I know what it's like to lose parents, but I can't imagine the pain when you've been so close . . ." Maria stops abruptly, realizing that the pain also belongs to Suzy.

Did Grace really use those words?

That they were *great*?

Something begins collapsing inside her.

A quiet sinking.

Grace hadn't even begun facing the truth, Suzy realizes. Moving back home might have been her attempt to bury the truth. Just as Suzy had invented the oceanfront house in her dreams, Grace might have told herself that none of it had happened, that her parents had never used her for their crimes, that they had never violated her conscience.

One day, if you find yourself alone, will you remember that I am too?

"What was his name?"

"I don't know. She never talked about him except that one time."

"When was the last time you saw her?"

"About a month ago, she dropped by suddenly. She said that she was in the neighborhood, which was unusual."

"Why unusual?"

"Because she never comes to Queens. It's almost like she avoids it. But that day, she said she was looking around to buy a store. When I asked her what kind of store, she said she'll tell me later."

A hundred grand, in one shot. A month ago.

Suddenly, pealing laughter halts the two.

"Mommy!" It is the tiny bundle of mess climbing up the stairs, smiling triumphantly, her mouth smudged in chocolate, and opening her palms to reveal a fistful of crushed cookie crumbs. "Look what I got for you!"

Bursting into laughter, Maria gushes, "Sweetie, thank you so much, that was so nice of you to think of Mommy and Miss Suzy." She throws one of the bigger crumbs into her mouth and then exclaims, "Yumm, it's really yummy, but now we've got to get you to the ladies' room to clean up!"

Maria Sutpen seems oblivious, which must be why Grace was drawn to her. Too ordinary, made to be a girlfriend, a mother. She even looks natural in a blow-dried bob. She takes whatever's given without much ado, even something as odd as a used ring or an entire house. The sort of woman you would find anywhere, whom you would never notice or remember, because, despite her mixed colors and name, she is your average all-American girl.

Finally, Maria looks up, her eyes glazed, as though her world has now ceased but for the little girl in her arms. "Please let me know if you hear from her. I'm worried about Grace. And about the letter, maybe we better wait."

Suzy makes no response. She barely hears Maria saying, "Since Grace specifically told me not to open it. I mean, she might have left me a message at home by now . . ." Without letting her finish, Suzy mutters finally, "Was it Grace who gave her the doll, the one named Suzie?"

"My fairy godmother did!" It is little Grace who jumps at the question. "She made me promise to take good care of her, because Suzie's all alone in the whole wide world!"

22.

ALL SHE CAN SEE ARE LINES. Lines to the entrance, lines for applications, lines for registration, lines for interviews, lines for hearings, lines to public bathrooms which are locked with "Out of Service" signs on all forty-two floors except three. She is not sure what made her come here. Everyone under the sun is here. The fluorescent blue makes everyone look sick. Or perhaps it is the perpetual wait that turns golden skin ashen. Men in stiff black uniforms trot back and forth with patriotic salutes. The objects of surveillance are aliens. Because here, at 26 Federal Plaza, "aliens" is the preferred name for immigrants. Ten-thirty on Monday morning, anywhere in the world would be better than here.

She could have said no. The call came at the last minute. The court's interpreter went home sick, and they needed a replacement. Immigrant hearings are rare. The court sticks to its own certified interpreters, and the agency mostly handles depositions that pay much higher fees. Even the voice sounded reluctant

when it left the assignment on her machine. But the minute
Suzy heard "26 Federal Plaza," she grabbed the phone. It seemed
unthinkable not to take the job.

26 Federal Plaza.

The largest civilian federal building in the country.

The home of the Immigration and Naturalization Service.

Returning to the scene of the crime.

Passing the metal detector, Suzy wonders if her parents were
summoned here regularly, if they were led through some secret
corridor, if they sold off their fellow Koreans in this very corner.
Suzy imagines little Grace next to them, her face lowered, her
eyes filled with tears. She surveys the crowd in the sprawling
lobby, searching for the INS employee who might have lured
her parents, who might have given the final order, who might
have turned his face away when they got shot. But nothing. Not
a trace. The INS is never clumsy in its tracks.

There are thirty-two courtrooms spread over three floors.
Courtroom 30 is located on the twelfth floor. By the door is a
young woman in a navy suit pacing the floor and whispering
into a cell phone, "No, it's not gonna take long. Just a formality,
really. Williams never grants relief." She takes no notice of Suzy,
who is now entering the room marked "Judge Jack Williams."
There are three wooden pews on either side, with two booths
and desks in front. Hanging behind the judge's bench is a circular bronze plaque that reads "*Qui Pro Domina Justitia Sequitur*,"
with an eagle perched in its center. It is a plain room, clean and
deeply worn. Yet enough to set one's nerves on edge.

Squatting in the right booth is a gray-suited man with his
nose buried in a pile of papers on the desk. All Suzy can see is
the wrinkled forehead and the drooping chin. But all too familiar. One thing she has noticed through the months of interpreting is how lawyers resemble their clients. They begin wearing

the same look. The same optimism, the same despondency. A quick glance, and she can usually surmise the situation. Whatever today's case is, there's not much hope.

Next to him is the defendant. Either she's been crying up until the point when she was summoned here, or her eyes are naturally swollen with dark circles. Her gauntness is alarming, the brown cardigan falling shapelessly over her bony shoulders. Her wizened face carries the yellowish hue of someone who hasn't breathed fresh air for a long time. It is hard to guess her age. Somewhere in her late fifties, although with immigrant workers one can never tell. She looks vaguely familiar, though, and Suzy leans for a better look. But unlike most witnesses, whose faces light up at the entrance of the interpreter, the woman does not even stir when Suzy slides into the seat next to her.

"Hi, I'm the interpreter assigned to the case," Suzy attempts. The woman seems not to hear her, muttering instead a few indistinguishable sounds under her breath. The lawyer barely acknowledges her. Occasionally Suzy has run into lawyers who don't address interpreters or stenographers directly. Some even snicker when she stumbles on a word and turns to a dictionary. They might sigh noisily or make a point of shaking their heads. Oddly enough, Korean lawyers are the worst. It might come from the country's long history of class hierarchy. Once, an attorney turned to her during a break and asked her to bring him a cup of coffee. Suzy collected her things instead and walked out. Sometimes bullying is a legal tactic to prevent a witness from being questioned: get the interpreter mad and bust the deposition. A cheap trick, but it works. Most depositions never get rescheduled. They cost too much. Before the second try, the case gets settled.

But no such play at an immigration court. No cocky lawyer, no tempestuous interpreter. There is a grimness here she cannot

shake off. Silence infused with doom. Like the end of a civilization, she thinks, peering at the woman, who still won't raise her
face.

Then, almost simultaneously, the young woman with a cell
phone strides in, and a lanky man in a black robe with bifocals
precariously perched on his nose emerges from the side entrance
by the bench. The new presence does nothing to lift the ominous air. The defendant recoils slightly.

"Let the record reflect that we are now commencing the removal hearing of Jung Soon Choi," the man with bifocals, who
turns out to be Judge Jack Williams, says, turning on the tape
recorder. At immigrant hearings, stenographers are rarely used.
The court does not have the budget. Facing both lawyers,
Judge Williams asks, "Do you, Counsels, wish to present your
exhibits?"

Right away, the young woman and the morose lawyer strut
to the bench. While the three are poring over the documents,
Suzy studies the defendant more closely. A creeping sense of familiarity; what is it? Why does her heart give at every frail motion of this woman?

When both return to their seats, Suzy rises and takes the
oath, as does the woman. As if on cue, Judge Williams pounds
and says, "For the record, please state your name." Suzy translates in a louder voice than usual, for fear that the woman might
not hear.

In a surprisingly clear and coherent tone, the woman answers, "Choi Jung Soon."

"Is that your lawyer sitting next to you?"

Mrs. Choi nods, at which Judge Williams orders her to answer verbally.

"Although I believe that the respondent is not even entitled
to a hearing, upon the request of the respondent's counsel, I am

willing to hear her side before making a decision. You may begin, Counsel."

Suzy translates, leaving out the part about her not being
entitled to a hearing. Why drain the woman of her last hope?

"When were you born, madam?" Her lawyer wastes no time.

"Nineteen forty-two. January 7."

Nineteen forty-two. The year her mother was born. The year
of the horse. Mom once said that no one wanted a girl born in
the year of the horse, because she was fated to die far from
home. The stars never lie, she whispered, as though imparting
an ancient wisdom. Suzy thought she was making it up.

"So you are fifty-eight years old."

If her mother had lived, she would have been fifty-eight. Still
a good age. Still young. The ripe age for a parent. It is not right
for a parent to disappear before.

"Where were you born?"

"Korea."

"When did you come to the United States?"

"Nineteen seventy-two."

"Do you speak or read English?"

"Little."

"What is the highest level of education you completed?"

"Objection!" the INS attorney lashes. "The counsel's wasting
everyone's time, Your Honor. His attempt to establish her background at this point serves no purpose."

"Sustained," Judge Williams rules. Get to the point, he
means. This is just a formality, the woman's as good as gone.

Surprisingly, Mrs. Choi replies anyway. "Graduate school,"
she says. "I received an M.A. in music from Ehwa Women's
University."

Not unusual. Many Korean immigrants are college graduates. It is a country with a nearly 100 percent literacy rate. Kore-

ans pride themselves on education. A man who owns a dry cleaner's might have once been an architect, or a pedicurist at a local nail salon might be a trained pharmacist. Their Confucian tradition dictates that learning is the basis of self-worth. But it also backfires. The difference between professionals and merchants is sharp. Most of them never get over the shame of being relegated to the working class. Thus a woman who's been a cashier at a deli for over twenty years will still hold on to her former life as a music scholar.

A momentary silence washes over the courtroom. Nothing about the woman suggests a music degree. The mass of gray hair gathered into a bun at the back of her head. The sallow face in desperate need of Maybelline or Lancôme or whichever product adds color. Then her cracked fingers, caked with dead skin, the nails chipped, which she quietly hides under her sleeves as though she too is surprised at her own revelation.

"Mrs. Choi, what is your status in the United States?"

"I am a permanent resident."

"Under what circumstances did you come to the United States from Korea?"

"I came on a student visa."

"Affiliated with any school?"

"Juilliard."

"And did you study there?"

"No."

"What happened?"

"My parents went bankrupt and could no longer send me money."

"So what did you do?"

"I got a job as a cashier at a Korean deli. I was planning on saving up and going back to school."

"And were you able to?"

"Objection! How is her education history relevant to any of

this?" The INS attorney looks exasperated. Suzy has seen this before, many times. Lawyers are always acting frantic. They are perpetually frustrated or running out of time. It must be the first lesson they teach at law schools: act like an asshole if the case is not going your way.

"Sustained," Judge Williams drones. Come on, his murky eyes suggest, do we really have to go through all this?

"Mrs. Choi, are you currently married?"

"Yes."

"Do you live with your husband?"

"I did."

"What do you mean?"

"I did until I was arrested."

"Any children?"

No answer. Suzy pauses as Mrs. Choi clams up. A silent response is the hardest for an interpreter. A pause signals difficulty. Sometimes the witness is confused or does not know the answer. Sometimes it is a ploy to avoid the question. But most times the witness is stuck because the answer is too painful.

"Mrs. Choi, do you have any children?

"Mrs. Choi, according to the record, you have one daughter, is that correct?

"Mrs. Choi, is your daughter's name Sue Choi?"

Leave her alone, Suzy pleads silently. Can't you see the sadness on her face?

"Okay, Mrs. Choi, let's move on to another topic." The lawyer relents, or puts the daughter on hold for now. "Where were you employed last?"

"Together Market."

"Where was Together Market located?"

"Between 125th Street and Lenox Avenue."

"What kind of business was Together Market?"

"A fruit-and-vegetable store."

"Who owned it?"

"My husband."

"What was your job or duty?"

"A cashier during daytime, and in the evenings I prepared food for the salad bar and made fruit cups."

Mom did that too, Suzy recalls. Although Dad never let Suzy, she saw Mom making fruit cups once. Long before they bought the Tremont Avenue shop. It was Grace who took her there. The store was in Manhattan, very far from Queens. It took nearly an hour on the Number 7 train, and at Grand Central, they got out and walked a few blocks. The woman at the cash register had the deepest double folds on her eyelids. Plastic surgery is common among Korean women to make their eyes bigger, like Meg Ryan's. Except the folds on this woman looked too fake, and her eyes seemed to pop out of their sockets, the skin around them pulled too tightly. The woman languidly pointed to the kitchen in the back, where Mom was squatting on a milk crate facing a cutting board and boxes of cantaloupes. She was carving melons into moon-shaped pieces before putting them into a plastic container, which she would tie with a rubber band. Then the process would begin again. And again. She was like Cinderella, with a mountain of chores, except the mountain was made up of cantaloupes and the midnight ball never took place. Suzy cannot remember what came next. Did Mom finally turn around and see them there? Or is it possible that before Mom could find them Grace pulled Suzy's arm with a sudden burst of anger and stormed out? How often had Grace gone there? Did she go back to watch Mom from the doorway? Why had Grace brought her there anyway? Suzy couldn't stand cantaloupes after that. Or Grand Central, for that matter.

For a while now, the questions have been circling around the store called Together Market—when did her husband purchase the store, how many hours per week did she work there, how much was her annual income. Then he finally zeroes in: "Let's go back to the night you got arrested, that would be December 2, 1997. Can you, in your own words, explain to the court what happened?"

For a second, Suzy notices Mrs. Choi's fingers clutching the edge of the seat. Then a curt response: "I stabbed a girl." Suzy hesitates before translating. She tries to think of a softer word for "stab" in English, but there is no such thing. Mrs. Choi did not mean it softly.

The lawyer seems frustrated by her response. He wants descriptions. Details. Whatever it would take to clarify the picture.

"Let me rephrase the question; please tell us the circumstances surrounding the incident in question."

"She was a customer, and I stabbed her," Mrs. Choi answers with not much feeling. And definitely no regret.

"I understand. But could you tell us how the situation specifically arose, or what exchange you had with this customer whom you claim to have stabbed?" He is losing patience. He knew that she would not be an easy witness. Legal Aid had warned him. Despite the language barrier, it is not hard to see that the woman has little interest in saving herself.

Suzy is also losing patience, adding at end of the lawyer's question, *Please say more. This might be your last chance.*

"I was making fruit cups and I saw the girl stealing."

"And then what happened?"

"I stabbed her in her shoulder with the knife I was using to cut fruit."

"Mrs. Choi, isn't it true that the girl punched you repeatedly before you pulled out the knife?"

"Objection!" the INS attorney barks. "The counsel is leading the respondent. Besides, the respondent has already served her sentence. The respondent is not summoned to this court for her crime; she's here because she is deportable!"

"Your Honor, it is very relevant. Her crime is exactly why she has been deemed deportable."

"Overruled, but, Counsel, I will not allow these types of questions for much longer." A warning. Judge Williams wants this show to be over with. Three more cases to go today: two asylum petitions, one status adjustment. Pardon them one year, detention centers get jammed tenfold in the following year. Is America up for grabs? Judge Williams adjusts his glasses, which slide down again almost immediately.

"Thank you, Your Honor. Mrs. Choi, did the girl you claimed to have stabbed provoke you in any way? Such as insulting you with racial slurs or attacking you physically?"

"I don't remember."

"Mrs. Choi, if you would please look at Exhibit A, in front of you, which is the transcript of your testimony from the criminal hearing that took place on January 30, 1998, you will find that you testified that the sixteen-year-old victim had stolen a six-pack of beer and a case of cherries and then called you 'Fucking Chink' several times, among other racial slurs, and then proceeded to punch you repeatedly in the face. Is that correct?"

It is then that Suzy remembers the headline from a few years back. "KOREAN WOMAN STABS BLACK TEENAGE GIRL FOR CHERRIES." It was all over the papers. The girl was out of the hospital in a few weeks, but boycotts spread like wildfire against Korean fruit-and-vegetable stores in Harlem and the Bronx. The *New York Post* called it the "Return of Rodney King"; Reverend Al Sharpton exhorted his people to fight back; 1010-WINS updated the news every half-hour. Suzy remembers the photograph of the distraught woman surrounded by a mob of reporters. Is that why she seems familiar? Where are those reporters now? Do people forget so quickly?

"Mrs. Choi, your silence is not helping," Judge Williams interrupts finally. "You do realize that, in the case of a green-card holder, an aggravated felony is grounds for removal?"

Without a glance at the bench, Mrs. Choi responds, "I've served almost three years in jail. I've lost everything. My husband, my daughter, my store. If that didn't kill me, nothing else will." It is the most she's spoken so far. But self-destructive. No use confessing her heart to a judge who never grants relief, or to the trial attorney sent by the INS. Yet Suzy has no choice but to translate.

Her lawyer then puts the cap back on his pen with an obvious look of irritation and fatigue. "I have no further questions," he sighs. Pointless trying to establish her as the victim, as the one who's lived here for a quarter of a century, whose husband and daughter are still very much alive in this country, for whom being removed permanently means being torn away from a home.

Then the INS attorney perks up, grabbing her notes: "I have a few questions." Suzy winces as she translates her words—the trial attorney from the INS, the source of everything that had gone wrong with her parents. "Madam, where is your daughter?"

Mrs. Choi then raises her eyes for the very first time. Dead eyes. Nothing there, Suzy notices. Nothing left over.

"Isn't it true that she ran away from home when she was seventeen?"

The question shoots out of nowhere and sticks. Suzy stumbles, as though it is her mother being examined, accused, sentenced. *Isn't it true that your daughter abandoned you because she couldn't stand you?*

"Isn't it also true that, before she left home, she had filed a complaint against your husband, Mr. Choi, for physical abuse, in which she alleged that he beat you as well?"

Mrs. Choi's face reveals nothing. Theirs was not a happy home, obviously, which is exactly what the INS attorney wants Judge Williams to consider. No one's breaking their home. They did that for themselves. Green cards were never meant for such undesirables.

"And isn't it also true that you have not once seen your husband, Mr. Choi, since the day you stabbed the girl in your store, almost three years ago?" The INS attorney fixes her gaze on Mrs. Choi for a few seconds, and then turns to Judge Williams. "Your Honor, I have no further questions."

The INS attorney spoke the truth on her cell phone earlier. Judge Williams's ruling is only a formality. Relief was never a possibility. Deportation had begun the minute she stabbed that girl. She should've known better. Immigrants are not Americans. Permanent residency is never permanent. Anything can happen. A teenage thief on one unlucky night. A pair of INS informers eyeing your store. A secret murder that is not so secret anymore. And Suzy, sitting across from the INS attorney on the twelfth floor of the INS building, about to translate a deportation sentence for a Korean woman exactly her mother's age.

When Judge Williams announces the removal date, Suzy chokes. Her voice is suddenly gone. She inhales deeply and then swallows once, twice. All faces are on her. Then she hears it again. The quiet murmur from Mrs. Choi.

Namuamitabul Kuansaeumbosal.

It's the Buddhist chant Mom used to utter when Suzy got sick. It always made her feel better. A lullaby. A dead woman's song.

23.

"HELLO, this is the Interpreter Hotline Services."

"Hello, this is a message for Korean interpreter Suzy Park."

"Hello, Suzy Park, please report to Job Number 009."

She presses "Delete" after each message. It is no longer possible. An interpreter cannot pick sides. Once she does, something slips, a certain fine cord that connects English to Korean and Korean to English without hesitation, or a hint of anger.

For the past three days, the phone kept ringing while she lay in bed. Michael, pleading into her machine. Even in her deepest dreams, she heard his sighs. He would fume, demand that she answer. Then, half an hour later, a softer, sweeter, *Suzy, please.* His calls stopped overnight, which could mean only one thing. He must be back in Connecticut. Even Michael would not dare calling his mistress during a Thanksgiving dinner.

A half-dozen messages have been left by Detective Lester. Suddenly he is eager to get to the bottom of the case. With each call, he seems increasingly confident that he is closing in, although the three ex-KK suspects are still claiming that it was a setup. He has no doubt that he could convict the gang of first-degree murder, although he seems unaware of their link to the Korean grocers. He never lets Suzy in on her parents' back-dealings with the INS, or with the police.

The girl from the accountant's office has called more than once. "Grace is missing," she squealed into the machine. "Grace still hasn't come by to sign the papers. Please call us back as soon as possible."

What is curious is how unmoved Suzy is, how unmotivated she is to pick up the phone. Instead, she is overcome by sleep. Her insomnia seems to have been miraculously cured. All she does now is sleep. No cigarette break. No water break. In between come those voices trailing off into the machine, voices from far away, voices belonging to dreams. The dream of the interpreter who no longer remembers her language.

"Hello, Miss Park?"

A woman, with a Jersey accent.

"Hi, this is Rose Goldman. I'm not sure if I have the right number."

Ms. Goldman. The English teacher subbing for Grace. Suzy reaches for the receiver.

"I hope I'm not calling at a bad time. I thought I'd just leave a message. I was sure you'd be gone for Thanksgiving." She must realize that Suzy, like Grace, has no family. "Oh, Koreans don't celebrate our Thanksgiving, please pardon me. I have so many Korean students, I should know." Ms. Goldman seems embarrassed at having been caught alone on Thanksgiving, although she is the one who called.

"Have you . . . heard from Grace?" Suzy asks, unable to shake off the persistent fatigue.

"No, not yet. But with Thanksgiving and all, the school's out until next week anyway."

Suzy is not sure why she is relieved. No news must be good news. Or is it?

"But yesterday, I remembered something. It's really nothing, but it bothered me. I don't know why, just a silly little thing."

"Yes?"

"Do you remember how I told you that I found it odd that her boyfriend was in the music business?" Rose Goldman sounds almost bubbly now, like a suburban housewife flipping through her copy of *Redbook*. "I finally remembered why. I remembered some kids saying that he was missing a finger on his right hand. And being a musician—although, now that I think about it, he could be a producer or something—but a musician with a missing finger is a bit strange, don't you think?"

They once each cut off their little fingers to honor their brotherhood, copying that crazy Yakuza ritual.

Closing her eyes, Suzy counts to three before firing the question: "Was it the little finger he was missing?"

"How did you know? Yes, that's what the kids said, like those famous gangsters in Hong Kong movies!"

DJ.

The last member of the Fearsome Four.

The one who split on his own after the gang's breakup.

The one smuggled into the country through the KK's adoption fraud.

An orphan, with no ties in the world but for Grace.

DJ was supposed to have been deported in November 1995, right around the time of her parents' shooting. Perfect timing, being sent back to Korea right after the crime. But, then, how is it possible that an ex–gang member who'd been deported reappears five years later, flaunting his BMW, picking up Grace after school? Why would Grace disappear with him? Why did Grace call Detective Lester out of the blue?

What was it that Detective Lester had said? *It's got KK finger-*

prints all over it. The way they do away with their enemies. The exactness of the shooting.

But the gang claimed that they were set up. They said that her parents were already dead when they arrived at the scene. According to Kim Yong Su, the grocers had never ordered KK to kill. If neither the ones who hired the gang nor the gang themselves had murder on their minds, is it possible that the murder might have been committed by someone else, with an entirely different motive? Someone intimate with the gang, who knew about their mission on that morning in 1995, who was not afraid to frame them? Yet who would have been clever enough to come up with such a plan?

The brave one. Someone so righteous that eliminating them would've been a necessity.

Suzy recalls the other clever setup. Maria Sutpen and her daughter, Grace, and a doll, Suzie, a cozy family portrait in her parents' final house. The little girl seemed happy, as neither Grace nor Suzy had ever been. It is an odd way for things to turn out. Their final house in America given away to a stranger. A half-blooded Korean woman, Dad would have balked. *Since when do you care about their wishes?* But what they had wanted was not Montauk, not Damian, not Michael, not mistress Suzy, not Christian Grace, definitely not a gang member with a missing finger.

Suzy begins pacing the floor. The cigarette smells of gasoline. She stubs it out instantly. She glances at the ashtray filled with barely smoked cigarettes. Then it comes back to her.

He won't crawl back to her. Definitely a changed man.

Grabbing her bag from the kitchen table, she pulls out a thin volume of stapled sheets, *1.5 Generation*, the student magazine from Fort Lee High School. She flips the pages and finds the photo of the car that belongs to the "dude rich enough for Miss Park," BMW M5, the same kind she'd seen parked outside Santos Pizza this past Saturday. Running to the closet, she rifles through the coats on the rack. Which one did she wear on that rainy day? Then, in one of the pockets, her fingers close on a crumpled piece of paper. She beeps the number and waits by the phone. It takes no more than a few minutes. These women waste no time getting back to clients. Even on Thanksgiving Day, which means absolutely nothing to an aging Korean prostitute.

"Mina here, someone beep me?" Her voice sounds noticeably husky, which must be her professional tone.

"Hi, I met you the other day," Suzy stammers.

"Hey," the woman cajoles in a low whisper, "don't be shy. We've got girls for all kinds of clients."

"No, no, no, that's not it." Then, hesitantly, "This is . . . Maddog's girl."

"Who? Oh, I remember now." Her voice sinks.

"Johnny . . ." Suzy says nervously. "When you said that he was a changed man, did he, by any chance, also change his name?"

"Jesus, is that why you beeped me?"

"Sorry, it's important."

"What does this have to do with you?" She sounds irritated, yawning loudly into the receiver before answering: "Of course Johnny's not the real name, no one in this business uses a real name, you think 'Maddog' is real?"

The BMW. The gang connection. The room salon in Queens. She does not even have to ask the next question.

"Did he use to call himself DJ?"

"So why you bothering me if you know the answer?" She is about to hang up when Suzy jumps in.

"What did Johnny do to cross Maddog years ago?"

No response. Silence at the end.

"Did Johnny tip off the cops this time?"

Anything to provoke an answer.

"Where is he now? Did he run off with Mariana?"

"*Mariana with Johnny?*" The woman lunges. "She would never! That bitch treats him like a dog." The woman is seething. She seems to have been holding back for years. Over a decade of unrequited love. "He wouldn't dare go running off to her now. What more does he want? I give him the car, I give him his Armani suit. He's a fucking fool. Always Mariana, Mariana, even after I packed him off to Korea to get him away from her. All he talks about is how she's the victim, how she needs to be saved, how she's all alone. But what about me? What does he think I've been doing all these years?"

Suzy stands motionless, feeling the blood suddenly draining from her face. She is still holding on to the receiver, long after the woman hangs up. It takes a while for her to walk to the futon and climb between the sheets, facing the wall.

DJ, or Johnny, whatever he calls himself.

Was it him? Was it all for Grace?

And Grace?

What did she know?

How much did she know?

Why did she run away with him?

"Fuck them," her sister chortles from the top bunk, sucking on a Marlboro. She is terrified, watching the door through which Dad might storm in at any second. "They'll never catch me, 'cause they don't want to." She wants to sneak one of her sister's cigarettes too, but she is only fifteen, still the younger one, still the one who never breaks rules. "Do me a favor, empty this for me, would you?" Her sister pokes her head from above, carefully handing her the full ashtray. A black plastic ashtray, which, upon emptying, reveals a cluster of white dots on its bottom.

Seven stars in a circle. A secret code. A girl by the name of Mariana.

Through the metal window-guards is the rain, the relentless rain. And the red tip of the cigarette.

One day, if you find yourself alone, will you remember that I am too? Because you and I, we're like twins.

24.

"MEET ME BY *SUNFLOWERS*."

A thirtieth birthday, suicide to spend it alone, Caleb insisted. "It'll be tattooed on your calendar, like the stupid sweet sixteen or the last date of your virginity!" Suzy had been inclined to stay home. She could not get out of bed. A celebration seemed impossible.

November 24th. The day after Thanksgiving. The Metropolitan Museum seems even more crowded than usual. It's been years since she was here last. The Met had always been Damian's territory. He had been a consultant for its East Asian Wing. He would come here whenever the mood struck, would retreat into one of its myriad rooms and disappear from Suzy. She would never accompany him. This was the world he kept separate from her.

She did not mind. He had thrown away everything for her, she thought. It seemed enough that they were together. It seemed enough to know that he would be with her from now on. She had jumped at the chance to play his young bride. She sat patiently and waited for him all day. She cooked elaborate Korean dishes. She threw on skimpy red lace and moaned harder each time she felt his attention drifting. Yet, once the initial shock of their escapade wore out, interminable silence hung in its place. Four years. It took her parents' murder. It took their death for the two of them to finally give up.

Damian contacted her just once after she moved out. It came during the second year of her living alone. "Suzy, enough," he commanded quietly into the machine. She did not pick up the phone. "Isn't this what you wanted after all, to be free?" He had no doubt that she would come back to him in time. He knew that she had nothing else. And she would have if she could. She wanted to, more than anything in the world. But on nights when she cried in her sleep, on mornings when she woke missing his arms around her, she heard gunshots, the tumultuous explosion of two exact shots.

Now the police have behind bars suspects who might have pulled the trigger, who might have wanted to pull the trigger, who might be filling in for the real murderer.

The guard points to the second floor. European Paintings. It's the nineteenth century she is looking for. Past the Grand Staircase, buried among the glorious pastels of Cézanne, Renoir, Seurat, Monet, are van Gogh's mad strokes against the wall. From the crowd gathering in front, it is easy to spot *Sunflowers*.

"Hey, birthday girl, you look not a day older than twenty-five!" Caleb exclaims from the wooden bench in the middle of the room. Twenty-five, Suzy's age when she first met him.

"Hi, how was home?" Suzy slides by his side, kissing him once.

"Rick told me we're finished if I ever bring him home again."

"Oh no, was it that bad?"

"Brutal. The funny thing is, they actually liked him. My

mom even went on to say that she thought he was *prettier* than Boy George. It was Rick who couldn't stand her. He said that she reminded him of Sally Jesse Raphael. I guess it was the glasses."

Suzy smiles, picturing Caleb's mother with her oversized red plastic frames.

"I had to rush back anyway to get ready for the opening. The artist is the newest British import. The next generation of the Sensation kids. He gobbles up classics and whips out blasphemous installations. A mannequin replica of one of Ingres's ladies that slowly turns into Princess Diana puking. A Botticelli painting where all the boys are sucking the Pope's dick. This time he's on to *Sunflowers*." Caleb turns to Suzy, rolling his eyes. "Personally, I don't see the appeal. I'm *so bored* by blasphemy."

Van Gogh's sunflowers look almost morbid. Not the usual perky, happy yellow faces, but a close-up of two withering heads, as if in torment. Beautiful, yet haunting. The madman's last reach for the sun.

"In Chelsea, no one gives a shit about the real thing. Everyone's just dying to know what new offense is about to be committed against the masterpiece. Except Vincent practically invented blasphemy. Look at his strokes, look how he twisted Impressionism senseless!" Glancing at the group of Japanese couples who are now following their tour guide to the next painting, Caleb continues, "In college, I was the only art major totally obsessed with Vincent. Everyone thought I was so passé. You fall in love with van Gogh, you study him in Painting 101, you copy *Starry Night* for your first assignment, but you don't obsess over him. While they all moved on to Mondrian, Beuys, Duchamp, I stuck loyal. Even now, *Starry Night* blows my mind. His cypresses make me weep. I used to read his letters every night before going to bed."

Suzy is suddenly struck by the image of the sky-blue bowling jacket Caleb always wore when they lived together. It had "Vince" stitched above its right pocket. She had assumed that it belonged to a former boyfriend. Strange how long it takes to know a person. Yet somehow reassuring that a person could have so many secrets.

"His letters? So that's what you were doing when you used to keep your lights on until dawn?" Suzy asks, half laughing.

"No, honey, I did other things too." Caleb winks before continuing. "But I used to read his letters religiously. They're painful. He was so damn alone. He wrote to his brother Theo almost every day. He told him every single detail of his life, down to the exact color of the sunset he'd seen that evening, the price of the paper he was writing on, the angle of his fingers gripping the pen. He was so needy. He begged women for love. He latched on to Gauguin for friendship. He threw himself into a painting frenzy. He even turned to God."

"God?"

"Vincent covered the whole nine yards. Studied theology, did the Evangelical bit, taught the Bible. But he didn't quite make it. He didn't fit. His loneliness was too deep, it really couldn't be helped."

So alone, so incredibly, desperately alone.

Something begins to break down inside Suzy. Something she has known almost from the beginning.

"Why was he so lonely?"

But the answer is there already. They are like twins. Suzy and Grace.

"Who knows? He was mad for sure. But there were other things, like his family, for example. His parents, his uncles, his siblings, including Theo. They sheltered him. They found him jobs, paid his rent, sent him paper and brushes. They had a strong hold on him, and Vincent was dependent and hated himself for it, although his family was by no means at the core of his problems."

"Then why write to Theo?"

"That's what makes those letters so fascinating. He felt suffocated by his family's love, and yet he couldn't help being a part of it. He choked Theo with his daily reports. There was a certain boundary he never learned. The suffocation he felt might've had something to do with it. No boundary with anything, with his family, with himself, even with something as common as sunflowers. Look at how he paints nature! His flowers are unique because there's absolutely no distance from the artist. For him, they're all the same, the self-portrait, the local postman, the sunflower. It's fun for us to sit back and analyze them, but for Vincent it must've been hell. You can only drive yourself crazy if you have no distance from the world."

Her face feels cold, as cold as her right hand against her cheek now, the curled fingers, the hollow of her palm. It is not clear which part emanates the chill, the hand or the face. It is the chill inside breaking loose. It is impossible to recall how long it's been there, this knowledge, this anger.

"Oddly enough, Theo died only six months after Vincent shot himself. They were connected by some desperate blood, like twins." Caleb shakes his head, still gazing at the painting. "Vincent paid for his genius, while Theo suffered for being sane."

Except that Suzy and Grace are not twins. Suzy's guilt is still tucked inside her unspoken. Suzy will continue to live.

"C'mon, enough culture for turning thirty. Let's go to Barney's to find you a dress. Your biological clock is seriously ticking, darling!"

Caleb is pulling her by the arm when Suzy notices a painting in the corner. A lime-green vase of violet petals against a pale-pink background. It is a tame still-life. Quiet, almost dejected, as if the artist has reached the requiem of his madness.

"Oh, *Irises*," says Caleb, following her gaze. "I'm not a big fan of his irises. They're a bit strange, tense. He painted that one at the mental asylum. It's like witnessing his death."

Irises.

It had to have been Grace who sent her irises each November. It was a letter to Suzy. A confession. A bouquet of Mom's last kiss. Because Suzy is the only one in the world who understood. The only one Grace could have reached out to. Where could she be now? Where has she disappeared to?

It is then that Suzy panics. Leaving Caleb frowning in confusion, she breaks into a run. She is flying past Cézanne, Renoir, Seurat, Monet. She is leaping through the narrow corridor of Rembrandt drawings. She skips down the Grand Staircase in double steps. People turn to look at her. Some move out of her way. A few guards even step forward to stop her. But Suzy sees nothing. All she knows is that something terrible is about to happen to her sister, if it hasn't already.

Then, running toward the coat check, Suzy stops suddenly at the sight of a man at the front of the line squatting before a bright-red stroller. With his back to her, the man seems to be adjusting straps across the infant's waist. His hair is dove gray, the color of Dad's Oldsmobile. His shoulders droop much lower than she remembers.

Damian, here on the ground floor of the Met, in the same line even, hunched over a baby. But it couldn't be. He couldn't ever be a father, ever deserve a home, ever own anyone in the world but her.

He does not see her. He does not sense her nearness. He is much too occupied with the baby's seat belt. The heavy black sweater is wrong on him. He never wore black. Too easy, he claimed, too young. Nothing else is recognizable to her. It is winter. He is covered under the layers. Nothing visible, not even his hands, buried in the stroller. Not even the back of his neck, wrapped in a scarf. She knows the scarf. She picked it out for him. The cream beige to suit his blue eyes. It looks different on him now, on that implausibly aged man in a black sweater bending over a baby, which might even be his.

But Damian could not be a father. He would have flinched at the thought. He would never have allowed it.

Then Suzy notices the woman standing next to him. Handing him a matching black coat, the woman is now stooping as well. It is hard to see her face, beneath the cascading blond hair. She is not much older than Suzy, late thirties maybe. Damian with a white woman. Suzy would never have believed it. He was too adept at caressing her olive skin, too skilled at kissing her black hair, too addicted to her Asian face. Suzy can almost hear the echo of Professor Tamiko's laughter—*He could never love an Asian woman.* How could he? His whole life had been about running from his whiteness. His purpose was searching the other. He couldn't even love his own kind. She was the antidote for his inability to love.

He raises his upper body, slides his arms through the coat sleeves. Turning around, he faces Suzy's direction for a second. Damian. She has not seen that face for so long. It has been so heartlessly long. Her first impulse is to jump the length of people in line, past the woman and the baby, and explode into his arms. But then she is suddenly not sure if it is indeed him. Perhaps another man who looks much like him. Perhaps her mind is playing tricks. All she can do is to stand still and stare straight at him. All she can do is stay where she is, continue standing. It is not clear if he saw her, although, from where he is standing, he must have. Then, before she can meet his eyes, before he can react, his face is blocked from Suzy as the woman lifts the crying baby from the stroller and dumps it in his arms.

Snatching her coat, Suzy starts running.

Before she can stop and catch her breath, before she can break into tears, she is already out of Damian's life.

25.

SUZY IS NOT SURE how she got here. She could have run the entire forty blocks. She could have hopped in a taxi. She knew she had to get out of the Met, although she had no idea where she was headed. But now that she is here, standing before a woman with a neat bob and a buttoned-up blouse surrounded by empty desks, it all makes perfect sense. Of course, this is where she had to come. From the moment she saw *Irises*, from the moment she realized that it had been Grace who sent her the bouquet, the next destination was clear. The New York Public Library. The only place to find facts, fast.

"I need to look up newspapers within the last two weeks."

She must appear strange to the woman, charging in like this, breathless, soaked in sweat despite the post-Thanksgiving chill outside. But the woman does not flinch. Anything can happen here. Free service. An open door to all New Yorkers. She must be used to all kinds of visitors. In a calm, friendly voice, she asks, "That would be in the periodical section. Is it local information?"

"Long Island. Montauk, actually." Her voice is strained, sounding almost foreign to her own ears.

"The best thing would be to look it up on Nexis, the online news search." The woman studies Suzy's face for a little longer and then adds, "But you need a library-membership number to access it. Do you have your card with you?"

No, she doesn't. Of course she doesn't. Even if she did, she could not remember where it might be.

"You okay?" The woman leans forward, as though alarmed by the look in Suzy's eyes. Such sad eyes, such immense sorrow. "I'll set you up at Terminal A. Better yet, I'll look it up for you if it's a quick one, there's hardly anyone here anyway."

"A boating accident, off Montauk coast," Suzy states numbly. She watches the woman's nimble fingers punching the keyboard. It is odd how calm she feels. This must be resignation. This must be the final relinquishment. She must have been afraid of such an end.

"That was easy!" The woman's face brightens with the researcher's delight at the correct answer. "Here are a few lines from the *Long Island Weekly*, dated November 19th, five days ago.

> *A couple disappeared when a boat sank off the Montauk coast. The cause of the accident is not known, police say. The body of an unidentified Asian male in his thirties has been recovered. The only distinct mark is the missing finger on his right hand. According to Sam Kelly, the boat's owner, the accompanying Asian woman could not swim. The police are continuing their search for her body.*

26.

THE FACE ON THE WINDOWPANE must be a lie. Dark eyes in which lights flash, splitting her in two. When did she grow into such a beauty? Little clueless Suzy? Little innocent Suzy? But Grace had been the beauty. She was the brave one. She was the first interpreter. Which one is she? Whose face is this? As she leans closer, the mirror shuts with a heartless snap.

A boat in November.

Montauk, a sure sign of trouble.

What's in that water?

Except the ashes of her parents, the tears of the woman who died childless, the blood of the man who'd chased the wrong girl.

Before boarding the train, Suzy made two phone calls.

Open the letter, she asked point-blank. *I don't give a shit about your loyalty crap. Open the goddamn letter before I throw you out of my parents' house.*

A will, whispered Maria Sutpen. *It's a will, in case she doesn't*

*come back. A will leaving everything to my little Grace, except for
a title to a store, a Korean market; it says you'll know what to do
with it.*

*Now the real question. What happened in that class? You never
learned how to swim. What about Grace, what happened to Grace?*

*Grace? No, not Grace. Grace passed with flying colors. She even
cocaptained the swim team. She could swim through any waters.*

There is no such thing as an accident.

Grace must have suspected him all along. She must have
known that he would do anything to save her. She must have
prayed never to find out. Except DJ must have crawled back
somehow, must have confessed to her at the parking lot of Fort
Lee High School. She would never have let him get away with
it. She would never have forgiven him. Since when does a good
Korean girl marry the one who's shot her parents, even if it had
all been for her? Love? Bury him in the same water, that would
be Grace's revenge. Never messy. No evidence. Not a chance of
suspicion. She would've fooled them all. Fuck KK boys. Fuck
grocers who hated her parents. Fuck INS. Fuck the Bronx DA.
And most of all, fuck Detective Lester.

Only Suzy would be spared. The silent witness. The bouquet
of white irises. A title to a Korean market—what's she supposed
to do with that? Give it to Kim Yong Su as an apology? A piece
of the American Dream? A family heirloom? What the hell's an
interpreter if she can't even interpret her own sister?

Tell us, Suzy!

Stop lying, Suzy!

Dear Suzy, my only family, this is your dream come true!

The pastel house by the shore. The sunlit faces of her parents. Not guilty, never guilty, never having crossed the line between what is family and what is not, what is right and what is
deadly wrong, what is Korea and what is not home. The line was
always there. The line had been marked from the beginning,

tightly woven around the two girls who couldn't find their way no matter how they tried, how hard they studied, how many boys they seduced, how many husbands they stole, which god they worshipped, unless their parents went away, unless their parents sailed a boat never to return, unless their parents drove to work one morning and never came back.

In the phone booth at Penn Station, Suzy made the final call, relieved that it was only the machine at the other end.

Detective Lester, this is Suzy Park. I know who killed my parents. I know it was the Korean grocers; a group of them had sent the gang that morning. I've got their names. Start with Kim Yong Su, and he'll tell you the rest.

Outside is no longer the city. No more Bronx, no more Queens, not even downtown Manhattan. The swaying is kind to her heart, to its beats of one, two, back to one. The sun is setting. The night is surging. The train is carrying her far, far away. At the end will be the lighthouse. At the end will be a new country.

She could swim through any waters.

Leaning back, Suzy closes her eyes. There is enough time until the arrival. Plenty for sleep. Soon it will be tomorrow. The end of Suzy's birthday. One more day until Grace's. For now, they will remain the same. Two girls with no parents, such fine American beauties.

ACKNOWLEDGMENTS

MY GRATITUDE to Suzanne Gluck and John Glusman. Thanks to my first readers: David France, Lisa Hamilton, Sean Kim, Kathryn Maris, Dara Mayers, and Amy Peterson. And to my sister, Sunny Kim, whose painting graces the cover.